THE
Serpent
GIFT

THE
SERPENT
GIFT

LENE
KAABERBOL

Hodder
Children's
Books

A division of Hodder Headline Limited

Copyright © 2003 Lene Kaaberbol

First published in Danish in 2003 by Forlaget Forum, Copenhagen
Original title: *Slangens Gave*

English translation copyright © 2005 Lene Kaaberbol
First published in Great Britain in 2005
by Hodder Children's Books
Published in agreement with Lene Kaaberbol,
represented by the Laura Cecil Literary Agency, London,
in association with ICBS, Copenhagen

2

A Catalogue record for this book is available from the British Library

ISBN 0 340 88363 4

Typeset in Bembo by Avon DataSet Ltd,
Bidford-on-Avon, Warwickshire

Printed and bound in Great Britain by
Clays Ltd, St Ives plc

The paper and board used in this paperback by Hodder Children's
Books are natural recyclable products made from wood grown in
sustainable forests. The manufacturing processes conform to the
environmental regulations of the country of origin.

Hodder Children's Books
a division of Hodder Headline Limited
338 Euston Road
London NW1 3BH

Contents

A note from the author

Any teacher worth her salt knows that glaring at an unruly class is usually more efficient than shouting at them. One of my students once handed in an assignment ahead of time – a rare event, but I still managed to forget about it. When I collected the essays, there was of course no paper on her desk. I looked at her. She protested indignantly, and I realised my mistake. I tried to smooth things over, saying that I hadn't actually told her off. 'No,' she said. 'But you gave me The Look.' And she was right.

I think we learn the power of The Look when we are children, from the receiving end. My mother was a master at it. Exceedingly few of my childhood crimes went undetected – she could look right through me when she wanted to. And when she scolded me, she would always insist that I look her in the eye. 'Look at me!' she would snap, as if that was part of the punishment. 'Look at me when I'm talking to you!'

When Dina's mother, the Shamer of this tale, takes on a suspected criminal, her first words are usually: 'Look at me!' And pity the poor wretch when he does, because the power of her gaze is so potent that it can bring hardened murderers weeping to their knees. I have certainly used my writer's right to exaggerate and enhance, but I know for a fact that the Shamers have learned a trick or two from my mother. And although Shamer is not a registered profession, nor indeed a word you can find in the dictionary, still the power of The Look exists, in our world too.

I am no longer a teacher. I no longer glare at people for a living (though I sometimes do it for fun, or because I think they have it coming). These days, the writing pays the rent (and the cornflakes and the stewing steak, and various other odds and ends). I live in Copenhagen, in a beautiful old warehouse, just across the harbour from the royal residence. I can wave at the Danish queen while brushing my teeth (so far, she hasn't waved back). I've arranged my desk so that I can watch the ships and listen to the seagulls as I write. 'Why do you always write fantasy?' my friends sometimes ask. Because I like faraway places and faraway times. And because there is, at the heart of every fantastical lie, a core of real truth. Like the small shiver that goes through a child when an adult says: 'Look at me when I'm talking to you.'

I
The Highlands
Dina's story

ONE

A Stranger

When I first saw him, I had no idea he would change our lives. There was no tremor from the ground, no icy gust of wind, not even a real shiver down my back. Just a small twinge of unease. I didn't even tell Mama about him. Maybe I should have? I don't know. It wouldn't have changed anything, not really. From the moment he caught sight of me, it was too late in any case.

It was supposed to be a good day. I had been looking forward to it for a long time – the Midsummer Market, when all the clans meet to trade, and talk, and entertain each other with races and contests and music from dusk to dawn. Mama and I had worked our fingers to the bone, drying herbs and making ointments and remedies for all sorts of ailments, and Rose, my foster-sister and best friend, had carved bowls and spoons and shelf ends, and little dolls and animals for the children. She was clever with her knife, and in her hands a bit of kindling would suddenly turn into a cow or a dog, as if the animal had been there all the time, hiding in the grain of the wood. My older brother Davin had nothing to trade, but he thought he might win a prize in one of the races with Falk, our skittish black gelding.

This would be my first Midsummer Market in the Highlands. The summer before there had been strife and hostility among the clans, and no real Market had been held. Kensie, the clan we lived with, had clashed with Skaya, and it was only at the last moment that we had managed to stop the battle in Skara Vale before they ended up killing each other. It had all been Drakan's fault, of course; Drakan who called himself Dragon Lord and ruled almost all the coastlands now, after having murdered the old castellan of Dunark. He was a bad enemy to have, was Drakan, both devious and ruthless. Instead of doing battle with the clans himself, he tricked them into warring with each other. And back when he killed Ebnezer Ravens, his daughter-in-law Adela and her young son Bian, he managed to have the castellan's own son Nicodemus accused of the murders. Nico would have ended up with his head on the block if it hadn't been for Mama. And me, a little bit. On that day, Drakan had become our enemy. And his reach was long.

We still couldn't go anywhere without protection. Callan Kensie had been Mama's bodyguard for two years now. He was big and steady and kind to us, and I liked him. But I still wished we didn't need him.

'Such a crowd,' said Mama. She had to keep a firm hold of the reins; Falk, who was serving as our cart-horse that morning, was not used to all the push-and-shove and hubbub. 'Where do you think we should go?'

I surveyed the crowded scene. At first it looked completely chaotic, with people milling about like ants in an anthill. But there was actually a pattern to the Market – streets and squares and crossroads, just like a real town, even if the Market town was made up of carts and wagons and tents instead of houses.

'There's a free spot,' I said, pointing. 'There, at the end.'

'Right,' said Mama, clicking her tongue at Falk. Our black horse snorted but walked on, stiff-gaited and suspicious of the crowd.

'Copper kettles,' yelled a peddler woman. 'Best copperware at even better prices!'

'Three marks?' said a broad-backed Skaya man. 'Bit steep for a pair of socks, if ye ask me!'

'Pork sausage! Smoked venison! Have a taste, Medama. Ye'll not regret it!'

Falk laid back his ears and became even more stiff-legged. The cart was hardly moving at all, now.

'Can't you make him move a little faster?' I asked Mama. 'Somebody else will grab our space.'

'He doesn't like all the ruckus,' said Mama. 'Dina, I think you had better lead him.'

I climbed off the cart and grabbed Falk's bridle. This made him move a little faster, but not much. And just as we were about to reach the slot I had decided was ours, a cart coming from the other direction swung into it.

'Hey,' I yelled. 'That's where we were planning to set up!'

'Is that so?' said the carter. 'Ye should have made better time, then.'

I glared at him. He was a thickset man with curly

brown hair and a smith's apron round his heavy middle. And he didn't look in the least bit sorry.

'You saw us! You knew this was where we were heading!'

'Hush, Dina,' said Mama. 'We'll find another spot.'

The carter seemed to notice Mama properly for the first time. Or rather, the Shamer's signet that hung fully visible on her chest. It was no more than a pewter circle enamelled in black and white to look like an eye, but at the mere sight of it, the man blenched and changed his behaviour completely.

'Beg yer pardon,' he muttered, one hand releasing the reins to slip behind his back, 'I had not seen . . . If Medama wants this space, then . . .' He hauled back on the reins one-handedly, forcing his tough little Highland horse into a sharp turn.

'No, that's perfectly all right—'

But he was already off, steering his horse and cart through the market crowd as quickly as the bustle permitted.

'Did you see his hand?' said Rose. 'Did you see it?'

'He made the witch sign,' I said tonelessly. 'But at least he did it behind his back. Some people make it right in your face.'

Mama sighed. 'Yes. It's sad. And it seems to be getting worse.' She raised a hand to touch her signet, but she didn't say it out loud – the thing we were all thinking: that it had gone from bad to worse since Drakan had begun to burn Shamers down in the coastlands. 'Well. We might as well take the space. Come on, girls. Let's set up shop.'

'If anyone will buy anything from the Shamer Witch and her family,' I muttered.

Mama smiled, but the smile didn't quite reach her eyes. 'Oh, they'll buy. For some reason they seem to think that my herbs work better than other people's.'

Mama knew a lot about herbs and the way they worked on the various illnesses people get, but what she did was not magic. Anybody could make the same infusions, and many did. But because Mama was also the Shamer, people assumed that there was witchcraft involved. In reality, there was only one thing Mama could do that others couldn't: she could look people in the eyes and make them confess their ill deeds – and she could make them ashamed of what they had done.

We unhitched Falk and pushed the cart into the neat row of stalls and other carts.

'Will you take Falk back to the camp?' I asked Rose. We had left the men – that is to say, Callan, Davin and Davin's friend Black-Arse – setting up the tent in the shelter of some rocks a bit further up the slope, away from the worst of the crowding.

Rose looked a little anxious. 'Can't you do it?' she said. 'With all those people around he might get a little . . . wild.' Rose was still not all that comfortable around horses. In Swilltown, the meanest and poorest part of Dunark, where Rose used to live, not many people could afford to ride or keep a horse.

I nodded. 'Yes, all right. You have your own stuff to unpack, anyway.'

★ ★ ★

On the slope, the men had finished their task. They stood there, side by side, looking at the tent as if it was a four-storey building they had just managed to erect.

'There,' said Davin, rubbing his hands. 'Nothing to it when you know what you're doing.' He gave me one of those big brother looks that clearly meant that girls were generally good for nothing except being a suitably admiring audience for manly deeds.

I pretended not to notice and hitched Falk to the tethering line so that he could graze with the other three: Callan's sturdy brown gelding, Black-Arse's dun mare, and my own beautiful Silky that Helena Laclan had given me last summer.

'Any sign of Nico?' I asked.

Callan shook his head. 'Not yet. But the lad will be around somewhere.'

Originally, Nico had meant to ride with us to the Market. But that morning when we came to fetch him, he and Master Maunus had been in the middle of a full-blown row. We could hear them yelling at each other even as we came down the hill. The voices cut through the morning silence, and Master Maunus was shouting so loudly that Nico's bay mare was all but choking herself, trying to tear loose from the post she was hitched to in the yard outside.

'What will it take to make you understand, boy? It's your damned *duty*—'

'Like hell it is. Don't preach duty at me. I couldn't—'

'Couldn't care less, yes, I've realized that. You would rather jig and dance and brawl with a mob of drunken peasants. And get drunk. Isn't that what you're planning on – Master Guzzle-Gut?'

'Don't call me that!' Nico's shout was nearly as loud as Master Maunus's, now.

'Oh? So truth is an unwelcome visitor?'

'Is it so unthinkable that I just want to have a bit of *fun* for a change? Must you immediately assume that it's all an excuse to get drunk? You don't trust me.'

'Have I *reason* to?'

The words seemed to hang there for a moment, a bitter accusation that Nico apparently could find no answer to. Then the door was flung open, and they both came out, Nico first, pale as death, and Master Maunus on his heels.

'Where are you going? Damn it, boy, you can't just run away like that!'

'Why not?' said Nico. 'You don't listen to a word I say anyway. And why should you? I'm just an irresponsible drunkard. Can't trust guzzlers like me, can you now?'

'Boy . . .' Maunus tried to put his hand on Nico's arm. 'Nico, wait . . .'

But Nico wouldn't wait. He threw one swift look at Rose, Davin and me, but it was as if he barely saw us. With a quick jerk on the tethering rope, he unhitched the mare from the post and leaped on to her back without bothering to use the stirrups. The mare, already half-panicked from the noise and the anger she could feel in him, practically took flight. She tore up the hill in a series of wild lunges, and within moments, both of them were lost from sight.

In Maudi's yard, Master Maunus came to a halt, looking oddly helpless. He was a large man, with greying red hair and beard and strong, bushy eyebrows. Standing there so bewildered-looking and empty-handed did not suit him at all.

'Damn the boy,' he muttered. 'Why won't he *listen*?'

Actually, Nico was no boy. Not any more. He was nineteen, and a grown young man. And the son of a castellan, to boot. Many people considered him the rightful lord of Dunark Castle, though Drakan ruled there now. But Master Maunus had been Nico's tutor throughout his boyhood, and ruling his charge had become a habit. He had very firm opinions about what Nico should and shouldn't do, and he would voice those opinions in no uncertain terms. Rows had become almost their normal way of talking, but even by their standards, this one had been a sizzler.

Master Maunus seemed to see us properly for the first time. He dabbed his forehead with a worn green velvet sleeve, trying to regain his composure.

'Good morning, girls,' he said. 'Good morning, young Davin. How is your lady mother?'

He always asked. Like most people, he had a great deal of respect for my mother.

'Good morning, Master,' I said. 'She's fine, thank you.'

'Glad to hear it. What can I do for you?'

I exchanged glances with Rose and Davin. Judging from the row, Master Maunus would not be thrilled with our errand.

'We came to ask Nico and you, Master, if . . . if

you were ready to ride to the Market with us,' Davin finally said.

Master Maunus looked at us for a moment. 'The Market. Yes. I see.' He raised his eyes to the morning sun and looked indecisive. 'I . . . I do not feel like going myself. And somebody has to stay here and mind the animals, after all. But the young lord . . . I think he has already left. At least, I think that is where he is going. And I thought . . . perhaps you would do me the favour of . . . keeping an eye on him there. If he is with you, then . . . well, I would feel better about it.'

You wouldn't be so afraid that he would drink himself senseless, I thought. But I didn't say it out loud.

Davin looked annoyed. Nico was not his favourite person in all the world, and acting as nursemaid to a nineteen-year-old 'young lord' was probably not what he had had in mind for his first Highland Market.

'Of course we will,' I said, before he could say anything.

Now it looked as if I might have cause to regret that rash promise. Merely finding Nico looked like a steep task in this circus.

'I'm not spending my time playing sheepdog to Nico's sheep,' said Davin. 'He's a big boy now. He can look after himself.'

'But we promised Master Maunus—'

'*You* promised. You look. I'm going to check out the racecourse.'

'Best ye stick together,' said Callan. 'I cannot mind ye all if ye go wandering off by yerselves.'

'But you don't have to,' I said. 'Callan, there are so many clansmen here. Nothing will happen to us *here*. Even if somebody did try something, I could just call for help.'

He looked at me for a while, then nodded slowly. 'So ye could. But . . .' he prodded my shoulder with one finger, 'be careful now, ye hear? Do not let me catch ye going off with strangers.'

'Of course not.'

He had reason to be cautious. Last year, when Drakan's cousin Valdracu captured me, it had been Callan who had to tell my mother that I was missing and that they feared I might be dead. It was not an experience he was likely to have forgotten. I hadn't either, of course, and I was sometimes scared that something like that could happen again. But here, at the crowded Market, surrounded by clansmen and market vendors, I felt very safe. All I had to do was raise my voice and help would be at hand.

Callan, however, had not quite finished with me yet.

'Perhaps I had best . . . it might be best if ye did not go alone.'

'Callan. *Please*. Nothing will happen.' It would be a very boring Market, I thought, if I had to have Callan trailing me everywhere I went.

He sighed. 'Aye, well. I cannot cage you, can I? Be off then. But watch yer step!'

'I will.'

Davin and Black-Arse were already headed for the racetracks, and I skipped off down the slope, to launch myself into the crowded Market once more. It was a little overwhelming at first: smells and sounds, people and animals . . . hawkers shouting at the top of their voices, mummers and mountebanks all eager to entertain you for the price of a copper penny. On one corner, a man was juggling three flaming torches; he had a trained dog that went around the watching crowd, sitting down in front of each of the onlookers in turn. It had a tin tied to its collar, and if you didn't drop a penny, it began to bark and howl and make a terrific fuss. It was fun to watch, but I hurried along all the same because I didn't want the dog to sit down in front of me.

I moved through the throng, searching for a familiar face, but Nico was nowhere to be found. Not at the races, where Davin and Black-Arse were watching the other contestants judiciously and making remarks like 'a bit narrow in the bone' or 'not enough chest'. Nor at the wrestling ring, where a mob of Laclan men were roaring their heads off, cheering for their man. I looked in every beer tent I passed, but didn't find him there either. Instead, I bumped into the carter who had nearly taken our space. I was so busy peering at the beer drinkers that I didn't notice him until I backed into his heavy aproned middle.

'Have a care, lass,' he said. And then he recognized me. 'Pushy, aren't ye?'

'Sorry,' I said, lowering my gaze from old habit. 'I didn't see—'

'I'll say ye did not. Nose in the air, I'll wager. But ye cannot go knocking decent people over just because yer mama is the Shamer.'

'I never meant to,' I said, trying to edge past him.

'Hold yer horses,' he snarled, snatching at my arm. 'Ye might at least have the manners to say ye're sorry.'

'I did.' I tried to pull away.

'Did ye now? Very quiet, it must have been, that "sorry". Quite silent, I think.'

This man was such a pain. I was beginning to get really angry.

'Let go of my arm,' I said. 'Or I'll—' Or I'll yell, was what I meant to say, but he didn't let me finish.

'Or what? Or ye'll get yer mother to curse me? Threaten an honest man, would ye?'

I wasn't scared, not really. I looked around quickly to see if Callan was anywhere near, but he wasn't.

'I'm not threatening anyone,' I said, as calmly as I could. 'And my mother can't curse people. And even if she could, she wouldn't.'

'A likely story.'

'A true story!' I glared at him. And right then, it happened. It wasn't anything I wanted. It wasn't anything I could control. Not any more. It was just a flash, a quick searing pain inside my head, and then it was gone.

He cried out and let go of my arm as if I had suddenly become too hot to hold.

'Witch brat,' he hissed, backing away, and this time he did make the witch sign in my face, fully visible to me and everyone else who cared to look.

I had looked at him with a Shamer's eyes. I hadn't meant to; perhaps it had happened because I was angry, or because he wouldn't let go of me. Now he wouldn't even look at me, much less touch me.

'Get away!' he cried, so loudly that people turned to stare. 'Keep away from me with yer devilry!'

Other people were making the witch sign now. A woman clutching a basket full of eggs backed away, trying to look and not look at the same time, and a black-haired man in a red shirt simply stood there and stared, as if I had turned into a troll or a banshee before his eyes.

Time to leave, I thought.

'Just leave me alone,' I told the carter and turned to go.

The black-haired man in the red shirt was barring my way. At first I thought it was an accident and tried to move past him. But he was still in my way.

'Excuse me,' I said, politely. One fight a day was quite enough.

He didn't move. And he was staring at me with the most peculiar look on his face, as if . . . I wasn't quite sure. As if he had found something, perhaps.

'What is your name?' he asked, and his voice had a strange sort of lilt to it. He did not sound like a Highlander, nor like any Lowlander I knew. And from one ear dangled a jewelled earring, a silver serpent with green gemstone eyes. The men I knew did not wear jewellery like that.

My heart was beating more rapidly than before. Who was he, and why was he interested in me? Was it because of the things the carter had shouted to the world, about devilry and curses and the like? I felt no desire to tell him my name.

'Excuse me, I'm in a bit of a hurry . . .'

Suddenly he put a hand on either side of my face and looked straight into my eyes. There was no roughness to his grasp, it was just so unexpected. I took a step backwards, and he released me immediately.

For a moment we stared at each other. Then I spun around and began to walk away, back the way I had come.

'Wait,' he said.

I looked over my shoulder. He was following me. Oh, *why* hadn't I waited for Callan? I started to run as best I could in the crowded Market street. Where was our own stall? I pushed through a narrow gap between two tents, leaped across a wagon shaft and dived beneath a table full of pottery, making the potter yell in surprise.

'Damn monkey!'

I didn't stop. I just ran. Was this our street? Yes, down there at the end was Callan, so reassuringly big and trustworthy, and Rose, dressed up in her Market best in a green skirt and white embroidered blouse. I looked back once more, and to my relief there was no black-haired, red-shirted stranger bearing down on me.

'Hello again,' said Rose. 'I've sold three of the little horses already, and a bowl! And the herbs are selling well, too.'

Mama was talking to a customer, getting her to sniff our thyme balm. She was careful to look at the jar, and not at the customer, but they were both smiling, and it looked like another sale.

'Great,' I said, pushing my fringe away from my forehead and trying to calm my breathing.

Rose peered at me. 'What happened?'

'Oh, I . . . bumped into the carter who tried to steal our space. He wasn't in a great mood.'

Rose giggled. 'I bet not. He missed a great space. Serves him right, too.'

I don't know why I didn't say more. Perhaps it was just that Mama looked so happy right then, and I didn't want her to become all anxious and worried again. But there might have been more to it than that. It was as if I could still feel his palms against my cheeks. His hands had been warm and slightly roughened. His hair and beard were carefully trimmed and black as night, like the fur of Maudi Kensie's favourite hunting dog. And the eyes that had looked so searchingly into mine had been green. Just like my own.

TWO

Heroes and Monsters

In the end, Nico found us. The light was beginning to fade, and we were packing up our little shop and thinking of supper. Or at least, my stomach was.

'That was a *good* day,' said Rose. 'I should have brought some wood along. I could have carved more of the little animals, they're selling like hot cakes.'

'Perhaps you should charge a little more for the ones you have left.'

Rose hesitated. 'I don't know. I like it that everyone can afford them. And it's not as if they cost anything to make.'

Not if you don't count the work, I thought. And the imagination, the skill and the patience..But Rose didn't seem to reckon that. She was just happy that people wanted to pay good money for something she had made.

Suddenly, Melli came to attention like a hunting dog who has caught the scent.

'There he is,' said my little sister and pointed. 'Look. It's Nico!'

She was right. There was Nico, slipping easily through the crowd because people moved out of his way – perhaps without realizing why they did so. It *was* a little odd, because he wore the same kind of clothes as everybody else now. There was nothing particularly lordly about his woollen shirt and jerkin. And yet . . . you could still tell. You could tell that he was no ordinary Highland peasant. I don't know if castellans' sons are actually born different. I mean, when they are babies I expect they squall, sleep and fill their nappies like any other child. But perhaps as they get older, they learn to move and talk differently. At any rate, it shows. And it's not just the clothes.

He had grown a beard since we moved into the Highlands. Most clansmen wore beards, so perhaps he imagined it made him look less recognizable. But it would take more than that, I thought. Even the careful courtesy with which he greeted us was somehow different from the Highland idea of good manners.

'Where is Callan?' he asked.

'Gone to fetch Falk,' I said. 'We're packing up for the day.'

'Was it a profitable day?'

I nodded. 'The salves are all gone, and Rose has sold a lot of her little animals.'

He picked up one of the carved dogs and weighed it in his palm. 'They're good,' he said. 'What do you charge?'

'A copper penny for the smallest ones and two for the others,' murmured Rose, her face colouring from the praise.

Nico frowned. 'Isn't that too cheap?' he asked. 'I'm sure you could charge more.'

'See?' I said. 'I've been telling her.'

'But that doesn't count,' Rose burst out. 'I mean, Nico isn't used to . . .'

'To what?' said Nico, suddenly very still.

Rose shuffled a foot and clearly wished she had kept her big mouth shut.

'Nothing,' she muttered.

'No, tell me. What am I not used to?'

'To counting the cost of things,' Rose whispered.

Nico put down the little dog figure, very carefully.

'No, you're right.' His tone cut all the way to the bone. 'People like me always have someone else to pay the price for us.'

He spun on his heel and walked away from us, and once more you could see people making way for him without even thinking about it.

'Wait,' I called, putting down the jars I had been packing. 'Nico, wait for me!'

'Don't trouble yourself on my account,' he said coolly, not stopping. 'I *am* perfectly capable of buying a mug of beer myself.'

In the crowded, twilit Market, he was almost lost from sight already. Oh, bother, I thought. We promised. We promised Master Maunus . . .

'Mama? Mama, can I go with him?'

'Yes,' said Mama, following Nico's dark head with her eyes. 'Perhaps you'd better.'

I eeled my way through the throng in Nico's wake, but he had longer legs than I did, and catching up with

20

him was not easy. I only succeeded because he had stopped at a liquor stall in the next street over. He stood there, hesitating, with the coin in his hand, but at least he had not yet put it on the vendor's desk.

I walked up to him.

'Nico – won't you eat supper with us?'

He spun. Apparently, he had not believed I would follow. He gave me only the briefest glance before lowering his eyes, and that made a sudden wave of misery well up in me.

'You can look at me,' I said quietly. 'I'm no longer dangerous.' Strange how that made tears sting at the corner of my eyes. It had been lonely, before, when I still had my Shamer's eyes, but it still felt . . . wrong, somehow, not to have them. As if I was no longer quite my mother's daughter. As if I was no longer quite myself.

Mama had said that the gift would come back, that it was only hiding, and I did sometimes get a flash as I had with the carter just now. But most of the time . . . most of the time absolutely nothing happened when I looked at people.

'Dina . . .' He touched my cheek, so lightly that it was only a fleeting warmth. 'Why do you mind so much? I would have thought you might enjoy being able to look at other people every once in a while, without having their darkest secrets leap out at you like a monster from a cave.'

'I don't know,' I said.

'You've had the chance to become *ordinary*,' he muttered. 'You've no idea how much I envy you.'

I didn't feel ordinary. I just felt . . . broken.

'I think it might be too late,' I said. 'I'm not sure I know how to be ordinary. I've never really had the chance to learn.'

'Then the two of us have more in common than I thought,' he said darkly.

'What do you mean?'

'If I had had a choice, I think I would have chosen to be . . . the son of a horsebreeder, perhaps. Or a merchant. Or a carpenter.'

'You only say that because you've never had to be hungry all the time at the end of winter when there's hardly any food.'

'I didn't say I wanted to be poor. Or to starve. But all my life, people have had a lot of fancy ideas about who I was, or ought to be. When I was a boy, I wasn't allowed to play with the guardsmen's children because I was the son of the castellan. I would have liked to make pots or work with wood, but no, I had to learn the sword. And when I didn't want any part of that, when I finally threw away my sword . . . well, you know what happened.'

Yes. I knew. His father had beaten him. Again and again, shouting all the while that 'a man is nothing without his sword'. But Nico had refused to fence any more, no matter how often or how hard his father hit him.

'And when . . . when it all happened, with my father and Adela and Bian . . . when they were all killed, everyone thought I had done it, and a lot of people think so still. To them I am Nicodemus the Monster, and they would kill me without hesitation, and boast about it afterwards. Did you know that there were people who came down to the dungeons of Dunark just to spit at me? People I knew. People I had grown up with.'

'But there are some – quite a lot, now – who don't believe those lies any more,' I said. 'The Weapons Master, and the Widow, and . . . and all the people they've gathered.' There was resistance now, down in the Lowlands, to Drakan and his Order of the Dragon. Secret resistance, but none the less serious for all that.

'That is true. And to them I am the Young Lord, and they want me to fight Drakan in some bloody battle and liberate all the conquered towns and cities, so that everyone can live happily ever after. They want a hero, I think.'

'Is that so bad? It beats being a monster.'

'Not by much. Have you noticed how often heroes die in battle? Afterwards everyone is very sorry, and a lot of pretty songs get made, but the hero is still dead. Stone cold dead. I'm in no particular hurry to climb up on my white steed and go slaughtering people until someone who is better or luckier than me spits me on his sword. No thank you.'

He looked both determined and ashamed at the same time, as if he really thought he *ought* to climb on his white steed and all the rest of it. I could well understand why he didn't want to end up dead, but all the same . . . I suppose I always did think that he would return to the Lowlands some day to fight Drakan.

'But then what?' I burst out. 'What do you want to do instead?' I couldn't quite see him working as Maudi's third assistant shepherd for the rest of his life, and to be honest, he wasn't much good at it. Only last week we had spent a whole day looking for a sheep he had lost.

Nico raised his head and for once looked straight at me.

'I want to be *me*,' he whispered. 'Is that so terrible? I just want to be Nico, not a lot of other people's hero or monster.'

'But, Nico, do you even know what that means?' Without meaning to, I glanced at the penny he was clutching in one hand, and Nico noticed it immediately.

'It means,' he said angrily, 'that I buy myself a mug of beer if I feel like it. Just like other people. And if you want to run home to Master Maunus and tell tales, go ahead and do so.'

I didn't know what to do. If Nico had a mug of beer . . . well, that in itself wouldn't be so terrible, of course. It was just that with Nico it was rarely one mug. Or even five or six. And that had actually been one of the reasons why it had been so easy to get him accused of murder.

Perhaps, if I had still had my Shamer's eyes, I could have stopped him. But I hadn't.

'Nico,' I said. 'When you've had your beer – won't you come and eat with us? We're camped up there, by those rocks.' I pointed.

Nico looked a little less tense.

'I will. Oh, go on, stop looking so worried. I will.'

I headed for the rocks myself. After a whole day of noise and bustle, it was quite nice to get away from the crowds for a while. I was pleased now that Mama had chosen a campsite here. The dew lay like a grey veil across the grass and the rocks, and my feet and ankles were soon soaked with it. The sun had almost set, with just a few pale golden streaks to show where it had gone. A soft twilight hugged the hills. This close to Midsummer, this was about as dark as it ever got up here. Wood smoke hung like mist across the valley, and I could hear the distant baaing of goats and sheep, and a little closer, dogs barking at each other.

Suddenly, there he was. Standing right in front of me, as if he had sprouted from the earth itself. The stranger. The man in the red shirt. I breathed in a little too suddenly and ended up having to cough from sheer surprise.

'I mean you no harm,' he said in his alien accent, softer and more lilting than the voices I was used to hearing. 'I just want to know your name.'

I didn't answer. I just darted sideways, away from him, and began to run.

It wasn't far to the camp. Our big hound, Beastie, gave a threatening *wrooof* when he heard me come charging up like that, and Callan, who had been nursing a small fire into life, got to his feet in one smooth, dangerous-looking move.

'What is it?' he asked, sharp-voiced.

'Nothing,' I said, catching my breath. 'A man. A man who—'

'Where?'

'There . . .' I waved a hand at the slope.

But the slope was empty. Only boulders, dew and wood smoke. The stranger was gone.

'No one there,' said Callan.

'He . . . he must have gone back down. To the Market.' But I didn't understand. How could he disappear so suddenly? Melting away, like he was a ghost or something, and not properly human at all.

'What did he look like? What did he want?'

'He just wanted to know my name.'

That sounded strange, even to my ears. But Callan nodded, as if that kind of thing happened every day.

'It is a good thing that ye're careful,' he said. 'But I do not think he wanted to harm ye.'

I didn't know what to think. He had said he meant no harm. But it would have been pretty stupid to say 'Come here and let me harm you' in any case. And after everything that had happened during the past two years, I felt I had reason enough to be suspicious.

I sat down by the fire and let Beastie keep me company while Callan took Falk down to fetch the cart. A little later Davin and Black-Arse came up, and then Mama and the rest. Even Nico. Mama had splashed out on smoked sausages for all of us, seeing that we had done such good business, and as we talked and joked, I nearly forgot about the stranger once more. It was the Midsummer Market. We had a bit of money for once. Davin was happy and proud because he and Falk had taken a prize at the races, and Mama promised that we could go down to the Market later, and listen to the music, and maybe even dance a bit. Life was good right then, and worrying seemed silly.

THREE

The Baying of Hounds

Mama was shaking me.

'Dina, wake up. We're leaving.'

'Mmmmh.' I didn't feel like waking up. It had been quite a late night, and I had ended up dancing till my head spun and my feet hurt.

'Are you awake? I need you to go and find Nico and Melli. I think they went down to the pond.'

I struggled free of the blankets and got to my feet, somewhat stiff-backed from sleeping on the ground. Trekking through the Market grounds in search of my rebellious little sister was not high on my list of favourite things to do this morning. But packing up the tent was not going to be a much more pleasing task, so after a visit to the latrines I set out for the shallow pond that served as a watering hole for most of the Market beasts.

I could hear Melli laughing long before I saw her. She was chuckling and snorting and giggling with laughter, and I sneaked in a little closer to see what was so funny.

It was Nico.

He was standing in the middle of the pond, with a long wet garland of water weeds across one shoulder. In one hand he held a stick as though it were a proper staff.

'I am Neptune, King of the Seas,' he called in a pompous voice. 'And I bid the winds and the waters rise. Let there be such a storm as never was before!'

And then he bent and blew at something – three little boats, I saw now, made from reeds and woven grass. The three boatlets rocked precariously, one of them threatening to capsize.

'They're drowning,' said Melli, her giggles coming to an abrupt halt. 'Nico, please, save them!'

'As M'lady commands.' Nico bowed deeply, a real courtier's bow. Carefully, he righted the little boat and sent it on its way.

I just stared. I had never seen him like this before – clothes soaked, hair and beard dripping with water, yet . . . luminous, somehow. His whole face was lit from within with laughter, with sheer unshadowed *fun*, and he looked as if he had never even heard of worries. I could hardly believe my own eyes. Here was the exiled heir to Dunark castle, playing the fool for the benefit of my six-year-old sister – and having a fine old time doing it, it seemed, with nary a thought for heroes and monsters now.

I was almost sorry to interrupt, but Mama and the rest were waiting. The Market was over, and we had a fair way to go.

'Oh, Great King Neptune,' I intoned. 'We're packing up.'

His head came up with a jerk. He obviously hadn't heard me coming.

'Dina,' he said, and I watched the laughter die from his eyes. 'Yes. Quite. We'll be with you in a moment.' He made a sudden gesture with one hand, spraying my skirt with a small shower of droplets in the process. 'I slipped, and gave myself a ducking. But perhaps Davin has a spare shirt I can borrow.' He brushed the weeds off his shoulder and headed for dry land.

'The ships,' objected Melli. 'They'll have no one to give them good winds now.'

'They'll have to manage on their own,' said Nico, wringing the tails of his shirt to rid it of the worst of the wetness.

Melli set her hands on her hips and gave me a defiant glare.

'I don't want to go home now.'

'Too bad,' I said, ''cause that's where we're going.'

'But I don't want to!'

I gave her a measuring look. Her cheeks were still flushed from laughing so hard, and her dress was stained with grass and mud and pond water. There was a stubborn set to her mouth, and she looked like a very angry and slightly chubby pond troll. She was perfectly capable of throwing herself on the ground, howling and screaming and generally kicking up a fuss.

'Come on, M'lady,' said Nico, settling to one knee. 'Climb up and let your trusty steed bring you to the ends of the earth.'

And lo and behold. The troll surrendered. Melli happily climbed on to Nico's shoulders and rode piggyback all the way back to our camp. No doubt that made her even damper and muddier, soaked as he was. But I didn't say anything.

I don't know how it happened, but by some mysterious magic everything we had brought with us had swollen to twice its original size, or at least that was how it seemed to us as we struggled to pack up the tent and the rest of the gear. Similarly, everything we had bought at the Market seemed bulkier than the stuff we had sold. It was a good long while before we were ready to hitch up and head for home.

We had been travelling for less than an hour when Beastie started to act strangely. He struggled against Rose's hold on his collar, and when she let go, he leaped off the back of the cart and began running around, circling us as though we were a flock of sheep he needed to protect. And then he barked. A series of short, sharp *wrooofs*, the way he often did when strangers approached the house back home. Silky danced uneasily, and I had to put a soothing hand on her neck.

'Mama, can't you get him to be quiet? He's scaring Silky.'

But Callan would have none of that.

'Leave him be,' he said. 'It's a poor hunter who will not heed the baying of the hounds. And Beastie is not a dog to sound off over nothing.'

Nico glanced at Callan. Callan shrugged his shoulder very slightly, as if to say maybe, maybe not.

'M'lady must ride in the carriage for a while,' Nico told Melli, who was perched on his saddlebow.

'But I want to stay with you,' said Melli.

'Perhaps later,' said Nico. 'Right now I need you to do as you're told.'

And once more, to my utter astonishment, Melli obeyed him, climbing into the cart and on to Mama's lap with no further ado.

'You really must teach me how to do that,' I muttered.

'Do what?'

'Get Melli to do as she's told without a tantrum.'

He smiled faintly, but his attention was elsewhere. He was sitting very straight on the bay mare, looking around him in a wary manner.

'Best I take a little ride,' said Callan. 'If yerself will stay here.'

Nico nodded silently. Callan dropped back, not suddenly but bit by bit, as if by chance. The road here wound its way around low hills, and soon he was lost from sight.

'Is someone following us?' I asked Nico, as quietly as I could.

'I don't know,' he said. 'Callan is checking.'

My whole body had gone stiff and tense at the thought, but when Callan reappeared a little while later, he was shaking his head.

'Nothing,' he said. 'Least, nothing I could see. The dog has caught the scent of some animal, it may be.'

'Yes, maybe,' said Nico. But he would not allow Melli back on his saddlebow, and his dark blue eyes kept flickering this way and that, left, right, ahead of us, behind us, all the way back to the cottage.

It was evening before we got there. Black-Arse called

31

goodbye and rode off home, and Nico also went off, home to Maudi's place and grumpy Master Maunus. Callan stayed around for a little while, to help us unload and unpack. We let the horses into the paddock and watched for a few moments as they slumped to the ground, rolling and kicking and sighing with relief. The chickens all came running, cackling and begging for food, so that I gave them a few handfuls of grain even though I knew Master Maunus would have fed them earlier.

'Can I go and fetch Belle?' asked Rose. 'Please?'

'Yes, do that,' said Mama. 'She'll have missed you terribly.'

Belle was Rose's dog. She was only about a year old and still quite puppyish, so Rose had not wanted to risk bringing her to the Market, among so many strangers and strange sights and sounds. Luckily, Maudi never minded looking after Belle, as it was Maudi who had given her to Rose in the first place.

'Can I go too?' I asked.

Mama frowned. 'We have to unload everything before it gets dark,' she said. But then she relented. 'Oh, well, we'll manage. Go on, be off. But hurry home, the both of you.'

Rose was so impatient that walking was too slow for her. Even though we were both tired, we ended up running almost all the way over to Maudi's place. And even before we came into the yard, Rose gave a shrill whistle between her teeth.

What a ruckus! *Wroof, wrooof, wouuuuh, woooouhhh . . .* yes, Belle had missed Rose, and she was busy telling the whole countryside, so much so that she soon had all of Maudi's other dogs barking too. Maudi opened the door, and a black and white arrow shot out between her legs and aimed itself at Rose. Belle was not a small pup any more, but she leaped straight into Rose's embrace, so that Rose keeled over backwards, her arms full of dog.

'Well, well,' said Maudi drily. 'Looks like someone is happy to see you.'

Rose muttered something into Belle's fur, but I couldn't quite catch the words. Belle's pink tongue licked everything within reach: hair, sleeve, neck and cheek. And I stood there feeling almost envious, because even though I knew I had Silky and Beastie, sort of, neither of them ever greeted me in that fashion.

We said goodbye to Maudi and headed up the hill. Belle was racing in large circles around us, playing shepherd the way Beastie had earlier, but in a much more light-hearted manner. She kept so low to the ground that her belly touched the grass at times.

It was dark enough now that the first few stars had appeared. Our cottage nestled in a hollow among the hills, protected from the strong Highland winds. On the tallest of the hills, the Stone Dance showed black against the darkening sky. There were few trees here, and almost all of those were birches. Other than that, yew and heather were the commonest of growing things, so on the day our cottage had had its first anniversary, we had made a neat sign to hang above the door: Yew Tree Cottage, it said, though most people still called it simply the Shamer's place.

Mama had lit the lamp in the kitchen and opened the shutters so that the glow spilled on to the dusty grass of the yard. As we came down the hill, Beastie came trotting slowly up to meet us. He had become a little stiff-limbed lately, especially when he had been lying still for a while. We had had him for a long time, and he was not young any more; not like Belle, who was busy greeting him with delighted little puppy noises, practically wagging her tail off.

Mama was frying onions, by the smell of it. Supper. Mmmmh.

'I'm soooo hungry,' said Rose.

'So am I.' Starving, actually.

Yet I still halted to stand for a moment, looking down at our small cottage with the tarred beams and the turfed roof, and at the stable and the sheep shed and the paddock where Silky and Falk were grazing. Behind the house the apple trees that Mama had planted last year were blooming, with pink and white blossoms like snowflakes against the black boughs.

'It was a great Market,' I said. 'But it's good to be home.'

'Yes,' Rose said simply.

FOUR

Fog

Two days later, the weather changed. We woke to a heavy, grey-white fog which clung so closely to the hills that we could barely see the sheep shed on the far side of the yard.

'It might lift once the sun is properly risen,' said Mama.

But it didn't. Finally, we had to go out and be about our tasks, even though the fog slowly seeped through our clothes, until it felt like wet fingers touching one's skin. Big fat drops of moisture collected in our hair and in the fur of all the animals. It would have been much nicer to stay indoors, but Mama had bought a lot of seedlings and seeds at the Market, and if we didn't get the planting done soon, nothing would come of it this summer.

'This is disgusting,' I muttered, pressing the dark soil into place around the stem of a baby cabbage plant. 'You can't breathe without getting your mouth and nose full of fog!'

'It probably won't last much longer,' said Mama. 'It's nearly noon, isn't it?'

'I can't tell,' I said irritably. 'The sun might as well not be there for all the good it does.'

'Let's eat,' said Mama. 'Maybe it will have cleared away by the time we're done.'

There was a lonely whinny from the paddock.

'I think I'll let the horses in first,' I said. 'Sounds as if Falk doesn't like the fog.'

'You do that,' said Mama.

I rinsed the dirt off my hands at the pump, wiped them on my apron and headed for the paddock gate. It was still the old, somewhat ramshackle paddock we had put up when we arrived, but Davin was making a bigger and better one, now that we had two horses. But even though the paddock was quite small, I could see neither Falk nor Silky. I heard hoofbeats and another plaintive whinny that I thought was Falk's – that was all.

'Silky! Falk! Come on, horsies!' I called out, then whistled the signal they usually obeyed if they felt like it. 'Want to come in out of the fog?'

Falk neighed once more. Now I could see him, at first only as a darker bit of fog, and then he came trotting out of the mists. But where was Silky? I peered into the mists behind Falk, but he seemed to be alone.

'What have you done with Silky?' I asked. Our black gelding merely snorted and shook the droplets from his lashes.

'Silky!' I called out. 'Siiiilky!' I whistled again. Still no Silky.

It was a little odd. But if I brought Falk into the stable, she would probably be standing by the gate by the time I got back – she didn't much care for being alone in the paddock.

'Come on,' I urged Falk. 'If Mylady wants to be coy, let her. There's no reason why you have to be wet and hungry.'

I put him in his stall and fed him a few handfuls of grain. But when I got back to the paddock, there was no dappled grey mare waiting by the gate. I wasn't sure whether to be irritated or anxious. She was not usually so difficult. Could something have happened to her? I climbed across the fence and trotted towards the far end of the paddock, whistling and calling. My sense of unease grew. Granted, a grey horse might be more difficult to see in the mists than a black one, but even so . . .

I reached the fence on the other side. And yes, the fog was dense, but not *that* dense. With a sinking feeling in my stomach I realized that my sweet-mannered Highland horse was not just being coy. She had disappeared altogether, and the paddock was empty.

'Silky is gone!'

Mama and Rose were setting the table and heating water for tea.

'Gone?' Mama put down the bread knife. 'What do you mean, gone?'

'She's not in the paddock!'

The kitchen went very quiet. All the little noises – the rattle of plates and mugs, the sound of Melli's feet kicking gently against the bench – had suddenly stopped. All you could hear was the hiss of the kettle.

'Are you sure?' said Davin. 'I mean – that's quite a fog . . .'

'Of course I'm sure! I went all the way around, following the fence, and . . . and I found a place where the top pole had come off.'

Davin cursed. 'I knew I should have checked that fence. Only, I was so busy with the new paddock . . .'

'She won't have gone far,' said Mama. 'The two of you can go and look for her. By the time you've caught her, Rose and I will have lunch ready for you.'

'We'll bring Falk,' said Davin. 'He'll neigh his head off the minute he catches Silky's scent, and she'll come running.'

I felt calmer now that we had a plan. And Mama was right. Horses rarely wandered far without their herdmates. If only there hadn't been such a fog. Perhaps Silky really wanted to come home but couldn't find the stable?

We saddled Falk, and Davin swung on to his back. I took a bucket and some oats to use as a lure.

'Let's start with just a quick circle round the house and the gardens,' said Davin. 'You go one way, I'll go the other. Or do you want to go together?'

'No, let's split up,' I said. 'We'll find her more quickly.'

'All right. But don't go too far from the house – it's easy to lose your sense of direction in this weather.'

Davin turned Falk around and made for the sheep shed corner. I went the other way, past the house and into the orchard. If Silky was eating Mama's new apple trees, I would have her hide! But she wasn't. The orchard was empty.

'Silky. Siiiilky!'

Wait. Was that a whinny?

I whistled the three soft notes that was my special signal for Silky.

Hoofbeats. I was almost certain . . . yes, there it was again. I stopped and listened, to get a better sense of where they were coming from. There, by the brook . . . *Clop-clop.*

'Siiiiilky!'

The path was damp and slippery, and I skidded down the slope to the brook, nearly dropping the bucket. I had to grab at a birch branch to stay upright. The mists moved in slow swirls over the mossy green stones, like elfmaids dancing. I could almost see them, even though I knew they weren't there – a curved arm, a graceful back . . . Music too. I froze. Music. Eerie and whispery, like a flute gone hoarse from the dew . . . I was nearly *sure* I could hear it, but . . . who would be wandering around playing a flute in this weather? And what kind of flute made a noise like that?

'Hello?' I called. 'Is anybody there?'

There was no answer, and now the music was gone again. Or perhaps it had never been there? It might have been just the rush of the water. Sounds behaved strangely in the fog, everyone knew that.

Then I caught sight of something that drove every thought of mysterious flute music from my mind. On the muddy bank on the other side of the brook I could clearly see several prints left by hooves – Silky-sized hooves.

I crossed the brook – Davin had laid down stepping-stones this summer, so that it was possible to get across it reasonably dry-shod – and climbed up the bank on the other side. A small copse of spruce and birch grew there, but I could see no grey horse shape among the pale trunks. Only the tracks, which showed up clearly in the leafy mould beneath the trees. She had come this way, at least. That much was certain.

There was a rattle and a flutter, and a small shower of heavy drops spattered my head and shoulders. I jerked, but it was just a woodpigeon taking off. It landed heavily on a branch a little further off, eyeing me with suspicion.

'Siiiiilky!' My voice sounded strangely lonely even though I knew I was only a very short walk away from the cottage. But even here in the copse, the fog hung like a heavy grey curtain, and when one could see no further than the next tree, it was easy to feel that one was all alone in the world.

If only the fog would go away. But it didn't, of course.

Wait. What was that? Something . . . something grey. More solidly grey than the mists . . . Silky, half hidden by the trees . . . I wanted to break into a run, but I knew that would only scare her off. I rattled the bucket instead and called to her in a low voice, moving forward with slow, easy strides.

But when I got there, she was gone again. Where was she now? I had heard no hoofbeats, and yet I could no longer see her. And where were the tracks? The ground looked completely untrampled here. This could not be where she had been standing when I spotted her. Perhaps a little further on . . .

I walked on, rattling the bucket and calling. She had

to be here, probably only just out of sight. Perhaps I should backtrack a bit and try to pick up her trail? But when I turned around, one tree looked exactly like the other. Where had I come from? Which way was home? Callan had told us plenty of scary stories about children who lost their way in the Highlands, only to end as a wolf's dinner or worse . . . captured by Underworld spirits, never to be seen again.

Calm down, I told myself severely. There is absolutely no reason to panic. Just walk back to the brook and follow it until you get to the washing stones. After that, the rest is easy.

But Silky? I'd *seen* her.

I hesitated. Should I go on looking now that I knew I was close? Or should I go back? I so wanted to find her. I was sure she was lost in the mists, lonely and scared and homesick. And what if there really were wolves? They did not often venture this close to human places, but perhaps the fog made them bolder?

I wished I hadn't thought of wolves. All of a sudden it was as if I could hear them howling; distantly, to be sure, but they could come closer any time. Poor Silky! There is no way I'll let you become a wolf's dinner, I silently promised. I will find you!

The copse fell behind. Hardly any trees now, just grass and rock and heather and mist. And still no Silky.

I stopped. This was no good.

I'm so sorry, Silky, I silently apologized. I'll lose my way if I keep going like this. It cut at my heart to think of my poor little horse astray in the fog, unable to find her own way home, and the thought of wolves made me even colder than I already was. But there was nothing else to do. I turned around and started walking back to the woods.

Only one thing wrong.

I couldn't find them.

I hated the fog. It wasn't just a matter of disliking it, I really *hated* it. I might as well have been blind, and I couldn't trust my hearing either; the fog could not really be full of flute music and the howling of wolves. Could it? When I tried to shout, the mists stole away my voice so that only a thin plaintive call came out. And no one answered. Davin couldn't be that far away. The *house* couldn't be that far away, or the woods, or the Dance, or . . . anything. Anything recognizable and familiar that would put east and west back where east and west ought to be and would tell me which way was home. And the longer I walked, the colder I got, because the dampness of the fog slowly seeped through my shawl and blouse and skirt. If I didn't get out of this stupid fog, I would grow *mould*, I thought viciously.

What if I kept walking downhill? Yew Tree Cottage was in a hollow, after all. Up and down were about the only directions I felt sure of. So. Downhill. Why did it seem to get colder the lower I got? I would have thought it would be less chilly here than on the hilltops, but not today. And then the ground started to get squishy underfoot, and when I lifted my foot, dark water collected in my footprints for a moment before slowly soaking back into the ground. Surely it wasn't this soggy around Yew Tree Cottage? The plants seemed different too – tall ferns, wolf's bane and gorse. And the soil was so dark it looked black, and smelled increasingly of bog.

I stopped. I didn't dare go on. The hollow I was headed into was not our hollow. I had to face facts: I was now completely and utterly lost.

I didn't know what to do. If I kept walking, I might be moving further and further away from the cottage with every step. I felt cold and wet and scared, and it was all I could do not to cry.

A lithe, scaly body slipped from the ferns and zigzagged across the black earth right in front of my foot. My heart jumped like a frightened frog, but it was just a grass snake; I could see the yellow spots behind its head. I knew it was harmless, but something about the black snaking form still made my skin crawl. No, I didn't want to be here. I wanted to be up where the ground was dry and firm, at least.

I tried following my own footsteps, but the ground was pockmarked with wet holes, many more than I could have made. Ferns slapped wetly against my legs, and around me the mists moved slowly, in lazy swirls. If I didn't carefully remind myself that fog was fog, the swirls turned into veils and white faces and pale arms reaching out for me.

Then I heard it once more, and this time there was no doubt. Someone really *was* playing the flute. The notes danced around me as though they were part of the mist, like a breath of wind through water reeds, or the first few drops of a rain shower. My heart was pounding along like a runaway horse now, because I was really hearing this music, and I could think of only one explanation: this was the spirits of the Underworld playing, trying to lure me into their den.

Suddenly I knew exactly what had happened. *They* had taken Silky. She was just the kind of horse they would love, fine-boned but strong, a real Highland horse without a single drop of Lowland blood in her veins. And the fog, of course, was their doing. Under one of the hills here, the Grim-Wife had lit her big cauldron. It was bubbling and boiling and pouring mist into the world, to trick and deceive unwary mortals. They were planning a feast tonight, the Grim-Wife and her people, and the music had already started. And I was horribly afraid that they meant for Silky to be the main course. They had a taste for horseflesh, it was said.

Oh, *why* hadn't I stuck with Davin? If only there had been two of us . . . and he had a proper sword, now, too, instead of that silly iron bar that broke the first time he tried to fight somebody with it.

I didn't even dare call out his name. The fog was listening. And in the stories, the spirits liked child's flesh even better than horseflesh. I couldn't even count on my stupid Shamer's eyes any more. Of course, they might not be much good against creatures like that anyway. *They* didn't know about good and evil, people said. It was possible to trade with them if one was clever and very, very careful. But no human could ever trust a creature of the Underworld.

I had been standing still for so long that I had started to sink into the soggy ground. When I tried to walk on, it was as if someone had hold of my feet from below. I wrested myself free, but it seemed the bog was loath to surrender its grip.

Not sure whether I was being brave, or just incredibly stupid, I started to walk towards the music.

There, in the middle of a small lake, stood the flute player. He was standing on top of the water, it seemed, while the mists curled caressingly around his knees, stretching up pale fingers to touch the hem of his cloak. The notes drifted along, almost a part of the fog, and whispered into my ears. And my eyes filled with tears, because the stories they told were so incredibly sad. I didn't understand everything the notes were telling me, but the sadness came through so clearly. The handle of the bucket slipped from my fingers, and I sat down as if I had no strength left in my legs at all.

He heard the rattle of the bucket and turned around. He had seen me, I knew he had. But still he kept on playing, kept blowing his sad notes across the lake and the reeds. Not until the tune had come to its end did he lower the flute.

'I thought you might come,' he said. 'Now, will you please tell me your name?'

It was only then that I recognized him. The stranger from the market, the man in the red shirt. And he wasn't standing on the water, as I had first thought, but on a flat rock half-hidden by the mists.

I was so relieved that he wasn't a spirit that I just told him. 'Dina.'

He nodded as if he already knew. 'You're looking for your horse,' he said.

'How do you know?'

He smiled faintly. 'Because a dappled grey Highland mare came this way a moment ago. May I help you find her?'

Silky, as it turned out, was not far away. We found her a little further up the hill, peacefully munching meadow grass as if she had not a care in the world. I was so happy to see her that I got all teary-eyed again, and at the same time I was angry with her for giving me such a fright. But I tried to sound calm and collected when I called to her.

'Silky! Come on, girl. Want some oats?'

She raised her head and pricked up her ears. And then she came forward eagerly to bury her muzzle in the bucket, and I gratefully caught hold of her halter.

'Thank you,' I told the stranger. 'I had almost given up on her.'

'One should never give up,' he told me in his alien, lilting voice. 'Did not your mother teach you that?'

I nodded hesitantly. Suddenly, I didn't know how to talk to him. What was he doing here? Had he followed us from the Market? I remembered Beastie's barking, and how Callan had circled back but found no one.

'Do you know my mother?' I asked. Should I be afraid of him? But he had found Silky for me. In a way, he had saved her from the Grim-Wife.

'I knew her once. If you let me walk home with you, perhaps we may become friends once more.'

I looked at him, trying to decide whether he was telling the truth, but without my Shamer's eyes, I couldn't be sure. He did not look like a liar, but one never knew. Mama would be able to tell. Perhaps bringing him to Yew Tree Cottage would be the right thing to do. If I could find it, of course.

'I'm afraid I'm slightly lost,' I said.

'Then it is fortunate that I am good at knowing where to go,' he answered calmly.

It was much further than I thought it would be. I had time to worry that he might be leading us astray. He had said he was good at finding his way, but I only had his word for it, and besides, he might deliberately be leading us in the wrong direction. But Silky walked with eager steps and pointed ears and looked like a horse headed for home and a warm stable, so I decided to trust her judgement. And after a while we heard voices calling – Davin and Rose and Mama.

'I'm right here,' I called back. 'I'm coming – and I've found Silky!'

'Dina!' Mama's voice was sharp with relief. 'Thank Our Lady. We were afraid you had lost your way in the fog.'

Davin took Silky's halter and led her into the stable, and Mama put her arms around me and hugged me tight. She had really been worried, I could tell.

'Mama, I did get lost a bit,' I said carefully. 'But then I met . . .' I hesitated, realizing that he hadn't told me his name. 'He says he knows you, Mama. He helped me catch Silky.'

Mama let go of me and seemed to notice the stranger for the first time. He was standing just inside the yard in his grey cloak and for a moment seemed almost a part of the mists. She stiffened. I could feel a sort of jerk going through her, and then her whole body hardened as if she had put on armour.

'What do you want?' she asked.

'Surely you can guess.'

'No.'

Her voice was hard as rock, and somehow you could tell that she wasn't saying No, I can't guess, but No, I know what you want and I won't let you have it.

'Melussina . . .'

'*No.*' Even more harshly, this time. 'Go away. Leave me and my children alone.'

'You cannot ask that.'

'Yes, I can. I want no part of you and yours.'

She still had her hands on my shoulders, and I could tell that they were shaking. Why was she so afraid of him? Or angry with him, or both.

'I have a right.'

'*Go away,*' said Mama, and this time she used the Shamer's voice so that he had no choice but to obey.

He bowed his head.

'As you wish,' he said, wrapping the cloak more closely around him. He turned and walked away, and within a few strides the fogs had swallowed him completely. But his voice reached us clearly even though we could no longer see him. It sounded much nearer than he was.

'You cannot deny me my right for ever,' he said. 'After all, I am the girl's father.'

FIVE

Beastie

It felt as if my legs no longer quite reached the ground. The girl's father. The girl. Did he mean me?

'Inside,' said Mama in a voice as grey and heavy as the fog. 'All of you. Inside. Now.'

On the kitchen table, plates and mugs were still waiting to be used. It was unreal. It was as if I had only closed my eyes for a moment, and now that I had opened them again, everything *looked* the same but was completely different. Mama closed and locked all the shutters, ordered Beastie on guard outside and barred the door. And then she did something I had often seen other women do, in Birches and in the Highlands, but never Mama. She took a bowl and brushed a little ash from the hearth into it. Then she spat on her finger and drew sooty black Xes on the door and all the windows. It barred evil from entering, they said. Mama never used to do such things. Perhaps she felt it wasn't necessary for a Shamer. But why, then, had it become necessary now?

'Mama . . .'

'Not now, Dina. Get the fire going again. Rose, light the lamp.'

It was midday. Were we supposed to burn expensive lamp oil in daylight hours? Everything was wrong. Everything. *The girl's father.* I stood there with a strange buzz and prickle in my whole body, like the deadened feeling in an arm when you've fallen asleep on top of it.

'Mama, he . . .'

'We will not talk about that, Dina. Not until the fog is gone. Now we will sit and eat our lunch, and afterwards Davin will tell us all a story.'

She looked at each of us in turn in that way she had which made it impossible to disobey. We all sat down, but I hardly tasted whatever it was I put into my mouth, and on the bench opposite me, Melli was on the brink of tears because she could feel that something was wrong. Belle cowered at Rose's feet the way she did when a thunderstorm was coming. And at first, nobody said a word.

'Davin — perhaps you can begin the story while we eat?' Mama finally said.

Davin looked at her searchingly, almost as if he was checking to see if she was ill.

'Which one do you want to hear?' he asked.

'I don't know,' said Mama. 'One that deals with good things. Fun things. A story that makes you laugh.'

Davin was the best storyteller in the family, probably because it had always been his job to tell bedtime stories to Melli and me whenever Mama was out, or too busy. But I could see that it was difficult for him to concentrate right now. Finally he started on The Tale of the Pig Who Wouldn't Be Dirty.

'Once upon a time there was a very clean little pig by the name of Persival.' Davin put on his storyteller's voice, deeper and slower than his normal one. 'While the other piglets rolled and wallowed and had mudfights, this little piggy liked nothing better than to scrub his pink hide until he shone with cleanliness. "Just because one happens to be born a pig is no reason to behave like one!" he said, to the despair of his mother, who was a very proper and dirty sow.'

Melli was already beginning to look less tense. She took a large bite out of the bread slice she was holding and chewed away as she listened.

'At first Persival's mother tried to reason with him, explaining how mud and dirt was naturally good for the skin. Persival wouldn't listen, and continued to scrub away as if soap and water had been invented specifically for him. All the other pigs in the field laughed at him and called him names, Soapy and Cleanie and Flower-Stink and worse things, but Persival turned up his piggy nose at them. "Sticks and stones may break my bones, but filth will never touch me," he said. His sibling piglets were ashamed of him, and more than once they ganged up on him and pushed him into the biggest mud hole they could find. But as soon as they let him up, he went straight to the nearest stream for a nice clean bath. And Persival might have grown up to be the cleanest pig in the world, had it not been for two wolves who happened by one day.'

At the mention of wolves, Melli sat up straight and

began to look anxious, and Davin hurriedly explained that the wolves had just eaten and were not very dangerous. They really just wanted to tease the pigs a bit.

'But Persival didn't know that,' he continued. 'So when he heard the wolves discussing which pig to catch and eat, he was so frightened that his pink skin became nearly green.'

Melli giggled at the idea of a green pig, and Mama gave Davin a small nod of approval.

Davin put on a growly deep wolf voice.

'Let's eat that one over there,' he growled, and answered himself in an even deeper voice, 'Naw . . . too dirty. Let's go for that nice little clean one instead.'

Melli put a hand to her mouth. 'That's Persival,' she whispered. 'They want to eat Persival.'

'Not really,' Davin reminded her. 'But Persival thought so. With a squeal he headed straight for the deepest wallow in the field and rolled and rolled and rolled until he was the filthiest piglet of them all.'

Melli grinned. 'And the wolves went away?' she asked.

'The wolves went away,' said Davin reassuringly, and Melli breathed a sigh of relief.

I felt much calmer now, too. More like myself. My head was still full of questions, but the deadened feeling was nearly gone.

'One more,' demanded Melli. 'Davin, tell another one! The Squirrel Story, please . . .'

Davin looked questioningly at Mama. Mama nodded. And Davin began to tell The Squirrel Story.

It was almost like those thunder nights when we

would all get up and gather by the hearth to drink tea and sing and tell stories until the storm had passed. But it was still daylight outside. And this was only fog, not thunder. And suddenly Beastie began to bark, one short sharp *wroof* after the other.

Davin paused in mid-story.

'Go on,' said Mama.

'But Beastie . . . we have to look!'

'No. Go on with the story.'

Davin opened his mouth to object. Then he closed it again. Mama was holding her mug so tightly that her knuckles looked white, and Melli's lip was trembling again. Belle wrested herself free from Rose's grasp and ran to the door to stand growling, all her sharp young teeth showing.

Hesitantly, Davin picked up the thread of his story. But outside, Beastie's barking rose to a furious howl, then abruptly became a fighting snarl. And then he wasn't barking any more. He screamed. He squealed like a puppy.

'I'm going outside!' said Davin, surging to his feet.

Mama caught his arm. 'No, Davin. There's nothing you can do. You'll only make it worse.'

'Make *what* worse? Mama, what is happening?'

Silence descended outside, with all the suddenness of a thunderclap. As if the whole world was holding its breath. Mama muttered a few words I didn't understand. A foreign language, I think. It sounded like a prayer. Slowly she set down her mug and pressed her fingertips to her temples, the way she sometimes did when she had a headache.

Something had happened. We could all feel it. Belle gave a brief howl and started scratching at the door with one paw. On the floorboards in front of the shuttered windows, pale strips had appeared. Strips of sunlight.

'The fog is gone,' said Davin. 'Can I go outside now?'

'Yes,' said Mama in a tired voice. 'Now, you may.'

Beastie lay by the woodpile next to the sheep shed. One side was dark with blood, and his neck and muzzle and throat were bloody also. He was still breathing when we found him. But before Mama had time to do anything for his wounds, he gave a strange, stumbling sigh, and died.

SIX

Blackmaster

I couldn't stop crying. Beastie. He had been with us for ever. Ever since I was small, anyway. He guarded us when Mama was away. He was the only animal who had come into the Highlands with us, the only one Drakan's men hadn't chased off or butchered. I knew he was old for a dog and that he had to die some day. But this was different. He hadn't just died. Somebody or something had killed him.

Mama sat with Beastie's head in her lap, pale as death, stroking his neck over and over again even though he could no longer feel her touch.

'Why did you tell him to guard us?' I screamed at her. 'Why couldn't he stay in the house with us and be safe?'

She didn't answer me. 'Davin, get Callan,' she said. 'Ride as fast as you can.'

Davin made no objection. He just saddled Falk and rode off, going up the hill at a full gallop.

Nervously, Belle crept up to Beastie's still form. She sniffed at him, and began to make a low whining noise in her throat. Rose wrapped her arms around her and buried her face in black and white fur – lucky Rose, who still had a dog to hug. Melli was looking at Beastie in white-faced silence. She wasn't even crying. Perhaps she hadn't quite realized that he was dead.

I fetched a bucket of water from the pump and began to wash away the blood from Beastie's grey flank. I'm not sure why. I probably just wanted him to look more like himself again. Instead, it only made his wounds more visible: two long slashes along the ribs and a deep stab close to his heart. Someone had used a knife on him.

No. Not just 'someone'. It was him – the stranger. The one who had said he was 'the girl's father'.

'Mama, who is he? Is he really my father?'

'No more than a serpent is mother to the eggs it lays.'

That meant yes, didn't it?

'And Davin? Melli?'

'No. Just you.'

Just me.

It was just me who had a serpent for a father. Just me.

I stared at my hands, pink from water and blood. Then I got to my feet. I couldn't stay still any more, not even for a second. If I didn't move, I'd burst. I spun around and took off.

'Dina! Stay here!' called Mama, sounding frightened. But I couldn't. It was all I could do to stop running when I reached the orchard.

Davin wasn't fully my brother. And Melli wasn't fully my sister. I might have known. I had always been the strange one. I only had to look in the mirror. Davin and

Melli looked like Mama – they all had the same silky-smooth auburn hair. I was the only one who had coarse black troll's hair. Just me.

'Dina.' Mama had followed me. 'Please, my love, go into the house. You mustn't run off like that, it's dangerous.'

I was shaking all over. Suddenly I felt so dizzy I had to sit down. The slender apple trees were completely black, and the daylight very white.

'What is his name?' I asked.

'Sezuan.'

'That's a weird name.'

'He is not from around here. He comes from Colmonte.'

'So do we. Or so you've said. The Tonerres.'

'Yes, but . . . in a different way. It's a long story. The important thing is not what he is called, but what he is. Do you know what a Blackmaster is?'

'A sort of wizard.'

'Not really. No more than a Shamer is a sort of witch.'

'Is a Blackmaster like a Shamer?'

'No, not that either. A Shamer sees the truth and forces other people to see it too. A Blackmaster does the opposite. He can throw a glamour on you so that you see things that aren't there, or so that you cannot see the things that are.'

'Did he make the fog?'

'Perhaps. At any rate, he used it. The glamour comes more easily when it is hard for us to see clearly in the first place. Dina, he is very, very dangerous.'

'Why did you send Beastie out to fight him, then?'

'Because animals are often harder to fool than people. They depend more on senses other than sight. And Beastie did defend us. It is because of him that we are still ourselves. That Sezuan did not manage to sway us to his will. But he'll be back, Dina. He will try again.'

Mama sat down beside me in the grass and put her arm around me. Now we'll both have wet bottoms, I thought, with the part of my head that went on noticing things like that even when it didn't matter.

'That's why we have to leave,' said Mama.

At first I didn't think I'd heard her right.

'Leave?' I said cautiously. 'To go where? And for how long?'

'Just . . . away from here. And Dina, it might be . . . for good.'

'No!' She couldn't mean that. Not again. Not now when everything had become . . . become almost ordinary again. We had planted apple trees. We had built the cottage. 'You can't . . . we can't just . . . run away from him. Just because he is a Blackmaster.'

'I ran away from him before you were even born,' she said sadly. 'I can barely protect *myself* from him. I do not know how to protect my children.'

'Me, you mean. It's just me he wants. I'm the only serpent spawn in this family.'

'Dina! Don't talk like that!'

'Why not?' I said bitterly. 'It's true, isn't it?' I rose. 'But what I don't understand . . . what I really, really don't understand . . . is how you came to have his child. Why was I even born?'

Mama opened her mouth, but I gave her no time to answer. I just walked off and left her. An apple twig brushed my shoulder, and I ducked to avoid damaging the tender buds. And then I thought, it doesn't matter. If we're leaving anyway, why should I care if there are ever apples on this tree?

SEVEN

The Leaving

Callan tried to talk my mother out of it. The Tonerres had friends here, he said. The Kensie clan would protect the Shamer and her children. Mama merely shook her head and kept packing things. In the yard outside, Davin was burying Beastie. 'Let him lie where he can see who is coming and going,' Mama had said. 'That's how he likes it.'

'If ye leave, who will be protecting ye?' said Callan, opening and closing his big hands as if he wanted to wrap them around something. 'The lad shows promise, I'll grant ye, but he is still too young. Medama, this is recklessness.'

'I'm sorry, Callan. I have no choice.'

'Let me get some good men together. We'll rid ye of the bastard.'

'Swords and good men are no use against a Blackmaster,' said Mama. 'How can you hit something you can't even see? And you will see Sezuan only when he wants to be seen.'

She would listen to no one. Not to Davin and me

and Rose and Melli, not to Callan, not to Maudi. Not one night more would she spend in Yew Tree Cottage. Callan barely managed to persuade her to stay the night at Maudi's and set off in full daylight, at least. I had trouble sleeping. On the other side of a thin wooden wall, I could hear the murmuring voices, Callan's, Mama's, Maudi's, arguing and making plans. But that was not what was keeping me awake. Every time I closed my eyes, I saw him: the flute player, standing in the middle of a lake making his music, while the mist curled and danced around him like a living thing.

Next day, in the grey dawn, we packed up the last of the things we could bring. There wasn't much room in the cart when you considered that it would soon hold everything we had in this world. So much of what we had worked for or made or bought during the last two years had to be left behind.

I felt so miserable. The leaving itself was bad enough. But at the same time I felt as if it was my fault that we had to leave at all, because it was my father we were fleeing from.

Sometimes, especially when I had been angry with Mama about something, I had dreamed of finding my father. He would be nice, of course, and brave and strong. He would have a fine-looking horse and beautiful clothes, silks and velvets and the like. And most importantly: he would have been searching for me all his life, and now that he had found me, his face would shine with happiness and joy. That's how I had dreamed it. Instead, I got Sezuan Blackmaster.

There was a bare spot of dark brown dirt in the yard where Davin had buried Beastie. I felt like leaving a flower, or something, but Beastie wouldn't care about flowers. He would rather have a bit of sausage and a good scratch behind the ears, and I could give him neither of those things now. I hoped there was a dog heaven somewhere, where he could run around all day sniffing at exciting scents, digging holes wherever he wanted to, with a good bone to chew whenever he felt like it. He deserved that, and more. What he didn't deserve was for his family to leave him when he was barely cold in his grave.

I hated Sezuan. And I came close to hating Mama for making us leave.

'Dina,' said Mama softly, from the carter's box. 'It is time.'

I leaned my forehead against Silky's warm neck for a moment. The last thing I wanted was to get up on her back to ride away. But there was nothing I could do. Davin was already mounted on Falk, and between the shafts of the cart stood a strong dun mare that Maudi had told us to take, so that Falk wouldn't have to play cart-horse.

'Shall I give ye a leg up?' asked Callan. He had agreed to go with us on the first part of our journey. Until we were clear of the Highlands at least, and perhaps even further than that; he hadn't really said.

I shook my head. I could do it myself, I just didn't want to. Not quite yet.

Nico and Master Maunus had come to see us off and to say goodbye. Now they were fighting – as usual. What was *un*usual was that they did it in whispers instead of yelling at each other the way they normally did.

'You have a duty. An obligation!' said Master Maunus in a furious low voice, looking over his shoulder to see if Mama had heard.

'Yes – but not the one you think. She saved my life!'

'One life – when the lives of thousands depend on you. Bad enough that you skulk around up here playing the shepherd. You simply cannot go traipsing all over the countryside like a . . . like a common tinker!'

Nico took a deep breath and spoke out in very calm and measured tones:

'Scold all you want, Master. My mind is made up.'

And then he smiled, embraced his tutor and kissed his furrowed brow.

Master Maunus looked completely flustered.

'Well, that . . . well, then . . . but . . .' he stuttered. And then ran out of words completely.

'Stay with Maudi, Master. Or move in to Yew Tree Cottage. When this is over, I'll come back. Or send for you. I promise.'

And so it was that when we left Yew Tree Cottage, Nico came with us. And Master Maunus stayed behind.

II
Loclain
Davin's story

EIGHT

Owl Night

The night before we left Yew Tree Cottage I had a row with my mother.

I couldn't find my sword. I had just finished burying Beastie, and the only thing I could think of was how soon I could find the evil bastard who killed our dog. No way was I going to let myself and my family be driven out of house and home by a puff-adder like him. But when I dug into the thatch on the sheep shed where I usually kept my sword, all I could find was straw. I searched all along one side and practically buried my arm to the shoulder, thinking it had to be there somewhere.

'It's not there,' said Mama.

Startled, I spun around to face her. I hadn't meant to involve her in this.

'Where is it, then?' I tried to sound matter-of-fact.

'Davin, this is not something you can fight with a sword.'

I knew then that she had taken it, and a surge of anger ran through me.

'What did you do with it?'

'Listen to me, Davin. You must not try to find him.'

She had no need to say his name – we both knew who she was talking about.

'He kills our dog. He kills Beastie – and you think he should get away with it?'

She dropped her glance but did not answer.

'Maybe you think it doesn't matter. Maybe you think, oh, he was just a dog. Nothing to get excited about. Just a dumb dog.'

'I'm as grieved as you are.'

'Well, you could have fooled me!'

Mama merely looked tired.

'We're sleeping at Maudi's place tonight,' she said. 'And tomorrow morning, we leave.'

Now it was my turn not to answer. If I had to do without the sword, I would. I had my bow. Well, Callan's bow that he had lent me. And in any case, an arrow might be a better weapon against sorcerous scum like him – that way, I wouldn't have to get in close. And if only I could find him tonight, there would be no need for us to go anywhere tomorrow.

Sometimes I might as well be made from glass. Mama could see right through me without even trying.

'You will not do it, Davin,' she said. 'I need you. What would I do, what would the girls do, if he lured you into some bottomless bog, or made you step off a cliff so that all we ever found of you were the shattered bones?'

'Mama . . .'

'No. I'll not let you. You can have the sword back

68

tomorrow. Tonight, you will stay indoors. *Do you understand?'*

There wasn't much I could do, not when she spoke in that voice. But I couldn't just meekly stand by either.

'Only cowards run without a fight!'

'Then I suppose that makes me a coward,' she said. 'But it will be as I have said.'

'But *why?'*

'Because we have no other choice.'

Mama didn't give me back my sword until we were ready to leave the next day. I took it without saying anything and tied it across my back where it would be within easy reach. No matter what Mama said, if Sezuan Puff-Adder tried anything, I'd be ready!

Dina would be riding Silky, and I had Falk. Mama and Rose and Melli rode in the cart. Maudi had told me to take a Kensie horse for the cart, and I had picked a strong dun mare we hadn't yet chosen a name for. It was one of the ones we had taken from Valdracu's men after the battle of Hog's Gorge last year, so I felt I had just as much right to it as anybody else.

Black-Arse had come to say goodbye. He patted me clumsily on the shoulder and didn't know what to say. Suddenly I felt horribly envious of Dina. Rose was coming with us. I was the only one who'd be losing my best friend. But after the mess I'd got him into last year, one could hardly blame Black-Arse's mother for threatening him with hellfire and retribution and no supper for a year if he so much as thought about coming with us. And anyone who knew Black-Arse also knew that the no-supper threat had a real sting to it.

'When ye find somewhere,' said Black-Arse. 'Somewhere to live, that is. Ye can send word, can ye not? And I could visit some day.'

I nodded. 'Yes. That would be nice.' And highly unlikely, I thought. I looked at the ground, at Falk's black legs and hooves. 'Take care of yourself,' I said. 'Stay out of trouble.'

Black-Arse's eyebrows rose until they nearly met in the middle. 'Why is it we cannot just kill this . . . this Blackmaster?'

'I don't understand either,' I said. 'Mama says swords are no good against him because you can't see him. But yesterday I saw him just fine.'

All the same, I had this constant unease, like an itch you couldn't scratch. Where was he? What did Mama mean when she said that you couldn't see Sezuan unless he wanted to be seen? How close could he come without being noticed? The hill above us? The sheep shed corner? Or might he suddenly appear right under Falk's soft, black nose?

We never actually said goodbye, Black-Arse and I. He just slapped me on the shoulder once more, and then I climbed on to Falk's back. The cart rolled out of the yard, and I followed. Black-Arse was left to stand with Maudi and Master Maunus, watching us leave. As we crested the hill, I looked back one final time. Would we ever see the three of them again?

Silky followed the cart, too, but not because Dina was guiding her. My sister looked as if she was barely taking in what was going on around us. Tears were streaming down her cheeks.

'Dina . . .'

She shook her head. 'Just leave me alone,' she said, pulling up the hood of her cloak so that I could no longer see her face.

The cart was no racing chariot, and even though the dun mare was a strong-hearted little lady, it was still an effort to pull the load up the steep slopes of the Maedin range. When the sun began to set, we had barely reached the boundaries of Kensie land.

'Perhaps we should camp here for the night?' I suggested. 'It's best to have a bit of daylight left to gather firewood and suchlike.'

Mama shook her head. 'We have to reach Skayark tonight.'

Skayark. That was a long way off.

'But it'll be hours and hours before—'

She didn't answer. She just looked at me.

'Mama, it'll be pitch dark. They might not even let us in.'

And Skayark was very much a fortress town. I had seen those walls, and they were not meant for scaling.

'Skayark,' said Mama stubbornly. 'We do not sleep until we have walls and people around us.'

I looked at Callan to see if he would back me up, but apparently he had no intention of gainsaying Mama today.

The sun dropped behind the Maedin range. It became more and more difficult to see the road in front of us –

71

and the potholes. All we need now is for a wheel to come off the cart, I thought. Trying to fix that in the dark would be no picnic. Then I caught myself and hurriedly gave three loud whistles to ward off any mischievous road spirit who might have heard my thought. You have to be careful what you wish for in the mountains. Especially at this hour, on the threshold between night and day.

'What did ye want to do that for, lad?' asked Callan in some irritation. 'The whole mountain can hear ye.'

'Sorry,' I muttered.

A cold wind came whistling through the valley, and I shuddered. Such sudden gusts are not unusual in the mountains, particularly near dawn and dusk. But it was not just the cold that made me shiver. It felt so hostile, that wind, as if it would hurt us if it could. The sun had completely disappeared now, and the first stars showed in the sky, cold and white against the darkness. Falk did not care for the wind, either. Snorting, he laid back his ears and stiffened his legs and spine.

'Callan,' said Mama, 'light a torch.'

'He will see us coming a mile off,' objected Callan.

'Do it anyway. In the darkness, we are easy prey.'

For a moment, I thought Callan would protest again. Then a sort of sigh made his wide shoulders rise and sink.

'If ye think that is the wisest way,' he said. 'I do not know how to deal with wizardry and the like. Robbers and highwaymen, now . . .'

He sounded almost as if he would like to be attacked by an honest robber just so that he would know what to do. And in a way, I understood his feelings. Cold winds and misty visions — what is a man to do against such things? I still did not clearly understand how Dina had come to lose her way in the fog and return to us in the Puff-Adder's company. Sezuan. Even his name sounded like the hissing of a snake.

'I'll fix us a torch,' said Nico, leaping off his bay mare. 'Go on, I'll catch you up.'

'No,' said Mama. 'We stay together. No one goes anywhere alone.' She pulled back on the reins, and the dun mare came to a halt — gratefully, it seemed. 'Davin, give the horses a little water.'

I slipped off Falk's back and fetched the bucket from the back of the cart. My fingers were stiff with cold. This was supposed to be summer!

'Is it far?' asked Rose quietly.

'A fair bit yet,' answered Callan. He stayed on horseback, very straight and alert in the saddle.

'Mama.' Melli rubbed her eyes. 'I'm tired. I want to go home now.'

I didn't want to explain to my smallest sister that we weren't going home. Ever. Apparently, neither did Mama.

'Lie down,' she said. 'Rest your head in my lap. You can sleep as we drive along.'

'We're not driving along,' objected Melli. 'We're not going anywhere.'

'No, but in a minute, we will.'

I offered the bucket to the dun mare first. There wasn't a lot of water left, even though we had filled it at the last stream. The mare slurped and finished what there was.

'It's not nice here,' said Melli defiantly. 'It's cold and disgusting and not nice at all. I want my own bed.'

Nico had cut off a stout birch branch and wrapped one end with rags soaked in oil from our meagre store, and it looked as if the fire had finally caught properly. He tied the torch to the front of the cart.

'Do you know the tale of Little Flame?' he asked Melli.

She shook her head sullenly.

'Well, do you want to hear it?'

Melli was clearly more in the mood for a good sulk. On the other hand, she loved stories, and in the end she surrendered, nodding royally.

'Once upon a time there was a small flame who wanted to see the world,' began Nico, hoisting himself into the saddle once more. 'One day it simply leaped from the hearth where it had been born and began its journey...'

We continued our own journey. The flickering torchlight fell on rocks and heather and ferns, and made the shadows flutter about us like black birds. The wind had brought new clouds, and most of the stars had disappeared. I could see only the two lowest now, like two pale eyes staring down at us. The cartwheels rumbled across the uneven ground, and from somewhere in the dark came a shrill, piping scream. Melli gave a startled little mew.

'Do not fret yerself,' said Callan. 'It is only a couple of owlets, begging for food.'

Nico had stopped in the middle of his story.

'Where is Dina?' he suddenly said.

I waved a hand. 'Right behind—'

But she wasn't. Not any more. The darkness hugged us closely, a cart and three riders. Of Silky and my sister there was no trace at all.

'Dina!' I called.

There was no answer.

Mama hauled on the reins so hard that the dun mare practically sat back on its haunches. For a moment, she looked utterly terrified. Then she flung the reins to Rose. 'Here. Stay where you are. Davin, give me Falk.'

'No,' I said. 'I'll go back. It's better that you stay with Melli.'

She probably would have objected, but I had already turned Falk around and urged him into the fastest pace I dared, what with the darkness and the stony ground.

'Wait,' called Nico behind me. 'I'm coming too.'

I slowed my pace just enough for him to be able to catch up. My hands had suddenly become so damp that the leather reins felt slippery and hard to hold. How could Dina have disappeared like that, right from under our noses?

'Dina!' I yelled, trying not to think of the last time I had ridden like this, calling and calling, with no answer except the silence. When Dina disappeared on me last year, it had been months before we got her back, and she still wasn't quite her old self.

Falk stumbled slightly in some pothole I had overlooked. Instinctively, I reined back, and he tossed his head in irritation.

'Ease up,' said Nico quietly. 'Give him his head and let him set the pace. He can see better than you can.'

Usually I became irritated when Nico corrected me, but right now there was no time for irritation. I let the reins slide between my fingers, and Falk immediately became both faster and more surefooted.

How long had it been since I had actually seen her? It felt as if she had been there, right behind me, only moments ago. How could we have let her fall behind like that? And why hadn't she said anything, why hadn't she called out? In my mind, I heard Mama's voice again: 'What if he lured you into some bottomless bog, or made you step off a cliff so that all we ever found of you were the shattered bones?' Could he really do that – the Puff-Adder?

'*Dina!*' I was yelling at the top of my lungs now. But all I could hear were the hoofbeats, the night wind and the hungry owls.

And . . . and something. A flute?

'Nico? Did you hear that?'

'What?'

But it was gone again. It had probably been the wind. Or some shepherd in the neighbouring valley, playing a tune to keep himself awake. Miles away, maybe. Sound carried differently in the mountains.

'There she is,' said Nico.

She was sitting stock-still on Silky, in the middle of the road. I was so relieved to see her that I immediately lost my temper. I don't know why, but that's how it usually works.

'What do you think you are doing?' I snarled. 'Mama is beside herself!'

She looked . . . strange. Stone-faced. Almost as if she hadn't quite seen us yet.

'I heard someone calling,' she said slowly.

'Of course you did! We've been yelling our heads off. Why didn't you answer?'

She looked at me uncertainly. 'I didn't know it was you.'

'Dina, what's *wrong* with you?'

'Nothing.'

'Why did you stop? Mama told us to stick together.'

She stared at Silky's white-tipped ears. 'I . . . must have fallen asleep.'

'Without falling off?'

'People do that!'

It sounded defiant and somehow . . . wrong. Yes, people did sometimes doze in the saddle. But that didn't explain why Silky had stopped. Horses did not normally let themselves be separated from the herd like that, and Dina . . . Dina didn't look like someone who had been asleep. More like someone who had had a wide-awake nightmare. And why hadn't she answered when we called her? What did she mean when she said she didn't know it was us? Who else would it be?

Something was wrong with my sister. It took no Shamer to see that.

'Dina . . .'

'I told you, I fell aleep!' She was staring at me with a strangely hostile glare. 'Are you calling me a liar?'

'Come on now,' said Nico. 'Let's get back to the others as quickly as we can. There's no reason to frighten them any more than we have to.'

★ ★ ★

I thought Mama would scold Dina, but she didn't.

'Dina. Into the cart, *now!*' she said, with precisely enough of the Shamer's tone in her voice to make it impossible for Dina to disobey. 'Rose, can you ride Silky?'

'Maybe,' said Rose dubiously.

'Then do it!'

The words came like the crack of a whip, and Dina had barely changed places with Rose before Mama slapped the dun mare's quarters with the rein so that it set off with a startled lunge. She drove the mare into a gallop, and the cart swayed dangerously, leaping and bouncing down the trail. I caught a brief glimpse of Melli's white and frightened face, then I had to urge Falk onwards to keep up.

'Have a care, Medama,' shouted Callan. 'Mind the wheels! Mind the horses' legs!'

'There's no time,' answered Mama, ice in her voice. 'I have my daughter's soul to think of.'

What did she mean by that? But there was no time for questions, either. It was all I could do to keep up. There were no cosy bedtime stories now. Hooves thundered across stony ground. White foam flew in tatters from Falk's mouth, and his dark neck steamed with sweat. Suddenly, the torch tied to the cart went out, either because of the wind or our breakneck speed, but not even that made Mama stop. It was a miracle that the wheels held up. It was a miracle that no horses stumbled. Perhaps it was a miracle, too, that all of us reached Skayark safely – my incautious little sister included.

NINE

Skayark

'We owe much to the young Shamer,' said Astor Skaya.
'And I tell ye, this Sezuan shall not pass.'

He proudly showed us his defences – the yard-
thick walls, the towers manned by archers, the guards
in their blue and black uniforms, with the Skaya eagle
embroidered in gold on the chest. Skayark lay like a
coiled dragon across the pass, with crenellated walls
that zigzagged from one mountainside to the other.
There was no way around this fortress, unless one had
wings.

'It will at least slow him down,' said Mama
thoughtfully.

'Slow him down? Medama, in three hundred years
no enemy has penetrated these defences. Think ye that
this Sezuan is capable of such a feat single-handed? I tell
ye, it is not possible for a mortal man.'

'Not by force, no. But perhaps by cunning? Be
watchful, Skaya. Be very, very watchful. He can make
men see things that are not, and trick them into not
seeing what really is. He can take on a hundred different

forms and make his direst enemy shake his hand as though he were a brother.'

For the first time, Astor Skaya seemed a little worried, and looked at his walls less smugly.

'Is there a way to recognize him?' he asked. 'If he can take a hundred forms, how are we to know him? We cannot clap every traveller in irons.'

'He has a mark,' said Mama, suddenly looking embarrassed. Embarrassed? Mama? Who always seemed so certain of things, and most of all of herself? 'A tattooed serpent. It is his family mark, he wouldn't and couldn't erase that.'

'And where is this serpent?'

'Coiled around his navel,' said Mama, blushing furiously.

And it was only then that I realized that Sezuan really was Dina's father. That my mother had seen that tattoo and maybe even . . . maybe even touched it. And that she had borne a child to this man who now had us fleeing like mice when the reapers come.

Anger surged through me, with such force that I could barely stand still. I wanted to shake her and yell at her. How could she do such a thing? She who was always telling the rest of us off about right and wrong. How could she?

Astor Skaya was watching us curiously. I bit back my angry words because I didn't want him to hear them.

'I think I'll go to bed now,' I managed to say. And I walked away from her, down the stone steps into the barbican below. Mama and the Puff-Adder. *Sezuan.* How could she?

Even now, in the middle of the night, Skayark was not completely asleep. Torches were burning, and guards were waiting to relieve those stationed on the walls and in the towers. A game of dice was in progress at the foot of the stairs, and I stopped, not wanting the players to see the expression I couldn't hide. I stood in the dark stairwell, leaning against the rough wall and keeping my face in shadow. How *could* she?

From the bridge above me I heard her voice.

'If my daughter has ever earned Skayark's favour . . .'

'She has. Many times over. Medama knows we owe her countless lives.'

'Yes. I do know that. And that is why I ask in her name for Skaya's aid. Astor Skaya, close the gates of Skayark for ten days. Let *no one* in or out. No one at all.'

'Ten days,' said Astor Skaya slowly. 'That is a long time. In the middle of the trading season, too. There will be a lot of angry people outside that gate.'

'I need that time, Skaya. Ten days of safety, to hide our trail and make it impossible for him to find us again.'

There was a moment's silence.

'Aye then,' said Astor Skaya. 'Ten days it is. Ye have my word on it.'

'Thank you,' said Mama quietly. 'You lend me hope.'

Yes, well, that's all wonderfully touching, I thought. But if you hadn't . . . if you hadn't let that dirty snakespawn take you to his *bed*, we wouldn't have needed ten days. We wouldn't have needed to flee like this, away from Yew Tree Cottage, away from Black-Arse, away from everything that had begun to make life bearable and *fun* once in a while.

Mama and Sezuan. I couldn't even bear to think it.

Callan and Nico and I slept in a low-ceilinged room above the stables with half a score of snoring Skaya guards. Astor Skaya had offered us his guest chambers, but it would have taken half the night to get them ready, and we were all tired. The Castellaine herself, Astor's wife Dia, had taken Mama and the girls under her wing, and they had disappeared into some woman's world where men were not generally invited. A world full of clean sheets and lavender scents and the like, I supposed. This place, on the other hand, smelled more of horse and dog and male sweat and a chamberpot that hadn't been emptied. But the straw mattress was clean and quite soft enough, and even though I was still furious with my mother, I fell asleep in the middle of my angry thoughts.

'Come on, lad. Get ye up.'

Up? What did he mean, up? I had only just lain down.

But the morning sunlight fell golden-bright on to the floorboards, and when I forced my eyes open properly, I realized I was the only one still abed. Callan had obviously been up and about for quite a while.

I groaned, but swung my legs out of the alcove. Nothing else for it.

'Coming,' I muttered. Sleep blunted the edge of my voice, which broke hoarsely.

'Ye'll have to use yer ten days well,' said Callan. 'No time to waste.'

'Us? You mean . . . you're not coming?' I suddenly felt much more awake. Unpleasantly so.

He shook his head. 'I might have come along with ye for another couple of days. Or some weeks, it might be. But yer mother has asked me to stay here.'

'But . . . why?'

He threw a look across his shoulder, but the only Skaya man still in the room was busy repairing a falconer's glove. He hummed tunelessly as he worked and had eyes for nothing except the tiny stitches.

'She wants to be certain that Astor Skaya really keeps his gate *shut*. That he doesn't let some rich merchant pass, some important trader he doesn't want to offend. If I'm here, shut means shut.'

I sat quite still on the edge of the alcove. Somehow, I had imagined that Callan would be with us always, even if we were no longer in the Highlands. It hurt to find out that I had been wrong about that.

He put his hand on my shoulder for a moment, big and heavy like a bear's paw.

'Ye'll do fine, lad,' he said. 'You, and Nico. Ye'll have to look after the Shamer now.'

'Nico . . .' I snorted. What use was Nico, what with him and his *I don't care for swords*.

'The young lord has a sensible head on his shoulders,' said Callan. 'As long as he decides to use it and grow up. And the same goes for you, laddie. Ye'll have to learn to think, not just charge in believing ye can meet every kind of trouble with yer sword. Ye have a charge, now.'

I cleared my throat. 'I wish you were coming,' I said when I was able to control my voice.

Callan nodded. 'Aye. And I'll miss ye all. But if ye are to be safe, Sezuan must not follow ye. And I promise – he'll not get past me.'

In his own way he looked as unmoveable as the fortress of Skayark itself. And if we couldn't have him with us, I thought, at least there was a great deal of comfort in knowing that he stood between us and Sezuan.

Shortly before noon we left Skayark – Mama, the girls, Nico and me. The horses were tired and tender-footed, and the wheels of the cart looked dented and cracked from the crazy pace Mama had set us the night before. Melli went from shrew to crybaby and back again in seconds flat, what with being so tired; Dina was pale and silent; and I didn't even want to look at my mother because I was still so angry with her. A jolly party we made, I thought, as we crossed through the Skayler Pass and began the long descent into Loclain.

TEN

The Soot-Monster

Loclain was neither Highland nor properly Lowland.
There were no true mountains, but the hills were fairly
high. There were lots of streams and lakes and woodland.
And ferns and moss and mites, and clearings full of tall
grass and strawberries, and an incredible number of birds.
Sometimes they blackened the skies.

There were more people here than in the Highlands.
More villages, and bigger. Some had more than one
mill, and more than one inn. But of cities like Dunark
and Dracana, there were none.

Nor were there castellans and the like. The villages
had names like Kettletown, Whittler's Place and
Ropeham, and that was actually quite telling. In Loclain,
any self-respecting village had at least three or four
respected craftmasters who were among the best in their
craft. People came from miles away to learn pottery from
Potter Laurenz in Clayton, or smithcraft from Master
Hannes of Kettletown. And when decisions had to be
made in the villages, the masters had the final say.

★　★　★

We arrived in Clayton late in the afternoon, on the tenth day since we had left Skayark. Tomorrow morning Astor Skaya would once more open his gates, and even though his men would keep an eye out for Sezuan, the risk that he would fool them had grown into almost a certainty – I couldn't see the guards stopping every single traveller, asking them to show their navels.

At least we had put our ten days to good use. We were many, many miles from Skayark now, and the roads we had travelled by had been small and well-concealed. We had even sold the dun mare and bought a small round-backed black gelding just to look different. And Mama hid the Shamer's signet beneath her blouse and carefully avoided looking at people we met, so that no one would report that a Shamer had travelled this way.

We hadn't meant to stop at Clayton. But as we rolled into the square between the smithy and the inn, there was a loud crack, and the cart swayed ominously. Mama braked and yelled for Rose and Melli to get off the cart. As she jumped clear herself, there was another crack and a tearing noise, and then one front wheel came off, and the cart seemed to kneel down for a moment, like a tired old priest, before crashing on to its side. The black gelding fought to stay upright, and Nico hurriedly cut it from its harness.

'Oi,' said a woman who had been getting water from the well. 'That doesn't look good.'

And it didn't. The axle was broken, and everything we had in the cart lay scattered across the fired clay tiles of the square.

'That won't take you far,' said the woman.

I could see as much for myself. I looked at her tiredly and might have given her a sharp reply if there had been the least little hint of malice in her smile. But there wasn't. She was just being helpful, as it turned out.

'Tell you what, my Amos is prenticed to Cart-Maker Gregorius in Wheelton, just down the road a little way. He would be pleased to mend the axle for you. You can stay at Minna's inn the while.'

'Is it expensive, the inn?' Mama asked cautiously.

'Well, not expensive, perhaps. But not cheap either. But if you don't mind the inconvenience, there is always Irena's cottage. It's not much good, to be honest, and a long walk from town, but I'm sure she'll let you stay there for next to nothing.'

'Where can I find this Irena?' asked Mama.

The woman pointed to the smithy.

'Right there. She married the smith last year, and the cottage has been empty since.'

It was no palace. The thatch was green and black with moss, and the daub walls leaned more than was sensible. There wasn't much space either – just the one room, with a fireplace at one end and an alcove at the other, and then a ladder leading up to a dark loft.

'Not much in the way of furniture,' said Irena Smithwife, who had shown us the way. 'But I'll get my stepson Olrik to bring you some clean straw so at least you'll have decent bedding.'

Mama paid her the ten copper pennies they had agreed on.

'Stay as long as you like,' said Irena. 'It'll do the old place good to be lived in once more.'

It felt strange to have a roof over one's head again. A roof that was almost our own. Strange, but good. Even if there were mice in the thatch – you could hear them scrabble and squeak.

'If we're going to live here, we'll need a cat,' said Rose.

And suddenly we were all looking at each other. It sounded so right: to live here.

'It's only for a night or two,' said Mama. 'A week at the most. It won't take them longer than that to mend an axle and one wheel.'

No one said anything right then, but I'm almost certain we were all thinking the same thing. Why not here? We had to stop somewhere, had to live some place.

'Ten days,' whispered Dina, and you could hear the longing in her voice. To belong somewhere. To stop travelling, stop drifting with no other goal than to get away. 'Isn't ten days' distance enough?'

Mama hesitated.

'I don't know. And we don't know what sort of a place this is. Let's not get our hopes up too soon.'

I woke up the next morning and needed to pee. I couldn't seem to find my boots, so I climbed barefoot down the ladder and opened the door. The sun was shining, and it was already quite a warm day. Grass and errant lupins grew knee-high in the small garden in front of the cottage. I waded through the grass and went around to the back of the cottage to find a quiet spot for a pee. I was barely done when Belle came scampering up to me, tail waving like a flag. She was still only a big pup, and she probably missed having someone to play with. No one had really been in the mood since . . . well, since Sezuan Puff-Adder turned up to ruin our lives. I laced up my trousers and picked up a long stick.

'Go on, girl,' I said. 'Take it if you can!'

Eyes shining with delight, Belle clamped her teeth around the other end of the stick, and we tugged it back and forth between us all over the back yard, trampling grass and goldenrod so that it looked as if a whole herd of wild pigs had passed by. Finally, the stick snapped. Belle chewed contentedly on her end for a while before coming up to drop it expectantly at my feet. I picked it up. It was all wet with spit and dog drool, but one would have had to be a whole lot more hard-hearted than I was to resist the expression in Belle's dark eyes. I threw the stick as hard as I could, and Belle pelted after it, through grass so tall that all I could see of her sometimes was a black and white tail.

'Davin!'

It was Mama calling.

'Back here,' I yelled.

'Can you come and help for a minute? Something is blocking the chimney.'

I went back in. And she was right. Looking up the chimney, I could see only the tiniest pin-prick of daylight and a lot of black something. We tried to poke at the something with a long stick, but it was up too high. A lot of soot fell down, and most of it lodged itself in my eye. Ouch. That really stung!

'Dina, get the bucket and the rope and see what the water is like in the well outside,' said Mama. 'Davin, don't rub your eye, you'll only make it worse.'

Mothers are at their most annoying when they are right. I clenched both hands in an effort not to rub my stinging eye, and a few moments later, Dina came back with a bucketful of well water.

'Smells all right,' said Mama, before taking a sip. 'Tastes fine, too. Davin, come here and let me rinse it.'

'I can do it myself,' I muttered.

'Probably. But I can see what I'm doing, and you can't.'

She washed my face and dabbed carefully at my soot-infested eye. I suddenly felt like a small boy again, being taken care of by my Mama.

I was still angry at her over the Puff-Adder, but just not all the time. You can't be angry at someone every waking moment, not when you have eaten, slept, travelled and worked together for ten days. Sometimes the anger boiled inside me, at other times it was almost gone. Right then I couldn't feel it at all.

'Is it better now?'

'Yes,' I said, and thought to myself that everything was, really. Today we didn't have to bounce along woodland trails. And if we ever managed to clear the chimney, we could eat a meal that had been cooked in a proper hearth, not over a hurried campfire.

In the end, I climbed on to the roof with the aid of our longest rope, which Nico managed to toss so that it coiled around the chimney. I scrambled up the mossy thatch until I could sit astride the ridge, and Nico then tied a long stick to the rope so that I could haul it up and use it as a poker. I bent over the chimney and looked into its dark mouth.

'Looks like a bird's nest,' I said, prodding at it with the stick. It wasn't easy, and I had to stand up in order to be able to reach further into the chimney.

'Careful,' called Mama.

'I am.'

I poked and prodded until sweat was trickling down my face. You would have thought the nest had claws, the way it seemed to cling. Finally, something happened. With a scratchy noise the nest slipped down the pipe and landed with a thud in the cold ashes of the hearth. A new burst of soot exploded up the chimney, but this time I closed my eyes in time.

'Huh-huh-huh-huh-huh!' I yelled.

'And what is that supposed to mean?' asked Mama.

'It means, Gracious Lady, that the deed is done! Victory is ours! Sir Davin of the Stout Stick has finally vanquished the Soot-Monster!'

Melli looked up at me, wide-eyed and open-mouthed. Then she started laughing. I swung the stick in a circle over my head and repeated my victory cry:

'Huh-huh-huh-huh-*huuuh*!'

'Yes, all right,' said Mama. 'But come down before you fall down. You might break something.'

ELEVEN

Homeless Mice

A week later, we were still living in Irena's cottage. The garden was nowhere near as overgrown now; the horses must have thought they had died and gone to heaven – no work for a week and all that juicy grass.

Some of the villagers were nice, others a bit more wait-and-see. Well, that was fair, I supposed. They didn't know us yet. Of Sezuan there had been not so much as a whisper, and in all the time we had been in Clayton, no strangers had come by, only people from the nearby villages of Wheelton and Weaversham.

On the seventh day Mama and I went to Irena Smithwife to ask if we could stay, and how much it would cost.

We found her behind the smithy, hanging out laundry to dry in the morning sun.

'Stay?' she said, fastening a peg to the corner of a sheet. 'For how long?'

'I don't know,' said Mama. 'Through the winter. Maybe even longer.'

A half-grown kitten was sneaking up on the laundry basket. In a magnificent hunter's leap it attacked a shirtsleeve that dangled temptingly over one side. Irena pushed away the kitten before it could deliver more muddy paw prints to the clean clothes. She wiped her hands on her apron and stretched, resting both hands against the small of her back. She was pregnant, I suddenly saw. Not showing hugely, not yet, but when she stretched like that it was pretty obvious.

'Come in for a while,' she said. 'I'll make us some rosehip tea.'

We followed her into the house, a solid and well-built brick house with a tiled roof. The smith and his family lacked for nothing, it seemed. And of course Irena had a beautifully crafted iron stove, rather than a simple open hearth. She stirred up the embers, put fresh fuel on the fire and set the kettle to boil.

'Why do you want to settle in Clayton?' she asked, her back still turned.

'I think we can make a home here,' said Mama quietly.

'Where are you from?'

'The coastlands.' Mama mentioned neither Birches, our old village, nor Dunark, though that, at least, was a name Irena was sure to have heard before.

It was quiet in the kitchen for a while. The kettle on the stove began to hiss softly. I sat there on Irena's kitchen bench feeling awkward, as though I were a beggar who had come to ask for a boon. But then, perhaps I was. Compared to a well-to-do household like this one, we were a bunch of homeless paupers, and what little money we had would not last us long if Irena demanded more than a few copper marks for her rent. I had never felt poor before, not even when we first came to Baur Kensie and had practically nothing. Poor wasn't the same as not having much. Poor was when there was something you really, desperately *needed*, food, shelter, or fuel, and you could not afford it.

Slowly, Irena turned to face us.

'You never look anyone in the eyes,' she told my mother. 'How come?'

Mama sat stock-still for a long moment. Then she reached inside her blouse and drew out her signet. 'Because of this,' she said.

Irena nodded. 'That's what I thought. Will you do Shamer's work here?'

'No. I . . . have some knowledge of herbs and healing. I will hold to that. And I would ask you not to mention my Shamer's gift to anyone.'

Irena looked at her more kindly now. 'I have heard of the Dragon Lord and what he does to Shamers in the coastlands,' she said, compassion in her tone. 'Here, it is different.'

'I still ask your silence.'

'I shall have to tell a few people,' Irena warned us. 'And it is a difficult thing for you to hide in the long run.'

'I would just rather not have the rumour spreading throughout Loclain,' said Mama.

'No,' said Irena. 'That I can understand.'

She took the kettle from the stove and poured tea into three tall earthen mugs.

'Welcome to Clayton,' she said, setting the mugs in

front of us. 'We would be fools to turn away a good herbwife.'

'But . . . the money,' said Mama. 'I have to know if we can afford it.'

'Money? You gave me money already. Didn't I tell you that you could stay for as long as you liked?' She laughed and stroked her rounded belly. 'And if you will help bring this rascal into the world, I have already made a good bargain!'

We didn't say much, Mama and I, as we walked home through the woods. Home. It was a good feeling that there was once again a place you could say that about. And at the same time I felt a funny tension in my stomach, because it was also a dangerous word. Once you began thinking like that, you started to have feelings for a place. And the fonder you got, the harder it would be if – no, I didn't want to think of the Puff-Adder now. I wanted to *allow* myself to be happy.

The path leading to Irena's cottage – our cottage – was just a narrow trail. A stranger would see no particular reason to follow it. The cottage was invisible until you were quite close. It was almost as if the woods closed around it and shielded it from harm.

Belle began to bark and yip delightedly, and then came charging up to us, tail wagging furiously. Then she sniffed in surprise and tried to get her nose into the basket Mama was carrying. Rose was sitting in front of the cottage whittling clothes pegs, but when she saw us, she leaped to her feet.

'What did she say? Can we stay here?'

Mama smiled. 'We may have to,' she said. 'Because we now have a cat. Tell Belle to stay outside for a little while.'

When the bottom half of the cottage door was closed, Mama opened the basket. Out tumbled the tabby kitten Irena had given us.

'There,' said Mama. 'The mice will have to move out, now.'

'It doesn't seem quite fair,' said Rose. 'After all, they were here first.'

TWELVE

Beans and Letters

We planted beans. It was about the only winter crop that would do us any good this late in the year. Preparing the soil was back-breaking work. There was a garden of sorts behind the cottage, but the woods had had a free hand with it for nearly two years, and it showed. We borrowed a dung fork from the smith. We had a spade ourselves – or at least, we did until Nico managed to lose it.

'I don't understand,' he said and looked about in confusion. 'It was here a minute ago!'

I didn't understand it either. How could anybody lose a spade? I mean, the thing was *big*. It wasn't like losing a button.

We searched for it.

'Think,' I told Nico. 'What were you doing with it? And where?'

'Errrhh . . .' Nico looked dubious. 'I was digging . . . there, I think.' He pointed to a corner of the garden that had been partially dug. No spade in evidence. I lost patience.

'How on earth could you lose a spade?' I hissed at him. 'That takes real talent, that does!'

Nico blinked and ran a filthy hand through his hair. 'I'm sorry,' he said, contrite.

He really was sorry, anybody could see that. But sorry didn't get us our spade back.

One couldn't call Nico clumsy, not really. Slightly butter-fingered, perhaps, with things he hadn't done before, and there were quite a few of those. Castellans' sons didn't do much crafting and gardening, I supposed. But the worst of it was that he didn't seem to have his wits about him when he was working. He didn't take proper care of things. Left the saw in a half-sawn stump so that the blade was bent. Put the hammer down on the ground and forgot where he had put it. Dropped a nail and failed to pick it up. Dropped a whole handful of spinach seeds in the yard, which made the birds happy but didn't really please me much – we needed every crop we could get. And so on, and so forth. But the spade was a low point, even for him.

'We can't afford a new one,' I told him through my teeth. 'And if we don't get those beans in, it'll be a very hungry winter. Has the Young Lord understood that much?'

Nico bent his head like a whipped dog. 'I'll find it,' he said quietly.

A little later, Mama called us in for the midday meal. 'Where is Nico?'

'Looking for the spade.'

'Davin!'

I spooned some porridge into my bowl. It was so thin it looked more like gruel.

'We need that spade,' I said. 'And it was Nico who lost it.'

'He's trying.' Mama looked at me, and I looked at my porridge. 'He just wants to help.'

'Yes,' I said. 'But he's not very good at it, is he?'

We didn't find it until the next day, in a cluster of nettles where Nico had flung it instead of leaving it upright in the bean patch the way any normal person would have done.

And it was only the day after that that the rabbit thing happened.

I had left snares in suitable places – might as well take advantage of the fact that we were living in the woods. Every morning and every night I walked my round and checked all of them, and sometimes we'd been lucky. That day I had caught a rabbit, a small pale brown one. It leaped and fought and tried to get away when it heard me coming and didn't seem to understand that it would do no good. I seized it by the neck and gave a quick twist. Meat for the pot tonight – and we didn't get that often, these days. I was feeling quite pleased with my efforts, walking back to cottage.

Nico was sitting in the grass outside the door playing with Melli. He held up a handful of twigs. 'How many?'

'Four,' said Melli instantly.

Nico put that hand behind his back and held up the other. 'And here?'

'Six.'

'Good. And how many altogether?'

99

Melli hesitated. 'Nine?'

Nico let her see both hands at the same time. 'Count them,' he said.

Melli's lips were moving as she counted the twigs. '. . . eight, nine, ten,' she murmured. 'There are ten!'

'Correct. That's good, Melli.'

Melli caught sight of me. 'Look,' she said, proudly holding up a contraption of strings and twigs. 'This is an M. That's the first letter in Melli!'

I could feel my temper rising. The beans weren't in yet, the hen-house had no door, the horses still had to be tethered because we hadn't had time to build a fence. We barely had a bench to sit on, or a table to eat at. And there he was, sitting on his backside fooling around with Melli. When there were a thousand useful things he could have done instead.

'Here,' I said, throwing him the rabbit. 'Skin it and give it to Mama.' He could do that much, couldn't he? I had even gutted it for him already.

He turned pale. Carefully, he lifted the rabbit off his lap and laid it on the grass. He held his hands stiffly away from his body, and I could see that there was a bit of rabbit's blood on them. Was he afraid of getting it on his shirt?

'I can't,' he said hoarsely and got to his feet. He went straight to the well and washed his hands meticulously till they were quite, quite clean. And then he left. Just walked off into the forest, without a word of explanation.

I simply didn't get it. He had to have been hunting with his father hundreds of times. That was one thing castellans' sons did do. Why was it then such a big deal for him if a bit of blood got on his hands? And you couldn't get him to lift a sword to save his life, practically. If I hadn't known that he had once killed a dragon, I would have thought that he was simply a wimp.

It was nice of Nico to come with us, I suppose. It was just that I couldn't quite see what earthly good he was.

'Three birds,' said Melli. 'No, wait, four! Look, Davin. Four birds!'

'Yes, Melli. Come on, now.'

'Two slugs. Two slugs and four birds, that makes six altogether.'

I wish Nico hadn't started on the numbers thing. Melli counted everything, now: grey stones and white stones, hazel bushes, horse poop, brambles and footprints. All the way from the cottage to Clayton. Houses, fencing posts, chimneys. Bags of flour at the miller's, horseshoes at the smithy. It was enough to drive a man crazy.

I had come to town to try to sell the black gelding. We couldn't afford to keep four horses through the winter. Possibly not even three, but Falk and Silky would not be sold unless we were practically starving, and we could hardly ask Nico to sell his horse as long as we insisted on keeping our own two.

'A good little worker,' said the smith, picking up each of the black gelding's hooves in turn. 'Sound legs, too.'

'Does Master Smith know anyone who might buy such a horse?'

The smith let go of the last hoof and straightened his back.

'Hmmm. I might. Not impossible, no.'

'Eleven, twelve, thirteen. Thirteen nails!' said Melli.

'Melli, be quiet now.'

'Thirteen nails and three hammers and one horse, that makes . . . that makes . . . that makes seventeen in all.'

'That's a bright little girl you've got,' said the smith. 'Who taught her that?'

'The . . . errh, my cousin Nico.' We had decided that it would be best if we pretended Nico was part of the family, but I hadn't quite got used to it yet.

'I can spell Melli, too,' said Melli proudly. 'M-E-L-L-I. And smith starts with sssss . . . an S.'

There was a grunt of laughter from the smith. 'Whatever you say, missy.' Then he looked at me. 'Tell me . . . this cousin of yours . . . do you reckon he could teach my Olrik his numbers? I've tried, but it doesn't seem to take. And if he can't do his sums and the like, he'll get hung out to dry too often by people who can.'

'I can ask,' I said, somewhat dubiously. I didn't know what Nico would say to being appointed tutor to the smith's half-grown son – in Nico's world, tutors were hired and fired as one needed them. One bought the best, of course, but they were not always granted the respect their skills merited.

'Tell you what, if Cousin Nico can teach my Olrik his sums, we have a couple of laying hens we can spare. And leave the horse here, I'll see you get a decent price for it.'

'Done,' I said instantly and held out my hand. Eggs again! Nico had better hold up his end of this bargain, or I'd tell him what for.

The smith grasped my hand, and the deal was done.

'Five knives and a kettle,' said Melli. 'But the kettle is broken, how do you count that?'

'I don't know,' I said. 'You'll have to ask Nico.'

To my surprise, Nico brightened like a sunny afternoon when I told him about the bargain I had struck on his behalf.

'Of course I will!' he said.

And the very next day he went off to Clayton, whistling loudly like a man on his way to a tryst. I shook my head at him and began mending the hen-house.

A couple of days later, Agneta Bakers came to ask politely if Master Nico would agree to school her Cornelius as well? Master Nico. Well, that was one for the book. But Agneta saw to it that we had fresh bread twice a week, so it seemed Nico was good for something after all. For some reason, he appeared to like it, and soon the whole village was talking about Olrik Smithsson who could do sums like nobody's business now, even though everyone knew he used to take two and two and make three.

By and by, Nico's class grew until he taught nine of Clayton's children two mornings a week. And Dina and Rose went with him, despite my protests.

'But we can't do without both of them! There is so much to do here.'

'Rose needs to learn how to read and write,' said Mama firmly. 'And Dina can help with the littler ones.' She looked at me pointedly. 'A bit of book-learning would do you no harm, either, Davin.'

But there had to be limits. Me, sitting with the children listening solemnly while Nico taught us how to spell 'I don't want to get my hands dirty'? No way. Never. Over my dead body.

THIRTEEN

Strange Looks

It was a school morning. Nico and the girls had left shortly after dawn, so Mama and I had to do everything by ourselves: watering the horses, feeding the chickens, weeding the bean patch, collecting firewood . . . all the little chores that still had to be done while His Self-Importance was busy playing schoolmaster to the village children. It was later than usual by the time I was ready to see to my snares. In the third one, there was an incautious water rat, already dead. We weren't *that* hungry, I thought, bending to loosen the snare. A yellow-green hissing head shot out at me, and I was so startled that I tripped over my heels and fell over backwards into a prickly bramble hedge. Arrow-snake. Ill-tempered and lightning fast, but not venomous. Good thing it wasn't a coppertail. But even though the arrow-snake's fangs had no venom, they were still very sharp. And the snake apparently considered the dead rat to be its lawful prey. I had to cut the snare and let the reptile win the day.

The snare was ruined now. I was filthy and wet, and

one hand sported a number of bramble scratches. And then it began to rain. Of course. It was that kind of a day.

Suddenly I saw Dina come walking through the rain. There was a really strange expression on her face, and she didn't seem to be headed for home.

'Dina,' I called. 'Where are you going?'

She stopped, looking about her uncertainly.

'Is that you, Davin?'

'Yes,' I said. 'Who else would it be?'

She didn't answer, just stood there looking at me as if she still wasn't sure I was me.

'Where are you going?' I repeated.

'Home.'

'Dina, home is that way.' I pointed.

'Yes,' she said, for all the world as if she hadn't just been going in practically the opposite direction.

'Why are you home so early? Has the Oh-So-Learned Master Nico finished his teachings for the day?'

For a moment she looked almost her old self. 'Why are you always so hard on Nico? You eat the bread he gets us!'

'Yes, and he eats the rabbits I snare. As long as he doesn't have to get blood on his hands, that is.'

'What do rabbits have to do with it?'

'Nothing.' I brushed the rain off my eyelashes. 'Is school over, then?'

She was back to looking stone-faced. 'No,' she said and walked on.

'Dina, wait. Has something happened?'

'Happened? Why would anything have happened? I just don't feel good, that's all.'

Was she crying, or was it the rain?

'What's wrong?'

'Nothing. I just have a stomach ache.'

She moved on. At least she was walking in the general direction of the cottage now. And perhaps she really did have a stomach ache. But I would talk to Rose about this later, I promised myself.

'I don't know,' said Rose. 'We were supposed to practise letters on the clay tablets Irena has made for us. Dina dropped one, and it broke. And then she just left.'

'But . . . did anyone scold her? Nico or somebody?'

'No. Nico never scolds anybody. Well, hardly ever.'

'But . . . doesn't she like this school business?' She ought to, I thought. She was so good at reading and writing herself and, very much unlike me, she actually cared for that kind of thing.

'Well, yes . . .'

'But?' Because there *was* a 'but' to it, I could tell from Rose's tone of voice.

'The littlest ones – Katrin and Beth – they're a little afraid of her. I think they can tell that she's not so used to other children. And even though Dina hasn't got Shamer's eyes any more, or at least not all the time, there is still something . . . something not ordinary about her.'

I sighed. Ordinary was probably not a word anyone would ever use about Dina. But couldn't she at least try? Sometimes it annoyed me. Couldn't she ever just be happy? Why did she always have to be so serious and hang-dog, and . . . and *weird*, so that nobody wanted to talk to her or get to know her? That wasn't how you made friends, I knew that much at least.

A couple of days later I had a fight with Rose that nearly blew the roof off. It all began with something Irena said when I came to return the dung fork we'd borrowed.

'Are you doing all right out there, Davin?' she said, giving me this strange look.

'Yes,' I said. 'We're fine.'

'And you have what you need? Food on the table, and everything else?'

'Yes. We have bread and eggs now.'

'Because if you're really short, all you have to do is say so. All right? We'll figure something out.'

Why was she looking at me so strangely? As if there was something she wasn't saying outright.

'We manage just fine,' I said, slightly offended. Of course that wasn't quite true, there were hundreds of things we needed, but nothing we couldn't make, get, or earn. 'We don't need anybody's charity.' I tried not to think about the ridiculously low rent she asked of us.

'Well, good,' said Irena. 'And don't be offended, I only meant to help. There are a lot of people in Clayton who would be sad if you had to leave.'

What kind of talk was this? And there was another one of those looks. Something was going on here, but I couldn't tell what.

Irena walked me to the door. Across the square, Minna the Innkeeper was shaking out the tablecloths. When she caught sight of me, her face went all tight and twisted. I greeted her politely, but she didn't answer. She just stood there glaring.

'What on earth did I do to her?' I asked Irena.

She hesitated. 'Nothing,' she said. 'She's just in a bad mood because she lost a couple of chickens. The fox got them, I expect.'

Curiouser and curiouser. Why would Minna be mad at me because a fox had taken her chickens? I said goodbye to Irena and headed for home, somewhat confused.

I had reached the outskirts of the village when something hard hit me on the shoulder. I looked about, but couldn't see anybody. Then another missile came flying, and as I ducked, I noticed the direction. Up there in Andreas Farmhand's apple tree, two of the cobbler's cheeky brats were sitting, pelting me with hard little green apples.

I grinned. Asking for trouble, were they? Well, I'd give them trouble aplenty. Quickly, I picked up one of the apples and got ready to give them a taste of their own medicine.

'Dirty thief, dirty thief,' yelled one of them.

I stiffened. 'I never stole anything!'

'What happened to the mince pie that went missing from our pantry?' shouted the brat, so loudly that all of Clayton must have heard.

'How would I know?' I yelled back, angry now. 'Cheeky brat!'

I took aim and threw the apple, hard and straight as I could. There was an offended 'Ouch!' from up the tree.

And I hope it hurt, I thought viciously. What a thing to say to decent people!

It wasn't until I was half way home that two and two started to make four. Irena's strange looks and 'if you're really short, all you have to do is say so.' Missing chickens. Stolen pies. Somebody had begun to steal things around the village, and of course suspicion homed in on us. The new people. The strangers. Never mind that none of us had ever stolen anything in our lives!

I stopped abruptly. Because that might not be entirely true. Rose. Rose who came from Swilltown where a lot of people had to steal to survive. Rose who could whistle a danger signal so that even a blackbird would think it was only another blackbird calling.

No, that's too silly, I thought. Rose would never steal chickens. What would she do with them?

But Rose had a dog. What about Belle? Belle, who happily followed the girls to class on school days. And there wasn't much meat to be had at home. What if Belle had taken Minna's chickens? Or Rose had taken the pie for Belle? I got all dizzy with strange suspicions and no longer knew what to believe. Perhaps Rose didn't know how important it was to behave decently to one's neighbours. *Especially* when one was a stranger. I had to talk to her.

Slap! The sound echoed through the cottage, and it felt as if my head was about to come off. Belle leaped up and started barking like mad.

'How can you say such a thing!' There were furious

tears on Rose's cheeks, and her eyes were bright with anger and hurt.

'I only asked . . .'

'Whore's brat from Swilltown, that's what you were thinking. Dirty thieving vermin, the lot of them. Don't you think I've heard that kind of thing before?'

'But I—'

'Damn you to hell. I never stole anything in my entire life!'

'But you can . . . whistle like a blackbird.'

'Why, so I can. How terrible. I have to be a thief, then!'

'Rose . . .'

'If you really want to know, then . . . we smuggled things. Sometimes. My wretched brother and me. Which is not the same as stealing from your neighbours!'

'It's still illegal . . .'

'So it is. So hang me.'

'It's just that it's so important that we don't—'

But Rose was no longer listening. She whistled a sharp signal at Belle and tore out of the door. I felt my cheek tenderly and thought that now was not the time to follow.

'Well, that was pretty stupid,' said Nico, upstairs in the loft.

I spun. I had thought that Rose and I were alone in the cottage.

'Somebody did steal something,' I said defensively. 'And that kind of thing can get us run out of town!'

'Rose has been living with you for two years now,' said Nico and stretched his legs so that they dangled off

111

the edge of the loft. 'Has she ever stolen anything from anybody in all that time?'

'No,' I muttered.

'So when you asked her like that – it was actually just because she comes from Swilltown.'

'Yes, all right, I get it.' I waved an irritated hand. 'I've been horribly stupid and insensitive, and I'm sorry. But if Rose and Belle didn't do it – who did?'

'I don't know,' said Nico thoughtfully. 'But it might be a good idea to find out – before the rest of Clayton judges as hastily as you just did.'

'We haven't time to go thief-hunting,' I said. 'There's work to be done.'

'Mmmmh,' murmured Nico, his mind clearly elsewhere. 'I think I'll have a word with my young scholars all the same.'

FOURTEEN

Coppertail

Rose was in a terrible mood for days after that. As I was patching the hen-house roof the next morning, I heard her yelling at Dina in the bean patch.

'Oh, so *you* think we're a couple of thieves too, do you? Me and Belle.'

'No, I—'

'Some friend you are!'

Rose rounded the corner of the cottage with angry tears in her eyes and sent me a look that by rights should have made me fall down dead from the hen-house roof. She disappeared into the woods, a worried-looking Belle at her heels. Belle hated it when we fought, but she knew which human was hers.

'That wasn't what I meant!' Dina, too, came round the corner, looking no happier than Rose.

'What did you say to her?' I asked.

'Nothing,' said Dina. 'Just . . . to take good care of Belle.'

'I don't think it was Belle who took those chickens.'

'I know that! That wasn't what I meant.'

'What did you mean, then?'

'Only that she should be careful that Belle didn't . . . run off. Or get hurt. Or something.' Dina's voice grew smaller and smaller, until it was hardly more than a whisper.

'Why would she? Belle is no stray.'

Dina didn't answer. She went back to the beans and the weeding. I shook my head and tried to thread a handful of straw into the old thatch without making more holes than I mended. I thought Dina was acting really strangely these days. What was wrong with the girl?

My foot slipped and went right through the roof. Damn! We ought to tear down the whole miserable half-ruin and build a new coop.

'Dina!' Mama was calling. 'Any eggs today?'

'I don't know.'

'Well, find out, can't you?' There was some irritation in the last remark, because it was normally Dina's job to collect the eggs.

Dina came back into the yard. She hauled up a bucket of water from the well and washed away the garden dirt from her hands. Then she went into the hen-house without even looking at me. Well, never mind, I was only her brother. Nowhere near as important as hens and eggs and suchlike.

She stayed in there for quite a long while, I thought. Long enough for me to get curious. I lay down carefully on the patchy roof and looked down through the hole I was supposed to be mending.

Dina was holding something in her hands. An egg.

But not a hen's egg. This one was painted in black, red and white spirals. Dina grasped the top and the bottom of it and tugged, and the egg came apart in the middle. It had to be made from wood or metal or something. And in the hollow space inside rested a small note.

My curiosity grew no less. Who was sending Dina letters by this curious egg mail? Did she have a boyfriend I didn't know about? Perhaps this was why she had acted so strange lately, what with all her silences, the stomach ache and the droopy looks. But if she was in love, it didn't seem to make her very happy.

Dina unfolded the letter and began to read. Then she suddenly flung it away from her and began to cry.

I slid down the roof, leaped on to the grass and flung open the door to the hen-house. Dina looked at me with startled eyes and tried to grab the letter on the floor, but I was too quick for her. 'Dearest Dina, I never meant to frighten you,' it said. That was as far as I got before Dina snatched it out of my hand.

'Give it here,' I said.

She shook her head vehemently. 'None of your business.'

'It is so my business. I'm your brother, and if some village lout thinks he can break your heart and get away with it . . .'

She gave me a strange look. 'You think I have a boyfriend?'

'Don't you?'

'If I do,' she said slowly, 'that's a matter between me and him.'

'Not if he makes you cry!'

She opened her mouth, then closed it again. The tears had stopped, it seemed, as suddenly as they had started. She put her hand on my chest and patted me, almost as if she was scratching Belle's ear or something.

'Sometimes you're really rather sweet,' she said. And while I was still trying to work out what to do with that remark, she slipped past me into the yard and let the letter fall into the well.

'No eggs today,' she called to Mama.

I picked up the painted egg. It was very light, too light to be made from wood, I thought, but I couldn't tell what kind of material it was. I put the two shells together. The design wasn't just random spirals, I could see now, but the coils of some kind of animal, a dragon or a monster serpent. It shone with a greasy gleam, as if the paint was still wet. It looked delicate and foreign and not at all like the kind of thing a village boy would make. And wasn't it a strange way to start a love letter? 'I never meant to frighten you . . .' Not that I had a whole lot of experience in that field, but if I was to write to a girl, that wouldn't be how I'd choose to start my letter.

'Dina,' I muttered. 'What kind of trouble have you got yourself into?'

It was not a cheerful supper that night. The smith had just come round with the black gelding. He couldn't find a buyer for it after all, he said. But he was staring at the ground when he said it, and wouldn't look in Mama's direction at all.

'It's all right,' said Mama. 'We'll just have to find a buyer ourselves.'

He nodded. 'It's a good little horse,' he said. 'Maybe you should try in Weaversham, or even further south. There are probably people there who would buy such a good little horse.'

But apparently not in Clayton, I thought. Were the stolen chickens still haunting us?

The smith left, and we sat down at the rough table I'd nailed together for us. Bread and nettle soup. I almost wished we really had stolen those chickens or that pie. My rabbits were practically the only meat we got. Dina was picking at her food and looking pale, and Rose was still in her thundercloud mood.

'Could we please ease up on the long faces?' said Mama. 'We'll sell that horse. And sooner or later the village will realize we didn't steal anything; if not before, then when the real thief is caught.'

Nico cleared his throat. 'Katrin – remember Katrin?'

Mama nodded. 'The small dark-haired girl. The youngest of your students.'

'Yes. Katrin says she knows how to get into the inn's hen-house. Perhaps we might consider setting up a guard?'

Mama shook her head. 'Let the village deal with it,' she said. 'It's best that we stay out of it.'

Dina got up and put on her shawl.

'And where might you be going, young lady?' asked Mama.

'I left the hoe and the basket out by the bean patch,' she said. 'I'd better fetch them before it gets dark.' And she was out of the door before anyone had a chance to say anything more.

I got up as well.

'And what did you forget?' asked Mama sharply.

'Nothing. I just wanted to make a start on the dishes.'

'Davin – are you sick?'

I could feel my cheeks heating.

'Very funny. Of course not.'

I grabbed the empty earthenware bowls and carried them out to the well, but instead of washing them I merely dumped them into the empty bucket and sneaked around the corner until I had a clear view of the bean patch.

Dina wasn't there. I saw just a quick glimpse of her before she disappeared among the trees.

Just as I thought. She'd gone off to meet this boyfriend of hers.

I returned to the well and began cleaning and wiping the bowls. By the time I was done, Dina still hadn't returned.

'Careful, Dina,' I muttered to myself. 'You're heading for trouble.' Mama must already be thinking that it was taking her an unduly long time to fetch a hoe and a basket.

I went back to the corner and looked towards the woods. Still no Dina. I would have to go and look for her soon, I thought. She was only twelve, and it was getting dark. And there was that strange sentence from the letter: 'I never wanted to frighten you'. The more I thought about it, the more uneasy I became.

'Davin?' Mama was standing in the open door.

'Yes.'

'Where is Dina?'

'I can't see her right now,' I said. 'But she's around somewhere.'

'Go and find her,' said Mama, and I understood the anxiety in her voice perfectly well. I only nodded and headed for the place where I had seen Dina disappear into the trees.

I had barely reached it when I caught sight of her. She was walking towards me, sobbing and out of breath, and she was holding one arm awkwardly away from her body.

'A snake bit me,' she said. And then she collapsed on to her knees, and I had to carry her the rest of the way home.

Two streaks of blood on Dina's lower arm, two fang marks.

'It fell on me,' said Dina. 'From a tree.'

I didn't think the snakes around here climbed trees. But that had to wait.

'Which colour was it?' asked Mama sharply, tightening the leather thong she had wrapped around Dina's arm. I knew what she was thinking. If it was yellow-green it might be just an arrow-snake like the one I had seen by the snare. Bad-tempered, but not venomous.

'Black and orange,' said Dina.

Coppertail.

'Davin,' said Mama in an unnaturally calm voice, 'give me your knife.'

I gave her my knife. My hand was shaking. I didn't

understand how hers could be so steady. But maybe it was because it had to be. She was the one who would have to do the cutting.

Coppertail. Its venom could kill. How much of it was now in Dina's blood?

'Light the lamp,' said Mama. 'I can't see what I'm doing.'

Nico lit the oil lamp and held it so that the light fell on Dina's arm. Dina was lying on the table now, where the nettle soup had been only moments ago.

'Rose, take Melli into the loft. Tell her a story.'

Rose nodded and took Melli's hand. Melli stared at Dina's arm and looked frightened, and at first she wouldn't move.

'Go on, sweetie,' said Mama. 'Go with Rose.' And Melli went.

Mama held the knife into the lamp's flame for a moment. Then she looked Dina in the eyes. 'It'll only take a moment, my love,' she whispered.

Dina stared at her without saying anything, and I could tell that she was clenching her teeth.

Mama rested the point of the knife against Dina's arm, directly above the fang marks. Then she cut, a fast, deep cross. Dina moaned once, an out-of-breath sound that hurt me to the bones, but Mama had already put her mouth against the cut to suck and spit, suck and spit. I hoped it was true that you could get rid of some of the venom that way. She kept it up for a long time, and Dina just lay there, not moving a muscle, not making a sound, though I was sure it hurt her. In the loft we could hear Rose's voice, trying to tell Melli a story. She kept getting stuck and repeating the same phrase twice or even three times, but Melli didn't object. I doubted she was listening.

'Get my basket, Davin,' Mama finally said. There was blood all around her mouth. 'And the kettle.'

I got the basket and the kettle. Mama took a small earthenware flask from the basket.

'Spirits,' she told Dina. 'It will sting, but it will cleanse the wound.'

She poured what seemed like quite a lot of the clear spirits on to Dina's arm. Dina hissed and bit her lip.

'It hurts,' she whispered.

'I know, love. But the worst is soon over now.'

If only that were true. I had never seen anyone die from venom, but I had heard ghastly tales aplenty, of gangrene and blindness and people who gasped themselves blue before dying. But that wouldn't happen to Dina, I told myself. She had come walking on her own two feet; it might have been a fairly superficial bite. And being bitten by a coppertail was not always fatal. Far from it.

Mama soaked a bandage with the steaming hot water from the kettle. She only let it cool for a moment before putting it on Dina's arm.

'Clean sheets in the chest,' she told me. 'Change the bedding.'

I got the sheets and started to make up the bed. Mama loosened the thong, and once more there was a thin moan from Dina. Mama stroked her forehead.

'The rest is up to you now,' she said. 'Remember what I always tell you when you're sick?'

'The body is only half of it,' Dina muttered tiredly. 'You also need to use your head to get well.'

Mama nodded. 'That's right. Picture it to yourself – that arm is fine again, and you are well. The venom is gone. Believe it. See it in your mind.'

'Yes.' The word was just an exhausted, miserable sigh.

'Dina! You have to promise to fight as hard as you can!'

Dina was silent for a moment. 'Things would be easier if I didn't,' she said, so softly that the words were nearly inaudible.

Mama looked stunned. 'Child! What a thing to say.'

There was a hoarse croak from Dina. It was a moment before I realized it was meant to be laughter.

'It's a little silly, isn't it?' she said. 'I mean, being bitten by a snake when you're serpent spawn yourself.'

Mama stood completely still for a draggingly long moment. Then she put a hand on either side of Dina's face and looked her in the eyes.

'*Forget about him*. You are *my* child. Not his. Do you hear me?'

Dina closed her eyes.

'Do you *hear* me?' said Mama once more.

'Yes, Mama,' whispered Dina. But it sounded as if she didn't quite believe it any more.

Nobody slept much that night. Rose and Melli made their beds in the loft where Nico and I usually slept. Dina kept complaining that she was cold even though we kept a fire going in the hearth all night, so we took turns lying next to her, trying to keep her warm.

I waited until Mama and Nico were a little way off, sitting by the hearth and speaking together in low tones.

'Who is he?' I whispered into Dina's ear.

'Who?' she murmured.

'Him. The bastard who is sending letters and luring you into the woods to throw snakes at you. *That* him.' My voice was shaking with fury.

'That . . . wasn't what happened.'

'No? Coppertails don't climb trees, Dina. *Who is he?*'

Silently, she stared at me. Her face was shiny with fever, her hair sticky with sweat. For a moment I thought she might actually give me an answer. But then she shook her head.

'I don't know what you're talking about,' she said.

Her eyes closed, and she pretended to be asleep. But I knew she wasn't. Her breathing was much too troubled.

At some point, I fell asleep without meaning to. I kept dreaming of that wretched egg. Dina was opening it, and instead of a letter, it contained a snake, a red, white and black serpent. The snake wound its way up her arm, opening its maw to show two long venom fangs . . .

'No, Dina,' said Mama. 'Dina, you mustn't!'

'I want it off . . .'

'No, love . . .'

I woke up. Mama was bending over the bed, holding Dina's wrists. She noticed that I was awake.

'Davin,' she said hoarsely. 'Help me. Hold her for a little while.'

'Hold her?' My head was still full of hazy serpent dreams.

'So that she doesn't tear off the bandage. Davin, wake up!'

I sat up. Dina was looking at me, but her eyes were glassy, and I don't think she actually saw me. My heart pounded in fear, because she looked like someone who was already half in another world.

'Hold her!'

I put my arms around my sister and seized her wrists. They were slippery with sweat.

'Let go,' begged Dina. 'I want it off. It hurts!'

She tried to break my grip, but it was easy to hold her. Far too easy.

'She mustn't spend her strength like that,' said Mama, as if Dina couldn't hear her at all. 'Try and see if you can calm her down, Davin.'

'How?'

'Talk to her. Sing to her. Tell her a story. Anything.'

My head felt completely empty. I couldn't think of a single story.

'Let go of me,' whispered Dina. 'Let go. Let go.'

I started to sing. An old lullaby I had long since forgotten about, except that it was still there, apparently.

'Little star, close your eye . . .'

It seemed that it did make Dina calmer. Perhaps I had sung it to her when we were both much younger. I couldn't recall all the words, but it hardly mattered. I could hum. What mattered was that Dina grew less tense.

Mama returned with a mug full of one of her brews.

'Raise her head a little,' she told me, 'so she can drink.'

She held the mug to Dina's lips, but Dina turned her face away.

'Smells bad,' she said, and her voice sounded sulky and babyish, as if a surly three-year-old had taken over inside her.

'Look at me,' said Mama.

Dina wouldn't.

'*Look at me*,' said Mama, and this time she left Dina no choice, because the voice she was using was the Shamer's voice. '*You made me a promise. You promised not to give up. And I'll hold you to that promise. Do you hear me?*'

Dina hung limply in my arms like a rag-doll, but for a moment her voice and her eyes were completely her own.

'Yes,' she said. And obediently drank what Mama gave her.

Dina slept. And kept on sleeping. She didn't even wake when Mama changed the bandage on her arm. The skin around the wound was reddened and inflamed, but Mama looked less worried all the same.

'No streaks,' she said. And though I had less interest in Mama's healing arts than Dina, I still knew that she was checking for signs of blood-poisoning. No streaks – that had to be a good sign.

At noon the next day, Dina woke and wanted a drink of water. She still had a fever, but she was herself again. And the morning after that, the fever was gone.

'Nice job, Sis,' I told her. 'Takes more than a dumb old coppertail to keep you down!'

That earned me a smile – a very small one, but still a smile. Then she went back to sleep.

'Make sure she drinks something every time she is awake,' Mama told Rose.

'Where are you going?' I asked.

'To Clayton.' Her voice lacked any special emphasis, but I knew her well enough to tell that she was angry. That she had in fact been angry for days, but was only now able to do something about it.

'I'm coming with you,' I said.

She looked at me for a little while.

'Yes,' she said. 'Perhaps you'd better.'

It was shortly after midday when Mama and I rode into Clayton town square. Mama halted Falk in front of the inn, but she didn't get off. She just sat there. Stock-still. And Falk, who was usually none too obedient, knew better than to stamp a hoof or throw his head about. He stood without moving a muscle.

Mama sat there on Falk so long and so silently that a small crowd began to gather.

'What is she doing?' whispered one man to his neighbour, not quite softly enough.

Mama looked at him, and he jerked.

'I'm waiting,' she said, and released his gaze the way a falcon lets go of a prey that holds no interest after all. The man rubbed his face and retreated a few steps.

'What for?' asked some brave soul.

'For the man or woman who tried to kill my daughter.'

After that, there was no pretending that this was just

an ordinary summer afternoon in the square. All other talk petered out. Nobody tried to buy anything or sell anything, nobody came to get water from the well, nobody sat down to enjoy a mug of beer outside the inn. It was as if a sort of whisper ran through the whole village, and within half an hour I would have bet good money that every single living person in Clayton knew where my mother was, and what she had said. And most of them had come to hear the end of the story.

There was a clear space around Falk and Silky, but other than that, the square was packed. Some tried to talk quietly, but the chatter quickly died, to silence or to a low, murmuring whisper. And when Mama suddenly pulled herself up even straighter on Falk's back, the whispers died too. Silence reigned in the square, eerie and complete.

'My daughter was bitten by a coppertail,' said Mama, and although she did not speak particularly loud, there was no one there who couldn't hear her. 'She nearly died. It may have been an accident. I hope it was.'

She let her gaze pass over the crowd, scanning each face. If they didn't know it before, they certainly knew it now: they had a Shamer in their midst.

'*Only the lowest of the low would hurt a child that way. If you mean to hurt us, stand forth. If you know anything, stand forth. If you are a human being, you must face your action and its consequence in the light of day.*'

Silence. No one moved. Mama's eyes went through the crowd, seizing one, releasing him, moving on to someone else. No one said anything. No one stood forth.

Not until Irena took one uncertain step towards Falk.

'Shamer,' she said, and her voice trembled slightly. 'We haven't hurt your child. We are decent people.'

Mama nodded slowly.

'I believe you,' she said. 'No one here did it. It may well have been an accident. I must choose to believe that.'

Then she turned Falk around and left the square. And no one in Clayton wanted to get in her way as she rode off.

'Did you mean that?' I said, when we were nearly home. 'About it being an accident?'

'Maybe,' said Mama. 'It certainly wasn't anyone in the square. But I noted also that there were some who didn't come. Andreas Farmhand. The cobbler. And Minna Innkeeper's eldest son. If anyone did do anything, it was one of those three.'

I couldn't quite see any one of them in the role of Dina's secret boyfriend, not even Minna's eldest. He was much too old for Dina, older even than I was. But perhaps the letter was not from her boyfriend, but from someone who pretended to be him. Or perhaps there *was* no boyfriend. Or perhaps someone else had heard of the secret tryst and taken advantage of it. If it had been a tryst. Or any kind of meeting at all. Ifs and perhaps fluttered about in my mind like confused bats, and the only thing that was clear to me was that I would have to speak to my sister. This time, she would tell me – or else.

But when we got home, Dina was asleep again, and I

was not hard-hearted enough to wake her up just to interrogate her. I was still too grateful that we had been allowed to keep her at all.

FIFTEEN

Torches in the Night

Belle was barking. A loud, sharp, warning bark that had me halfway out of my bed before I was properly awake. Downstairs by the door, I could hear Rose trying to hush her dog, but Belle wouldn't listen.

I crawled towards the ladder and peered into the living room below.

'What is it?' I whispered to Rose, though I could barely see her in the dimness. Belle's white ruff was the most visible thing down there.

It was a moment before Rose answered.

'I think someone is coming,' she said, and her voice was low and anxious.

I turned to rouse Nico, but he was already awake.

'Get your bow,' he said.

I nodded. If someone was coming to our cottage in the middle of the night, it *might* be because there was an illness or an injury that needed Mama's aid. But after what had happened in the last few days, I was afraid it—

'Medama Tonerre!' A rapid knocking on the door, an out-of-breath voice. It sounded like—

'Open up, Rose,' said Mama. 'It's Irena.'

And it was. She was breathing so strangely, and her face looked so strained, that at first I thought something was wrong with her baby. That was Mama's first thought too, it seemed.

'Sit down,' she said sharply. 'Are you bleeding? Davin, get us some light.'

Irena waved a hand in refusal. 'No,' she said, still breathing hard. 'It's not me. It's – it's . . .'

'Wait till you catch your breath,' said Mama.

Irena did sit down, but she was still shaking her head. 'There isn't time,' she said. 'They found Katrin – Tim Saddler's Katrin. And she . . . there's something wrong with her. She was found in the inn's hen-house, unconscious, and no one could rouse her. And she . . . someone had painted a sign on her chest. In blood.'

'In blood . . .' Mama looked merely confused at first. Then, slowly, she asked, 'What sort of sign?'

Irena looked down at her hands. 'Two circles, one within the other. Like . . . like a Shamer's signet.'

I nearly dropped the lamp just as I had managed to light it. Mama stared at the smith's wife, who still wouldn't look at anything except her own hands.

'Irena . . .'

'I know you didn't do it.' Irena raised her head with a look of defiance. 'Whatever it is and whoever did it . . . I know it wasn't you. But . . . a lot of other people are saying this is the Shamer's vengeance for what happened to the Shamer's daughter. You have to leave. You can't stay here. You have to go now, at once.'

My thoughts were whirling round my head. What

had happened to Katrin? I knew her. She was one of Nico's little students, a quiet girl with dark brown curls and a gap between her front teeth. No more than seven, or thereabouts. Who would hurt a little kid like that?

'She said she knew how to get into the inn's hen-house,' said Nico quietly. 'Perhaps she . . . surprised the thief, or something.'

'Davin, get my basket,' said Mama. 'I have to see if there's anything I can do.'

'Aren't you listening?' Irena suddenly shouted. 'You can't stay! The cobbler, Andreas, Minna's eldest . . . how long will it be, do you think, before they arrive here with torches and clubs and whatever else they think they need? You have to go, I tell you. Now!'

Only then did I realize. That we had to move on again. That we were homeless again.

Belle began to bark once more, louder than before.

Irena looked scared.

'It's them,' she said. 'They're coming.'

There wasn't time for the cart. Just a few moments to yank the bare neccesities from pegs and shelves and get out of the cottage. I had to carry Dina in my arms as we rode; she was still too weak to manage Silky. At the last moment Rose managed to catch Tabby, our kitten, for Irena to take away with her. Off we went, me on Falk with Dina, Mama with Melli on the black gelding, Nico and his bay mare alongside, and Rose, scared and pale-faced, on Silky, holding the reins too tightly because she still wasn't used to riding.

We used the small path behind the cottage. The cart

132

trail would have been faster and easier in the dark, but we didn't dare go that way. The way Belle was acting up, they had to be quite close now.

'Make her be quiet,' I hissed at Rose. 'She'll give us away!'

'Easy for you to say,' Rose hissed back, but not with quite her usual snappishness. She probably felt she had enough trouble with Silky. She tugged at the rope she had slipped into Belle's collar and scolded the excited dog, but to no effect whatsoever. Belle understood only that something was terribly wrong and that she had to defend her family. Upset by Belle's barking, Silky shied sideways into Falk. Rose grabbed at Silky's neck to stay in the saddle – and dropped Belle's leash. And Belle took off like an arrow, snarling and howling, headed for the enemy that threatened her humans.

'No!' screamed Rose, flung herself off Silky's back and ran after her wayward dog.

'Rose! Stop!' I yelled after her.

But Rose didn't stop. I threw a despairing look at Mama.

'Turn back,' she said. 'We can't go anywhere without Rose.'

It seemed the whole yard was milling with horses and men. I don't know how many there were, or who they were – they had put something over their heads, like a bag with holes for their eyes and mouths, and the light from their torches danced and flickered, so that all I could see was a glimpse of an arm, a hand, a glint of eyes through the holes in their masks.

One of them had a hold of Rose's arm. Another was

trying to chase Belle off by swinging his torch like a club. Belle was barking and snarling like mad, and nipping at the horses' legs.

Suddenly Mama was in the midst of it. I hadn't even seen her get off her horse.

'*What is your business here?*' she said. And she spoke in the voice that made everyone stop and listen. Even Belle became quiet and cowered down, knowing she had done something wrong. Rose tore free of the man holding her and wrapped her arms around her disobedient dog.

At first, none of the men seemed willing to answer. Then one of them cleared his throat – the one riding a horse that seemed very reminiscent of the inn's dappled grey gelding.

'You don't scare us, witch,' he said. 'We have a score to settle.'

He would probably have liked to sound tough and determined, but he didn't quite succeed.

'What score is that?' asked my mother. I don't know how she managed to sound so calm, but there was no uncertainty in her voice.

'A just cause! As you well know.'

'If your cause is so just, why are you wearing masks? *Are you ashamed to show yourselves?*'

The men stirred uneasily.

'Katrin,' said one of them. 'Little Katrin is lying there, and may be dying. With your filthy witch mark on her chest!'

'Let me see the child. It may be that I can help her.'

'You'll never touch her again!'

'Where is the child's father?' asked Mama. 'What does he say?'

Again, no one seemed to want to answer. Then the man on the dappled grey said, 'He's with the child.'

'Maybe that is where you should be, too. I have no part in her illness.'

'But the mark,' said the other. 'The witch mark. What about that?'

It sounded like a sincere question, as if he had really begun to doubt who was guilty of what. It was a moment when anything could happen – perhaps even the right thing.

Then the rider of the grey gelding straightened.

'Witchcraft,' he snarled. 'Can't you feel it? She is confusing our minds so that a man no longer knows how to do what he came to do.'

He raised his torch as if he meant to hit Mama with it. Dina made a fearful, croaking sound and tried to struggle free of my arms.

'Be quiet,' I whispered into her hair, and felt like setting my heels to Falk and charging in between my mother and the masked men. If they hit her . . . if they so much as touched her . . . I wanted to be at Mama's side, but I couldn't leave Dina and Melli. It was tearing me apart.

'Stay with your sisters,' murmured Nico, and walked up to Mama's side. Without so much as a dagger to defend himself with. He was no coward, whatever else he was.

'Good evening, Andreas. Good evening, Peiter

Innkeeper's. Good evening, Cobbler. And Vilman Carpenter is here as well, I see. How is Vilman Junior getting on with his sums these days?'

Nico apparently recognized the men with no trouble at all, in spite of their masks. But then he had had more dealings with the villagers than I had.

They didn't much like being known, and mentioned by name, that much was clear. They would rather have remained unfamiliar strangers in the dark.

'I'm truly sorry for Katrin,' said Nico, and it was obvious that he meant it. 'Whatever we can do to help her, we will gladly do.'

'There's nothing you can see,' said Vilman. 'She is just . . . asleep. But no one can rouse her.'

'Let me help,' begged Mama. 'Let me see what I can do. There are herbs—'

Peiter suddenly turned his grey horse and rode off as if all the evil spirits of the forest were at his heels. The others hesitated for a moment, then followed him. The hoofbeats grew faint, and the torchlight faded among the trees.

I could hardly believe it. They were gone. And they hadn't attacked us.

Melli had begun to cry, soundlessly, as if she was afraid they would hear her. I slid slowly down from Falk's back so that I could hold both her and Dina.

'Hush,' I whispered. 'They're gone. It's over now.'

But it wasn't.

All at once there was a drumming of hooves, and three riders came sweeping down the cart trail. They didn't stop, and they didn't speak. They just flung their torches on to the roof of the cottage.

The thatched roof.

I let go of Melli and Dina and ran to the well.

'Help me,' I yelled at Nico and hauled on the rope, too impatient to use the handle. The roof was old and moss-grown; perhaps we would have time to put out the fire before it really caught. One torch had rolled off by itself, but two still lay there, burning.

Nico seized our own water bucket from the pack his mare was carrying, and I poured water from the well bucket into it. Then I started hauling up yet another bucketful. Out of the corner of my eye I could see Nico trying to toss the water on to the roof. It didn't splash anywhere near high enough. He put down the bucket and disappeared among the trees.

What was he doing? Had he given up already?

'Nico!'

There he was again, with the bay mare. He leaped on to her back and stood there, balancing like a juggler at a carnival.

'Rose, pass me the bucket!'

Rose gave him the bucket, and he tossed the rest of the water on to the roof. This time, one of the torches went out. If we could only get the other one . . .

From out of the wood came another three riders, or the same three with new torches. The bay mare gave a startled sideways leap, and Nico had to slip down to sit astride. This time, only one of the torches stayed on the roof, but up near the ridge where it would be hard to get at. Already, the thatch had begun to smoulder and burn. And in the darkness under the trees, we could hear the next wave of galloping horses approach. Mama put her hand on my arm.

'Let it burn,' she said tiredly. 'We couldn't stay here anyway.'

Miserably we watched as the flames began to lick the thatch. Belle whined, and Melli was still crying in her new scared and soundless way.

'See what your boyfriend has cost us,' I hissed at Dina. '*Now* will you tell me who it is?'

'Oh, Davin, don't be stupid,' Dina said quietly. 'I don't have a boyfriend.'

'I'm not the stupid one. It wasn't me who went off into the woods at sundown because of a letter from some village lout.'

'Letter?' said Mama. 'What letter?'

Dina didn't say anything.

'Dina. **What letter?**'

Dina's breathing sounded all wrong, almost like when she had been bitten by the coppertail.

'He said he never meant to frighten me. That it wasn't he who killed Beastie. That he just wanted to get to know me better.'

Dina was right. I had been stupid. Horrendously stupid. *Sezuan*. The egg letter had been from Sezuan.

Mama's eyes shone with fear and despair. 'Oh, Dina,' she said. 'And you *believed* him.'

'No. Not at first. And not . . . no, not really. It was just . . . everyone seemed so happy to be here. And I couldn't bear it if we had to leave again. Because of me.'

Mama was silent for a long time. *Please don't scold her,*

I prayed. *Please don't scold her now.* I had never heard my sister's voice so small, so fragile. She sounded as if she would fall completely to pieces if anyone spoke harshly to her right now.

'How long has he been here?' Mama sounded calm, but it was not the sort of calm you could trust. It lay like a mask over something else – fear or anger, or both.

'I don't know.' Dina's voice was so small it had almost disappeared. 'One day at school he had written something on one of the tablets. I saw it when I was handing them around. It must be . . . a week ago now.'

'Nearly two,' I said hoarsely. 'It was the day you came home with a stomach ache.'

Dina nodded.

There was a sharp owl-like cry from the woods – the sort of cry that didn't come from a proper owl.

'We have to go,' said Nico. 'Standing in front of the flames like this . . . we're easy targets if anyone has a bow.'

It was almost as if they heard him. Suddenly, an arrow hit the ground only a few paces away.

'Get out,' came a shout from the darkness. 'We want no witches in Clayton!'

'Into the trees,' ordered Nico. 'If they get the horses too, we are in deep, deep trouble.'

That finally prodded Mama to move. She hauled Melli up on her hip and ran clumsily for the cover of the woods. Nico swept Dina into his arms and followed.

'Come on,' I told Rose, who was still clutching Belle. 'And this time, keep a leash on that savage beast of yours!'

★　★　★

They chased us all night. Every time we thought it was safe to stop and breathe, we heard their damned owl's cries, and then there would be an arrow. They were playing with us. They knew the woods better than we did, and as long as they kept a safe distance, there was nothing much we could do to defend ourselves. They didn't mean to kill us – if that had been their intention, we would have been dead long since. But it was still a lethally dangerous game because they couldn't see well enough to be certain of *not* hitting us. Once they nicked the little black gelding so that there was a long bloody furrow across his shoulder. And once it was only a sixth sense and a quick duck of his head that saved Nico from an arrow through the eye.

Not until dawn did they let us alone. One last arrow struck the ground in front of Silky, who was almost too tired to shy away from it.

'Get out of Loclain,' called a voice I couldn't recognize. 'We don't need your kind here!'

Four days later, the woodlands of Loclain were behind us, and we trudged instead over the plains west of Sagisloc, with no firm goal in mind. We had even less now than when we left the Highlands – very little except life and limb and the clothes on our backs. If I had hated Sezuan before, it was nothing to what I felt now.

III
Sagisloc
Davin's story

SIXTEEN

The Foundation

Sagisloc was a wealthy city. It showed from miles away. The roofs glittered with copper and glazed tiles, and I had never before seen so many glass windowpanes in one place. Nearly everyone was richly dressed. Silk waistcoats gleamed as they stretched across well-fed bellies, silver buttons flashed in the sun. Sagisloc could afford life's luxuries and saw no reason to hide that fact.

'It looks very expensive,' I said to Mama. 'Do you think they have room for people like us at all?'

'We have to try,' said Mama. 'This can't go on.'

She was right. We desperately needed rest and shelter. Melli had begun to cough, a horrid, wet-sounding cough that shook her whole body when the fits came on. We were all of us tired and pale, and Dina was still a ghostlike shadow of her usual self.

We asked a man in the street if there was a place we could find shelter. To my surprise he answered readily and pleasantly that there was a 'hostel for travellers of no means' on the outskirts of town, and gave us clear directions on how to find it.

It was right near the lake, on the eastern edge of the city. It was big, far bigger than I had expected. Whitewashed buildings with red tile roofs lay on both sides of a neat gravel road, like a small village in its own right. The road was blocked by a large and heavy gate, crowned by a coat of arms with two dragon heads on it.

Nico halted his horse and looked up at the double dragon with a worried frown.

'What is it?' I asked.

'That's the arms of the Draconis family,' he said.

'The dragons up there?'

He nodded.

'Does it matter?'

He grimaced. 'Probably not. But . . . if anybody asks, my name is Nicolas, not Nicodemus.'

It was easy to see where you were supposed to go. The road led through the gate and right up to an open door, and above the door was a sign showing a hand stretched out in welcome. Nico stayed with the horses while I went in with Mama and the girls to see if they had room for us.

It was a strange room. The walls were covered with slates, from floor to ceiling. Even the door had its load of slates. In the middle of the room stood a tall desk, and the man behind it had the double dragon embroidered on his grey and black suit.

'Welcome to the Draconis Foundation,' he said, smiling pleasantly. 'What can I do for you?'

It wasn't easy to stand there, empty-handed and 'without means', as they called it. To stand there asking for something, knowing you couldn't pay for it.

'We heard that . . . that travellers might seek shelter here,' said Mama.

'Yes, of course,' said the man. 'That is what we are here for. How many people in your household?'

'Six.'

'Six . . .' He made a note on a clean slate. 'Age and sex?'

Mama mentioned us by age, starting with Melli and moving up. The man put down his little slate, fetched three others down from one wall, and started to make notes on those.

'Any household animals?'

'Three horses and a dog.'

He raised an eyebrow. That was probably more than most travellers without means brought with them.

'They will have to go to Foundation stables,' he said, and made yet another little note. He rang a bell, and two people appeared – an elderly man in grey shirt and trousers, and a young girl in a grey dress and white apron. 'Paulus, see to it that the animals outside are brought to the stables. And if Olina will show the four ladies to their quarters? That will be Block C, rooms 2 and 5. The two gentlemen will please come with me.'

Nobody moved right away.

'We would rather stay together,' I said, rather loudly and firmly. 'As a family.'

The man was already halfway out of the door.

'I regret,' he said with the same pleasant smile, 'but that is not possible. We do not have the appropriate facilities. Here, men and women have separate quarters.'

Appropriate whatsits? It wasn't a word I had ever heard before.

'What does that mean?' I asked Dina. 'That faci-something word.'

She shook her head tiredly. 'Maybe it's something to do with bed linen,' she said.

Melli coughed.

'We have to,' said Mama. 'At least for a couple of days, so we can rest and gather our strength.'

She and the girls followed Olina out of the door and to the left. Accompanied by the man with the pleasant smile, Nico and I went the other way, to the right, into what was apparently the men's quarters.

Everything was very clean and tidy. The paths and little squares had had their gravel neatly raked, the walls were recently whitewashed, and the woodwork on the stairs and walkways smelled of fresh tar. Here and there, old men in grey clothes were sweeping or raking the paths. Three little boys, hardly more than six or seven, were kneeling in the courtyard, nipping weeds with their bare fingers. They too wore grey trousers and shirts. Did everyone here have to dress like that?

'Room 8,' said our guide and opened a black door exactly like every other black door we had passed, except that this one had the number 8 and the letter E painted on it in white. He threw open the shutters to let in a bit more light, and we could see the room we were meant to sleep in.

It was not exactly spacious. On both sides of the aisle some wide wooden shelves had been built, in three tiers.

That's where one slept, apparently. Two to a shelf, one after the other, so to speak. At the end of each shelf was a wooden box, nailed to the wall. There was no other furniture, nor was there room for any. But at least the beds were made up with clean white sheets, a thin grey mattress and grey blankets.

'It is the responsibility of the room's inmates to keep the facilities tidy and hygienic,' said our guide. 'Personal belongings are to be stored in the boxes. If the space there is not sufficient, surplus property may be brought to the common stores.'

I looked at the boxes. They weren't very big. As little as we had managed to bring with us, we would still have quite a lot of 'surplus property'.

'The top bunk and the middle one there are free. I ask you to take note of the bunk number. This is Room 8, Block E. Your bunk number, young man, is 10. In other words, you are 8-E-10, if anybody asks.'

'Wouldn't it be easier just to tell people my name?' I said in some confusion. I couldn't see what good all those numbers and letters would do, except perhaps to make it easier to find your bed at night.

'We cannot learn the name of every traveller passing through,' said our guide. '8-E-10. It isn't too difficult for you, is it?'

'I suppose not,' I said.

'You can leave your belongings here while we go to the bath house.'

The bath house? Now? I would have liked to see how Mama and the girls were doing. But I supposed scrubbing off some of the travel dirt wouldn't hurt.

The bath house was very posh; or at least, I had never bathed in anything so fine. There were two pools, a hot one and a cold one. First you stepped into the hot tub – large enough that several people could bathe at the same time, and deep enough for you to dunk yourself completely if you wanted – and then into the even larger cold pool to rinse off. It made the blood rush faster, throbbing under the skin, and I quite forgot how tired I was. Instead, I felt like teasing Nico a bit, the way I sometimes did with Kinni and Black-Arse. Or had done. Would I ever see Black-Arse again? But I didn't want to think of that now. I dived beneath the surface and tugged at Nico's ankle so that he got a ducking he wasn't expecting.

When he resurfaced, he looked quite offended for a moment. But then a teasing gleam showed in his dark blue eyes. He tossed back his dark, wet hair, took a deep breath and dived. And we had a glorious splashy water-fight with every kind of dirty trick and sneaky dodge. He knew quite a few, did Nico. More than I did, actually.

Afterwards we sat on the edge of the pool, breathing hard. I looked at him sideways. He was quite thin now, but then, so was I. You could count our collected ribs with no trouble. Food had been sparse for months, and neither of us had had much in the way of fat before that.

Then I noticed some funny little scars he had all over his upper body. Short nicks and scratches, no more than an inch or so long.

'What's that?' I asked.

He followed the direction of my gaze. 'What? These?' He rubbed at one of the marks with a thumb.

'Yes.'

He grimaced. 'My fencing teacher's work. The first time you made a mistake, he would hit you. The second time, he cut you. Just a nick. He told us that a little blood made you remember the lesson better.'

I stared. There were scores of them. At least a hundred. Perhaps it was no wonder that Nico didn't like swords much.

'That must have hurt. Was that why you didn't want to fence any more?'

He shook his head. 'Not really. When I threw away my sword, I knew what my father would do to me when he found out. And he had a much heavier hand than the fencing master.'

'But . . . why, then?'

He shrugged. 'It's not so easy to explain. It was just . . . I could see it. I could see what my father wanted me to be like. Which was basically a man like him. And I . . . I just didn't want to.'

Maybe I was lucky not to have had a father. Or even to know who he was. Look at Nico. Look at poor Dina, who woke up one morning and discovered she had the Puff-Adder for a father.

The man with the pleasant smile returned. His smile stiffened a bit when he saw the mess we had made – there was water everywhere – but he didn't say anything. He merely showed us into the third room in the bath house, where we were meant to dry and dress ourselves.

'Where are my clothes?' I asked.

'They were brought to the laundry,' said the man. 'We have laid out clean ones.' He pointed to two neat piles of folded grey clothing. 'When you are dressed, we will proceed to the Refectory.'

I looked questioningly at Nico, because that was yet another word I hadn't heard before.

'Dining hall,' he murmured.

Well, that sounded encouraging. And the grey clothes fitted reasonably well. There was a drawstring to tighten the trousers with, and the shirt was loose but comfortable. And yet . . . I didn't like them. It was as if they turned me into something other than what I really was.

Nico looked at himself. 'What elegance,' he said in a nasal drawl. 'What delicacy of style.'.

I had never heard courtiers speak about fashion, but when they did, they probably sounded exactly like Nico did right then. I couldn't help laughing at his antics.

'Mesire,' I said, and gave him my best effort at a courtier's bow. 'Shall we proceed to the banquet?'

Nico smiled. 'Let's do that,' he said. 'Before I start chewing on the towels.'

When we came to the dining hall – or the Refectory, as they called it – I couldn't see Mama and the girls at first; naturally, they were now just as grey as the rest, and the women had to wear scarves, too, so you couldn't even see the colour of their hair. But then I heard Melli cough.

It didn't suit her at all, this grey clothing. Well, it hardly suited any of us, I suppose, but it was worse on Melli.

She looked like a little lost sparrow. Her natural chubbiness had all but disappeared, and the grey scarf made her face look even more fever pale. I wanted to tear it off her and get her into her own night dress and then into bed, and feed her hot broth, cranberry juice and bedtime stories.

'Shouldn't she be in bed?' I asked Mama.

'Eating in the dormitories is not allowed,' said Mama. 'I'll put her to bed as soon as she's had a little food.'

Dina sat hunched around her snake-bitten arm, staring at the empty tin bowl in front of her. She looked oddly numb and uncaring, as if she was too tired even to feel. Rose, on the other hand, had furious red blotches high on her cheeks, a sign that her temper was very close to boiling point.

'What is it?' I asked her cautiously.

'They put Belle in a cage! With a lot of other dogs.'

'Why? Did she bite somebody?'

'Of course she didn't!' Rose looked mortally offended. 'They said they couldn't have stray dogs in the grounds. As if Belle would ever stray! She was right by my side the whole time!'

'It's only a couple of days, Rose,' said Mama in a comforting tone.

'If one of those mangy mongrels bites Belle, I'll . . . I'll make them sorry!'

Somebody tapped my shoulder.

'You're not supposed to sit here,' said one of the grey women. Her voice was neither sharp nor apologetic, merely toneless, as if that was the way the world was, and there was nothing she could do about it.

'Why not?' I asked.

'Those aren't your seats.'

'What do you mean?'

She pointed to the bench, and I noticed that numbers had been painted on the boards. Numbers like those on the bunks.

'This is 2-C-4,' she said. 'That's my seat.'

I moved along the bench so that there was room for her, but it seemed that wasn't good enough.

'You have to go to your own seats.'

'Does it matter?'

She nodded tiredly. 'Nobody gets fed until everyone is in their proper place.'

This Foundation with all its rules and numbers, I thought. I could get tired of it very quickly. But I noticed that Nico and I were the only men in this part of the dining hall, and we were already collecting sullen looks from the hungry people all around us.

'We'd better move,' I told Nico. 'Let's see if we can find 8-E-10 and 8-E-11.'

SEVENTEEN

The Reeds

After the meal – barley soup – we were put to work, or at least, Nico and I were, I wasn't sure what had happened to the girls. We were told to go down to the lake, where they were harvesting reeds for thatching and the like. Two men in black tunics were in charge, it seemed, while the actual harvesting was done by workers dressed in grey just like Nico and me. They gave us each a sickle to cut the reeds with.

'Don't drop it,' I advised Nico. 'I think they might take it badly if you lost it.'

Nico sighed. 'I have actually managed to use a tool without losing it, every once in a while.'

'Yes, all right.' Just not all that often, I thought, but I didn't say it out loud. There was no point in fighting.

I rolled up my trousers and took off my boots. There was a flat-bottomed barge, but apparently that was meant only for the reeds we cut. The workers just had to get their feet wet. Feet, and ankles, and thighs. As for the trousers, I might have saved myself the trouble, they were soon soaked anyway. The lake bottom was so slick and slimy that it felt almost like walking on the back of some living creature. And there was life of a sort, I supposed, what with all the bristle worms and other crawlies. Black mud seeped up between my toes, and I tried not to think of leeches and other bloodsuckers.

It was hard work. Very soon, the small of my back ached uncomfortably, and my hands and arms got sore, too. At first, the water had felt nearly warm, but it sapped the heat from my feet and lower legs all the same so that they became chilled and bloodless. And then there were all the irritating little bugs that buzzed and swarmed and stung and bit at you.

It was probably worse for Nico. I had helped with the harvest often enough back home in Birches, and except for the fact that we were wading in water up to our knees, this was not so different. Nico didn't even know how to hold a sickle at first. Of course this made him slower than the rest of us, and it didn't take long before one of the uniformed overseers noticed.

'Move along, you lazy dog,' he yelled. 'What's your number, greyling? Yes, you. What's your number?'

Nico had to think for a moment. '8-E-11.'

'I have you down!' The overseer waved a slate. 'Don't think you can put one over on me. This is the only warning you get: you don't work, you don't eat.'

'What does he mean?' I asked one of the other workers.

'If they don't like the way you work, they put you on half-rations at supper,' he said. 'And that's hardly enough to keep a man alive.'

I didn't like the sound of that. We needed a chance to regain our strength, not a starvation diet.

'Can't you work a little faster?' I whispered to Nico.

'I'm trying,' he muttered. 'I'm trying.'

And he was. He was doing the best he could, without complaint. But his best still wasn't very fast. Finally the overseer rode his horse into the water and crowded Nico so hard that he could barely straighten without banging his head into a dripping muzzle. The man kept up a storm of abuse directed at Nico, almost as if he *wanted* him to answer back. Nico didn't. He set his jaw and kept working, bending and cutting, bending and cutting, without saying a word. And if Nico could keep his mouth shut, then so could I, I supposed. But it was *not* easy. And while I heard that vicious bastard going on and on about Nico's incompetence, laziness and general clumsiness, I couldn't help thinking of all the times I had nagged at him. The words I had used may have been less coarse, but then they probably stung all the more because they came from me, and not some stranger.

They kept us at it until the sun hung huge and orange, practically touching the rooftops. Fair enough that we should work for the room and board the city gave us, but it seemed to me they piled on the labour with a fairly heavy hand. And when we handed back our sickles to the overseers, I noticed that Nico's had large reddish-brown stains on the handle.

'Show me your hands,' I said.

He just shook his head. 'There's no point.'

'Nico!'

'What would you do about it? Wash them in rosewater and wrap them in silk? I'll get calluses soon enough. I'll have to, won't I?'

At supper there were only half-rations for 8-E-11. I sneaked a few spoonfuls of my lentils on to his plate.

'I don't want any favours!' whispered Nico furiously and tried to give them back.

'Nico, please. Just shut up and eat.'

Our room was almost full – only two bunks were still unoccupied. Ten men in such a small space made for a pretty muggy atmosphere. I opened the shutters in the hope of catching a few mouthfuls of breathable air now and then.

'The mosquitos will be up from the lake, then,' said 8-E-6.

'Do you want me to close them again?'

'No,' he said. 'Can't hardly breathe then, can you?'

I took off my shirt and climbed on to my bunk. There wasn't room to sit upright. It was a shelf for sleeping on, and no more.

I had succeeded in having a quick word with Mama after supper. She had graciously been allowed to stay with Melli because Melli had a fever, but Rose and Dina had beaten flax all afternoon and were just as work-weary as Nico and me.

I closed my eyes and promised myself that we wouldn't stay here. Not a day longer than we had to. As soon as Melli was a little better, the Foundation could kiss us goodbye.

EIGHTEEN

The Black Men

'Anyone here know how to use a hammer and saw?'

Nico nudged me. 'You do.'

I hesitated. 'I'm not sure it's such a good idea to volunteer for anything around here.' And if I did, that would leave Nico alone in the reeds. The thought worried me.

'Whatever it is, it can't be any worse than cutting reeds. Go on, do it!' He practically shoved me forward, and the person who was asking, a small man with a slate in his hand, caught sight of me.

'Number?'

'8-E-10.'

'And you have experience with carpentry?'

'Yes.' Some, anyway.

'Right, then. Report to Mesire Aurelius in Silver Street. Seems they want a bigger coach shed.' He gave me a flat wooden token with the double dragon of the Draconis Foundation on one side. On the other, there was a hollow filled with wax. 'Give Mesire the token. When he is satisfied with your work, he will set his seal in the wax, and you will bring it back here.'

I turned the token over in my hand a few times. Where was Silver Street? Well, I supposed I could ask directions along the way.

'Good luck,' said Nico. 'See you tonight.'

'Yes,' I said slowly. He would need the luck more than me, I thought, and hoped he would get through the day without slicing off his thumb or getting into a fight with that malicious overseer.

As I walked through the streets of Sagisloc, I noticed quite a few people who wore the Foundation's grey clothing just as I did. Mostly, they seemed to be doing chores like sweeping horse dung off the street, or carrying sacks or boxes, or scrubbing the stone steps in front of the houses. Once I even saw a small cart drawn by two greylings, harnessed almost as if they were horses. From the cart a velvet-clad citizen waved amiably at other velvet-clad citizens along the way. He didn't wave to me. As a matter of fact, he seemed to look right through me – I might as well have been a ghost. But then, I hadn't paid much heed to the grey forms on my first day here. Silk and silver buttons were more apt to catch the eye.

'Excuse me,' I asked a woman holding a little boy by the hand. 'How do I find . . .'

She continued past me, and when the child turned and wanted to stop, she hauled him along and scolded him, as if he had been about to sit down in the dirt.

She was either very rude or in a tearing hurry, I

decided. Or both. Well, there were other people in the street. Like the two elderly gentlemen chatting on the next corner. I stopped, waiting for them to pause in their conversation, but they didn't seem to notice me. They were deeply engaged in a talk about the price of linen in various places in the country.

'If one can get a caravan safely through to Campana, one may demand a very decent price, I have heard. As much as ten marks the yard . . .' One of the men waved his silver-headed cane for effect. The other nodded, fumbling for his purse.

'Excuse me,' I said. 'But—'

'Yes, all right, then,' said the man with the purse. 'Here is a penny. Run along now. I thought the whole idea was that you shouldn't beg any more.'

He threw me a copper penny. Reflexively, I caught it. Then I felt the heat rising in my cheeks and knew that my face had gone lobster red.

'I don't want your penny,' I said angrily and flung it at his feet. That put paid to any more talk of linen prices. But even though I walked off as quickly as I could, I still heard their offended remarks.

'The cheek of the boy!' said one. 'So a penny isn't good enough!'

'And when you consider that nobody has to beg any more, now that we have the Foundation,' said the other. 'But I expect there will always be a few hopeless cases. No pride, I suppose. No shame or ordinary decency.'

I wasn't about to make the same mistake a third time. I found a man dressed in the same kind of grey shirt I wore and asked him for directions. And he told me how to get to Silver Street; to the house of Mesire Aurelius.

It was a stone house, with a shiny black door and a knocker shaped like a lion's head. It was so gleamy bright I hardly dared touch it – I was beginning to understand, at last, that my grey shirt made me one of the lowest in this city. But I had been told to come here, so I knocked.

A greyling girl opened the door.

'What do you want?' she asked. 'Mesire is out, and we haven't ordered anything.'

I showed her the token. 'Something about the coach shed?' I said.

'Oh, that. Go round the back and I'll let you into the kitchen.'

She shut the door in my face, apparently not expecting any reply. I walked along the front of the house until I came to a gateway leading into a closed courtyard at the back.

'Down here,' called the girl.

The kitchen was in the basement, but even there the windows had glass panes in them, and quite a lot of light came in from the yard.

'You'll have to wait until Mesire comes back,' said the girl. 'He can tell you what needs to be done. Would you like a cup of tea? And a bit of bread? There are some leftovers from Medama's breakfast tray.'

'Thank you.' A far cry from the reeds, this.

'My name is Ines,' she said. 'Who are you?'

'Davin.'

'New here, aren't you?'

'Why do you think that?'

'Haven't seen you around the Foundation.' Her brown eyes were watching me curiously.

'We came here the day before yesterday,' I said.

'Well, then. Haven't quite got used to it, then, have you?'

'I'm not going to get used to it,' I said, surprised at how much anger I felt at the mention of the Foundation. 'We'll only be here a few days.'

'That's what they all say. But take it from me, my friend. That shirt is easy to put on – but getting rid of it again is another matter.'

'How long have you had yours?'

'Four years.'

'Four *years*?' I couldn't imagine how anybody... I mean, just sleeping on that miserable wooden shelf. For four years?

She shrugged. 'What can you do? Not a lot. Did they show you your debtor's board yet?'

'My what?'

'Didn't think so. You see, at the Foundation, nothing is free.'

'So I've noticed. I've worked in the reeds for nearly two days!'

'Yes, and your labour is duly noted on one side of the line. On the other is the sum you owe them for food and housing and baths and clothing. And that is a little more. Not a lot. Just enough so that you probably won't be able to pay them the difference.'

'But I worked my tail off... we harvested barge

after barge of those miserable reeds. They have to be worth more than a bunk and a few bowlfuls of barley soup.'

'The Foundation decides the price of things. Both your labour and the barley soup.'

'They didn't tell us that when we arrived!'

'Course not. They're not stupid, see? They're always smiley-kind-and-nice to the newcomers. At first.'

'But . . . but that's not fair!'

'Welcome to Sagisloc.'

'But what if you leave?'

'That's called theft,' she said. 'If they catch you, it's the Sagisburg for you.'

'The what?'

'You really are new, aren't you?' She looked as if she could hardly imagine anyone not having heard of the Sagisburg. 'That's where—'

She got no further. A door slammed, and feet came clattering down the stairs at a stumbling run. Long before the girl child actually entered the kitchen, we could hear her crying, in the loud tones of someone who feels she has been wronged.

'He hit me. Ines, the man *hit* me!'

Velvet bows in blonde curls, red velvet dress with a white lace collar and silver buttons on the shoulders. Oh yes, this was very much an upstairs child.

'There, there,' said Ines. 'Show me, where?'

The girl held out her hands. There was a red mark across one palm.

'He hit me with his ruler. I hate him!' Tears poured down her angry red cheeks.

A grey-haired man in a black robe came down the stairs at a far more dignified pace.

'I must ask the little miss to return to the schoolroom immediately!' he said. 'She has barely begun her exercises.'

'No, I won't,' yelled the little miss. 'You are a stupid old man, and you smell bad. I hate you!'

There actually was a none too pleasant smell about him — somehow both sweetish and decaying, like rotten hay. But he probably didn't relish being told so by a girl no older than Melli. He practically gulped with indignation.

'Really . . .' He spun and meant to storm out of the kitchen, but he couldn't. The doorway was blocked now by a woman wearing a velvet dress matching the girl's, only in a more adult version.

'Master Rubens,' she said. 'Do tell me what the problem is.'

'I resign,' he snarled. 'Immediately! And then we shall see if Medama can find anyone to teach the little monster. I very much doubt it!'

'Oh, no,' moaned the lady of the house. 'What has she done now?'

'The impertinence of the child! Defiant. Wilful. Unheard of!'

'He hit me,' said the wilful child in question, holding out her palm.

'Oh no. Master Rubens, I hardly think hitting Mira is going to—'

'Medama intends to lecture me on method, now?'

'No. No, of course not . . .'

'The child is unteachable. Rebellious. There is a proclivity in her, yes, I will say it plainly, a flaw in her character. Where one ought to find natural womanly obedience, there is only rebellion and savagery.'

Natural womanly obedience? He had obviously never met Melli. Or Dina. Or Mama.

'She misses her brother.' Medama Aurelius was pleading now. 'I'll speak to her. Strongly. And tomorrow, everything will be much improved.'

'Possibly – but without my services. I hereby advance my resignation.' He bowed to the child's mother in a measured fashion and strode up the kitchen stairs.

'Oh, no,' said Medama for the third time. 'Please . . . Master Rubens, you mustn't do that. We can . . . I'm sure my husband is willing to raise your fee . . .'

But Master Rubens was not about to stop.

'It is not about money,' he spat. 'It is about the proper respect!' And he walked through the door and slammed it behind him.

For a moment, the woman stood looking up the stairs, as if she was half expecting him to come back. Then she collapsed on to one of the kitchen benches, weeping helplessly.

'Oh, Mira,' she said, hugging the child. 'What have you done!'

'But . . . he hit me, Mama,' said the girl uncertainly. 'Mama, please don't cry.'

I couldn't understand the mother's helpless tears. Personally, I wouldn't have gone out of my way to keep the services of the good Master Rubens.

'I told you, Mira-love,' she murmured into her daughter's hair. 'You have to be good and try to learn. Or they'll take you away from me.'

That had the child crying again, hiccoughing loudly. 'But I don't want to, Mama. I don't want to go away with the black men.'

'Oh, my sweet love . . .'

'What black men?' I asked.

The mother seemed to notice me for the first time. 'Who are you?'

'My name is Davin.' Damned if I would introduce myself as 8-E-10. 'I'm here for the coach shed. Who are the black men that Mira is afraid of?'

For a moment she seemed to consider whether it was really suitable to share such personal troubles with a lowly greyling. But I think she was too miserable to keep silent.

'They call it the Law of Rightful Education,' she said bitterly. 'But I think they should call it wrongful education instead. All citizens' children have to attend an annual test of their knowledge and skills. If they do not pass it, then . . . then they are sent away for schooling.' She clung to the child as if she could already feel Mira slip away from her. 'They've taken Markus. I couldn't bear to lose Mira as well.'

An idea stirred somewhere inside my head.

'How long is it before Mira has to take her test?' I asked.

New tears ran down her mother's cheeks. 'A week,' she said, so choked the words were barely audible. 'Oh, Mira, why couldn't you be nice and behave?'

I took a deep breath. 'My cousin is an excellent teacher . . .' I began.

It was no easy task to convince her that a greyling might be able to help her child. She had probably never considered that there might be people at the Foundation who could actually read and write, and if she had been able to think of any other way out, she would never have accepted. But in the end we agreed that I should fetch Nico right away. Whatever else, I thought, it would at least get him out of the reeds for a while.

Ines saw me to the door.

'You have a way with you,' she said admiringly. 'This cousin of yours, does he really know about such things?'

'Yes, he really does.'

'Good. Mira may be a brat at times, but you should have seen Markus the last time they let him come home. That's no way to treat a child.'

When we got back to the Foundation that night, Nico and I asked to see the family's debtor's boards. And Ines had it right: we already owed eight copper marks altogether. Not a princely sum, perhaps, but more than we could afford to pay.

'You'd almost think they had gone through our purse before coming up with the amount,' I told Nico.

He looked thoughtful. 'Maybe they did,' he said. 'While we were bathing that first day.'

'This place is a trap,' I said bitterly. 'They invite you in with open arms. And then they have you.'

★ ★ ★

The next couple of days, Nico and I went along to Silver Street every morning – me to build them their new and larger coach shed, Nico to see if he could make the necessary words stick in Mira's stubborn head. When the weather was decent, he usually came out into the yard to share whatever Ines gave us for lunch.

'They teach the children strange things around here,' he said. 'Look at what they want her to copy out.' He gave me a piece of parchment with some awfully curlicued letters on it.

'Errm . . . it might be faster if you read it out loud,' I muttered.

Nico looked at me for a moment. 'Are you sure you don't want me to help you study a bit yourself?' he asked. 'At some point? It's quite a useful skill to have, and we needn't tell anybody.'

'I can read!'

'Yes, I know. But if you never practise, you might forget.'

'Go on and read it, Nico,' I said. 'You can make a clerk of me some other day.'

'You? A clerk?' Nico laughed. 'I don't think so. It's just not in your nature, is it?'

'Read the stupid paper,' I said, brushing a few crumbs off my shirt.

He smoothed the paper and read it to me.

'Who is the Ruler of the land? Arthos Draconis. What are the true names of Prince Arthos? Courage, wisdom and justice. What is the will of the Prince? The health and happiness of his citizens. What is the will of the citizens? Their proper service to the Prince. What is the fate of those who do not serve? Ill indeed. What manner of enemies exist? Those within and those without. What is the fate of the enemy without? To be stricken by the Prince with terror, swords and blood. What are the enemies within? Traitors all. What is the wage of treason? Death.'

He paused. 'Is that a proper thing to teach a six-year-old girl? No wonder she finds it hard to remember.'

'But this is what they want her to know?'

He nodded. 'Or they will send her to be schooled by someone they call the Educators.'

'The black men.'

'Yes, they wear black robes. And Mira is scared witless of them. She saw what happened to her brother.'

'Why do people put up with it?'

Nico shook his head. 'There are actually quite a few people in Sagisloc who send their children to the Educators of their own free will. Because if you want an important office, or the right to trade in cloth or copper or something else that can make you rich . . . well, then you have to be a graduate of one of the Draconis Academies.'

'He has it all figured out, hasn't he? This Prince Arthos. Anyone you know?'

Nico grimaced and looked about quickly. The groom was wiping one of the carriage horses dry, but he paid us no heed. We were greylings, he wasn't – he put some store by that.

'Actually,' said Nico, 'he is sort of my uncle. Or whatever you call it when he is my aunt's father.'

'Your aunt's . . . do you mean Dama Lizea? Drakan's mother?'

'Precisely.'

'Nico . . . remember Valdracu?'

'I certainly do.'

'How is he related to Prince Arthos?'

'As near as I can make it . . . his grandchild. His son's son. So it might not be a good idea to talk too loudly about the fact that you killed him.'

I looked down at the paper with all its words about enemies without and within, and terror, swords and blood.

'That's what I was thinking,' I said.

NINETEEN

The Tell-tale

I found myself whistling as I walked. Not loudly and piercingly, so that people would turn and stare, but a quiet, nearly tuneless sound. Things were definitely on the mend. Melli's cough was all but gone, I was nearly finished with the coach shed, and Mesire Aurelius had praised my work and given me five pennies 'for yourself', as he put it. He was paying the Foundation a much larger sum for my work, I discovered. But the best of it was that he had promised Nico twenty silver marks if Mira passed her test today. Twenty marks! With that money, we could pay off the Foundation and still have something left so that we would not be beggars 'without means' wherever we went next.

'She will pass, won't she?' I asked Nico, who was walking next to me.

'I think so,' he said with what I thought was heartening confidence. 'She knows her lessons when I test her. But I still think it's awful to force children to learn such things.'

'As long as she knows her stuff.' Twenty marks. That money could save us all.

'She does.'

I whistled a little louder. Secretly, I had begun to savour the thought of leaving Sagisloc and its Foundation for good. We could go south, towards Campana. Somewhere Prince Arthos's shadow did not fall quite so heavily upon the land. On a clear day, you could actually see the Sagisburg, where he lived, in the mountains across the lake.

'Come in,' said Ines. 'Markus is coming home today! Mesire has gone to fetch him, and Medama is beside herself with the whole thing.'

We sat down on the kitchen bench and ate the breakfast leftovers with Ines. We didn't have to wait long before we heard Mira's rapid clattering steps on the stairs.

'Nico!' she called, and practically flung herself into his arms. 'Sing me the Frog Song!'

Nico laughed. 'If Mylady insists.'

'If I what?'

'If you say I must.'

'I do!'

And Nico sang the Frog Song. I knew it well, it was an old one about a clever frog who cheated the stork, but between stanzas Nico had changed it so that the stork questioned the frog: 'Who is the Ruler of the Land?' and the little frog in its croaky voice said 'Arthos Draconis', and so forth.

Aha. So that was how he had coaxed the impertinent little miss into learning her lessons, I thought. Though that probably wasn't the entire secret. Nico liked children, that much was obvious. And I didn't think Master Rubens did.

'Mira? Mira, my sweet, where are you?'

'She is down here, Medama,' called Ines. 'Nico and Davin are here.'

'Oh, good,' said Medama Aurelius, coming down the stairs. 'Mira, let me look at you.'

Mira obediently bounced off Nico's lap and turned around, pirouetting like a dancer. She was wearing black velvet this morning, with a starched white collar that practically reached her ears. Medama Aurelius fiddled with the collar and brushed a bit of lint off the black velvet.

'Aren't they back yet?' she said anxiously. 'We really can't be late today. We really can't!'

At that moment, we could hear trotting hooves and the rattle of carriage wheels outside.

'Papa!' cried Mira happily. 'Papa and Markus!' She rushed to the kitchen door, tore it open and shouted: 'Papa! We're down here!'

Mesire Aurelius entered. He, too, was stylishly dressed, in brown velvet with silver hooks. At his side was a boy of about nine, fair-haired like his sister, but with the hair so closely cropped that his skull seemed almost naked. He looked strangely formal and serious for a child.

'Markus!' Medama Aurelius reached for the boy and hugged him tightly. 'My sweet boy, how have you been?'

For a few moments, the small form yielded to her embrace. Then he freed himself.

'Excellently well, Mama,' he said.

'Better than last time? You look so pale, my love.'

'I am quite well, thank you.'

Why did he sound as if he was lying? Possibly because the words seemed much too grown-up for him.

Ines wiped her hands on her apron and held out her arms.

'Come here, you rascal!' she said, moving forward. 'Give us a hug.'

She clearly expected him to come running to meet her. But he stared at her with a chill that made her halt abruptly.

'I do not associate with the likes of you any more,' said young Mesire Markus. And when I saw Ines's face, so crestfallen, so deeply hurt, I wanted to take hold of that pompous little Master Prim-Face and whack his behind for him. But it wasn't really he who deserved the beating. Someone, somewhere, in the time that had passed since his last visit, had taught the boy that greylings weren't people. At least not people of the kind you could have feelings for.

Even Mesire Aurelius looked taken aback. 'Really, Markus,' he said. 'You may say hello to Ines.'

The boy merely held his arms stiffly along his sides, as if they would snap if he had to hold them out to anyone. And Ines turned away quickly and began fumbling with the cups from the breakfast table.

'Doesn't matter,' she said. 'If the young master doesn't want to, I'd as soon he didn't. Besides, I have work to do.'

Markus's face was masklike in its blankness. It was impossible to tell what went on underneath it.

'Ah, here is my star pupil,' said Mesire Aurelius and lifted Mira up to stand on the kitchen table. 'How fine you look. Well? Let me hear you.'

Nico gave Mira a slight nod, and Mira rattled off the whole thing, flawlessly.

'Who-is-the-Ruler-of-the-Land-Arthos-Draconis, what-are-the-true-names . . .' and so on and so forth. Without hesitation. Without stumbling at the difficult words.

'Bravo!' said the proud father. 'She certainly knows her lesson.' And then, more quietly, to Nico: 'But why does she say *quack-quack* at the end?'

'Errrm . . . perhaps you had better not do that, Mira,' said Nico. 'The Educators might not know that song.'

'Markus,' said Mesire Aurelius. 'This is the man who has taught your sister. It is thanks to him that we are allowed to keep her at home for another year.'

Markus turned his cold stare on Nico. His face was still expressionless, and yet I could almost see the cloud of hostility that radiated from his thin body. Was it Nico's grey shirt, or was Markus jealous because he had to go off to school while his spoiled little sister got to stay home?

Mesire Aurelius seemed not to notice his son's coldness. He watched Nico for a while and then extended his hand the way he would to an equal.

'My thanks, Nicolas,' he said. 'I have to admit that I doubted my wife's plan at the outset, but you have put my doubts to shame. And when Mira has passed her test a few hours from now, I will keep my promise to you.'

★ ★ ★

174

The whole family left. For the first time, Nico was beginning to look nervous, but then, he had nothing to do for the next few hours except sit in the kitchen with Ines and bite his nails. I was happy enough that there were still a few things to be done in the coach shed so that I wouldn't have to sit and think.

Finally, though, there was nothing left that needed sanding or planing, and not a single shaving that hadn't been swept from the floor. And still no sign of the Aurelius family. I went back to the kitchen, where Nico had begun pacing the floor.

'She knows it,' he muttered. 'I know she knows it.'

'Will you sit down?' I said. 'Watching you is enough to make anybody seasick.'

He sat. And began drumming his fingers against the tabletop.

'Do you suppose she forgot the words after all?' I said. 'Or lost her nerve in front of a bunch of strange old men?'

'How would I know?' snapped Nico. 'I'm not psychic.'

How on earth had we reached this point, I thought, with our whole future hanging on a six-year-old girl's ability to remember a meaningless rigmarole?

'Settle down, Nico,' I said. 'If she flunks, we'll think of something else.'

He stared at me. 'If she flunks, they'll take the poor girl away from her family and her home and put her through . . . through . . . through whatever they did to the other one. Her brother. Didn't you see him? That's no child, that's a dead thing. If you think it's the twenty marks that's making me sweat, think again!'

175

My conscience smarted at that, because I had to admit I hadn't thought beyond the money.

There were footsteps outside, but it wasn't the family returning. These sounded more like the tramping of soldier's feet.

We heard the street door open. A lot of boot heels rapped against the floor above our heads, and I was beginning to get a really bad sense of trouble.

'Nico,' I whispered. 'Something is wrong. I think we'd better get out of here.'

He still sat unmoving at the table. 'Why?' he said. 'We haven't done anything wrong.'

Ines laughed bitterly. 'Think that matters? In this city, greylings are always guilty until proven innocent.'

Steps on the kitchen stairs, now.

I latched on to Nico and pulled him to his feet.

'We're leaving,' I said.

Finally, he moved. I opened the door to the courtyard.

And found myself facing a couple of uniformed guards who were apparently quite aware that a fox's hole has more than one exit.

Behind us, more guards were already filing into the kitchen, along with Medama Aurelius and Markus. Medama was pale as death, and of Mira and the master of the house, there was no sign.

'Who is it, then?' asked the guard captain.

'Him,' said Markus, pointing at Nico. 'There is the greyling who has poisoned my sister's mind!'

TWENTY

The Court's Justice

They dragged us through the city in chains. It was hard to believe that I had walked through the same streets a few hours earlier, *whistling*.

'Why couldn't you stay out of it?' Nico hissed at me. There was a cut above his left eye, and a thin thread of blood trickled down the side of his face. 'Why did you have to start a fight?'

Was that all the thanks I was getting?

'I only wanted to help!'

'Right. And what about your mother? What about the girls? Who is going to look after them now?'

'But . . . they'll have to let us go,' I said. I was having a hard time breathing; there had been a bad kick to the ribs, and I wasn't over it yet. 'We didn't do anything wrong!'

'Oh . . . apart from head-butting the guard captain, you mean?'

Yes, well, that might not have been the cleverest thing I'd ever done. But when two soldiers are hanging on to your arms it's the only way you can fight back,

177

and when he had begun hitting Nico . . . well, what was I to do? Nico hadn't even resisted. He was just trying to talk his way out of it, until that bastard of a captain started shouting about 'greyling impertinence'. And hit Nico. More than once. Which was when I butted him.

Clutching his nose, the captain had roared even louder. He swung at me, but I pulled away from one of the guards holding me and stumbled back so that he missed me entirely. The table was overturned, bowls and cups went sailing through the air and hit the tiled floor with a crash. Potshards everywhere, and total confusion. The guards were trying to catch me, and I was trying to avoid being pummelled half to death. Nico had begun to fight back as well, now, but there were six soldiers in all and not much doubt about the outcome. They wrestled me to the floor eventually, on top of all the shards, and chained my hands behind my back. And the bloody-nosed captain kicked me in the ribs with a vengeance. I was almost sure one of them was bent or broken.

Which was why we were now being marched through the street in chains, guards on both sides of us, for the good citizens of Sagisloc to stare at. And Nico was right. I had been stupid. If they locked us up for a couple of weeks, or whatever they usually did to greylings who dared resist, who would look after Mama and the girls?

They locked us up in some basement room beneath the courthouse. There weren't any windows, and they didn't bother to leave us a light. A tiny crack of daylight showed beneath the door, and that was that.

'Are you hurt?' asked Nico.

'I think I may have broken a rib,' I muttered. They had left the chains on, so I couldn't even touch my ribcage to find out. 'What about you?'

'No,' he said. 'Nothing much.'

'How long do you think they'll leave us here?'

'I have no idea. I don't even know whether greylings get a trial the way citizens do, or whether they just hand out your punishment without further ado.'

We were both of us quiet for a while, and I don't think Nico's thoughts were any more cheerful than mine.

'I don't understand,' he finally said.

'What?'

'Why they came to arrest us. What is it they think we've done?'

I sighed tiredly. 'You heard him. The pale little rat. Markus. Apparently, a greyling is not allowed to masquerade as a tutor. Or maybe they don't like it when you turn the Draconis rigmarole into a song about a frog. What do I know?'

'But how was I supposed to know that? Not even Mesire Aurelius knew.'

'You think they care?'

There was nothing to sit on except the floor, which was gritty and cold. I tried to pull up my knees to keep warm, but it hurt too much. Every time I moved, those damned chains clinked so that I felt like a donkey or a chained watchdog, or whatever. Something less than human, at any rate.

I heard Nico move in the darkness. He was pacing. Back and forth, from one wall to the other.

'They might have left us a light,' he said, hoarsely. 'They didn't have to leave us here in the stinking dark so that we can't even see where we are!'

I didn't see that it made a huge difference. We were in a cold, bare basement room under the courthouse. What was there to look at? But it obviously mattered to Nico. And then I realized. This was not the first time Nico had been in a dungeon. The first time Dina met Nico, he had been locked up in a cell in Dunark Castle, accused of having murdered his father, his sister-in-law and his small nephew. If Dina and Mama hadn't helped him then, the executioner would have chopped off his head. And it must be hard for Nico not to think of that time now. Darkness in a cell in Sagisloc probably wasn't very different from darkness in a cell in Dunark.

I tried to think of something to say, something that might make it easier for him. But my chest hurt, and I was freezing cold. I might have said 'It'll be all right', or something like that, but right now it would be really hard to sound as if I believed it myself.

They came to get us. I don't know how much later; it was impossible to keep proper track of time in the darkness.

'Out,' said one of the guards gruffly.

I got to my feet with some difficulty – it isn't easy with your hands chained behind your back and a body full of bruises that have stiffened in the cold. I wasn't quick enough, it seemed; the guard grabbed me by the arm and hauled me into the passage outside. I had to squeeze my eyes shut. The light from the window at the end was blindingly bright after hours of darkness.

They dragged us up two flights of stairs and into a hall with tall, narrow windows on all sides. On a dais raised a few feet above the floor sat a row of men in black cloaks. I wasn't sure whether they were Educators or some other kind of official.

Standing in front of them was Mesire Aurelius. He had not been chained, but it was still obvious that he was being accused.

'Does he admit to having used a false teacher, a greyling even, as a tutor for his daughter?' said one of the men on the dais.

'Yes, M'lord Courtmaster, I do so admit,' said Mesire Aurelius. 'But only out of ignorance. I had no idea . . .'

'Ignorance is no excuse. The law is clear, and it is a citizen's duty to know it: only Educators and tutors authorized by the Prince may teach our children.'

A whisper went round the hall, and I noticed that the balcony at the end of the room was crowded with onlookers. The Courtmaster threw a sharp glance at the audience, and the whisperings died. Then he raised the Sword of Justice, a cumbersome thing loaded down with gemstones and scarlet tassels, and spoke his judgement:

'Mesire Aurelius is fined a hundred silver marks. And the child is to be brought to the Educators at Sagisburg.'

'No,' moaned Mesire Aurelius. 'The money, yes, I'll pay it gladly, but Mira . . .'

The Courtmaster rose and looked down on Mesire Aurelius. 'The charge could have been one of offence against the Prince's name, Mesire. Does he know the penalty for that?'

Mesire Aurelius's voice was barely audible. 'Death,' he said.

'Precisely. You should compose yourself, sir, pay the fine and count yourself mercifully judged. Next case.'

The guard next to me cleared his throat. 'M'lord Courtmaster . . .'

'Yes?' It clearly did not please the Courtmaster to be interrupted.

'The two greylings . . .'

'Oh, yes. Six years' labour at the Sagisburg. Next!'

Six years. Six years?

'Don't we get a say?' I shouted.

Apparently not. The guard whacked the back of my neck so hard that I stumbled and grew dizzy.

'Apologies, M'lord Courtmaster,' he said. And to me he snarled, 'Shut your mouth, cur, or I'll break your jaw.'

The Courtmaster looked as if he had just discovered something unpleasant in his food. 'Clear them from the room,' he said. 'And see to it that they are shipped to the Sagisburg this very night.'

The guard grabbed my shoulder in a no-nonsense hold, forced me around and pushed me towards the door. And that was when I saw him, up there among the riveted onlookers on the balcony. Sezuan. I was certain it was him. That black hair, and the eyes, so like Dina's . . . He stared at me for a long moment. Then a man in front of him got up, and suddenly Sezuan was gone. But he had been there. I was sure of it. And he had wanted me to see him. *No one see Sezuan unless he wants to be seen.* But why? To mock me? To drive me wild with fear at what he would do to Dina and the others now that I wasn't there to protect them?

If that was his purpose, he succeeded. My gut was one big icy lump of fear.

Mama, I thought. Dina. Melli. Rose. Surely, these people couldn't send us off without at least letting us speak to our family?

But it seemed they could.

At dusk that night they dragged us from the cellar, put us in a boat with poor Mira, and sent us off across the lake to the Sagisburg.

IV
The Mountain Road
Dina's story

TWENTY-ONE

Six Years

Beating flax was hard and dusty work. It made my arms and back hurt, and soon my cough was nearly as bad as Melli's.

'It should be our last day here,' said Mama comfortingly. 'When Nico and Davin come back with the money, we can collect our belongings and leave.'

I could hardly wait. The working day dragged along at snail's pace.

But by the time we got to supper, neither Davin nor Nico had turned up.

'Where are they?' I asked, anxiously.

'Perhaps the Aurelius family has asked them to stay for dinner,' said Mama. 'To celebrate.'

But I could tell by the look in her eyes that she was worried too.

I felt like sneaking into the men's quarters that night to find them, but I didn't dare. There was probably some silly fine if you got caught, and if that made it impossible for us to leave the Foundation . . . it didn't bear thinking about. So all night I lay on my shelf, dozing for a while, then lying awake with my anxious thoughts, then dozing again.

At breakfast, still no Davin, still no Nico.

'Where *are* they?' I hissed at Mama.

'I don't know,' she said. 'But we shall have to ask.'

We went to the Inscriptorium, the building where our names had been entered into the record slates of the Foundation the very first day.

'Pardon me,' said Mama to the Scriptor. 'But I don't understand . . . my son and my nephew, we haven't seen them since breakfast yesterday, and I was wondering . . .'

He looked at her in irritation, as if that was none of his concern. She kept her eyes lowered, but it was obvious all the same that she had no intention of moving before he gave her an answer.

He sighed. 'Number?' he rapped out.

'8-E-10 and 8-E-11.'

He brought the 8E slate down from its hook on the wall and carefully held it so that we would not be able to see what was written on it. Then he put it back and turned to us with a chilly smile.

'They've been arrested,' he said. 'Sorry.' He didn't sound very sorry.

'Arrested?' said Mama. 'Why?'

'For having falsely tutored a child without authorization, for spreading treason, for having attacked an officer of the Prince's guard and for resisting lawful arrest.'

'What?' Mama looked completely stunned, and when I took her hand, it was icy cold to touch.

'They got six years,' said the Scriptor and smiled his pleasant smile. 'At the Sagisburg.'

Mama wanted her own clothes back. She was going to the courthouse, and we all knew she wouldn't get much of a hearing if she showed up in a greyling shirt. At first the Scriptor wouldn't hear of it, at least not until Mama turned her Shamer's eyes on him.

'Is this the way you treat a fellow human being? Is this the way you would want to be treated yourself?'

The colour left his face and he muttered something inaudible. And suddenly it was quite possible to get ordinary clothes from the laundry; not our own, perhaps, but anything was better than the greys.

'Now he knows you're a Shamer,' I said as we hurried through the streets.

'There's no help for that,' said Mama. 'It had to be done.'

The courthouse was a big, square grey building of the kind that has been built to make people look small. It didn't seem to bother Mama. She marched up the stone steps as if they were her own kitchen stairs.

'I wish to see the Courtmaster,' she said to the first person she saw, a guard in a black uniform tunic. And even though she used neither the Shamer's eyes nor the Shamer's voice, there was such a forcefulness to her that he merely obeyed and said, 'This way, Medama,' though she was dressed somewhat drably and looked like nobody special or powerful at all. It wasn't until he paused in front of a door on the first floor that he seemed to hesitate.

'Erhhh . . . who may I say is calling?' he asked cautiously.

'Melussina Tonerre.' She added nothing to her bare name, just left him to sort it out for himself.

He knocked, and when a come-in sort of grunt sounded from inside the room, he poked only his head in, as if he was less to blame if less of him was visible.

'Medama Tonerre,' he said. 'Will M'lord Courtmaster receive her?'

But M'lord Courtmaster never got the chance to make up his own mind on that score. Mama moved swiftly past the guard, and I followed her into the large, well-lit room where the Courtmaster had been enjoying an early lunch.

'Mesire,' said Mama. 'I've come to talk to you about my son.'

And Nico, I added in my own mind, let's not forget Nico. But perhaps it was wise of Mama not to start talking about her 'nephew Nicolas' right now. She was the worst of liars.

The Courtmaster looked somewhat taken aback. He let go of the drumstick he was chewing and put his hand reflexively to his chest, leaving grease stains on his black robe.

'I do not believe we have met,' he said pointedly. 'Nor do I have any idea who this son of yours might be.'

'Yesterday Mesire sentenced him to six years' labour.'

He frowned. 'I did not pass such a sentence on any citizen yesterday.'

'It is possible,' said Mama in her sharpest voice, 'that

Mesire did not consider him a citizen. He was dressed in Foundation clothes.'

'Oh, one of the two greylings.'

'Yes. Mesire, my son has not deserved such punishment.'

'Medama. I do not recall the details of the matter, but I know I followed the laws of the land.'

'*Did Mesire also follow his own conscience?*'

Normally, weeks passed by without my mother using her powers. Now she had done so twice in one morning. It caused a wobbly sensation in my insides, because using the Shamer's gift was often the next best thing to prodding a hornets' nest. It might take a moment or two before something happened, but after that, leaving in a hurry was a really good idea.

The Courtmaster's own eyes were nearly hidden by heavy folds of skin, and at first it was hard to tell whether Mama had struck a nerve or not.

'They were greylings,' he finally ventured. 'If he was not guilty in this instance, I'm sure he had committed other acts deserving of punishment.'

'Why? *Because greylings are not citizens? Not human like you and I?*'

He stared helplessly down at his dead chicken. 'Judgement has been passed,' he said. 'There is nothing I can do now.'

'Is that so?' Mama spoke with icy contempt. 'I demand the immediate release of my son and his . . . companion. And I believe this to be within the powers of a courtmaster.'

Tiny beads of sweat glittered on his lined forehead, but he did not surrender completely.

'The boat has sailed,' he said. 'The two convicts have already been brought to the Sagisburg.'

There was perhaps just a touch of malicious pleasure in his voice. Mama stared at his bowed neck, and I almost wished she would use her voice and eyes on him again, to make him cringe and admit his fault, and his shame at it.

She didn't. Mama had taught me not to abuse the gift, and I had never seen her do so herself. But I think she came close, that day in the Courtmaster's office.

The boat has sailed. Nico and Davin were on their way to the Sagisburg now. How long would it be before someone found out that Nico was the old castellan's son? And Davin. Davin had killed Valdracu – Prince Arthos's own grandson. How long would they let him live if they found out about *that*?

'Mama?'

We were standing on the steps outside the courthouse. Had, in fact, been standing there for a while. Mama had stopped halfway down, as if her feet had suddenly sunk into the stone and she no longer had the power to move. And I grew even more afraid than I already was, afraid in a new way. Because if Mama couldn't go on, if Mama gave up . . . then it really did seem hopeless, and the world might as well come to an end right away.

It felt to me as if we had been standing there for ever. Then Mama finally raised her head.

'Which street?'

'Mama?'

'Mesire Aurelius's house. Which street, Dina?'

'Silver Street,' I said and felt the worst, most terrible fear seep away. Mama was still here. She hadn't given up.

Ines, the maid, showed us into the parlour. Everything in there seemed to be some shade of white or pale blue, and it might have been quite a cheerful room on most days. Right now, it seemed haunted, not by dead people but by the living, the master and mistress of the house and their son Markus. They all sat still as statues, looking at no one; a table had been set for tea, but it looked as if the boy was the only one who had eaten anything.

'Medama Tonerre,' announced Ines and left the room as if the devil might catch her if she stayed. But the sound of her footsteps halted as soon as the door had closed behind her. Was she listening by the keyhole?

'Medama Tonerre,' said Mesire Aurelius tonelessly. 'I'm afraid I'm not acquainted . . . have we met?'

'I'm Davin's mother.'

That made him raise his eyes from his saucer. He got up.

'Medama . . .' He eyed her pale green skirts as if he thought they ought to have been grey. 'I regret. I must ask you to leave my house immediately.'

'Mesire. My son and Nico have suffered judgement and imprisonment because they tried to aid this house. And you want me to leave without having spoken?'

Why was Mesire Aurelius suddenly looking at his son? A quick sideways look, as if to see whether Markus was listening.

'This house is obedient to the will of Prince Arthos,' he said in a loud and hollow-sounding voice. 'We do

193

not consort with enemies of the Prince. Leave, Medama, before I have the guards called.'

He seized my mother's hand and arm for a moment, as if he meant to push her out of the door with his own two hands. She looked at him coldly.

'Mesire, I am perfectly capable of walking on my own.'

'Then please do so.'

There wasn't much else to do. We turned our backs on the statue family and left the room.

'Mama . . .'

'Hush,' said Mama, eyeing Ines who was busy polishing a door handle a little further down the passage, a door handle that looked gleamingly clean to me already. 'When we're outside.'

In the streets a few moments later, I could no longer keep my mouth shut.

'Mama, why were they like that? As if they had been turned to stone?'

Mama shook her head slowly. 'I don't know. But I think Mesire Aurelius is afraid of his son. And I think he would like to help us if he could. He gave me a silver coin.'

She held it so that it glinted in the afternoon sun.

I hadn't seen him give her anything. Perhaps when he had seized her arm?

'Why would he be afraid of his own child? That's weird.'

'Yes.'

'What can a . . . how old is he, ten? What can a ten-year-old do that a grown-up needs to fear?'

Mama looked thoughtful. 'Perhaps . . . tell tales,' she said.

Suddenly the door opened again. Ines poked her head out, looking left and right.

'Mesire asked me to say he will send word,' she said softly.

'When?'

'He didn't say. But I should think . . . when the young master has left.'

Ines ducked back into the house and quietly closed the door. We didn't have time to ask when that might be. And I wasn't sure how much help we could count on getting. A silver mark was no mean sum, to be sure, but it would take more than that to release us from the Foundation. And that would only be the first step. We still had to work out a way of freeing Davin and Nico.

'We have to go back to the Foundation to wait,' said Mama. 'If he sends word today or tomorrow, fine. If he doesn't . . . we'll just have to think of something ourselves.'

Yes, but what? I didn't ask the question out loud, because I knew she wouldn't be able to answer it.

TWENTY-TWO

Dinner at The Golden Swan

We had barely reached the Foundation when we were called down to the Inscriptorium. There, the Scriptor eyed us with suspicion.

'A gentleman has asked for you,' he said. 'He wishes to hire you for a task, the exact nature of which he would not disclose. I feel bound to draw your attention to the fact that the Foundation does not permit its clients to perform acts of indecency or any other form of lewdness.'

Acts of indecency? Mama? Me?

'I can assure Mesire that neither my daughter nor myself has any intention of acting indecently,' said Mama with a coldness that should have left him an icicle from the ears down. She didn't look at him, not quite, but I think he remembered what had happened the last time she did so.

'No,' he said quickly. 'No, of course not. The gentleman has sent a carriage.'

A carriage. How extravagant.

'Who is he?' asked Mama.

'The gentleman did not leave his name.'

'Do you suppose it's Mesire Aurelius?' I whispered to Mama.

'Let's hope so.'

It was a beautiful carriage, drawn by two dappled greys that reminded me a bit of Silky. The coachman politely offered Mama his arm to help her into the carriage, and then did the same for me.

'Do you work for Mesire Aurelius?' I asked.

'This is a hired carriage,' he said. 'I work for whoever pays me.'

He gave my mother a courteous bow, closed the carriage door and mounted the block. The carriage took off with a jerk.

'I should have asked where he was taking us,' I said.

'I know of nobody else who might be this interested in us, *and* pay for a carriage,' said Mama. 'He is trying to clear his conscience, I wager.'

But when the carriage came to a halt, it was not outside the house in Silver Street. A liveried servant opened the door for us, but I didn't recognize my surroundings at all.

'Where are we?' I said, a little nervously.

'At The Golden Swan,' he said. 'If Medamina will step this way . . . Mesire has arranged for supper.'

An inn. That soothed my nerves. Probably Mesire Aurelius dared not meet us at the house in Silver Street where Markus's pale eyes noted everything that went on.

We followed the usher into a handsome red building. Lamps were everywhere, and waiters in blue waistcoats and white shirts were busy lighting them to shine softly in the dusky evening. The floors were wooden, so dark that they were nearly black, and so shiny that one could practically see oneself mirrored there. Several of Sagisloc's good citizens were already seated at white tables enjoying what looked like an exquisite meal – capon, salads, grapes and wine.

'Mesire's guests are here,' said the usher to one of the blue waistcoats.

'Ah, yes. This way, Medama, Medamina . . . Mesire thought it would be pleasant to enjoy dinner in the orangery, as it is such a warm evening.'

He led us through the house and into a tiled courtyard where apple trees, pear trees and peach trees stood in long rows, like pillars in a church. From a glasshouse at the back, a soft light was shining on to the tiles.

It was like something out of a fairytale. A house of glass. Like a tiny crystal palace. So many panes . . . even the roof was mostly glass. I was almost afraid to shout or sneeze or make sudden movements. What if it broke?

The wide doors were open to the orchard, and inside, among lemon trees, fig trees and vines, a table had been set. A silver candelabrum sported a whole forest of candles, it seemed, and a young girl in a starched white apron was already serving the first course.

'Please be seated,' said the waiter in the blue waistcoat and held the chair for my mother and then for me. I had not been treated this way since . . . no, I had never been treated with this kind of courtesy in my life.

I was sitting on a white chair with a blue velvet

cushion. On the platter in front of me, a rolled-up fish rested in a small pool of orange sauce. Thin strips of orange peel had been arranged delicately on top, and I couldn't help thinking of Melli and Rose who were sitting down to another round of the inevitable barley soup at the moment, or to boiled lentils and pork trimmings, if they were lucky.

The waiter and the serving girl both retired. The third chair was still empty. Where was Mesire Aurelius?

'Fine meals and silver candelabra,' murmured my mother, eyeing the fish. 'All very well. But I would rather have the money so that we could free ourselves from the Foundation and . . . and see what can be done for Nico and Davin.'

'You aim too low, Melussina,' said a voice. 'Why make it either, when you can have both?'

Mama leaped to her feet, so abruptly that her chair crashed back and fell over.

'You,' she said softly. 'I might have known.'

Sezuan came out of the orchard shadows, so soundlessly that he seemed to glide rather than walk.

'Will you not be seated?' he said. 'I can help you. Melussina, you know I can.'

'In return for what?' said my mother bitterly. 'You never give anything freely. There is always a price.'

Sezuan hesitated. 'Sit down,' he said coaxingly. 'When did you last eat? You've probably had nothing all day. I promise you, this dinner is yours to enjoy, free of any . . . cost.'

The light gleamed in the short red silk jacket he was wearing, and in his serpent earring. Mama was staring at him, but although he didn't meet her gaze, he didn't seem afraid of her. Not at all afraid.

'Come. Sit,' he repeated, making a gesture towards the table and the fish on the platters.

Any hunger I might have felt had vanished at the sight of him. And I could hardly believe my own eyes when my mother slowly nodded.

'Very well,' she said. 'Let us at least eat together. And talk about what we might do for each other.'

She smoothed the green skirts of her borrowed dress and stood waiting while he picked up the fallen chair and held it for her.

'Wine?' he said.

'Yes, please.'

He pulled the crystal stopper and poured golden wine into one of the three glasses that waited by Mama's plate. He stood behind her when he poured, like a waiter does. I couldn't help notice how beautiful his hands were, long and slender, with deft straight fingers. The hands of a flautist.

'Dina?' He held out the carafe.

'A little,' said Mama. 'But you will drink water with that, Dina.'

I dutifully watered my wine. My hands were shaking a little. I didn't understand why we were sitting here pretending to be the best of friends. Was he suddenly all right now? Was it just a silly mistake that we had fled hell for leather to get away from this man?

Mama began to eat her fish, just as if everything was perfectly normal.

I can help you, he had said. Was that why we were still

here? Because Mama hoped to buy his help somehow? But what did we own that might interest him, he who had money to stay and eat at the most expensive inn in town?

'I was at the courthouse when Davin and the young castellan's son were sentenced,' said Sezuan, taking a delicate bite of fish. 'It was a most speedy trial. The fastest I have ever seen.'

'Castellan's son?' said Mama, raising an eyebrow.

'Come now. Did you think I wouldn't guess? Yes, I know who "Cousin Nico" really is.' He smiled – not maliciously at all, more as if we shared a delicious secret.

You can't trust him, I told myself. Remember who he is. But it was hard to do when he sat there, smiling, meeting my eyes without fear. Drakan can meet my gaze too, I told myself sourly. But Sezuan did not look in the least bit like Drakan. He looked like me. Same black hair, same green eyes. Just like mine.

Mama put down her fork.

'All right. You know who Nico is. Is there a price for that secret too?' she said, her voice hard like a bargain-driving peddler's.

'Why do you always assume that I mean to hurt you?' asked Sezuan.

'The benefits of harsh experience.'

'Melussina. I have never forced you. I have never harmed you. I never wanted anything except . . .' he hesitated, as if afraid of what she might do. 'I only wanted to love you,' he finally said.

I couldn't even begin to guess what was going on

inside my mother's head. She sat stone still, not moving a muscle.

'And your mother?' she said. 'Your family? Did they also want to *love me*?'

He lowered his eyes and could not look at her.

'My mother is dead,' he said, rolling the stem of his wineglass between his fingers, so that the wine was forced into a very small maelstrom inside the glass. 'My aunt is head of the family now. I know . . . I know that my family has done things you find it difficult to forgive. Things few people would be able to understand. But I am here with you, now. Not with them. Doesn't that tell you anything?'

Horrified, I saw that tears were streaming down my mother's face.

'You are so clever,' she said, and in her voice there were no tears, only anger, anger like a rockslide that buried everything else. 'You are all so clever. You can turn night into day, evil into good. You never wanted to love me. Your mother sent you to me the way they send a stud to a mare. Because she believed the offspring would be interesting. Can you look me in the eyes and deny *that*?'

The circling motion of the glass stopped. He sat very still for a moment, the light gleaming in the serpentine curves of his earring.

'No,' he finally whispered. 'I cannot deny that. A child that might have both the Shamer's power and the serpent gift . . . it was too great a temptation. But . . . I can deny the accusation that I never loved you.'

'Don't lie to me. Not again, Sezuan!'

'I'm not lying.' And he raised his head and looked her in the eyes for a brief, painful moment before dropping his glance once more.

That shook her.

'Dina,' she said in a very odd voice. 'Go. Go to the inn and . . . get us some more wine.'

I stayed where I was.

'We can call the waiter,' I said. I was not about to leave her alone with him, no matter what she said. Not the way she looked right now, with tears still on her cheeks and hands she couldn't keep still.

Mama looked straight at me.

'*Go*,' she said.

I was on my feet without meaning to be. It is no easy thing to gainsay a mother who has the Shamer's gift. Sometimes it is downright impossible. I took the carafe and left the table. But as soon as I had moved far enough into the crowding shadows of the orchard that she wouldn't be able to see me, I stopped.

Mama waited until she thought I was out of hearing. Then she wiped the tears from her face with an angry motion and drank the last of the wine in her glass.

'Well, then,' she said in a harsh voice I hadn't ever heard her use before. 'Let's discuss the price.'

'Melussina . . .'

'No,' she said. 'No velvet words. No waking dreams. No lies. What are you offering when you say you can help us?'

'The money you need. The help that can bring your son and young Nicodemus Ravens out of the Sagisburg.'

'You are certain you can do that?'

203

He shrugged. 'Nothing is certain in this world. But the serpent gift is a great help, isn't it? Who can pass the guards unseen? Who can make the turnkey dream sweet dreams while his keys go for a walk? A Shamer cannot do such things, Melussina. But a Blackmaster can.'

My mother slowly nodded. This was why, I thought. This was why she hadn't stormed out of the glasshouse the moment she had heard Sezuan's voice. We *needed* the help he could give us. And to save Davin she must almost be willing to do a deal with the devil himself.

'And the price?' she said.

'Are you so sure there is one?'

'Yes. And I will not go one step further until I know what it is you want.'

'What were you thinking of offering?'

'Don't play with me.'

'I'm not. Make me an offer, if you are so sure that my aid is a thing that may be bought and sold.'

My mother rose. She smoothed the pale green linen skirt with a nervous movement that made it look as if she were wiping her palms.

'Dina doesn't have the serpent gift,' she said.

'How do you know?' he asked. 'You have hardly tried to teach her. Not if I know you.'

'Believe me. She doesn't have it.' My mother's voice was as tense and hard as a drawn bow. 'But . . . I am still young enough to bear another child. A child that your family may have.'

I nearly dropped the carafe. She . . . she . . . she couldn't do that! In my mind's ear I heard the Scriptor warn us against 'acts of indecency and other lewdness'.

What I had just heard my mother suggest had to be the most indecent thing I'd ever heard of. Far worse than the more ordinary kind when a woman offered her body for money. Mama stood there offering to sell an unborn child!

It seemed she had succeded in taking even Sezuan aback. For a moment, he looked . . . perhaps not crestfallen, but certainly bemused. Then he too got to his feet and walked to stand directly in front of her. He put a hand on either side of her face, almost as he had done with me the day he met me in the market crowd. And I knew that my mother had closed her eyes. She could have sent him staggering back with one look, she could have made good and sure that he wouldn't dare touch her. She didn't.

I raised the carafe. If I threw it as hard as I could, right through the large windowpanes of the glasshouse . . . I could almost see it, the glass breaking and splintering, cascading like icicles down on the lemon trees, the white tablecloth, Sezuan and Mama . . .

He kissed her. And then he laughed, softly and gently.

'Oh, Melussina,' he said in an affectionate tone. 'You are the worst liar in the world.'

She stepped backwards, out of his grasp.

'What do you mean?'

'Let us say for a moment that a child did come of this. Do you seriously mean to tell me that you would give it up?'

Mama hesitated. 'Wasn't that what I just said?'

But even I could hear that she didn't mean it. I lowered the carafe again.

He shook his head. 'Thank you for your most generous offer,' he said, 'but I have very keen and unfond memories of last time. I would not have thought a pregnant woman with a small child would have been able to cover that many miles in such a short time. Determination must have lent you wings.'

She took another step away from him. Suddenly she looked afraid, far more scared than angry.

'What do you want, then?' she asked.

'Time.'

'Time?'

He nodded. 'Time with Dina. Time to get to know her.'

'Time to see whether she has the serpent gift, you mean.'

'No,' he said. 'Not just that.' He turned his back on her, walked back to the table and took a swallow of wine from his glass. 'She is the only one,' he said finally. 'The only child I have.'

'Oh, really,' said Mama scornfully. 'Would you have me believe I was the one and only? Your mother must have really lost her grip. I would have thought she would waste no time in procuring you another few . . . brood mares.'

He rubbed his forehead absently and suddenly looked smaller and more tired. More ordinary.

'There have been others,' he said in a peculiarly flat voice. 'But it would seem I am not very . . . fertile.'

'How disappointing. For your mother.'

'Could you possibly *not* mention her in every other

sentence? She is dead. Let her rest in peace. Listen, Melussina. Is it so unnatural? That a father wants to know his daughter?'

Mama slowly shook her head. 'No,' she said. 'You are not getting Dina.' She sounded as unyielding as a mountain.

'Do you mean to say that you will deny me a few days of my daughter's company – even though your refusal may cost your son his life?'

'We will manage on our own,' said Mama harshly. 'We always have.'

Suddenly, something touched my arm.

'Pardon me, but may I serve—'

Startled, I spun round. The carafe slipped through my fingers, and though I made a frantic catch at it, I knew it was too late.

Crash. It sounded like a thunderclap.

The girl in the white apron held a hand to her mouth in consternation. Mama and Sezuan both turned to look directly at us. And I knew they knew I had heard the whole thing.

'May I serve the main course?' asked the girl.

'No,' said Mama. 'We are through here. Come on, Dina.'

On the way back to the Foundation, she spoke not a single word to me. And I didn't dare say anything to her. Only when we were nearly at the gates did I venture to open my mouth.

'Mama?'

'Yes.'

'Couldn't we . . . I mean, if all he wants is a few days? And if he really can save Davin and Nico?'

She stopped in her tracks.

'Do you know what he wants to do to you?'

I shook my head mutely. 'Get to know me, he said.'

'Dina. *Never trust him*. He hopes that you have his gift. The serpent gift. So that you may become a Blackmaster just like him.'

'You said I didn't have it.'

'And I don't think you have. But . . . he is your father. It *is* possible. But it isn't . . . I won't . . . If he can, he will awaken it within you. And then . . . Dina, I wouldn't be able to bear it if you . . . became like him.'

Serpent kin. Serpent spawn. I wasn't so sure I'd be able to bear it myself.

TWENTY-THREE

Trading with the Devil

Mama was a long time falling asleep that night. I know that because I lay awake myself, waiting. She kept tossing and turning, making the bunk creak at each turn. But finally all the little noises stopped, leaving only the sound of her breathing, and when I poked my head out of my bunk to look into hers, she had the blanket drawn up to her chin and was fast asleep.

Right now it would have been useful to be able to move as silently as Sezuan – to glide along like a snake, rather than to have to climb out of the bunk warily and slowly, inch by inch, to set my feet as quietly as I could on the creaking floorboards.

It was dark inside the crowded room, of course, but the shutters were open to give us at least a chance at some fresh air. In the sky outside hung a summer moon, huge and yellow, and the moonlight fell through the window on an arm, a foot, a blanket fold, and whatever else poked out from the bunks. It wasn't necessary to get dressed. Foundation comforts didn't run to night robes, so you slept in the grey clothes or in nothing at all. All I had to do was lace up my bodice and sneak towards the door.

'Dina?'

I turned slowly. Mama's voice was hoarse and sodden with sleep, and she was only half awake.

'I have to pee,' I whispered.

She didn't say anything. I think she went back to sleep. I opened the door and tiptoed out on to the balcony outside. There was no guard at the gates to the Foundation; two watchmen walked their rounds occasionally, but that was probably mostly to prevent people from breaking into the kitchen stores. It wasn't hard to hide behind the Inscriptorium until they had gone past, and then slip through the gates and into the sleeping city.

The streets were deserted. Pale yellow moonlight fell on cobbles that were dark and shiny with the dampness of the night. Somehow, it felt too obvious to walk boldly in the middle of the street, so I kept to the side, in the shadows cast by the houses.

It wasn't that I wanted to be here. Tension made my chest and belly ache, and it was as if I could barely breathe properly. It felt a little the way I had felt before climbing on to one of the highest branches by the swimming hole in Birches, knowing that I didn't really have the nerve to jump. And yet I had jumped. Because Davin had been there. 'You can do it,' he had shouted. 'Come on, Dina.' And so for a moment I had felt as if I was flying, wind in my hair, butterflies in my belly, all the way down. And he had been so proud of me afterwards and had boasted to the Miller's second-eldest son.

But the leap I was about to make now wouldn't make anybody proud. Certainly not Mama. She would be beside herself if she knew where I was going.

The Golden Swan lay on the other side of town, as far away from the Foundation as it was possible to get and still be within the city walls. Walking back this afternoon with Mama I had carefully noted the way, so finding the inn was no problem. But when I reached it, it was as dark and shuttered as everything else in town. A solid-looking gate blocked my way into the yard, and for a while I just stood there, looking at it, and feeling lost. Somehow I think I had been expecting Sezuan to be there, waiting in the open door. But he wasn't, of course.

I knocked tentatively on the gate. There was no answer, not even when I banged it a little harder.

'Hello?' I called cautiously. 'May I come in?'

Silent as the grave, I thought. Everybody must be asleep in there, behind the white shutters. I walked around to the back, looking for another way in. And I found it. Not quite the convenient back door I had imagined, but still . . . A big chestnut tree grew by the orchard wall. And even though I didn't climb like a squirrel the way Davin did, I thought I might be able to reach that big branch up there, the one that stretched across the top of the wall.

It was an old tree, full of cracks and furrows and knobs where branches had once snapped off. I slipped once and got myself a few scratches and a moss-coloured scrape along one arm, but I did finally succeed in hooking my leg over the branch I wanted, so that I could pull myself up and sit astride it. Cautiously, I wormed my way along it, until I could see the orchard and the glasshouse, directly beneath me. There were no candelabra now, but the table was still there, with its white tablecloth gleaming softly in the darkness.

It was as if I was hearing Mama's furious accusation against Sezuan once more. *Your mother sent you to me the way they send a stud to a mare. Because she thought the offspring would be interesting.* The offspring, that was me. Was that how Sezuan thought of me?

The branch shook beneath me. I held on tightly, thinking at first it might be a gust of wind. But then it happened again. And this time, I was certain there had been no sudden gust.

Somebody else was climbing the tree.

I twisted my neck, trying to see. But though the branch was trembling like a living creature, I could see no movement, only leaves and darkness and . . . wait. Wasn't there a glint of something pale, eyes, teeth, or maybe . . . maybe a weapon? There really *was* someone.

I held still. Still as a frightened mouse. I knew it was stupid, I knew it would be better to make a break for it, slip down on to the wall beneath me and from there to the ground . . . but my arms and legs were frozen like ice. And he might not have seen me, he might simply have taken it into his head to climb this tree, not knowing that I—

Thunk! Something hit me hard between the shoulder blades, and I nearly lost my grip on the branch. I looked about wildly. Where—

Thunk. Once more, high on the arm, with force

enough to numb. This time, I did lose my balance, swinging round to catch desperately at the branch with the arm that was still working, until I hung beneath it like some three-legged sloth. And now I could see him, above me, on a branch a little higher up. It was only the briefest of glimpses: black hair, white face, red shirt. Then he swung his powerful stick once more, hitting my hand. My fingers opened nervelessly. For a second I hung on by my legs only, and then I fell, plummeting like a stone, through the air, through the glass roof and on to the table, which broke beneath me. Around me, broken glass tinkled against the tiles, a strange, crisp sound, like icicles hitting the pavement. I lay still. I couldn't see, couldn't move, couldn't breathe. For the first few moments, it didn't even hurt.

The glass shards crunched and tinkled. He was coming towards me, I could feel it, even though I couldn't feel much else. Something touched my ankle – the tip of boot, I thought. And then things began to hurt, not just my leg or any particular place, just everywhere. I moaned a little.

'My dreams,' hissed a voice. '*Mine*. Won't let you take them!'

I had no idea what he meant, but there was so much hatred and fury in the voice that panic pounded through me at the sound. Away. I had to get away. He wanted to hurt me, I could hear it. I tried to sit up, but my arms wouldn't work.

Cold bony fingers touched my neck.

Then there were other noises: footsteps and voices. I could see light, light flickering among the apple trees.

'Who goes there!' called a commanding voice.

He hissed like a cat that didn't want to let go of its mouse. His fingers dug into my neck for a moment, then he let go, and I could hear his tinkling steps for a moment before he disappeared into the darkness.

I should disappear as well, I thought dizzily. They wouldn't be pleased when they saw what I had done to their glasshouse. I made it to my knees, but that was as far as I got before a tall, fat-bellied man in a nightshirt and bare legs showed up in the glasshouse door, a frying pan in one hand and a candlestick in the other.

Open-mouthed, he stared at the devastation.

'Holy Saint Magda!' he exclaimed.

Another man, thinner and younger, appeared beside him.

'What happened?'

'The thieving little brat has smashed the orangery,' said the fat one, picking his way across the broken glass. He dropped the frying pan, seized my arm and hauled me to my feet. 'Come here, you little vandal, and I'll give you what's owing!'

'I didn't mean—'

But he wasn't listening. He slapped my face so hard it made me even dizzier.

'She's bleeding,' said the younger one. 'She must have cut herself on the glass.'

'No more than she deserves, the little thief!'

It was only now that I realized that blood was streaming down my arm. Where was the damage? Somewhere at the back, close to my shoulder blade.

'I'm no thief,' I said.

'No?' said the fat one. 'Then I beg her pardon. No doubt the Medamina has her reasons for climbing people's walls in the middle of the night and smashing up their orangeries.'

'But I—'

'Save your excuses for the Courtmaster, girl. Adrian, lock her in the root cellar. Tomorrow, the city guards can take her.'

'No! I need to—'

'You need to go along with Adrian, that's what you need. And be grateful I haven't given you the hiding you deserve!' He cast a black look at the ruins of his beautiful orangery, and an even blacker one at me.

Adrian took my arm, the one that wasn't bleeding.

'Come along,' he said. 'It's better not to make any trouble.' His hold on me was a lot gentler than the fat man's, and his warning sounded more like well-meant advice, rather than threat.

That was when I heard the flute. Very faintly, a soft and soothing melody. Both men stopped in their tracks, like dogs hearing the distant whistle of their lord and master. Then the melody stopped, and Sezuan came out of the darkness with soundless, gliding steps. He was wearing a long blue robe of some kind.

Blue robe.

I had seen only a brief glimpse of the man who had attacked me, but I had thought . . .

I pressed my free hand against my temple. It had looked like Sezuan. But now that I saw him . . . no. It hadn't been Sezuan who had hit me with the stick. But . . . who else, then?

'Is there anything I can do to help?' he asked, in a quiet, courteous voice.

Adrian had let go of my arm. The fat grey-bearded man stood there holding the candlestick in front of him almost like a shield, but he suddenly sounded oddly subservient.

'Did we disturb Mesire's sleep?' he said. 'I am very sorry. It's only a thief who—'

Sezuan laughed his soft laugh. 'That is no thief,' he said. 'That is my daughter.'

'Ohhh . . .' The greybeard looked as if the thief he had caught had suddenly turned out to be a princess in disguise. 'I see. But then . . . we really do apologize . . .' He sputtered to a stop.

'Naturally, I shall pay for the damages to your orangery,' said Sezuan.

'Naturally,' murmured the greybeard. 'Thank you kindly, Mesire. Is there anything else I . . . may do for Mesire and . . . and . . . his lady daughter?'

'Bring me some hot water.'

'At once. Here, or . . .'

'In my room.'

'Of course. Yes. Adrian, take the candle and accompany Mesire and Medamina to the room.'

'Give me the candlestick,' said Sezuan. 'We'll find our own way.'

Adrian and the fat man withdrew, each with a formal bow. Sezuan watched me for a moment in the candlelight glow.

'I thought you might come,' he finally said. 'But couldn't you have used the front door?'

The bed did not look as if it had been slept in, so perhaps he really had been waiting for me. On the table was an open book, and the oil lamp was still lit.

'Sit,' said Sezuan and pointed to one of the three chairs by the table.

I sat. I still felt dizzy and battered by my fall, and the shoulder was very painful by now. I didn't lean against the backrest; it would have hurt too much.

Sezuan did not sit down. He remained standing a little distance from the table, looking at me.

'You've come because of your brother,' he said.

I nodded.

'You heard everything your mother and I said to one another, didn't you?'

'Yes.' My voice was hoarse and croaky, the way it often was when I grew nervous.

'But your mother does not know that you are here.'

'No,' I whispered. I didn't even dare think about what she would do when she found out.

He smiled slowly. It was not a nice smile. There was a hard and glittering edge of triumph to it, as if he had won, and Mama had lost.

'Poor Melussina,' he said. But it didn't sound as if he was really sorry for her, and his tone made me angry. There just wasn't a lot I could do with my anger, not if I wanted him to help Davin and Nico.

There was a knocking at the door. Sezuan opened it, and Adrian entered with a pitcher of hot water and some linen strips.

'For Medamina's injury,' he explained, bowed to me and to Sezuan, and left.

'Wash yourself,' said Sezuan. 'Both the wound and the rest. I cannot abide filth, it is so unsavoury.'

There was no special weight to the way he said it. I couldn't even figure out whether it was meant to be insulting. But he made me feel small and dirty and vaguely disgusting, and I was loath to loosen my bodice and take off my blouse while he was watching.

'Well?' he said, after a while. 'Will you get on with it?'

'Not with you watching,' I said, embarrassed but also stubborn. I meant it.

He raised one eyebrow. 'I beg your pardon.'

He took the book from the table, deliberately turned his back, and presumably began to read.

I took off my bodice and eased the blouse off the injured shoulder. The grey material was dark with blood and had a tear in it as long as my hand. I twisted my neck, but the wound was too far down for me to see it.

The blouse wasn't worth much now. I took it off, soaked it in the hot water and used it for a wash cloth. It wasn't easy to cleanse a wound I couldn't see. It was harder still to manage some kind of a bandage out of the linen strips that Adrian had brought. I couldn't help thinking that it should have been Mama doing this, she was always the one who took care of us when we were hurt or ill. It would be a long time now before I saw her again, and if Sezuan had his way . . . if I really did have the serpent gift and he managed to awaken it in me . . . would my mother still want me?

I sniffed back a couple of tears and tied the last knot

on my clumsy bandage. Then I put the bodice back on, but without the blouse I still felt somewhat bare.

'May I turn around now?' asked Sezuan.

'Yes.'

He put down the book and studied me for a while. I couldn't tell at all what he was thinking.

'Are you afraid?' he suddenly asked. 'Are you afraid of me?'

The answer to that question was yes, of course. But I didn't want to tell him that. I didn't want him to think that he could make me jump just by saying boo.

'Will you help Davin?' I asked instead.

'Perhaps,' he said. 'And if I'm willing . . . what then?'

'Then . . .' I had to swallow and start again. 'Then I will do what you want me to do.'

For a moment, something showed in his face, some sort of deep emotion, but I couldn't tell which.

'Do you even know what that is?' he asked.

'You want to see if I have . . . the serpent gift.'

Again, he watched me for a long time, but this time his face was as expressionless as a reptile's. Then he nodded. 'Yes. I would like to know that.'

I don't, I thought. But I couldn't see any other way out of this for us.

'And if I let you do that,' I said as firmly as I could manage, 'then you will pay the Foundation to let us go and you will help free Nico and Davin from the Sagisburg. Won't you?' I looked him straight in the eye and wished like anything that I had my Shamer's gift back, just for a moment, so that I could be sure he wasn't planning to cheat me. Nothing happened. Now, when I needed to be my mother's daughter more than ever, my gift failed me completely. It was enough to make you weep.

'If I pay off the Foundation, your mother will be at our heels in a moment,' he said. 'Even if we do not, she will try to find us and stop us . . . but at least it will be more difficult.'

I bit my lip. 'You told Mama you would pay.'

'Yes. And if she were here, doing her own bargaining . . . it would be different.'

Yes, I thought, because she would be able to tell if you were lying.

I got to my feet. 'If you don't do it, I won't come with you.'

'Oh, really?' he said without batting an eyelid. 'All of a sudden, you do not care about your brother after all?'

But I did. That was the hell of it. When you know you have to buy no matter how outrageous the price, you drive a lousy bargain. If only. If only I could make that man ashamed of himself, even for a moment. But my gift stubbornly refused to come to my aid.

'You may have the money after we get back,' he said.

I shook my head. 'What if we don't?' A lot could happen. And I had talked to people who had been at the Foundation for seven years, ever since it began. Seven years — it didn't bear thinking about. 'I want to free Davin and Nico, yes. But what good will that do if Mama and Melli and Rose are still trapped?'

'The Foundation is hardly as cruel a prison as the Sagisburg,' he said.

I didn't answer. I just stared at him with the best imitation of a Shamer's look that I could manage.

'Very well,' he said. 'I will take care of the Foundation.'

I sank back on to the chair as if I suddenly had no legs. Had it worked? Had I succeeded in giving him just the tiniest pang of conscience? Perhaps there really was a bit of the Shamer's gift left, even though I couldn't quite feel it myself.

He took pen and paper from a small chest by the bed and started writing. Then he pulled at a bell-rope by the bedpost, and shortly afterwards Adrian appeared at the door.

'Mesire wishes?'

'Do you know how to read?' asked Sezuan.

'Yes, Mesire.'

'Good. Follow the instructions I've written here. Here are the monies for the Foundation, and this coin is for your trouble.' He gave Adrian a grey leather pouch and a silver penny. Adrian bowed.

'Thank you, Mesire. Thank you very much. Mesire may be sure that everything will be as he wishes.'

He turned to go, but I stopped him.

'Wait. I want to see the paper.'

Adrian looked questioningly at Sezuan, who gave a small nod. Adrian held out the paper. It said that the sum enclosed, twenty-five silver marks in all, should be used to ensure the release of Melussina Tonerre, her daughter Melli and her foster-daughter Rose. And then it said: 'This release shall take effect ten days from this day, the eighth day of the Harvest Moon.'

Angrily, I turned to Sezuan.

'No. It has to be now. Tomorrow!'

He shook his head. 'No. These are the best terms you will get. Take it or leave it.'

I stared at the paper and wanted to rip it apart. Ten days. Ten days would be an eternity to Mama, Melli and Rose.

'Well?' he said. 'Do you want a deal with me or no?'

Tears burnt hotly at the corner of my eyes, but I had no choice. I returned the paper to Adrian.

'Is that a yes?' asked Sezuan.

I nodded. 'Yes,' I whispered, though the word tasted bitter in my mouth.

'Good,' he said, waving Adrian off. He sat down on his bed and stretched like a pleased cat. 'Now it is *her* turn to feel what it is like to sit there looking at a locked gate for ten days.'

Oh, I thought. This is his vengeance for Skayark.

He kicked off his boots and lay back in the pillows. 'Put out the light before you sleep,' he said and closed his eyes. And very shortly afterwards it seemed that he had fallen asleep himself.

I stood there in the middle of the floor in nothing but my skirt and bodice. He did not seem particularly worried that I might run away. He hadn't even locked the door. But then, where would I go? I had made a bargain with the devil, and now he owned me.

222

TWENTY-FOUR

The Music of the Flute

When we left Sagisloc, it was on foot.

'Why aren't we sailing?' I asked.

Sezuan shook his head. 'There are monsters in the lake,' he said, and I wasn't quite sure whether I was meant to believe him or not.

'It would be faster,' I said stubbornly.

He stopped and looked at me with an irritation he didn't bother to hide. 'Are you going to argue with me all the way to the Sagisburg? It will be a very long trip, then, Medamina.'

It would be a long trip anyway, I thought. He hadn't even hired horses for us. Instead, he had bought a small grey donkey that carried all our belongings, and a new blouse and skirt for me so that I no longer looked like a greyling. Couldn't he at least have bought a mule, so we could ride? He didn't seem to be short of money.

He was doing it on purpose, I decided. He *wanted* this trip to be a long one, so that he had more time to 'get to know me', as he called it. But he would not succeed in making a Blackmaster of me. Not even if it took us the rest of the year to get to the Sagisburg.

I kicked at a rock that went flying down the path. The donkey twitched its ears and snorted. Sezuan threw me an irritated glance, but didn't say anything.

The road followed the bank of the lake for the first few miles. I could see the grey-clad workers harvesting the reeds, just like Davin and Nico had done the first few days. If there really were monsters in the lake, the workers would have been eaten, I thought. I might get used to the fact that half of everything Sezuan said to me was a lie. The trouble lay in deciding which half to believe.

We walked in silence most of the morning. I had a headache, and my shoulder ached, and I kept thinking of Mama, and of Davin and Nico. The sun was burning, and the road dust made my eyes water, and when there was finally a breeze from the lake, it was full of little pesky creatures that bit or stung or swarmed so closely that they kept getting into your nostrils when you breathed. Every once in a while carts rumbled by, drawn by oxen or horses. We didn't meet anyone else who was stupid enough to travel through the noontime heat on foot.

A little past midday we came to a small town, not much more than a village, but big enough to have a sizeable inn. And I was so heavy-headed and dry-mouthed by then that I was glad of the rest, even though it slowed us down even more.

I couldn't see how Sezuan did it. On the road, people had passed us without a second glance. But as we trudged into the dusty little square in front of the inn, he grew taller and more important-looking with every step. When he called for the stable boy in a firm voice, the lad came running to take the donkey as though it were a four-horse carriage with plumes and silver buckles and a coat of arms enamelled on the door. When the people at The Golden Swan had treated Sezuan as though he were a prince royal, I thought it was because they knew he was rich even though he didn't always look it. But how could a stranger like the stable groom know that before Sezuan had even loosened his purse-strings? People who came wandering in with a donkey were not usually the ones who crossed your palm with silver at every opportunity.

It continued as we entered the dining room. Respectfully, our host apologized for the fact that his 'establishment' could only offer us a single course, a humble lamb stew. But if Mesire's time permitted, he would be pleased to slaughter a few pigeons or a capon?

'No, thank you,' said Sezuan. 'Lamb will be perfectly adequate. And if we may have a pitcher of wine and a pitcher of water?'

The stew arrived, and I ate some of it even though my headache didn't leave room for much in the way of appetite. I drank a lot of water, which helped. Or water with a bit of wine in it, because Sezuan insisted.

'There is no knowing about the water in a place like this,' he said. 'And there's nothing more unsavoury than a vomiting child.'

Would a vomiting adult be more wholesome? I didn't think so, but I obediently drank what he gave me, even though the wine added a sour-sweet, yeasty flavour to the water.

'Is the meal to your liking?' asked our host tentatively. He looked as if he wished he had killed a capon for us.

'Delicious,' said Sezuan. 'My good man, I do believe this is the best lamb stew I have had in my life. Mesire may be proud of his inn and his kitchen.'

A delighted flush spread across our host's face, from the tip of his thinly bearded chin to the top of his balding crown.

'Mesire is too kind,' he said, bowing deeply. 'Perhaps we may offer a small almond cake for dessert? On the house, of course.'

I had to hand it to him – Sezuan had a way with people. But the strangest thing of all happened when we left. Sezuan handed the host a single coin. I was fairly certain it was copper, and a copper penny was certainly not what one usually paid for two helpings of lamb stew, water, wine, a good feed for the donkey, and so on. But the man acted as if he had been given a gold mark. He beamed from ear to ear, bowing and scraping, and wished 'his lordship' a pleasant journey. The groom got nothing at all except a few words of praise, but he too bowed and smiled and wished us well.

When we had gone a little way, I gathered my courage.

'That copper penny?'

'What about it?' said Sezuan.

'The innkeeper . . . he thought it was gold, didn't he?'

'He may have.'

'But . . . but that means you cheated him!'

'How so? Did he seem unhappy?'

'No, but . . .' But he had still been cheated. 'What happens when he finds out?'

'He won't. He will remember that his inn had a visit from a fine gentlemen who praised his food and paid him royally. He will remember it with happiness and pride, and he will boast about it to his neighbours. That is a sort of payment too.'

'But . . . that won't feed his family.'

'Not feed their bellies, perhaps. But joy has a value too, doesn't it? That innkeeper's heart has been well fed. And because of the sum I had to put up to release your precious mother from the Foundation, we are not exactly wealthy, I'll have you know.'

Was that why he hadn't hired a boat? And why we didn't have horses? He wasn't as rich as I'd thought, apparently. Or else he was lying to me, and was as rich as Prince Arthos himself. If only I knew what to believe.

'You cheated him,' I said stubbornly. Mama would definitely think he should be ashamed of himself. But he didn't seem to be. For a moment, he merely looked thoughtful.

'I didn't let him kill the capon,' he said finally.

We spent the night on a farm, a large and busy one which had a whole crowd of greylings right then to help with harvesting the hay. The farmwife, a thin dry woman who looked at first as if she never even smiled, was soon blushing and giggling at Sezuan as if she was no older than me. It was 'Mesire' this and 'Mesire' that and '. . . if it pleases the gentleman'. And all that for the price of another copper coin. After we had eaten, the greylings outside at a rough plank table and the proper farmhands inside with us, Sezuan brought out the flute and began to play.

I tried not to listen. Covertly, I took a bit of bread and rolled it between my fingers and put one bread plug in each ear, but it didn't do much good. The notes moved against me like a cat who wants to be stroked, and they brought sights and sounds with them, of things that weren't there. A starlit night, a shower of roses, a horse's nose. Everything soft and beautiful and lovely. The scent of clover. Mama's lips against my cheek as she kissed me goodnight.

I was crying. Tears were running down my cheeks like raindrops down a windowpane, and I wasn't the only one. While dusk was falling softly around us, no lamps were lit, because everyone sat still and unmoving, even the greylings outside. But I was the one Sezuan was watching as he played, I was the one his eyes rested on. And I knew it was for me he played.

I got up.

It wasn't easy: the music wanted me to stay. But perhaps my sticky little bread lumps did some good after all. Because while all the others were still sitting as frozen as if they never meant to move again, I staggered through the kitchen door, past the listening greylings, and on to the rainwater barrel by the gable. I took a deep breath and stuck my head in the barrel, never caring that leaves and drowned insects floated on the surface.

So unfair. That such music should come from such a man.

I stood there with water soaking my shirt, and probably with my hair full of dead mosquitos, and all I wanted was for all of us to be home, Nico and Davin, and Mama and Melli and Rose, home at Yew Tree Cottage when we had never even heard of Sezuan and his flute.

Silence fell inside the house. The notes stopped coming, and it was quite a while after that before anyone dared break the spell by talking. Only very slowly did ordinary chatter start up again.

Sezuan came outside.

'Dina?' he called softly, peering into the darkness.

I didn't answer. But he came unerringly towards me, as if he had some kind of invisible leash on me.

'Didn't you like the music?' he asked.

'No,' I lied. 'I suppose I'm not very musical.'

I had actually hoped that he would be hurt, and perhaps angry. He wasn't. On the contrary. He smiled so widely that his teeth glittered in the darkness. As if I had finally done something right. As if I had done something he had been waiting for for a long time. Did he know I was lying?

'Come inside, my daughter,' he said. 'I won't play again tonight.'

'Don't call me that!'

'What?'

'Daughter.'

'Why do you dislike it? I thought you and your mother were all set on telling the truth.'

I didn't know what to say.

He smiled again, in his slow, lazy way. 'Don't stay out too long, my daughter,' he said, and went back inside himself.

I stood there in the gathering dusk and didn't know whether to go or stay. If I went in now, it would seem as if I came out of obedience to Sezuan. But being out here all night on my own, tired, road-weary and down-hearted, wasn't very appealing either.

I ended up climbing the fence of the paddock where they had put our donkey. It wasn't the same as cuddling up against Silky's warm, smooth neck, but it was better than nothing, and the donkey good-naturedly allowed it and even seemed to think being cuddled was quite nice for a change.

Suddenly its long, furry ears came up.

'What is it?' I asked. 'Can you hear something?'

I don't know why I always talk to the animals when they can't talk back, but I do. And in a way I suppose the donkey did answer me. It snorted, reared back from me and took off at a gallop.

I stared into the summer dark, which by now had become quite dense and starless. Clouds hid the moon and crowded heavily above the lake and the hills.

'Hello?' My voice sounded very wobbly and uncertain. Was there a rustling over there by the barn? A . . . a presence? 'Anybody out there?'

There was no answer. Perhaps it was just a cat. Or a greyling. But a greyling would have answered me, wouldn't he? I didn't know. And I was far from brave enough to walk boldly up to the barn to look. I just climbed back across the fence and hurried back to the house, where there would be lights and people. Even if one of the people was Sezuan.

Before we walked on the next morning, the farmwife gave us a big bundle full of bread and ham and other good things. That was the best we had for quite a while, because even though people kept on receiving Sezuan as though a royal entourage had arrived, farms became fewer and further apart, and the people who lived on them had less to share. The soil was poor and sparse here at the foot of the Sagis Range. The fields were small terraces surrounded by stone walls to retain what farming soil there was, and it took a lot of stone-dragging and water-fetching and careful nurturing to make a crop grow here. Grazing animals were few as well, so the meals were mostly made with beans and onions and a special kind of small, mealy potato they grew here. Luxury was a rabbit stew.

It felt as if we were walking and walking without ever really getting anywhere. The road was steep and rocky and wound uphill in serpentine curves so that you could walk for miles and still look down to see the same tree you passed seven loops ago. It was enough to make anyone lose heart.

We had paused in the midday heat to eat and catch our breath and let the donkey graze a little. The grass was dry and yellow and full of grasshoppers, but that means nothing to a donkey worth the name. It was so hot that the air flickered across the rocks, and the lake by now was mostly a memory and every once in a while a distant glitter to our right.

Sezuan brought out the flute. He always had it with him, I had realized, usually in a sort of sheath on his belt, the way another man might have worn a sword. In the two days that had passed since that night at the farm, he had not touched it. Now he held it out to me.

'Do you want to look at it?'

I stared at it as though he was trying to give me a venomous snake.

'No, thank you.'

He smiled. 'The flute hasn't hurt anybody. You do not need to be scared of it. Here, go on. Try.'

I shook my head.

He looked at it for a while as if considering whether to force me to take it. Then he put it on the ground between us.

'I'll fetch us some more water,' he said, and disappeared down the mountain path with our water skin at his back.

I eyed the flute. It had been painted in red and black spirals, like the egg he had once given me. It reminded me a bit of the markings on a salamander. And it was like no other flute I had ever seen. It was much longer, and not even the most nimble-fingered flautist would have been able to reach the holes furthest from the mouthpiece if it hadn't been for a clever system of vents and stoppers that looked like . . . looked like it was made from bone. I shivered a little even in the heat. What – or who – had provided the bone for this?

It was beautiful, in an alien sort of way. And it wasn't really the fault of the flute that it belonged to a man like Sezuan. I reached out and stroked the smooth black finish. I wondered how those vents really worked.

I looked around quickly. No sign of Sezuan.

I raised the flute to my mouth. Tentatively, I blew.

Nothing happened, or nearly nothing. A thin hiss of air with no tune or melody to it, that was all.

I blew a little harder. Then harder still. And finally as hard as I could.

'It's not enough to blow hard. You have to purse your lips. Make it more . . . precise.'

I pursed my lips and tried to make it more precise. At once I could feel that this was how it was done. And from the flute came a single, plaintive note, like a lonely bird on a mountain.

'Put your finger here. It will deepen the tone.'

I put my forefinger where he told me. Then the next finger, and the next. The note deepened and became darker, became a shrieking owl, a cold night breeze blowing through a lonely cave.

It was a wonderful flute. I never wanted to let go of it again.

Sezuan smiled. He was standing right in front of me. Had, indeed, been standing there for quite a while. And suddenly I came to my senses again. I put the flute back on the ground – I would have liked to just fling it away, but I couldn't bear to think that it might break.

'You tricked me.'

'How so?' he said. 'Did I pick up the flute and put it in your hands?'

No. I had done that. Me myself. And I felt sick to my soul, because what if . . . what if that meant that I really did have the serpent gift?

233

'You played beautifully,' he said. 'Not many people can coax a note from the flute in their first attempt.'

It was as if he knew my fear and deliberately fanned it. I got up, so hurriedly that I nearly stumbled, and began walking, almost blind with tears. In front of my feet the grasshoppers sprang into the air and floated for a moment on red wings, like little butterflies, before they landed and became grasshoppers again. I too had been a different kind of being for a brief moment, when I had floated on the notes of the flute. But it wouldn't happen again, I silently promised. I was my mother's daughter, and Sezuan would not succeed in making me his.

'Dina. Wait.'

I didn't want to wait, but I still slowed my pace a little. I needed his help to save Davin and Nico. Once they were free, though, I would oust him from our lives. Whatever the cost!

Suddenly there was a series of sharp cracks and a longer rattle. I looked up just as something hit me on the shoulder and threw me down on to my hands and knees. A shower of stones and dirt tumbled down on me and continued down the mountainside. I coughed and got a mouthful of dust and gravel and coughed again, and several more pebbles rained down on me so that I ended up on my belly with my arms folded around my head, just waiting for it to stop.

'Dina. Are you all right?'

Sezuan pulled me up with one hand and brushed dirt and gravel off me with the other. And wasn't he the one who couldn't abide filth? I thought in some confusion.

Now he would get dirty himself, wouldn't he?

'Are you hurt?' he repeated, and did actually look both frightened and worried.

'No,' I muttered. 'I don't think so. I think the cut on my shoulder is bleeding again, though.' I could feel a wet and sticky sensation by my shoulder blade.

He peered up the mountainside.

'Did you see what happened?' he asked. 'Did you see anybody?'

My attention suddenly sharpened.

'What do you mean, anybody?' I said. 'Did *you* see anybody?'

He shook his head. 'No. Not . . . not that I am sure of.'

I suddenly remembered the man in the chestnut tree, and the noises by the dark barn.

'Is someone following us? Or following you?'

He looked at me without answering.

'If you are unhurt, we should move on,' he said.

But I wasn't about to let it go.

'Who is it?'

'Nobody. The sun and the wind. A mountain goat. Come on.'

I couldn't wring an answer from him.

But after we had walked for a bit, he said, 'Stay close to me. I don't want you to fall too far behind, or get too far ahead. It isn't safe.'

TWENTY-FIVE

Dreams

Being afraid of Sezuan was bad enough. Being frightened also of some mysterious creature following us . . . it was almost more than I could bear. All day I stuck closely in his shadow and kept eyeing the mountainside above us, or throwing nervous glances downhill to see if there was anyone behind us. When a pair of grouse flew up from the shrubbery right under our noses, I leaped like a startled foal. My shoulder was hurting again now, and I had dirt everywhere: in my ears, in my nose, in my hair. Even in my navel.

Maybe your belly can only handle one fear at a time. At any rate, I was almost grateful that Sezuan was there. When he walked beside me, solid and visible and real, he didn't seem anywhere near as frightening as he had been back when he was mostly an invisible threat, a voice in the mists, a distant scary presence that spoke to me through words scratched on tablets or letters hidden inside hollow eggs. I might almost start to think that he cared about me and would look after me if anything happened.

And then my thoughts stopped short. Because wasn't that what he would want me to think? *Never trust him*, Mama had told me, more than once. There might not even be anyone following us. Perhaps the rockslide had happened by itself. Or perhaps Sezuan had made it happen, by throwing a stone, or . . . or loosening a boulder when he went for water, or something. The noises by the barn might have been anything.

But the man in the tree. That hadn't been Sezuan.

Or had it? At first I had thought so, when I caught a glimpse of black hair and a red shirt. and perhaps I had been right first time. There had been time, hadn't there, for him to throw away the red shirt and appear in his blue robe, pretending that the noise had disturbed him? And there was Beastie. And the coppertail. Who other than Sezuan would have known that I would be walking along that path at that precise time? After all, he was the one I had been going to meet.

Thinking this hard could make a person dizzy. I stared at Sezuan's back and wanted to be able to look inside him, into his heart. Black or white?

Perhaps he could feel my eyes. At any rate, he turned around and smiled at me, a bit more tentatively than he usually did.

'Do you want to borrow the flute?' he asked. 'You could practise as we walked?'

'No, thank you,' I said sharply.

'You liked it,' he said in an oddly gentle tone. 'I could see that.'

'I don't want it!'

I was practically shouting at him, and his smile

237

vanished. His face closed up again, almost as if ice had formed on the surface.

'As you please.'

We walked on in a chill kind of silence. The hooves of the donkey beat against the hard ground in a swaying, clip-clop rhythm. It was practically the only sound we could hear.

Then I could no longer hold back the question. It struggled out of me, the way a chick forces its way out of the egg.

'Do I have it?'

'Do you have what?'

'Your . . . your gift. The serpent gift.'

He stopped. So did the donkey, as he was holding its lead. He looked at me across its woolly grey back, and something moved in his face.

'Would that make you very unhappy?' he asked.

Tears stung my eyes. I didn't say anything, but it probably wasn't difficult for him to see the answer.

'Dina. It is not some horrible and evil power. It is also . . . the ability to make people dream. Is that so terrible?'

My stomach was a rock at the bottom of a lake. Hard, cold and slimy.

'*Do I have it?*' Don't lie to me, I prayed. Don't lie.

His silence seemed to me to last a small eternity.

'How would I know?' he said. 'Some things you have to find out for yourself.'

And I didn't know whether he was lying or telling the truth.

★ ★ ★

That night we found no farm to stay at but had to camp in a small laurel grove. I lay for a long time, thinking, and when I finally did fall asleep, I had a horrible, horrible dream I couldn't wake from. I was walking through endless underground tunnels looking for Davin, and the tunnels were full of fog and darkness. I called and called, and finally I heard his voice answering. I ran towards the sound, and suddenly I was in a cell exactly like the one I had shared with Nico in Dunark. I raised my torch and caught sight of Davin. He had been chained to the wall; but what held him wasn't ordinary chains, but snakes. Fat, scaly snakes, opening their mouths to hiss at me.

'Get them off me,' screamed Davin. 'Dina, get them off me.'

I didn't dare. I simply didn't dare. I was so afraid they would bite me.

Something touched my leg. I looked down and saw that a snake had wound itself around my ankle and was slithering up my leg. I screamed and kicked and tried to get it off me, but suddenly there were snakes everywhere; one fell down from the ceiling and wrapped its scaly length around my neck; there were snakes on my arms, on my legs, and when I opened my mouth to scream I found I couldn't, because something was coming out of me, there was a snake *inside me*—

'Dina. Hush now, Dina, it's only a dream.'

I knew that, sort of, but I couldn't wake. I could hear myself crying, and I could feel somebody touching me, but at the same time I was in the dungeon with Davin, choking on snakes, hundreds of them now, I was buried in them, they crawled over one another and over me, and I could feel their cold scaly bodies against my skin.

'Dina. Look at me.'

It sounded almost like Mama, and somehow I wrested my eyes open. But it wasn't Mama. It was Sezuan.

I tried to stop crying, but it was hard. The snakes were still there somewhere, waiting for me. And Davin *was* a prisoner, together with Nico, and suddenly it seemed perfectly hopeless to think that we could free them, just Sezuan and me.

'Stop crying now,' said Sezuan, patting my shoulder awkwardly, as if he wasn't quite sure how it was done. 'Wait. I'll drive away the bad dreams.'

He took out the flute and raised it to his mouth.

'No,' I whispered. 'Not the flute.'

I could only just make out his face in the glow from the embers of our bonfire. His eyes glittered, and at first I thought he might be angry with me. But I don't suppose he was. At any rate, he put away the flute, sat down on the ground next to me, and started singing instead.

> 'Nightbird is flying through the darkness
> Nightbird is bringing me a dream
> A dream as fine as you are
> A dream as fine as you.
> Night winds are blowing through the valley
> Night winds are bringing me your name
> A name as fine as you are
> A name as fine as you
> Often have I dreamed I found you

Often have I thought of you
Were you happy? Were you strong?
Did you never think of me?
Nightbird has closed her eyes now
Tucked her beak under a dark wing
Sleep, my daughter, sleep and be easy
The night winds bring nothing ill.'

He didn't have a particularly beautiful voice. It was not at all like when he played the flute. When he sang, he sounded like an ordinary human being. But that felt better. I grew calmer. The snakes slipped away from my half-waking dream, one by one. And he stroked my hair as if he hadn't even noticed that it was actually quite filthy and 'unsavoury'. Never trust him, Mama had said, but there wasn't anyone else, and I needed so badly to trust *somebody*.

'Did you make it?' I asked. 'The song?'

It was a while before he answered.

'Yes,' he finally said, very quietly.

I grew very quiet myself. Because if that was true, then he had made it for me. He had no other children, he had said. *Often have I dreamed I found you*. Had he really dreamed about me?

'How long have you been looking for me?'

'For years,' he said. 'Twelve years, to be exact.'

Somewhere in my chest something tight loosened, and I could breathe more easily. In the end I fell asleep, without evil dreams, while my father sat stroking my hair.

TWENTY-SIX

The Donkey Thief

The next morning, the donkey was gone. The donkey and most of our supplies. The water skin. The flatbread. The rye biscuits and the white goat's cheese that Sezuan had bought at the last farm we had passed.

'Did it get loose, do you think?' I asked.

'Picking up two saddlebags as it went?' said Sezuan. 'Hardly. This thief had hands.'

I wanted to look for the donkey, but Sezuan said that would do no good.

'If this was done by robbers, we must be grateful they didn't just slit our throats while we slept,' he said harshly. 'I should have kept better watch.'

'What do you mean, *if this was done by robbers?*' I asked.

He looked at me searchingly, as if to gauge my mood.

'There is another possibility,' he said. 'If it was him, then . . . the donkey will come back by itself, or not at all.'

I knew it. There *was* somebody following us.

'Who is he?' I asked sharply. This time, I wanted the truth.

Sezuan hesitated. 'A sick man,' he finally said. 'A wretch, but a dangerous wretch. Once his name was Nazim, but you mustn't call him that any more, it makes him furious.'

'What do I call him, then?' I asked. 'If I see him.'

Sezuan heaved a sigh. 'I hope you won't.'

'But if I do?'

'He calls himself Shadow.'

'That's not a name.'

'No. But then . . . he is no longer a . . . a proper human being. Dina, if . . . if something happens, and I'm not there, speak nicely to him. Don't anger him. And don't look at him too much, he doesn't like that. Often it's better to pretend that you don't see him at all.'

The sun had already begun to heat the rocks around us, but I still felt shivers down my back.

'Why is he following us?' I asked, aware that my voice was a thin, uncertain thing.

'Because he is mad.'

'That can't be the only reason.'

'To Shadow, it is reason enough,' said Sezuan tersely and would say no more.

There was nothing we could make breakfast with. We didn't even have water. The only remotely suitable container we had left was the tea kettle still sitting in the remains of last night's fire. I shook it, but it was dry as bone.

'I'll get us some water,' I said.

'No,' said Sezuan. 'We'll go together.'

'But . . . what about our things? What if he runs off with the rest?' The blankets, for instance. The nights would be cold without them.

'We shall have to take them with us.'

It wasn't much we had left, but without the donkey and the saddlebags, it was still a cumbersome burden. We had to bundle everything up in the blankets and carry them like sacks at our backs. Mugs and spoons rattled around as I walked, and the ungainly bundle kept banging me in the small of my back. Sezuan carried our small axe in his free hand; I had the tea kettle.

We stopped at a little stream and drank as much as we could. Then we filled the kettle and walked on. My belly hardly knew whether to slosh or growl. Cold water wasn't breakfast, but if we didn't find the donkey thief soon, or some kindly mountain peasant who would take pity on us, then the next meal might be a long time coming.

The sun rose. So did the path – up and up in twists and turns. We saw no living creatures except for lizards and the like. No donkey thieves. No peasants, kindly or otherwise. Not even so much as a goat. Only hard sun and even harder rocks. Dust. Thorny bushes. Stones, stones, stones.

My calves had begun to ache from walking uphill all the time. And when we finally reached the crest and could see what waited on the other side, the way ahead looked every bit as stony and steep and deserted as the road behind. At least we would be walking downhill, I thought, rubbing my poor calves. That had to ease some of those aches.

It did. At first, anyway. Then my thighs began to ache instead. My back was soaked in sweat, and my fingers had turned into stiff sweaty claws from clutching the heavy wool blanket. About halfway down the next slope, my grip slipped, and clothes and mugs and spoons cascaded on to the mountainside. As if that wasn't enough, I managed to drop the tea kettle as well in my attempt to save the blanket bundle. Now our drinking water was nothing more than a wet spot on the path.

I rubbed my tired eyes. This heat, and then no water. Not good. You could get sick from that. And who knew when we might come upon the next brook or wellspring? Gushing streams and cool forest lakes weren't exactly crowding each other in these parts.

Sezuan didn't scold. He merely helped me pick up the stuff and get my bundle together again. But he made no move to walk on.

'This is no good, Dina,' he said. 'I shall have to use the flute.'

'What good would that do? There's no one around.'

'It may be that we are alone,' he said. 'But you never know. Wait and see.' He pointed to a cluster of wolfsbane by the side of the path. 'Sit there,' he said. 'And pretend you aren't here.'

I looked dubiously at the tall violet flowers. Wolfsbane, Mama's voice said in my mind, also known as monkshood or aconite. Poisonous. But then, I wasn't planning to eat them, just hide among them. If possible – it didn't look like a very effective hiding place.

'Do you want me to hide in those?' I said uncertainly.

He shook his head. 'No, not hide. Just sit down and imagine you aren't there.'

It sounded like a very peculiar thing to do. He might be able to hide in broad daylight in that fashion – *no one sees Sezuan unless he wants to be seen*, or so Mama had said – but I wasn't Sezuan.

'Just sit,' he said when he noticed my hesitation. 'And do not talk.'

Well, that much I could probably manage. I sat down among the tall flowers and let yellow flies and small golden bees buzz undisturbed around me.

I didn't see him raise the flute, but suddenly the music was there, huge and overwhelming, harsh as a mountain. Not at all like when he had played for me. No roses and clover scents now, this was all thunder and trumpets, like a signal calling soldiers to battle. 'Come,' shouted the flute. 'Obey!' The notes marched across the valley in straight columns, and it almost made me want to march along. But I was not the one he was calling, so I remained where I was, on the ground among nodding wolfsbane flowers.

Nothing happened. No mysterious Shadow peeked out from behind the boulders. No robbers either, for that matter. In fact, nothing and no one appeared.

Sezuan didn't give up right away. He played until there was a glistening sheen of sweat on his face and neck. But finally he lowered the flute.

'Maybe he really is not here,' he murmured.

I got up slowly. Sitting on the ground, so still and for so long, had stiffened my back and legs.

'What do we do? Walk on?'

'I suppose we shall have to.'

Sezuan put his flute back in its sheath. I collected my bundle and swung it on to my back. We walked on.

He stood on the path in front of us, suddenly, as if he had shot up from some hole in the ground. His mouth was hanging open, and he was breathing in shaky gasps, like an injured animal.

My heart jumped into my throat, and I dropped my bundle once more. *Don't look at him*, Sezuan had said, but it was hard not to. His faded red shirt was soaked in sweat, and his hair that had probably once been neat and short like Sezuan's now stuck straight up into the air like a coxcomb. It was so sticky and clotted with clay and ashes that he had to have done it on purpose, and this made it impossible to tell its original colour, but it wasn't black, I thought, the way I had believed after that first glimpse in the chestnut tree.

Because it was him. There was no doubt. Even the long stick was still with him. He stood there clutching it, and it was hard to say whether it was for support or because he wanted to hit us with it.

Without a word, Sezuan raised the flute. The man's eyes followed every move, but other than that he stood stock-still. Sezuan blew a short signal-like tune, like whistling for a dog. The stick clattered on to the ground, and the man – Shadow, I would have to learn to call him – fell to his knees in the dust at my father's feet.

'Master,' he whispered. 'Master . . .'

Sezuan lowered the flute and looked down at the

kneeling form. I had no idea what he was thinking or feeling.

'Where is the donkey?' he asked, and his voice was so cold that I almost pitied the man on the ground.

At first, Shadow didn't answer him. Instead he raised his head and looked straight at me, and there was no doubt what *he* was feeling. Hatred narrowed his eyes into slits.

'Little Serpent,' he said, and his voice sounded as if he hadn't used it for a long time. 'Little Serpent, beware. Or the big serpent will eat you.'

Once again, my heart jumped in my chest. I had been feeling sorry for him a minute ago. Now, I was afraid of him. And I didn't like the name he had given me. Little Serpent. Did he know that Sezuan was my father?

'Where is the donkey?' asked Sezuan again, and this time his voice was even more glacial.

'Gone away and run away,' chanted Shadow. 'Gone, gone gone.' He smiled, and I could see that he had a tooth missing. 'What will Shadow get if he can find it?'

He looked up at Sezuan, and his face was lit up with expectation, like a child who knows that Grandfather has something nice in his pocket. And apparently, Sezuan knew perfectly well what Shadow wanted.

'A dream,' he said gruffly. 'Show us where the donkey is, and I'll give you a dream.'

The donkey was tethered to a thorn bush half a mile further down the track. The saddlebags were there, too, but they were empty. Shadow had torn them apart, and all our belongings were scattered over what looked like half the valley. Everything that could be opened had been opened, and everything that could be torn apart had been torn apart. The flatbreads were nothing more than dirty crumbs in the dust, and what looked like a powdering of snow on the rocks was probably the contents of Sezuan's little bag of salt. I crouched down and stared at the devastation with a sense of hopelessness.

'Why did he do that?' I whispered to Sezuan. I was so afraid of Shadow that I was almost too nervous to look at him. The idea of talking to him was too scary to contemplate.

Sezuan didn't answer me.

'I haven't got any,' he snapped at Shadow. 'You could have saved yourself the effort.'

Haven't got any what? I thought.

'Master promised Shadow a dream,' said Shadow sulkily. 'Shadow found the donkey for Master, and now he wants his dream!'

'You didn't find it, you stole it,' said Sezuan.

'Master promised!'

'Yes,' said Sezuan softly. 'So I did.' He looked at me. 'Dina, take a walk.'

Take a walk? When we had been doing nothing *but* walk for days and days? But I understood him well enough. He wanted me out of the way while he gave Shadow his dream. Reluctantly, I got up.

'Where to?' I asked.

'Take the water skin. I think there may be water down there by the willows.' He pointed further down into the valley, to some crippled-looking saplings that didn't look as if they would ever be trees.

I didn't want to go trudging down there on my own. I suppose I was curious too — what was it that Sezuan didn't want me to see? But at the same time there was something about the way Sezuan was acting, and Shadow too, that made me wish I was anywhere but here.

'Go,' said Sezuan. His eyes were deep and dark green like bog water.

I went. The empty water skin hung across my shoulder, limp like a drowned kitten. Had Shadow drunk the water, or just poured it out on the ground? At least he hadn't ripped it apart, the way he had with the saddlebags. Behind me, I heard the flute now, soft and kittenish. I wanted to stick my fingers in my ears, because the notes seemed almost to stick to the skin, sweet and somehow rotten at the same time, like syrup gone bad. Unhealthy. Wrong.

There was water by the willows, a thin trickle barely deep enough for me to fill the skin. I dipped both hands in it and rubbed my face and neck, trying not to hear the flute. Not until the notes stopped did I dare return to Sezuan, Shadow and the donkey.

Sezuan looked strangely absent-minded. Shadow, on the other hand, was stretched out on the ground with his arms flung wide like he was waiting to embrace somebody. His eyes were only half shut, but even though his pupils were visible, huge and dark under the heavy lids, it was obvious that he didn't see anything. A thin thread of spittle seeped from the corner of his mouth.

I shuddered. 'What's wrong with him?' I asked.

'He is dreaming.'

'I dream almost every night, but I don't look like that while I'm doing it!'

'Some dreams are dangerous. If you don't know how to control them.'

'Control them? Who does? I can't decide what to dream.'

Sezuan silently held out his hand for the water skin. I passed it to him, and he poured a little water into his palm, drank most of it, and wiped his face with his wet hands.

'Some day, you may,' he said. 'It's possible to learn.'

'For people who have the serpent gift?'

'Not just for us. But it makes it easier.'

I shut my mouth and didn't ask any more questions. I didn't like the way he had said *us*, as if he and I were the same. But all of a sudden, Sezuan seemed only too willing to talk.

'You asked me why he did this,' he said, nodding at the ripped-up saddlebags.

'He was mad. Or mad at us, at any rate.'

'No. He was looking for something.'

'What?' I couldn't hold back the question, even though I had decided I really didn't want to know any more about this.

'We call it dream powder. It's made from a particular kind of nut that grows down south. Some Blackmasters use it when they are training an apprentice, so that the apprentice may learn to understand the nature of dreams better. It takes a long time to learn how to control dreams — your own and those of others. The dream powder is a sort of . . . short cut. But it is a hazardous

251

short cut. One you should avoid.' He looked at me seriously, but I didn't quite see the point of these warnings. I wanted nothing to do with his serpent arts, with or without dream powder.

He looked as if he expected an answer, but I didn't know what he wanted me to say. In the end, he just sighed, drank more deeply from the water skin and gave it back to me.

'You drink too,' he said. 'Or you'll give yourself a headache.'

I drank obediently. I looked sideways at Shadow, still on his back staring straight up at the sun. Wouldn't that harm him? I almost wanted to put something over his face, but at the same time I was scared of touching him.

'Is that why he looks like that? Because you gave him . . . dream powder?'

Sezuan shook his head. 'No. I told you I didn't have any. And a Blackmaster who is strong enough does not need the powder. But that was how it started for Shadow. When everything began to go wrong. Today he is a slave of the dreams, not their master. And that is . . . not good.'

I looked at Shadow's empty eyes and gaping mouth. *Not good.* No, he could say that again.

Sezuan picked up Shadow's stick and looked at it for a moment. Then he flung it as far away as he could. It whirled through the air in a lazy curve to land in a cluster of goatleaf further down the hill.

'We have to move on,' he said. 'Help me get him on to the donkey.'

I wished we could just leave him. But an animal might

come, perhaps even a wolf. And the way he was now, he couldn't even defend himself against an ant. He moved not a muscle to help or hinder when Sezuan hauled him up and tried to push him across the donkey's back.

'You will have to help,' said my father. 'Take hold of his wrists and pull when I lift.'

I looked resentfully at Shadow. I didn't want to touch him. He smelled – a sour, unwashed smell. Worse than the donkey, which after all only smelled the way donkeys ought to smell. But I did take hold of his arms and pulled, the way I had been told. There was something wrong with his skin – small flakes of it came off and stuck to my fingers after I had touched him. I rubbed my palms against my skirt and then wished I had chosen something else to wipe them on. The thought of having tiny bits of Shadow stuck to me was sickening.

The donkey moved in an irritated manner, and Shadow's limp body nearly slid right off again.

'Hold him,' ordered Sezuan. 'I have to find something I can tie him with.'

Reluctantly, I took hold again, although this time so far up that I didn't have to touch his bare, skinny wrists. Sezuan took the tethering rope and managed to secure the awkward burden on the donkey's back. It was almost as if Shadow had stopped being human and had been turned into a cumbersome bit of baggage.

'There,' said Sezuan, tightening the last knot. 'That ought to hold him.'

The donkey tipped back its ears and looked extremely unenthusiastic. And now that it had enough to do carrying Shadow, we still had to carry everything else ourselves. Everything, that is, that Shadow hadn't made completely unusable. But at least we had the water skin now.

The sun was so harsh the rocks looked nearly white. A reddish-brown lizard stared at us with bulging eyes. Apart from that, the valley seemed deserted.

'Come on,' said Sezuan. 'There must be people somewhere.'

My belly, which had had nothing but water, rumbled hungrily. People. Bread. Maybe even a bit of goat's cheese? But what were we going to do about Shadow? No peasants would welcome him under their roofs, no matter how charmingly Sezuan played to them.

And even that was getting ahead of ourselves. First, we would have to find a peasant.

I clicked my tongue at the donkey, and we began to walk again. Slowly, because Shadow was a heavy burden for a small donkey like ours. *Shanks's mare will get you anywhere in time*, Mama used to say. But the Sagisburg was still a long way off, and right now it felt as if we would *never* get there.

V
The Sagisburg
Davin's story

TWENTY-SEVEN

The Wyrm

Quietly, the boat slid through the dark waters. The oars broke the surface softly and carefully, and the creaking of the rowlocks was the only constant sound. No one spoke. In the bow, two men armed with long spears were gazing warily into the waters of the lake. They had been standing like that for more than an hour now. I wondered what the spears were for – fish, perhaps? We weren't short of supplies. Two newly butchered lambs lay in the shadow of the bow.

A thin haze covered the lake. Each time an oar dipped into it, the veil was swept away for a brief moment so that we could see the black mirror surface. The waters ran deep here. If anyone was to drop something over the side, they would never get it back.

I squirmed, trying to find a position that would make my ribs hurt a little less. My motion caused the chains to rattle, and one of the guards turned around angrily.

'Quiet!' he said. 'Or we might use you instead.'

'For what?' I asked, although I knew that that would probably make him even angrier.

'For the Wyrm,' he said. 'So better not tempt me!'

Worm? What worm? I looked questioningly at Nico, but he shook his head faintly. He didn't know either.

Around us, the cliffs rose like the walls around a fortress. The sun had disappeared behind the mountain ridge, and now there were only a few golden streaks left to show that it hadn't quite set. Other people, elsewhere, could still see it. It was only here in the shadow of the Sagisburg that night had already fallen.

Mira began to whimper with fear and homesickness and huddled against Nico even though he couldn't hold her properly with his hands chained the way they were. It didn't exactly improve matters when one of the guards hissed at her to 'shut her silly gob'.

'Leave the child alone,' said Nico. 'It isn't her fault.'

Even though he said it very softly, one of the guards rapped the back of his neck with his spear butt and told him to shut up, and then, of course, Mira started crying for real. Her high, clear girl's voice rose like a seagull's cry, echoing across the still waters of the lake.

Something was moving down there. Something big. Hidden forces caught at the boat like a current, turning it sideways. The oarsmen fought to right it, then backpaddled as if our lives depended on it. And no wonder.

In front of us, less than three oars' lengths from the bow, rose a . . .

Waterspout? Giant fish?

No.

It was a head. A scaly grey head longer than Mira's

entire body. It rose above us and kept rising, on a neck like a . . . a tree. Or something bigger still. A cloud column. The neck of a tornado. Something too big to be alive.

But it was alive, the Wyrm. Black eyes stared down at us, lightless like the eye-holes in a skull. Mira screamed, a thin, hoarse cry of terror, and hid her face against Nico's shoulder.

'The lamb,' called one of the spearmen. 'Toss her the lamb, now!'

His partner seized one lamb and heaved it across the gunwale, as far away from the boat as he could. The Wyrm didn't seem to care. It – she? – she kept staring down at the boat with those eyes of hers, dark and deep like mountain caves. A single mouthful, I thought. She could snap the boat into halves with a single bite. She opened her maw a little, and a stench of dead water plants, ooze and rotting fish poured over us.

One spearman panicked. He drew back his arm, preparing to throw.

'No,' hissed the other, knocking the spear from his hand. 'That's no good against the likes of her. Save it for the smaller ones. Toss the other lamb!'

Splash. The other dead lamb dropped into the lake a good distance from the boat.

Slowly, the Wyrm turned her head. She snorted, spraying us with droplets of lake water and wyrm drool. Then she sank back into the waters. Staring down, I could make out the darkness that was her body, huge and massive like a reef. To her, we were no larger than fleas in a dog's pelt.

'Row on,' barked the man still holding his spear. 'Let's get docked before she returns.'

The oarsmen dug in with a will. The boat shot across the waters, and soon an opening appeared among the cliffs.

'Now, that was the Wyrm,' said the spearman. 'She is the biggest of them all. She has quite a few children, though. Just thought I'd mention it, in case anyone was thinking of swimming out of here.'

The opening turned out to be the entrance to a cavern. Jagged spears of rock jabbed out at us from above and below, like the fangs of some giant monster. It took a great deal of skill and caution to manoeuvre past the entrance reefs without getting the hull ripped open, but once we were in, the boat glided smoothly over a black and unrippling surface towards the landing, where a small group of men awaited us.

Some were obviously castle guards, in leather armour reinforced with iron bosses, and with the double dragon of the Draconis family painted on their chest-plates. The last two were . . . well, they had to be Educators, I supposed, though they didn't look anything like I had imagined.

Dressed in black, yes. I knew that. Even their hands were covered by black gloves. But the most striking thing about them was their faces.

It was almost impossible to tell the two of them apart. Black hoods clung closely to head and neck and left only their faces free, and those faces were . . .

Not old. Not young. Beardless. Hairless. Not even a

trace of eyebrows. It was as if everything that might have made them slightly human had been covered or removed. So that was what an Educator looked like. Like something hatched from an egg, rather than born. They looked as if they had never been children.

Mira literally squeaked with fear and began to cry once more. After meeting the Wyrm, I didn't see how she could be frightened by two men, no matter how black-clad they were. But then, I wasn't six years old and far away from home for the first time in my life.

One of the city guards climbed out of the boat and on to the floating dock to give a roll of parchment to one of the Educators, who took it and began to read from it.

'Mira, daughter of citizen Anton Aurelius. Greylings Davin and Nicolas.' He gazed at us in a measuring way, like a farmer would look at livestock he was thinking of buying. 'Some are brought to the Sagisburg to learn, others for punishment. But I say to you, there is no punishment that is not also a lesson. And whosoever receives his tutoring with an open mind and heart may walk away from it unbent and unblinded, like a true prince's man. But he who closes his heart and will not receive his lesson, he shall abide in darkness for ever.'

I had no idea what he was talking about. What did he mean that a punishment was a lesson? What exactly was I supposed to learn from having my hands chained and my ribs kicked in? But perhaps that was just the way Educators talked.

'Mira Aurelius,' he continued, 'follow Master Aidan into the House of Teaching.'

Mira clung to Nico and wouldn't let go. Nico whispered something into her fair hair, but it didn't make her any calmer that I could see, and in the end one of the castle guards lost his patience. He grabbed her hand so that she lost her grip on Nico's shirt, lifted her on to the dock and gave her a push towards the Educators.

I held my breath. Mira's flashpoint was low at the best of times, and if she began to scream and kick Master Aidan's shin the way she had done with Master Rubens . . . I didn't like to think what might happen.

But Mira was too scared to act in her normal manner. She just stood there, tears streaming down her cheeks. And when Master Aidan took her hand, she followed him unresistingly, stiff and silent like a small wooden doll.

'What about the greylings?' asked one of the castle guards.

The other Educator looked down at the parchment in his gloved hand. Probably every horrible crime that Nico and I were supposed to have commited was outlined there in detail.

'Send them to Mascha,' he said. 'He knows how to rid a body of the rebellious spirit.'

TWENTY-EIGHT

Blank-back

A long, long staircase wound its way up from the docking cave. Some of it was hewn from the rock itself, some was brick, some wood, a spindly column winding its way through caverns and shafts and tunnels inside the mountain. Squeaking bats darted this way and that, rapid fluttering shadows on their way to this night's insect hunts. I envied them their wings. We trudged upward, step by step – hundreds of them – and my ribs hurt me worse for every one of them.

The stairs ended in a narrow yard, surrounded by tall buildings. Above us rose the crenellated walls of the Sagisburg, with parapets and turrets and embrasures. A little ahead of us I could see Mira and Master Aidan the Educator. They were headed for a large black door, a door so tall it made even Master Aidan look like a child. Mira looked more like a very reluctant ant. Above the door letters had been carved, in huge sharp letters: IN EVERY THING A LESSON, it said, so it was probably the entrance to the House of Teaching. Ant-Mira cast a last, desperate look over her shoulder, and Nico raised his hands in a sort of wave. He intended it as a comfort, probably, but the chains made it a sorry-looking gesture.

One of the guards shoved me none too gently in the back.

'You,' he said sourly. 'Move. We haven't got all night.'

They marched us into another courtyard and then through a narrow door at the base of a tower. Greasy stone steps led downwards into a round, bare chamber with six identical black iron gates. The guard captain rapped the bars of one gate with his spear.

'Mascha,' he called. 'Hey, Mascha, wake up. Fresh dragon fodder for you.'

Dragon fodder? Did he mean us?

There was a rattle from the darkness behind the gate. Then a man appeared. He was beardless and bald, but this did not make him look childish or grandfatherly. Much the opposite. His naked upper body was marked by dozens of scars, some of them whip marks, others caused by what looked like knifings or sword cuts. He wasn't enormously tall, but there was a sinewy strength to him that made the idea of getting into a fight with him an extremely discouraging thought.

'Again?' he said. 'Can't Erlan take them?'

The guard shook his head. 'No, they're all yours. By Master Vardo's direct order. But if you disagree, I'm sure he would be happy to discuss it with you. Shall I ask him?'

Mascha's answer was just a wordless snarl.

The guard grinned. 'Thought so,' he said, unlocking the gate. 'Welcome to the Gullet, boys. Never fear. Uncle Mascha will look after you like you were his very own.'

It wasn't exactly a room, behind the gate. More like a vault or a tunnel, with a ceiling so low I had to duck my head. There seemed to be a gate at the other end, much like the one we had entered through, but it wasn't likely to be much use to us; the guards unchained our hands, sure enough – but they then clapped leg-irons on us and tethered us to the same long chain that held Mascha and eight other prisoners safely captive. They had us – and they obviously intended to keep us.

'Sleep tight,' said one of the guards with a grin that seemed rather malicious. 'Long day tomorrow, or so I hear.'

Then they locked the gate and went away, taking their torches with them.

Even in the dark, Mascha's voice was unmistakable – deep and rough and unvarnished.

'They always give me the pigheaded ones,' he said. 'The troublemakers. The rebels. Now, why do you suppose that is so?'

I didn't say anything. Neither did Nico. But apparently, he was talking to me, because when I didn't answer, he gave the chain a sharp tug, so that I nearly tumbled to the floor.

'Why do you think, blank-back?' he repeated.

'I don't think anything,' I said, tiredly.

'No? Well, maybe there's a bit of wisdom in you after all. Because up there in the daylight, it may be that things are run by Prince Arthos. But down here in the dark, in the Gullet, I am king. *King* Mascha. Understand, blank-back?'

I already hated him. I wanted to tell him to go to hell. But my ribs still hurt abominably, and the last thing I needed was more bruises.

'Understand?'

'Yes,' I muttered.

That was enough, apparently. Mascha's voice lost some of its threatening edge.

'Sleep,' he said. 'You'll need your strength tomorrow. And if you need to take a piss, do it in the gutter there. Try not to wet anyone else.'

There weren't any blankets or other luxuries, just a bit of old straw, thinner than the bedding I normally gave the horses back home. It stank badly and was probably full of lice and other pests, but I lay down anyway. My bruised and weary body was clamouring for rest.

With the torches gone, the darkness in the tunnel was so complete that it hardly mattered whether we had eyes or not. I could hear the others breathe. I could hear the occasional clanking when one of them moved, dragging a chain. And then I noticed another sound. A tiny rattle of metal against stone, rapid and regular like the beat of a moth wing against a windowpane. I listened to it for a while, not understanding what could make such a noise.

'Nico?' I whispered. 'Is that you?'

'What?' His voice sounded strangely breathless.

'That sound. Is it you?'

'Sorry,' he said, and the sound stopped.

Not long after it started up again. This time I didn't say anything. I just reached out and touched Nico's leg.

He was shaking. He was shaking so badly that the iron round his ankle vibrated against the stone floor, making that little noise, *ta-ta-ta-ta-ta-ta-ta*.

Mascha heard it too.

'Stop that racket, blank-back,' he snapped. 'Are you really so scared of me already?'

But it wasn't Mascha that had Nico shaking.

It was the darkness.

I knew it, from the courthouse cellar in Sagisloc.

'It'll be all right,' I whispered. 'You'll get used to it.'

'Yes,' he said. 'Of course.' And he made sure, after that, that the chain didn't rattle. But I don't think he stopped shaking.

'What is a blank-back?' he asked me, in a whisper.

I didn't know. But my neighbour did.

'Blank-back?' he said. 'That's what you call someone who hasn't been whipped yet.'

The walls around the Sagisburg were mountain-tall and solid, and most of them were wide enough that six men could march abreast along the top of them without even brushing the parapets. Below the outer wall lay the dragon pits, more than thirty yards wide in places and inhabited by scaly man-eating monsters like the ones Drakan kept at Dunark. From the guard bridge where we were standing I could see two of them sunning themselves on the hot rocks. From snout to tail they measured three or four horse-lengths.

Mascha noticed my interest.

'Mind how you go, blank-back,' he murmured. 'If you fall . . . well, they'd enjoy tender young flesh like yours.'

I gave him a sour, sideways look. If I did fall, I thought, I wouldn't have to worry too much about the dragons. The drop was quite enough to kill me without any help from the monsters.

All in all, the Sagisburg defences were the most unbreachable I had ever seen. But apparently that wasn't enough for Prince Arthos. He had ordered the outer walls built even higher.

'The wall from Hawk Tower to Lion Tower is your task,' said the Wallmaster. 'Erlan's lot will do the bit from the Lion Tower to the Dragon Tower. And the Educators want to know which gang finishes first, and which is last.'

He said it with no particular emphasis, but a strange sort of sound went through Mascha's gang, halfway between a moan and a snarl. And as soon as the guards undid our leg-irons, my fellow prisoners threw themselves into the task as though their lives depended on it. I had never seen men work quite that hard before.

'You. Blank-back. Ever done any masonry?' asked Mascha.

I shook my head. Saw and hammer, yes, but I'd never handled a trowel.

'You?'

'No,' said Nico. 'Never.'

'Pity. You'll have to haul rock, then. Go with Gerik, he'll show you what to do.'

The stone blocks for the wall were hewn from a quarry at the back of the Sagisburg, where the fortifications met the mountainside and more or less became one with it. Nico and I had to load the stone on to a sledlike cart and then haul the cart along the top of the wall to the section Mascha's gang was working on. That may not sound so bad, and the first load was no great strain. It was after the tenth haul, or thereabouts, that it stopped being hard work and became a torture instead. My ribs hurt so badly by then that I couldn't walk fully upright any more.

'Let's stop for a moment,' said Nico, who had watched me hunch up more and more.

I nodded. I didn't have breath left to speak.

While we stood there with the sled-cart, trying to catch our breaths, I saw two boys come running across the courtyard down below. They both had their hair cropped short like Markus the Tattle-Tale, one fair, one dark, and they both wore white shirts, black waistcoats and grey knee-breeches so I guessed they must be two of the wretched children from the House of Teaching. It seemed like they were racing each other, and I was quite relieved on Mira's behalf. I had thought the Teaching consisted mostly of being caged up in dusty classrooms learning endless nonsense chants like the one she had had to know for her test. But at least it seemed the children were allowed out to play every now and then.

How they ran. Legs milling, arms pumping. The goal line seemed to be the gate over there where one of the Educators waited. As they rounded the last corner, the dark boy drew a little ahead of the fair one.

Suddenly the fair-haired boy grabbed the dark one's collar and jerked at it, so that the boy lost his balance and fell. Little cheat! He won the race and got to the gate first because of that dirty trick, but I was sure the

Educator would have a thing or two to say to him about the way he won it.

But no. Apparently not. The Educator put his hand on the fair-haired boy's shoulder and praised him – or that was how it seemed, because the boy beamed like a small sun and stood a little taller than before. Together, the two of them went into the next courtyard and vanished into the House of Teaching.

The dark-haired boy had regained his feet. He had scraped his knee, and a thin trail of blood was trickling down his shin. He didn't even notice. He was staring at the Educator and the fair-haired boy as they disappeared, and I could suddenly see that the race had been no game. His face looked completely frozen, pale and numb with despair. He looked as if his world had just come to an end.

'Children should never look like that,' I muttered.

Nico followed my gaze.

'I think there are a lot of desperate children in that House,' he said darkly. 'The sooner we get Mira out of there, the better.'

I almost laughed out loud. Here we were, chained like mules to a sled, with barely a hope of seeing the outside world again for the next six years, and yet he spoke blithely of freeing Mira, as if it was only a matter of when, not if.

'Come on,' I said. 'Let's get on with it before Mascha sees us and tears our heads off. I don't mind being a blank-back yet awhile.'

It wasn't Mascha, however, but Gerik, who had noticed our breather.

'Are you mad?' he hissed and sounded almost more scared than angry. 'Get a move on! Or do you want Erlan's gang to finish before we do?'

I looked at him in puzzlement. 'So what if they do?' I said. 'What terrible things will happen?'

He stared at me as if I had lost my mind. 'Don't know that, do I? They never tell us in advance. But trust me — whatever it is, you won't like it. And if we lose because of you, Mascha will hear of it. That's a promise!'

When the day's work was finally done, the Wallmaster carefully measured how much we had managed to build, and how much Erlan's gang had done. And even though Nico and I were newcomers and apparently horribly slow, Mascha's gang had still added a yard more to their wall than Erlan's had. The Wallmaster made careful note of that, too, on a tablet that reminded me a bit of the debtor's slates at the Foundation.

The guards put us in leg-irons once more, and I thought we were headed back for the Gullet. But that wasn't where the guards took us.

'Where are we going?' I asked Gerik.

'To the Whipping Yard,' he said, as if that was the most natural thing in the world.

'Why? Did we do something wrong?'

'No, this is just the 'Count of the day,' he said. 'But today, it's on Erlan's lot.' He grinned with malicious humour.

Count of the day? What on earth did they mean by that?

They meant, apparently, that a man from the slowest

271

gang had to receive three lashes of the whip. That in itself was sickening enough, though it seemed that Gerik and the others hardly reckoned it. But it became even more sickening when I saw who had been appointed to do the whipping.

It was a boy of no more than eleven or twelve. One of the Teaching House boys, in waistcoat and knee-breeches, his hair cropped close to the skull. An Educator stood behind him, resting his hands on the boy's shoulder. And even from this distance, I could see how the boy's hands were shaking as he clutched the whip.

One of Erlan's men had already been unshackled from the leg-irons and tied instead to a stout post, facing it, his arms above his head.

'This man is an enemy of the Prince,' the Educator told the boy. 'Your arm must be strong when you punish him.'

The boy was staring at the man tied to the pole. Hesitantly, he raised the whip. Then he lowered it again.

'I . . . I would really rather not,' he whispered.

'Pavel,' said the Educator, 'Do you not love the Prince?'

'Yes . . .'

'And do you not hate his enemies?'

The boy nodded obediently.

'Then you must not be weak. Do your duty. You do not want to be one who fails, do you?'

The boy's face for a moment looked drawn with pure terror.

'No,' he said loudly, in a thin scared voice. 'I'll not fail. Never.'

He looked once more at the man's naked back. Old white scars and newer red streaks told their tale – this was not by any means the first time this man had stood at the whipping post. In a fit of determination, the boy raised the whip and brought it down on the man's back.

But not hard. Not hard enough by far, it seemed.

'Pavel,' said the Educator reproachfully. 'You have not even marked him! Is your hatred of the Prince's enemies such a weak and feeble thing?'

The boy had begun to cry, quite soundlessly.

'No,' he sniffled. 'I hate them. I hate them!'

'Then show us.'

But still the boy hesitated. Tears were coursing down his pale face, and he sniffed softly.

Suddenly, the man at the post turned his head and looked straight at the boy.

'Crybaby,' he snarled scornfully. 'Piddling little crybaby. Come on. Get it over with. Or don't you have the guts?'

That did it. The boy raised the whip and hit the man as hard as he was able, three times. Three new weals joined the collection on the prisoner's naked back.

'That was well done, Pavel,' said the Educator. 'You have served your Prince well.'

The guards released the man from the post, and we were all allowed to leave, this time to go back to the miserable holes we slept in.

'Why did he say that?' I whispered to Gerik. 'The crybaby thing, I mean. Anyone would think he *wanted* the boy to hit him.'

'Of course he did,' said Gerik. 'Anton is hardly stupid. If the boy doesn't make it, the guards finish the job. And which would you rather be whipped by, an eleven-year-old crybaby or one of the armoured swine?'

Put that way, it made a certain kind of sense.

'Why him, then? I mean, why him and not someone else from Erlan's lot?'

Gerik shrugged. 'That's for Erlan to decide. Or Mascha, if we lose.' He rolled his shoulders reflexively, in a way that suggested that he, too, had taken his turn at the post. 'In some gangs it's always the weakest ones who take the beatings,' he said, 'on account of them being the least use anyway, when it comes to the next day's work. Not with Mascha. We mostly take turns.'

That surprised me. After my first encounter with Mascha, I wouldn't have put him down as a champion of the finer points of justice.

'And Mascha?' I asked. 'Does he take his turn as well?'

Cold-eyed, Gerik looked at me.

'It happens,' he said. 'But don't get any ideas. Blank-back.'

It was clearly a dirty name in his book. Spoken in almost the same tone of voice as Anton had used when he called his whipping boy 'a piddling little crybaby'. Here, a man took his beatings, it seemed, with something almost like pride.

Of the ten prisoners in Mascha's gang, Nico and I were clearly the lowest. Even slump-shouldered old Virtus had more respect from the others than we did, even though he practically crept along the walls and cringed every time a guard even looked at him. He was always muttering to himself, a jumbled sort of chant that at first I couldn't make head or tail of: 'Zprinzescrate, zprinzescrate, zprinzescrate,' over and over again. Only gradually it dawned on me that he was saying 'The Prince is great'. No, he wasn't quite right in the head, that was for sure. His hands shook so badly he could barely hold the tools. Yet none of the others, not even Mascha, gave him a hard time. Nico and me he ripped into every time we so much as paused for a breather, but not Virtus. Not even when he dropped the plumb line into the dragon pit and we had to ask the guards for a new one and then wait for ever before it got there.

'Why do we have to put up with such a doddering old fool?' I muttered to Gerik. But he took offence.

'Hold your tongue, boy,' he said. 'You don't know anything. And Virtus is no older than I am.'

'How come he looks that way, then?' I said, eyeing the trembling hands and the hunched-up figure that looked almost as if his spine was crippled.

'None of your business, blank-back,' snarled Gerik. But a little later he added, 'You might end up looking like that. If we lose.'

Was he trying to pull my leg? I took another sideways look at Virtus. There was some grey in his beard and hair, and deep furrows on his brow and around his mouth. But it was probably true that he wasn't actually ancient, even though he acted like an old man most of the time.

'What is it they will do to us if we lose?' I asked Mascha later. What could make a man end up like Virtus?

'So that we may learn to be more obedient, the

Educators will come up with an entertaining little game for us.'

Mascha's growl was even deeper than usual, and his eyes glittered with hatred. It wasn't hard to figure out that this 'little game' was entertaining only to those lucky enough not to be part of it.

Five days went by. We slaved away at our wall-building for as long as the sun was in the sky. Come sunset, the Wallmaster measured the result of our efforts and noted it on his tablet. And then we went to the Whipping Yard. The first three days, Mascha's gang managed to stay ahead of Erlan's, possibly because we were a little closer to the quarry. Each night a new boy from the House of Teaching had to wield the lash. Not all of them were as reluctant as Pavel had been the first day. One of them really put his back into it, so that the prisoner he was hitting moaned loudly at the last stroke. The Educator praised the boy for his strength and his hatred of the enemies of the Prince. And the boy beamed and stood taller at the praise. It was enough to make you sick.

On the fourth day, we lost.

'Twelve yards and a quarter,' announced the Wallmaster. 'Against Erlan's full thirteen.'

My stomach contracted. This was it. It was our turn to face the 'Count of the day. And I felt absolutely sure that Mascha would pick on either me or Nico. My poor back was already so work-worn that it hurt even to think of it, and my ribs felt as if they would never mend. I wasn't at all sure that I would be able to keep my mouth shut and take my whipping like a man, the way the other prisoners had done, except for the last one.

Mascha's dark gaze rested first on Nico, then on me. His face was completely expressionless.

'Gerik,' he said. 'You'll have to do it today.'

I think my mouth dropped open. I had been so certain it would be one of us blank-backs.

Gerik didn't say anything. He merely nodded, as if that was as much as he had expected. Was it his turn? Or had he done something that Mascha didn't like? I didn't know. But Gerik let himself be tied to the post and took his three strokes with no more than a hiss between clenched teeth. And as we were marched back to the Gullet, he nailed me with a hard stare that said: That's how it's done. Could *you* have done as much – blank-back?

I don't think Nico slept much. I had expected him to get used to the darkness after a while, to stop being so afraid. He didn't. You could hear it in the way he breathed – gasping like a dog with a too-tight collar. And some nights he woke all of us up by yelling and fighting in his sleep, caught up in one of his nightmares.

The other prisoners didn't like him much, especially at first. There was something in the way he talked, and probably something about the way he walked, even fettered by those miserable leg-irons, something that set him apart. They knew that he was 'posh', or had been. That and the nightmares made them scorn him and mock him when they could.

He never fought back. Silently, he just took all the abuse they handed out and never lost his temper, not even when one or the other shoved him or 'accidentally' swiped him with the chain. If it had been me, I would have lost my head a hundred times over, and I was often so angry on his behalf that I snarled at them and gave them back all their dirty names with interest. On the morning of the fifth day, as we were being herded together for the day's work, I even got into a fight with Carle, one of the other prisoners in Mascha's gang. It began because he stepped back the moment Nico was stepping forward, so that Nico stumbled and fell on his face. When you spend at least ten hours every day chained to nine other men, you learn how to move with and not against each other, so I knew that Carle had done it on purpose.

'Stupid bastard,' I muttered, but softly, so that the guards wouldn't hear.

He gave me a fast, mean-eyed glare.

'Can I help if Prince Pee-In-His-Pants is a clumsy idiot?' he snarled back.

'You did that! You did it on purpose.'

'Shut up, Davin,' said Nico, getting to his feet again. 'Just shut up, can't you?'

Carle grinned, a superior and malicious grin. You could tell he thought Nico was hushing me up because he was scared.

'Pee-In-His-Pants,' he murmured. 'Prince Pee-In-His-Pants and his noble knight Sir Wet-Behind-The-Ears. What a pair!'

And then he made Nico stumble again.

I forgot all about sore ribs and sore arms. I was going to wipe that smirk off his stupid face if it was the last thing I did. And he was only one place down from Nico and me on the chain, so I had no trouble reaching him. My fist struck him right on the nose with a lot of pent-up fury behind it, and he toppled over backwards and went down.

Not for long, though. In a moment, he was up and at me, and I learned just how much I didn't know about fighting prisoner-style, with no room to move away but with lots of nasty ways to use the shackles as weapons.

The guards made no move to stop it. They just laughed and watched while Carle and I tried to half-kill one another. Or at least, that was what Carle was trying to do – I was busy trying to stay alive. Somehow I ended up on the gritty floor of the chamber, with a length of chain across my windpipe and one wrist, while Carle had a fine old time punching me in the belly with his free left hand. I tried to pull up my legs in protection, but the leg-irons got in the way, and breathing was becoming more and more difficult.

Mascha stopped it. I don't know what he did to Carle, but suddenly the blows stopped and the choking pressure of the chain went away. While I was still lying on the floor gasping and feeling blue in the face, Mascha bent over me, pinching my upper lip between finger and thumb. It was incredibly painful, and I batted at him with both hands, trying to get him off me. It was like trying to move a log.

'Who gave you leave to fight, blank-back?' he asked. 'If we lose today because you and Carle are too slow, who do you think will be going to the post, boy? Any ideas?' He finally let go of me with his hands, but not with his eyes. 'Get up,' he said. 'And if there is half an ounce of sense in your wretched body, you'll work today like you've never worked before. And pray we win.'

'Fourteen yards,' said the Wallmaster. 'Against Erlan's fourteen and a quarter.'

Mascha looked at me. His eyes were so dark they just seemed like holes. 'Told you so,' he said, and jerked his head at me. 'Him,' he told the guards.

'No,' said Nico. 'Not Davin. He is . . . Let me. Take me. It was my fault he got into the fight in the first place!'

Mascha sniffed contemptuously. 'Who asked you – Prince Pee-In-His-Pants? You don't make the calls here. And never fear – your turn will come.'

I couldn't help resisting as they dragged me to the post, but the guards had done this a hundred times, and it took them only a moment to haul up my arms and secure my wrists to the crosspiece. Just hanging there like that with my arms above my head hurt my ribs and my abused stomach. I twisted my neck to try to see who was to wield the whip today.

It was a skinny little boy, no more than perhaps ten years of age, and I breathed a little more easily. A runt like that – how hard would he be able to hit me? It wouldn't be so bad, probably.

The Educator started his usual cant about the enemies of the Prince, hatred, and punishment, and strength. The boy nodded eagerly, as if this was a lesson he was well acquainted with. But when they gave him the whip, his eagerness vanished.

'But . . . he never hurt me any,' he said in a small voice.

'He is an enemy of the Prince, Aril. Do you think he has not earned his punishment?'

Aril squirmed. 'Yes,' he muttered.

'Why, then, will you not punish him? Do you not yearn to serve the Prince?'

'Yes . . . but . . .'

'But what, Aril?'

The boy was silent for a while. Finally he spoke, so softly that I barely caught the words.

'Mama says . . . Mama says you shouldn't hit people.'

For an instant, the Educator stood utterly still. Then he bent over the boy.

'We have talked about this matter before, Aril. You no longer have a mother. The woman who *was* your mother – who is she?'

'An enemy of the Prince,' whispered Aril.

'And what are her just wages?'

'Death.'

'Louder, please, Aril.'

'Death!'

'Good. Now, hit this man.'

And Aril did. The lash left a stinging trail down my back, and I clenched my teeth, waiting for the next stroke.

It didn't come. The boy broke into tears and stood there, crying his eyes out, as if he had been the one to feel the lash. He threw the whip on the ground.

'I won't. I won't!'

And no matter what the Educator said to him, he

wouldn't pick it up again. Finally, the Educator took the boy's arm in a firm grip and led him away. And the guard captain pointed to one of his men.

'You will have to finish the job then, Brand. Two strokes, if you please.'

Brand was a big brute of a man, and he picked up the whip without hesitation, flicking it through the air with a loud crack. There was something about his practised ease that made a chill spread outward from my spine. I wanted to call for the boy to come back and finish it. I suddenly understood utterly and absolutely what had made Anton egg on his reluctant whip boy, until the child managed to complete the three strokes. I wished I had had the sense to do as much with Aril.

Brand swung the whip. And the blow went right through my body. My head jerked back so suddenly that I cracked my chin against the post, and a line of fire shot down my back.

Then the second stroke came, and this time, I couldn't bite back the sound. I roared like a steer being branded. Someone had cut two deep furrows in my back and poured sizzling oil into them. Or that was how it felt. Fire. My whole back was on fire. And something warm ran down the small of my back. Blood, it had to be.

I tried to stay upright when they cut me down, but my knees buckled and I ended up on all fours. I absolutely didn't understand how Gerik could have walked away from the post as if three strokes of the lash counted for less than a bee sting. I didn't understand how he and the others had been able not to cry out. Were they made of stone? Or had the skin on their backs gradually turned into leather so that they no longer felt the blows as other men would?

Nico had hold of one of my arms, Mascha the other. Mascha? *Mascha* was helping me?

'Come on, lad,' he was saying. 'Got to help us a little, here, can't bloody carry you, can we?'

Somehow, I made it back to the Gullet even though every step sent a shudder of pain through my back. As I sank down on to my knees and then on to my stomach in the dirty straw of the lock-up, I heard Mascha talking to the guards in low tones. Sweet Saint Magda. That anything could hurt this much. Three measly strokes. Or two, really, because the sting of Aril's efforts had disappeared completely in the roaring pain of Brand's blows. I knew that men had sometimes been sentenced to ten or twenty strokes. How did they survive? I would never whip a horse or a mule again. Ever. No matter how stubborn they were.

'Do it!' said Mascha, his voice suddenly much louder. 'You owe me. And you know it.'

The guard muttered something and disappeared. But he let the torch remain behind, and a little later he brought a bucket of water and some rags. And it was Mascha, to my surprise, who cleaned the furrows on my back and dressed them with sheep's tallow. And Mascha who made me eat and drink, even though I didn't really have the energy. I didn't get it. I thought he didn't like me. But perhaps it was just that he knew we had a working day ahead of us tomorrow. The thought made me cold all over. I couldn't. I simply couldn't. No way would I be able to get up tomorrow, and climb to the top of the wall, and spend the day dragging stone. Not if my life depended on it.

Carle held out the filthy rag of an old cloak that he usually used as a blanket during the night.

'Lie on this,' he said. 'Be real uncomfortable else, lying on your stomach all night.'

'Thanks,' I muttered, dizzy and confused to be so suddenly on their good side. I had cried out, hadn't I? Even though I had promised myself I wouldn't. I had acted like the wet-behind-the-ears blank-back that I was.

'That Brand is a real swine,' said Carle darkly. 'Didn't have to lay your back open like that, did he? Probably has *his* money on Erlan's team to win, I shouldn't wonder.'

'His money?'

'Sure. They bet on us, didn't you know? And if you can't work tomorrow, it'll slow us down. Filthy scumbag swine.'

The tallow helped a little. My head was buzzing like a beehive, and my body felt heavy and somehow not quite my own. Finally I dozed off, slipping in and out of sleep for a few hours. Once I woke to find Virtus next to me, clumsily patting my head.

'It's because he loves us,' he said.

'What?' I muttered, lacking the energy to brush off his touch.

'He chastises us so that we may learn. Because he loves us.'

Nico sat up abruptly. 'Shut up, Virtus,' he hissed. 'Leave him alone.'

Virtus withdrew his hand. 'The Prince is great,' he muttered nervously. 'The Prince is great.'

'He is mad,' whispered Nico. 'Raving mad.'

I didn't say anything.

Towards dawn I couldn't stand lying on my stomach any more. Inch by painful inch I managed to get to my knees. The torch had burnt itself out, but a pale glow of early daylight came through the grille at the far end of the tunnel.

Mascha had noticed that I was moving.

'How are you doing, lad?' he asked.

I wasn't sure what to say. I didn't know how to take the curious care and . . . well, tenderness almost . . . that he was suddenly awarding me.

'I'll live,' I finally said.

He watched me in silence for a while.

'What did you say your name was?' he said.

Why did he want to know? Why now? I stared at him suspiciously. But his beardless, baldheaded face was as expressionless as an egg.

'Davin,' I finally said.

'Davin? Hmm. All right. Have to try and remember that, then.' He suddenly grinned. 'Can't very well call you blank–back any more, now, can we?'

TWENTY-NINE

The Key to Wisdom

I did climb to the top of the wall that morning, but there wasn't much I could do. Almost any movement made the wounds on my back crack open, and after that it didn't take long before I got so dizzy it was sit down or fall down. Nico slaved like a beast to load and drag the sled almost on his own, but no matter how hard he worked, it went more slowly than before. That night Erlan's gang beat us by more than two yards, and Carle had to take three strokes. It was hardly noticeable in his work the next day, and I felt bad because I was still staggering like a sick calf, unable to lift my share of the load.

'Sorry,' I muttered to Nico the third time I had to drop out of the harness and sit down. 'I . . . I can't help it.'

'Of course you can't! You shouldn't be working at all.'

'Carle is working.'

'Yes. But there's a difference. Carle has three nasty weals that probably sting a great deal. You have two bloody furrows that split open and bleed down your back every time you bend!'

That night Erlan's gang were once again the winners, by a yard and a half. And this time Mascha chose to take the strokes himself.

'Why?' asked Nico hoarsely. 'Why not me?'

'Because I can take it better than you can – blank-back,' growled Mascha. But he had seen how Nico had worn himself to the bone, trying to drag the sled practically single-handed, and there was less of a sting to the insult than usual.

Mascha took his strokes without even a moan, and as we were marched back to the Gullet, they seemed to have made no difference at all to him. Maybe he really was made of stone. Even though his whip boy had been a big, stocky fourteen-year-old, the red weals hardly showed on Mascha's scarred, dark, sun-bitten back.

When the guards had locked the gates and retreated back up to the surface world and their leisurely pastimes, Mascha made us draw together in a huddle so that we could talk without being overheard by the gang in the hole next to ours.

'Tomorrow settles it,' he said. 'Erlan's are about ten yards short, we lack nearly twelve. For those of you who can count, this means that we have to beat them by two yards to finish before they do.'

Somebody groaned. Two yards was a lot.

'Can we do that?' asked Gerik.

'If we hustle,' said Mascha. 'And that means not taking a breather just because the next load of stones hasn't arrived yet. You bloody go and help get it instead. Understand? Everybody works *all* the time.'

'Perhaps . . .' Nico broke off, probably wondering whether anybody would listen to words of wisdom from Prince Pee-In-His-Pants.

'Perhaps what?' asked Mascha.

'At the quarry . . . most people choose the smaller blocks first because they are easier to lift, and that means you load the sled more quickly. Erlan's people do that, I've seen them. But if we got the biggest we could find, even if it takes two to lift them . . . the masonry would go more quickly, I think. And we have fewer masons than stone-draggers. All in all it would save time, I think.'

There was a thoughtful silence.

'I think he is right,' said Imrik, our most highly skilled mason.

'Good,' said Mascha. 'We'll do it. Any other bright ideas?'

'We must work hard!' said Virtus suddenly, very loudly. 'Work hard. Work hard.'

'Yes, Virtus,' said Mascha, with a gentleness I would never have guessed he possessed.

'The Prince is great!'

'Yes, Virtus. Anything else?'

No one else had anything to say.

'Right. Get some sleep. You too, Prince Pee-In-His-Pants. We need you.'

We worked like beasts. Like demons. Like something hardly flesh and blood and bone. Imrik's hands flew. Carle and Mascha hefted huge stone blocks as if they were logs. And Nico and I toiled in the harness as though we were mules, not men. The wall grew, yard by yard, closer and closer to the Lion Tower.

'We're ahead!' called Gerik towards the end of the afternoon, passing us with an empty wheelbarrow. 'We've caught them up and passed them, and we're ahead!'

Sweat was literally dripping off us, and I could feel blood and fluid seeping from the deepest of the wounds on my back, but Gerik's message put new life into tired arms and legs. We could win now. We could actually win! Both of us, Nico and I, leaned forward into the harness to get the sled moving just a little faster.

Crack! A loud, sharp noise, a splintering of wood, and then the crunch of stone on stone as our entire load listed sideways and slid on to the pavement.

We stared at our capsized sled in disbelief. One heavy plate wheel had simply split in half, and the front axle rested directly on the cobbles now.

Gerik came charging up.

'What happened?' he cried.

We didn't say anything. Nico just waved a hand at the wrecked sled, a dumb and helpless gesture.

'Can we get a new wheel?' I asked.

Gerik looked about ready to cry, and I had to repeat my question before he heard me.

'A new wheel? Before Erlan's lot get done? No.'

'But if we can't get the stones to Imrik . . . ' I didn't finish my sentence. There was no need. We all knew what I meant: if we couldn't get the stones to Imrik and his masons, the wall would not be finished.

'We'll have to use the wheelbarrow,' said Nico.

'Are you crazy?' said Gerik. 'It's not made for that. It'll break. And it only has one wheel. It'll be hell on whoever has to drive it.'

'Do we have a choice?'

Gerik was silent for a little while. Then he shook his head. 'I don't suppose we have.'

We did our best. And for a while it really did seem as if our narrow lead might hold. But while we were still feverishly working to get the last two blocks into place, there was a roar of triumph from the other side of the Lion Tower. Erlan's gang were done. They had finished before us.

The Wallmaster noted it on his damn tablet and sent it off to the Educators.

Most of our gang stood there, stoop-shouldered and gasping for breath. I let myself collapse on to one of the two not-yet-laid blocks.

'Now what?' I said, looking up at Mascha.

'Now? Now we finish the damn wall. And then we face whatever game it is the Educators have prepared for us.'

There was such hatred, such bitter gall in the last words that it sounded as if the words had been soaked in acid before he spoke them.

The next morning they took Gerik.

It wasn't the usual lot of guards. These were cleaner and more stylish, with boots and mail that glittered with spit and polish, and shiny buttons and buckles everywhere. The double dragon had been enamelled on their breast plates, not just painted on as with the regulars.

'Prince's Own Guards,' whispered Carle. 'Don't usually mix with our lot down here. Might get their boots dirty, see?'

The captain of the Prince's Own threw a quick look in our direction.

'That one,' he said, pointing at Gerik. And one of the usuals came over to unchain Gerik.

'Where am I going?' asked Gerik.

'Shut up, dog,' said the captain.

Mascha glared angrily at the guard he knew. 'Where is he going?' he growled.

But the guard just grinned. 'You'll find out soon enough – dragon fodder,' he said.

And they took Gerik away.

'Why do they call us dragon fodder?' I asked Mascha, because it wasn't the first time I had heard them do so.

He nodded towards the grille at the other end of our tunnel. 'That gate? It leads into the dragon pits. If we tried to rebel or escape, all they'd have to do would be to open the gate and let the dragons finish us. They like to remind us of that. You know why they call this place the Gullet? Same reason. We're half in the dragon's gullet already. And . . . when someone down here dies . . . why waste time and effort burying scum like us? And why waste a perfectly good cadaver, when dragons are quite happy to eat carrion?'

My stomach turned over. It was better than being served up to the dragons alive, I supposed, but a disgusting thought all the same.

'How many dragons does he have? Prince Arthos?'

'Don't know. A lot. Scores of them.'

The only other dragon owner I knew of, Drakan, only had about seven or eight now that Nico had killed off one of them. And his dragons had come from here, I knew, as part of a wedding present when Dama Lizea came to Dunark to be married. How on earth had they managed to bring them all that way? They were big beasts, from what Dina had said. But perhaps they had been younger and smaller, then.

'What do you think they want with Gerik?'

'How should I know?' said Mascha. 'Now, shut up with the questions, can't you, boy?'

Somewhat later, an hour or two perhaps, they came to get the rest of us. They led us into the outer courtyard, in the shadow of the wall we ourselves had toiled to make higher. Up there on the wall stood a very pale Gerik with a couple of the Prince's Own. And what had happened to the wall itself? It bristled like a hedgehog with spikes that had been hammered into the cracks between the stones. On each spike hung a key. There were . . . well, at least thirty.

Walls, galleries and windows were crowded with onlookers. Guards, courtiers and other castle folk. Educators and children. Quite an audience, all in all. Up there, beneath the red silk hanging . . . might that be Prince Arthos himself? Obviously, they were expecting some form of entertainment. I wondered what shape it might take.

An Educator stepped out into the courtyard. I thought

it might be Master Vardo, who had received us the first night, but I was far from certain. They looked so alike, with their beardless faces and black hoods.

Master Vardo – if it was him – raised his voice.

'These men have failed,' he said. 'They have not done their work with a diligence worthy of the Prince's servants. But the Prince is lenient. The Prince is just. He gives to each of us the chance to learn. And if these men are capable of learning their lesson, then tonight they shall dine at the Prince's own table. If they cannot – a just punishment will fall on them.' He pointed at Gerik. 'This man will be lowered into the dragon pits. These men . . .' this time he was pointing at us, 'may be his saviours. If they can find the key to wisdom.'

The key to wisdom? I glanced up at the many keys on the wall. Was it one of those? Next to each key a letter had been painted, I noticed. What was that supposed to mean?

From the courtyard a gate led into the dragon pits, probably so that the beasts could be let loose in the courtyard if an enemy ever succeeded in breaching the outer wall. Was it this key we were supposed to find?

'The essential key lies within this casket,' said Master Vardo, waving forth two boys from the House of Teaching who set down a large black casket in the courtyard and hurriedly withdrew. 'To find it, all you must do is answer one question: what is the true name of the Prince?'

A faint smiled curled his lips, as if he was quite happy with himself and the little game he had arranged. He raised his hand to signal the guards who were standing on the wall with Gerik.

'Begin,' he said.

Begin. Yes, but how? The guards had already started lowering Gerik into the pit out there.

Mascha's jaw was bunched like a mastiff's.

'We'll just get the damn keys,' he said. 'All of them. And try them one at a time until we find the right one.'

But the keys hung high, some of them extremely high, on the wall, and a good distance apart; just getting to them, particularly the topmost ones, would be a somewhat daring feat.

'There isn't time,' said Nico. 'Davin, help me, damn it. What is the true name of the Prince?'

What was he on about? How should I know? And then a small dim light did begin to dawn after all, something to do with Mira and a silly song about a frog.

'You were the one who taught her,' I hissed, trying to remember the words. Who is the ruler of the land? Prince Arthos Draconis. What are the true names of the Prince? My mind stood still. Completely and utterly. 'Nico, you must have said it a hundred times!'

'I can't think,' he said, looking pale. 'I can't think at all.'

What are the true names of the Prince? What are the true names . . . Goodness? No.

Courage, wisdom, and justice.

Suddenly I knew.

'Courage, wisdom, and justice,' I said. 'Nico, that's how it goes!'

'Yes,' he said softly. 'Yes. Mascha – get me the key next to the C.'

Mascha glared at him. 'The C? Do I look like a damn clerk? I can't read, boy!'

'There,' I said, pointing. 'Far left, three spikes up.'

One of the easy ones, luckily. Imrik perched on Mascha's shoulders, picked the key off the spike and threw it to Nico.

'Here!'

Nico stuck the key into the lock of the casket – or tried to. It didn't fit. He threw me a stricken look.

'It's not the right one!'

'All right, so it's not courage. Try wisdom.'

Carle climbed up to get the W-key, which was another of the low ones.

'No good either.'

'Justice,' I said. 'It has to be. And the Educator said so himself, didn't he? The Prince is just!'

J was one of the high ones, so high that Imrik had to stand on Mascha's shoulders, balancing precariously. He threw the key to me, and I tossed it to Nico. If it didn't fit . . . if it didn't fit, I didn't know what to do.

Nico shoved the key into the lock and tried to turn it. Nothing happened.

'It's no good,' he said. 'It's not the one.'

I sank to my knees. I felt like ripping the damn key out of Nico's hands and forcing it to turn. It *had* to be the one.

Nico's eyes were flickering across the wall, as if he was expecting the letters up there to flow together and make sense.

'There,' he suddenly said. 'There's another J.'

And there was. And this time there was a loud, blessed click, and Nico could throw open the casket.

Inside was . . . not a key. Another, smaller casket. Locked, of course.

Nico and I stared at each other.

'All of it,' he said. 'We have to spell the entire word.'

And I knew the same thought was going through both our heads: would there be time?

Nico and I were the only ones who even knew what the letters looked like. We had to direct the others to the right keys.

J. U. S.

Casket within casket.

Some of the onlookers, those that could read, at least, were realizing what we were doing. A murmur ran round the galleries, and a few of the castle's people, commoners mostly, even began to cheer, as though this was a cock fight they were watching.

T.

I had a small hope that 'just' would be enough, but no. Yet another casket.

We could hear Gerik shouting from the pit, now.

'Hurry,' he shouted. 'Hurry, damn it!' There was an edge of sheer panic in his voice.

The I–key was close to the top of the wall. Not even by standing on Mascha's shoulders was Imrik able to reach it.

'Wait,' said Nico. 'Let me. Davin, give me a hand.'

And he climbed up, nimble as a cat. A foot on my shoulder, a hand pressed into a crack in the wall, a foot cradled by Imrik's hand . . . and there he was, balancing on Imrik's shoulder, reaching for the key. And I remembered how once he had balanced on the back of his bay mare like a market juggler to douse our burning cottage roof.

There were certainly things he did without clumsiness.

He threw down the key. I grabbed it and ran to the casket and left it to Carle to help Nico get down again.

'Hurry!' screamed Gerik. 'It's coming!'

I shoved the I-key into the lock and opened it to find the smallest casket yet.

'C!' I called. 'Give me C!'

'We already have it,' said Nico breathlessly, slamming it into my hand. 'The first key we tried . . . Courage, remember?'

C-key in. Casket open . . . and this time, not yet another casket, but a key.

Mascha seized it.

'Is this the one to the gate?'

There was a scream from the pit, a scream completely without words.

'Try,' said Nico. But both he and I were thinking: JUSTIC.

What about E?

'Get it,' hissed Nico. 'We're sure to need it.'

And while Mascha unlocked the gate to the dragon pit, Nico leaped on to my shoulders and fetched down the E-key.

'He's chained,' roared Mascha from the pit. 'We need another key. *Now!*'

I sprinted through the tunnel. And came to an abrupt halt. Right outside, a few steps away from Mascha and the shackled Gerik, was a dragon. It opened its jaws and hissed at us, and a stench of carrion and rotting meat washed over us. A single drop of pearly white venom hung from the point of each fang.

I stared at the dragon's purply gullet and the dragon's yellow eyes, and for a long moment was unable to move.

'A spear!' roared Mascha at the guards on top of the wall. 'Give us a spear, for the love of the Lady!'

At first it seemed no one would. But then a long spear dropped to the ground right at Mascha's feet. He snatched it up and advanced a step towards the dragon.

'Get that chain off him, boy,' he hissed, 'before the beast eats all of us.'

Gerik had his arms shackled above his head, the way they had lowered him down. There was no colour at all in his face, and his breath was coming in great, heaving gasps. I turned my back on the dragon, hoping to all the saints that Mascha could keep it at bay long enough, and that the key would fit the lock.

It did. The shackles came open, and Gerik's arms fell bloodlessly to his sides like two pieces of dead meat.

'Now!' I yelled at Mascha.

He threw the spear at the dragon, turned and ran. We all rushed through the brief darkness of the tunnel and slammed the gate in the monster's face. And Gerik fell to his knees, as if someone had chopped his legs in half.

Around the galleries, walls and windows, people began to cheer and clap their hands as if we'd won a race. Some of the courtiers were tossing things down into the courtyard, some coins and a ring, a glove and a fluttery silk scarf. I stood there with my heart hammering against my ribs, staring at them, and what I felt most was disgust. Would they have applauded as loudly if the dragon had eaten Gerik?

Once more, Master Vardo came into the courtyard. So did what looked like an entire company of guards. Apparently they didn't want us to get any ideas just because people were cheering at us.

'What is the true name of the Prince?' asked the Educator, staring straight at Nico.

Nico stared right back. But the guards had us surrounded now, and he said what the Educator wanted him to say.

'Justice. J, U, S, T, I, C, E.' He spelled out the word slowly and carefully, each letter dripping with contempt. Master Vardo heard the contempt, but there was nothing he could do about it right now. We had won his twisted game, and now he had to deliver. He looked up at the row of children hanging from the windows of the House of Teaching.

'These men have learned a precious lesson. And tonight they shall receive their reward, and dine at the Prince's own table. May you also learn from what you have seen: the key to wisdom is the key to life, and the Prince's justice is all!'

Children and castle folk applauded once more. But as the guards took us away, I couldn't help thinking that that was hardly the speech Master Vardo had expected to deliver. Just how many prisoners could read? Apart from Nico and me, perhaps only one or two in the entire Sagisburg. No, the lesson he had meant the children to see was quite a different one: prisoners are stupid and ignorant. And those who don't learn to read will be eaten.

THIRTY

At the Prince's Table

'Dinner at the Prince's very own table,' said Carle. 'That's something, isn't it?'

His voice sounded weird, somewhere between cocky and not-so-confident-after-all. All in all, the gang was in a strange mood. There was relief that we had all survived Master Vardo's lesson, of course, and exhilaration at our victory and all the cheering. Some were feeling expectant, perhaps. And yet there was also this odd anxiety, as if this couldn't be true, there had to be a catch . . . like waiting for the hammer to drop.

'If they're really serious about this Prince's-own-table stuff,' I whispered to Nico, 'will that be all right? I mean, does he know you?'

Nico shook his head. 'He's never seen me before,' he said. 'But . . . it might be better not to be too noticeable.'

The hours were long that afternoon in the Gullet. The flies were buzzing, and the fleas seemed to bite worse than usual. I almost missed the work. It was too murky in here, even in the middle of the day, for us to do anything other than talk. Tell a few stories. Sing a few dirty songs. Or sleep, as Nico did, now that he finally had a chance to rest during the daylight hours.

In the early evening they came to get us, but not to take us to the banquet hall, or at least not right away. No, before we were allowed to set foot on such polished floors, we had to be cleaned up thoroughly, of course. They led us out into the narrow yard behind the stables and ordered us to scrub each other down with cold water from the pump.

That was almost the best part. To throw away the miserable rags of shirts gone stiff with sweat and dirt and Gullet filth and become clean again, really clean, so that one's skin felt smooth and warm, and not scaly and scruffy like the hide of some kind of reptile. They even gave us soap, two whole bars of it, which foamed and smelled of flowers.

Mascha sniffed suspiciously. 'What's that smell?' he asked.

'Lavender, I think,' said Nico.

Mascha snorted. 'Thought that kind of thing was just for the ladies,' he said.

Nico shook his head. 'No, at court everybody uses stuff like that. Some of the men even use rosewater and perfumed hair oils.'

'Well, well. Sounds like you know all about it, eh?'

'So I've heard,' said Nico quickly.

When we were more or less dry, they gave us clean shirts like the ones the guards wore under their armour, and loose grey trousers that reminded me a bit of the Foundation greys. No one would take us for courtiers, of course, especially not as we were immediately

302

fettered again, but it was still a great improvement. Even my sore back was feeling better, and for the first time since I had been kicked, I could breathe without feeling my ribs.

Six guards of the Prince's Own led us the last bit of the way into the Palace Court, through a colonnade and into the banquet hall itself. No one else had arrived yet, and the servants were still setting the tables, but then, I don't suppose any of the other guests needed to be shackled before they were allowed to sit down.

'They might have taken off the damn irons just for this one night,' muttered Gerik. 'The place is lousy with guards anyway.'

'They're probably afraid we'll go for the Prince,' said Imrik.

'Yeah – or for the ladies,' grinned Carle.

But when the other banquet guests began to arrive, the grins faded. Most of them pretended we weren't even there. But a few stared.

'They gape at us as though we were beasts in a circus,' said Imrik in a low growl.

'Ignore them,' said Nico.

'Do what?'

'Ignore them. Just pretend you don't see them.'

'Are you going to talk posh too? You're not a damn sight better than the rest of us, boy.'

'I never said I was,' said Nico. 'Ever.'

Imrik scowled, but I don't think it was Nico he was truly mad at. Nico was just the only one he could get to.

Suddenly there was a great braying of trumpets

somewhere above us, in the gallery, and all the guests hurriedly got to their feet. Even us, though it took a sharp bark and a shove from the guards to get Imrik out of his seat. A door at the other end of the hall opened wide, and a herald in dragon livery announced:

'His Greatness Prince Arthos Draconis the Just!'

I stretched my neck, curious to see this Prince who had sundered my family and put me and Nico in chains. He was more than ninety years old, I had heard, but he still seemed able to walk on his own with no trouble, and his back was far straighter than Virtus's. He did not look like a man in his dotage. His beard was coal black, and his head was covered by a hood much like the ones the Educators wore, except his was scarlet and richly decorated with gold thread and little gemstones that flashed whenever he turned his head. The beard must have been dyed, I thought, but his skin . . . it was almost as smooth as my own, just in a strangely dead and hard way. Like a shell. Egg smooth. Completely like the Educators, I suddenly realized. They might be father and son, he and Master Vardo. Or brothers. Hatched from the same egg.

But the herald had not yet finished:

'The Prince's own daughter and dear guest, Her Grace Dama Lizea,' he shouted, and in the Prince's wake a woman entered, dressed magnificently in sweeping blue silk, with a net of silver and pearls over her black hair. Two white streaks in the black looked almost as if they were there on purpose. But it was hardly on purpose that her face was so emaciated that it looked like a skull covered with just a thin layer of skin.

Lady Death. That had been Dina's name for her.

Drakan's mother – who knew Nico excellently well.

There was no way we could run. We couldn't even get up from the table. We were shackled to Mascha and the others, who in turn were chained to the heavy oak table. Nico could do nothing except duck his head and hope that Dama Lizea belonged to the ignore-them type of noble, and not the staring kind. Luckily, they hadn't been too literal about 'the Prince's own table' – there was quite a bit of distance from our corner of the banquet hall to the High Table, where Prince Arthos and Dama Lizea were now seated.

'What are we going to do if she sees you?' I whispered to Nico.

'Nothing,' said Nico. 'And especially not you. There is no reason to give them an excuse to chop *both* our heads off.'

Apparently, he was in no doubt what would happen to him if Lizea recognized him.

Another flurry of trumpets, and the first course was served. It was flounder, prepared with some kind of white sauce. Carle took a bit of fish with his fingers and was about to pop it in his mouth, but the guard behind him slapped his fingers and hissed, 'Not yet!' as if he were some kind of governess hired to teach proper manners to a bunch of unruly children.

An Educator – was it Vardo? I thought it might be – stepped forward from his position just behind the Prince's chair.

'Let us all thank the Prince for the meal he

305

so generously grants us, and let us pray that it may strengthen our limbs and nourish our minds so that we may better serve him. The Prince!'

'*The Prince!*' It was like a roar, reverberating round the hall, as if everyone except us was trying to see who could shout the loudest.

And only then was Carle allowed to eat his fish.

Nico sat bent over his plate, picking at the pale fish with his fork. He had grown a beard since coming to the Highlands, and right now it was even fuller than usual. Was it enough to disguise him? I doubted it. He looked very much like himself, beard or no.

I ate a bit of flounder. It tasted strongly of something very tart. Lemon, perhaps, from the orangeries of the Palace. My mouth was so dry that I had difficulty swallowing, but it would be too conspicuous if we didn't eat. Around us, the rest of the gang were shovelling food down their throats as if they had never had anything like it. Which they probably hadn't. Certainly not during the months and years they had been prisoners of the Sagisburg.

Another bray of trumpets. At once, people around us put down their knives and forks and were silent. The Prince had risen to his feet. He was watching the gathering with his head slightly tilted to one side. That and the hood made him look a bit like a bird of prey, I thought, a hawk, or perhaps an eagle.

'We have unusual company today,' he said. 'Men who this morning woke in the lowest dungeons of this castle are now seated in our midst, among silks and velvets. They learned. Let others be equally enlightened. He who once was low may be elevated. And they who sit in high places may be brought low – if that is the will of the Prince.'

The silence deepened. I think most of the guests held their breaths. This was a warning to them, that much was obvious. A warning not to feel too smug, too safe. All they had to do was look at us to know where they could end up if they displeased their Prince.

IN EVERY THING A LESSON it said above the door of the House of Teaching. And it seemed as if the entire castle was one big house of teaching, and the lesson everywhere was the same: bow before the Prince – or be broken.

Everyone was looking at us, even those who at the beginning had ignored us. I tried to read Dama Lizea's face, but she seemed not to have noticed Nico in particular.

The Prince sat down. Accompanied by yet more trumpetry the next course was served, and I breathed a little more easily. I glanced at Nico. Tiny beads of sweat glistened on his cheekbones and forehead, and although he continued to put food in his mouth, I don't think he tasted a thing.

I would never have thought anyone could long for a dark, evil-smelling, flea-infested dungeon. But right now I was sure that both Nico and I would rather have been lying on the dirty straw in the Gullet than sitting here staring down at platters full of pheasant and green grapes.

Hundreds of candles hung above our heads, on chandeliers the size of wagon wheels. Nico was not the only one sweating. Mascha's beardless face was flushed from the heat and the wine, and sweat beaded Carle's face too, as he cheerfully stuffed his face with pheasant meat, not bothering with such niceties as a knife and fork.

Suddenly the captain of the Prince's Own was at the end of our table.

'The Prince wishes to know which one of you has the ability to read,' he said.

Mascha hadn't drunk enough to lose his ingrained wariness. 'Why?' he said cautiously.

But Carle, who had drunk more than his fill, was less hesitant. 'My friend Nico here,' he said, slapping Nico amiably on one shoulder with greasy pheasant fingers. 'And Davin, the sneaky bastard. They know a thing or two, the pair of them. The Educators never reckoned on that, did they?'

The guard captain jerked his head at two of his men. 'Unshackle them,' he said. 'The Prince wishes to speak to them.'

'I'm the one who can read,' I said quickly, getting up. 'Nico was just following my orders.'

The man loosening Nico's fetters paused.

'Rubbish!' said Carle, loudly and none too clearly. 'Don't go takin' all the credit, now.'

Mascha, who had caught on to the fact that something was afoot, tried to hush Carle up, but it was too late.

'Is he coming or not?' said Nico's guard.

'Take both of them,' said the guard captain.

I looked around quickly, but we were surrounded by guards. It was impossible to run. And if we tried, they would know for sure that there was something fishy about us. What prisoner tries to escape just as he may be about to receive a princely reward?

They led us through the hall to the High Table. Only a few seats away, on the Prince's right-hand side, Dama Lizea sat talking to her neighbour, her face turned away from us. I fervently hoped the conversation was so fascinating that she wouldn't even spare us a glance.

Prince Arthos, on the other hand, tilted his head and looked at us in his predatory manner.

'And how is it,' he said slowly, 'that my dungeon has come to hold two men who know how to spell JUSTICE?'

'My friend is a tutor,' I said quickly, so that Nico wouldn't have to answer. 'We had no idea that a royal permission was necessary to teach a child in Sagisloc.'

'A tutor. I see. And what is the name of such a tutor?'

'Nicolas,' I said. 'And I am Davin.'

The only thought in my head was how to keep them from finding out who Nico really was. I didn't even consider lying about my own name. But as soon as the word had left my mouth, I knew I had been stupid. Because Dama Lizea's head snapped round as if pulled by an invisible string.

She looked at me. And then she caught sight of Nico, and really stared. And then she began to laugh. 'A tutor. Well, well. I suppose that is what he is best suited for, now that I think of it.'

Prince Arthos was clearly puzzled by her behaviour. 'Will Medama explain herself?' he said acidly.

Dama Lizea smiled. 'That,' she said, pointing at Nico with an emaciated finger, 'is Nicodemus Ravens. And if

309

I am not mistaken, his ragged friend there is Davin Tonerre, who killed My Lord Prince's own grandson.'

Prince Arthos stared at us for a long moment.

'Take them to the council chamber,' he said. 'Shackle them. And send for the executioner.'

We waited for a long time in the council chamber while Prince Arthos finished his banquet. He was not a man to rush things, it seemed, and what with the fetters, the shackles and four guards, it wasn't as if we were going anywhere.

Finally he came, with Master Vardo and four bodyguards. Even in the heart of his own castle, he apparently guarded himself as well as he guarded his prisoners.

He seated himself in a high-backed chair, not quite a throne, but almost, and regarded Nico and me for a while, as though we were some sort of puzzle he meant to solve.

'Ebnezer Ravens' son,' he finally said. 'What do you mean by coming here?'

Nico bowed as well as the chains allowed.

'Nothing ill,' he said. 'And I do not believe there ever was enmity before now between my house and the house of Draconis.'

A faint snort from the princely nostrils.

'Where are your men?'

'Men? I have no men.'

'Do not try to deceive me. I know well enough that my daughter's ambitious son encounters resistance to his plans. I have heard of ambush, weapon raids and espionage. If those men are not yours, whose are they?'

Nico inclined his head. 'I know that such things are done in my name. But I have no men, nor do I want any.'

There was a slight movement at the corner of the Prince's mouth – a disbelieving twitch. That Nico would not want to have anyone under him – that was too alien a thought for someone who had clung so tightly to his power for more than a generation.

'Is the executioner on his way?' he asked one of the guards.

'Not yet, My Lord Prince.'

'Why not?'

The guard looked ill at ease. 'He . . . he sometimes drinks a little, My Lord Prince. Perhaps they have difficulty in rousing him.'

'I see. It would appear we have need of a new axeman. Note that, Vardo.'

Vardo nodded. 'As My Lord Prince commands.'

'Is it My Lord's intention to have me executed?' asked Nico. He sounded almost as if he was inquiring into Prince Arthos's breakfast plans or some other insignificant thing. I didn't know how he could do it. But there was something about Nico now, something I was not used to seeing. A smooth coolness, a courteous self-control. Perhaps these were court manners. Perhaps this was what you learned when you were the son of a castellan.

'Most likely,' said Prince Arthos. 'But I am a thrifty man, young Ravens. I do not discard what may be useful to me.'

The door burst open, so suddenly that the Prince's bodyguard came close to drawing their swords. But it was not enemies from without who had entered the chamber; on the threshold stood Dama Lizea, the Prince's own daughter. She looked at Nico and me with an icy glare.

'Not yet dead?' she said. 'Why so indecisive, Sire?'

It obviously didn't please the Prince to be interrupted.

'My daughter has a hasty nature,' he told Master Vardo. 'So hasty as to border on shamelessness at times.'

'Sire!' Indignation made Dama Lizea's face look even tighter. 'I have not deserved such words of you.'

'No? Had you been less hasty, my dear, and waited to be wed *before* you went to your marriage bed, your son would now be the rightful heir of Dunark, and the House of the Dragon might have been spared much shame.'

Dama Lizea's glare was edged like a sword-blade as she stared at her father. She was silent for so long that it was obvious she had to struggle to maintain her self-control.

'My son,' she finally managed with only a slight tremor to her voice, 'is conquering the West. My Lord Prince and Father holds sway over most of the East. If you would but stretch out your hand to him as a grandfather should, he would make the House of the Dragon rulers of the entire Skay-Sagis!'

'He lacks nothing in ambition, one must grant him that,' said Prince Arthos with a certain dryness. 'But why should I support an upstart lordling who cannot keep order in his own house?'

'He is your own blood!'

'He is a bastard whose own father would not recognize him.'

'My Lord Father!'

'Is this not why his own people arm themselves against him? Yes, daughter, I have heard of the rebels you would rather not mention. I have heard of stolen weaponry and ambush and seasoned soldiers deserting to support *him*.' He jabbed a finger at Nico like a spear-point. 'Ebnezer's true-born heir. Well? What do you say to that, my daughter?'

A sound escaped her, a hiss of anger and contempt.

'Kill him,' she said. 'Execute him here and now, and all resistance will melt away.'

'If My Lord Prince acknowledges my heritage, he knows that killing me would be a grave misdeed,' said Nico calmly. 'Once we start executing true-born rulers – where will it end? Is any prince then safe?'

It was the first time I had ever heard Nico refer to himself as a ruler. He often fought over it with Master Maunus. Why should he risk his life to rule Dunark? But he had probably guessed that Prince Arthos would hesitate a little longer over the shedding of noble blood.

I covertly licked my dry lips. There was not a single drop of noble blood in my veins, so there was no reason for Prince Arthos to hesitate on my account.

Dama Lizea threw a cold look at Nico. Then she repeated her demand.

'Kill him, and all resistance will die with him.'

'Or increase tenfold because his death inflames the

wrath of the people? He serves us better as a hostage than as a martyr.'

'If you are too soft to kill him, leave him to me.'

Prince Arthos looked up at Master Vardo, who was still standing at his side.

'What do you think, Master? Should I let my axeman do Drakan the favour of killing off his rival? So that the dragonet my shameless daughter has spawned can grow another inch?'

'My Lord Prince put it well,' murmured Vardo courteously. 'It is foolish to discard what may be of use. And an heir to the House of Ravens may be useful indeed – if trained right.'

Prince Arthos regarded Nico keenly, as though Nico was a book in a foreign language that he must try to read.

'Tell me, Young Ravens . . . Did you love your father?'

The question clearly startled Nico, and I could well understand that. What on earth had that to do with anything? And in any case, I knew it was not an easy question for Nico to answer, after everything that had passed between the two of them.

'He was my father,' he finally said.

'Yes, at least you can say that much. More than young Drakan can swear to.' A strange sort of gasp followed, sounding as if he had swallowed something the wrong way – only this, I realized, was the Prince's laughter.

'I do not think my daughter loves me,' he said. 'But one need not love in order to serve. Though I must say she has been no faithful servant either.' He looked at her for a moment, and she returned his irritated glance with a rebellious expression. Then he turned his attention to Nico once more.

'If I let you live, Young Ravens – would you serve me?'

Nico was silent for a while. For much too long, I thought. Then he shook his head.

'I . . . cannot promise that.'

'Hmmm,' snorted the Prince. 'More honesty than wisdom, I see. Very well. I can appreciate an honest man. A shame one meets so very few. But if I released you. If I put you on the throne of Dunark . . . what then?'

Dama Lizea practically spat. 'My Lord Father, that would not—'

'Silence!' barked the old man, and his daughter bit her lip and subsided.

Nico might be honest, but he was not entirely stupid. 'Under whose rule?' he asked.

'Mine,' said Prince Arthos. 'And . . . Drakan's. He has the army. One must also recognize the power of the sword.'

He hadn't reached the age of ninety, I supposed, without learning a thing or two along the way. If Nico agreed, then the resistance the Weapons Master was trying to build would crumble like a badly built house. The rightful heir would be the castellan of Dunark. But Drakan would still remain as Overlord over the entire western coastlands.

Nico took a deep breath and grimaced. 'No,' he said. 'It wouldn't work. It's probably better that you kill me.'

Oh, Nico, why can't you lie? Couldn't you just say you agree, and then do as you please once we are out of here? But apparently he couldn't. You had to admire that stubborn honesty of his, I supposed, but right then I wished he had just a bit less of it.

Prince Arthos nodded slowly. 'The Ravens always were a stubborn family,' he said. 'Stiffnecks, the lot of them. But even stiff necks may learn to bend. Take him, Vardo. See if you can make me a faithful servant out of him.'

Nico looked uneasy. More so now than when the talk had been about executions and the like. I didn't quite understand him. Having acted in one of Master Vardo's little educational performances I was in no hurry to be part of another one. But it was still better, wasn't it, than being the main attraction on the scaffold?

Dama Lizea looked like a cat who had been cheated out of half its prey, but she knew better than to defy her father's will openly.

'The Shamer's son, then?' she said. 'We can execute him, at least. No one will make a martyr out of him.'

'People know him,' said Nico quickly. 'And they know his mother. His death will arouse much anger.'

Blood hammered through my body, loud enough to roar in my ears. If only I had been able to run, or hit somebody, *do* something. Standing here like this, bound and helplessly waiting while others coolly decided whether to kill me or not . . . it was unbearable. It was just as well that I had Nico to speak on my behalf, because I couldn't manage a single word. But I was afraid there wasn't much Nico could do. Dama Lizea was right – my death would not make half the stir that Nico's would.

She was smiling now.

'Oh, I doubt there will be much outcry because we hang a simple murderer,' she said.

'I am no murderer,' I said angrily, finding I had a tongue after all.

Now it was my turn to be spitted by the Prince's predatory gaze.

'Did you not kill my grandson Valdracu?'

I fought a strong urge to stare at my feet, but denying it would do no good. Dama Lizea obviously knew all about events in Hog's Gorge. A few of Valdracu's men must have escaped to tell the tale.

'Yes,' I said hoarsely. 'But it was . . . in battle.' While Valdracu was crawling through the mud of the Gorge, but I tried not to think of that. He would have killed Dina. I had had to stop him as best I could.

'There you are, Sire. He does not even bother to deny it.'

Prince Arthos tilted his head to look at me.

'We may execute him at any time. It seems to me a little . . . lacking in imagination. It would entertain me more to see what Vardo can make of him. Perhaps . . . an executioner. I seem to be in need of a new one. Yes. That would be very suitable. He seems to have the knack.'

I stared at him in disgust. Did the old vulture really think that I would ever lift a sword for him? Would kill at his word? No. Better my own neck on the block.

A servant came to whisper something in the Prince's ear. Prince Arthos nodded briefly. Then he rose from his chair.

'Take them both, Vardo,' he said. 'And teach them well.'

Master Vardo bowed, and I was almost certain that I saw the shadow of a smile play at the corners of his beardless mouth.

'As My Lord pleases,' he said. But it occurred to me that it might also please Master Vardo quite well. He regarded us for a moment. Then he nodded at the guards.

'Take them to the Hall of the Whisperers,' he said.

THIRTY-ONE

The Hall of the Whisperers

Vardo stopped in front of a massive-looking door on heavy iron hinges.

'Unchain them,' he told the guards. 'There is nowhere for them to run.'

He didn't say it in any threatening tone of voice, but it still sounded . . . ominous. I glanced at Nico. He looked uneasy too. I knew he would be thinking mainly of one thing: would it be dark in there?

The Educator unlocked the door and put his hand on Nico's arm. Nico didn't shrug it off, but he looked as if he wanted to.

'The Hall of the Whisperers,' said Vardo. 'Listen and learn.'

I stepped across the threshold without waiting for the guards to shove me, and so did Nico. There was no reason to give them an excuse to rough us up. The door fell shut behind us, and Vardo's key rattled in the lock. The Hall of the Whisperers? Why did they call it that?

At least it wasn't completely dark. Shafts of dim blue

light filtered down from somewhere above us. I took a few steps forwards, and Nico followed.

It wasn't so much a hall as a long gallery. Our steps echoed between grey stone walls, an echo that wouldn't go away. I looked up. And up. The vaulted ceiling was so high it hardly seemed like a ceiling, more like a . . . a distant, dark sky. Or dark treetops in a forest. And then there were the faces. They were everywhere – on the walls, the vaults and columns, even in the floor.

Stone faces, of course, and it wasn't as if I thought they were real, but it still unnerved me a little. Every single one of them had its mouth open, a dark and gaping hole that seemed bottomless. I shivered. It was almost as if one could hear their silent cries. Were they the Whisperers?

There was a door at the other end of the gallery. I tried the handle just to be sure, but it was locked, of course, and as massive as the one we had entered by. No escape. The Educator had been right – chains were unnecessary here.

At least it was not a dark, damp and flea-infested dungeon. It could have been worse.

Nico turned slowly, looking at the stone faces.

'They're watching us,' he said. 'Everywhere.'

His voice echoed strangely under the vaulted ceilings.

. . . watching us . . . watching . . . watching . . .

. . . ware . . . ware . . . beware . . .

'Watching?' I said. 'I think it looks more as if they're yelling at us.'

The echoes started up again, blending with the slightly weaker echoes of Nico's voice.

... yelling ... yelling ... yell ... hell ...

... ware ... hell ... ware ... hell ...

I shivered again. I didn't like the way the echo kept whispering at me. It made me almost afraid to talk.

I found a place where I could crouch without sitting on top of a face, and leaned back against the wall behind me. Then I straightened again. There was a strange rustling and buzzing as I touched the wall. As if it was a live thing. Not live as a human being, perhaps, but the way a forest was alive, or ... or something more alien and magical. What was this place? Even though Nico and I had both been quiet for a good while, it was still not silent. A tuneless whistling, a hissing, a whispering ... was there a wind somewhere, passing through the open mouths, in or out, as if they had breath? Perhaps their cries weren't as soundless as I had first supposed.

Nico spun, staring at me. 'What did you say?'

'Nothing. Not a word.'

... word ... word ... word ...

... word ... hurt ... hurt ...

His eyes looked haunted. 'I'm sorry. I thought ...'

... sorry ... sorry ... sorry ...

... thought ... ought ... ought ...

Nico didn't finish his sentence. I never found out what he thought.

... sorry ... sorry ... sorry ... the gaping faces kept whispering. And suddenly I thought I could hear something else, something more, something that couldn't just be the echo of what we had said:

... sorrow ... sorrow ...

... sorry and small ...

321

I got up quickly. The small noise of my rising surged through the gallery and came back to me sounding as if a hundred invisible people had suddenly moved, as if a hundred shoes had scraped against stone floors, and a hundred sleeves brushed against the wall.

. . . evil and small . . .

. . . cowardly small . . .

There *was* someone whispering. Narrowing my eyes, I peered at the faces, but didn't think mouths carved in stone could talk like living people. The masks stared back at me. I licked my dry lips. They really were staring at us. There was a glimmer of light in some of those empty eyes. No, I didn't believe it, but . . .

. . . sorry and small . . .

. . . cowardly creature . . .

. . . evil . . . evil . . . evil . . .

The accusing whisper kept on and on. Where was it coming from?

'Is there anyone here?'

. . . hear . . . hear . . . hear . . .

. . . anyone . . . one . . . one . . .

. . . one who has killed . . .

. . . here . . .

. . . here . . .

. . . murderer . . .

So softly. Almost inaudible — but I heard it. One who has killed. Murderer.

'I'm not a—'

I stopped myself with an effort before I flung that last word at the walls. I didn't want to hear them whisper *murder murder murder* at me for the next hour or so.

I stood there tensely, poised to run though there was nowhere to run to. My heart pounded along, and though my body was screaming for rest, I couldn't make myself sit down again.

'Shut up. Can't you be still?' cried Nico, loudly, desperately, so that I leaped like a frightened colt.

. . . still . . . still . . . still . . . whispered the walls.

. . . so still . . . so dead . . .

. . . dead . . . dead . . . dead . . .

Before my eyes, one of the stone faces changed into a human face, a face I knew. Or had known. It was Valdracu's face I saw, with Valdracu's dying gaze, and his throat half cut and the blood spurting.

'No!'

I couldn't hold back the word. And the echo seized it and gave it back to me.

. . . no . . . no . . .

. . . no life . . .

. . . coward and murderer . . .

. . . you . . .

I pressed my knuckles against my teeth to keep myself from calling out, from saying anything at all, from trying to drown the accusation in an angry shout. Valdracu stared at me, blood running from his throat. I closed my eyes and stumbled backwards, but when I opened them again, he was still there, only in a different place, four places, five places . . . a hundred Valdracu eyes were staring at me, dying, dead, like the eyes of a butchered pig. And it *was* me, I *had* killed him, hacking at him from behind while he was crawling in the mud. I had butchered him, yes – like one butchers a pig. Murder. Coward. Small and sorry.

I was crouched in the middle of the floor with no memory of having sat down. I wrapped my arms around my head like someone expecting a blow, but I still couldn't shut out the sound, the stubborn whisper telling me I was a murderer, a weak and sorry coward who stabbed people from behind.

. . . sorry . . . sorry . . . sorry . . .

'Davin . . .'

It took me a moment to realize that that voice was not one of the Whisperers', but Nico's. Slowly, I opened my eyes.

'Davin, please . . . tell me. Is there blood on my hands now?'

I stared at him. His face was grey, and his eyes utterly despairing. He looked like someone more than halfway mad. He held out his hands in front of him with spread fingers, keeping them stiffly away from his body, as if afraid of soiling his clothes.

'No,' I said. 'No blood.'

. . . no . . . no . . . no . . .

. . . blood . . . blood . . . blood . . .

He drew in his breath in what sounded almost like a sob.

'Are you sure?'

'Yes.'

'Thank God.'

But the walls kept whispering . . . blood . . . blood . . . blood . . . for a long time after that.

★ ★ ★

I don't know how long it was before they came to get us. It was dark outside, but it couldn't still be the same night. Could it? We had been in there longer. We had been in there for ever. Perhaps it was the next night. My lips were dry and cracked from thirst, but it didn't matter. The only thing that mattered was the silence. In the Hall of the Whisperers there was no sleep, only nightmares. Only one thing worse than being awake – and that was falling asleep.

They led us along a short passage and into two separate chambers. I was so dizzy that the guards had to support me, and when they closed the door behind me I didn't even think of checking whether they locked it.

The room was small and bare, with naked white walls. Moonlight streamed through a small square window. And it was silent.

Oh, the silence.

I drank it in as though it were water.

I dropped down on to the narrow pallet, drew the blanket over my head and fell into deep, deep sleep.

Only not for long. When the guards shook me awake, the moon was still in the sky. Same moon. Or at least I thought so.

Master Vardo waited until he was sure that I was not asleep on my feet.

'Here, my son,' he said, offering me a beaker. 'Drink.'

My hands were shaking, and I sniffed suspiciously at the cup, but it seemed to be just water. I drank in long greedy gulps.

'Look at the cup, my son.'

I turned it in my hand. The dragon mark of the Draconis was stamped into the metal.

'You have nothing. Everything good – water, food, rest and life itself – comes to you by the hand of the Prince. Show your gratitude, my son. Kiss the dragon.'

I looked at Vardo. Everything about him was clad in black except the hairless, beardless face. It floated over me like a mask, a mask with no body and no human soul behind it. He reminded me of the Whisperers.

'Go to hell,' I said hoarsely and slung the beaker on the floor. It hit the tiles with a bell-like chime.

Vardo did not move a muscle. His beardless features might have been carved from stone. He nodded briefly at the guards, and they seized my arms.

'Back to the Whisperers,' was all he said.

This time, I fought them. I dug in my heels and fought them with everything I had, hitting, biting and kicking, never mind that it made my back split and bleed all over again. But they were wearing mail shirts and gauntlets, and I hurt myself more than them, I think. One of them lost his patience and clouted my ear with a mailed fist.

Master Vardo stopped him.

'Guardsmaster. If you have to hit him, make it a body blow. His head must be clear.'

A clear head was the last thing I wanted. Passing out would suit me just fine right now, but I wasn't that lucky.

They dragged me into the gallery and flung me down on the grey stone floor. One of them kicked my stomach, rather casually, just to keep me occupied until they had left the Hall, I think.

I curled up, hugging the pain to me as if it could blank out everything else. There was a roaring in my ears, especially the one touching the cool, smooth tile.

. . . killer . . . killer . . . killer . . .

'Shut up,' I whispered. 'Leave me alone . . .'

. . . lone . . . lone . . . lone . . .

. . . leave . . . leave . . . leave . . .

The sound of the door opening and closing again momentarily drowned the whispering voices. Footsteps reverberated round the Hall.

'Davin?' A hand touched my shoulder.

It was Nico, of course. His face was still almost as grey as the stone, and there was a movement by one eye, as if some tiny animal caught under the skin was struggling to get out.

'Nico.' I began to sit up and then gave up the effort. It hurt my stomach too much.

'Did they hurt you? Are you . . . in pain?'

. . . hurt . . . hurt . . . hurt . . .

. . . pain . . . pain . . . pain . . .

I was, of course, to some extent, but I shook my head. It wasn't so bad, and I was feeling almost grateful for the pain because it had made it possible to think of something other than the whispering voices for a little while. But the faces behind Nico had already begun to change. They were glaring at me, full of scorn and accusation. Light glittered in the empty eye holes, cold as contempt itself.

. . . coward . . . they whispered . . . sorry . . . cowardly . . . killer . . .

Valdracu's eyes were on me again. The blood was dripping from his throat.

327

I turned to Nico, to the only face I was sure was real. He stood there hunched up with exhaustion, hugging himself, and hiding his hands in his armpits.

'Is there blood on your hands now?' I asked.

. . . blood on your hands . . . blood on your hands . . .

He nodded. 'I see it all the time now.'

'Why?'

'In Dunark . . . in the cell. I had blood on my hands then, and on my clothes. My father's blood, and Adela's, and little Bian's. And they didn't let me wash. Not until Dina came and shamed them into it. I sat there for a day and a night with my dead family's blood on my hands.'

I suddenly remembered the day I had tossed a dead rabbit at him. Now I knew why he had been in such a hurry to scour off the blood.

'It wasn't you who killed them,' I said.

. . . killed them . . . killed them . . . killed them . . .

. . . you who killed them . . .

'Davin, please don't say any more.'

any more . . . any more . . . not alive any more . . .

'But you didn't!' I persisted, loudly, so as to drown out the Whisperers. 'Drakan did!'

'And I made it possible! If I hadn't gone . . .' He broke off.

. . . gone . . . gone . . . gone . . . whispered the walls.

'When my brother died, I promised Adela that she could always come to me. That I would look out for her. But where was I when Drakan killed them? Dead drunk in my chambers. Or in hers. I don't even know that. Can't you see that it's my fault they are dead?'

His voice had risen to a shout. dead dead dead echoed

328

back and forth, so sonorously that for a while it overwhelmed the hissing scorn of the Whisperers.

'At least you didn't stab anybody from behind,' I muttered bitterly.

. . . stab from behind . . . stab from behind . . .

. . . murderer . . . coward . . . stabs from behind . . .

Nico tilted his head almost like Prince Arthos. He was listening to something, but I wasn't sure he heard the same things I heard.

'I think it's best if we say no more,' he finally said.

I only nodded, while the walls whispered their . . . no more . . . no more . . . the dead live no more . . .

Sorry coward. Killer. Murderer. Was it inside my head or outside? It wasn't just Valdracu's face I saw now. Dead eyes were staring at me from dead faces, and sometimes the faces were Mama's, or Melli's, or Dina's. At some point it occurred to me that I might be able to knock myself out. If I beat my head against the floor hard enough . . .

It didn't work. All I got for my pains was a worse headache than I already had. My throat was as dry and parched as if I had been screaming for hours. And the whispering voices had not faded. On the contrary. There was a constant rushing roar in my head, and the roar had words in it.

. . . evil . . . killer . . . sorry coward . . .

If only I could sleep. But when I closed my eyes, I saw even worse things than when I kept them open.

Nico shook my shoulder.

'Davin. Look!'

329

He held something up in front of my eyes. A . . .
a doll, I suppose it was meant to be. Clumsily made
from rags and string, with eyes and mouth drawn in
coal.

'I found it behind that column.'

His eyes were no longer so guilt-ridden and inward-
turned. They flashed with fury.

I couldn't quite understand his outrage.

'Don't you see what this means?' he said.

I shook my head numbly. And what did it matter
whether I understood or not. I was just a sorry coward
anyway. Coward and killer.

. . . killer . . . killer . . . killer . . .

'They do this to *children*!'

I licked my lips, or tried to. It was as if my mouth
contained no spit at all.

'That's a shame,' I croaked.

. . . shame . . . shame . . . shame . . .

'Davin. We can't let them win.'

I looked at Nico. The blood was pouring down his
throat. How could he talk when his throat had been
half cut? I closed my eyes. Opened them again. The
blood was still there.

'I'm not sure I can stand this,' I said. 'I just want it to
stop.'

. . . stop . . . stop . . . whispered the walls.

But there was no end to it, and no escape.

I was lying on the floor even though it made the
voices clearer. I couldn't keep upright any more. Master
Vardo was standing in the doorway. He was saying

something to Nico, but I couldn't hear the words, my ears were too full of whispers. Nico shook his head and turned his back on the Educator. A guard spun him around and forced him to his knees, and Master Vardo spoke again, holding out his hand. I don't know what Nico did, but it must have displeased Master Vardo, because shortly afterwards there was a cry of pain from Nico, loud enough to drown the Whisperers for a little while. He was lying curled up on the floor now, and the guards stepped over him and came towards me.

I tried to get up, but my legs wouldn't take my weight. The guards seized my arms and dragged me forward, until I was lying at Master Vardo's feet.

'How are you, my son?' he asked.

Old stoneface, I thought. A lot you care.

'Answer the Educator,' said one of the guards and hauled me to my knees.

'No,' said Vardo. 'He doesn't have to speak. It is sufficient if he shows his willing spirit.' He held out his hand to me. His gloved black hand bore a ring with the double dragon, crafted in silver. 'Kiss it.'

No way. Over my dead body. You can take your rotten dragon mark and go to hell.

That was what I thought, but I didn't say any of it. From the walls, Valdracu's dead eyes were staring down at me, and I felt small and sorry and cowardly.

I kissed the dragon.

'Well done, my son,' said Master Vardo. 'Now you may rest.'

★ ★ ★

It was still dark outside. Had another day passed? Two, even? Or had the sun decided never to rise again? The room was the same one, small and bare, just the pallet and the white walls. I lay down, stretching my bruised and battered body. Silence. Sleep. Thousands of people all over the world had both every night, every day, for hours. They had no idea how precious a gift it was, the silence. I closed my eyes.

small . . . sorry . . . cowardly . . .

killer . . . killer . . .

'No!'

I leaped to my feet. Looked around wildly. White walls. Moonlight. No stone faces. And yet, I could still hear them.

sorry . . . cowardly . . . killer . . .

My legs buckled, and I fell back down on the pallet. Tears burned my face. I had done what he told me to do. I had kissed his damn dragon, though it made me sick to think of it. And still I couldn't sleep. Still I felt small, and sorry, and cowardly. Even more so.

My breath came in harsh, jagged sobs. I wanted it to stop. I wanted everything to stop. I turned my face to the white wall and felt like the sorriest human being on earth.

THIRTY-TWO

The Golden Cup

He has courage, I'll say that. That's what people often said about me, or something like it. And I had been proud of that. I had this idea of myself as someone who dared more than most. Dared ride the fastest horses, and the wildest. Dared fight, even with those I knew were stronger than me. I admired brave people. Callan, for example, and others who put themselves in harm's way without showing fear.

I suppose I had also felt a fair amount of contempt for those who weren't so brave. Gutless. Wimp. Yellowbelly. Coward. Oh yes, there were names aplenty.

Nico was afraid of the dark. More than afraid – terrified. He didn't like swords and would rather run away than fight. He couldn't even skin a rabbit without getting the shakes. But Nico hadn't kissed the dragon. And I had.

And if they wanted me to do it again, what then? Or if they wanted me to do worse things? *It would entertain me more to see what Vardo can make of him*, Prince Arthos had said. *Perhaps . . . an executioner.* And I had sworn to

333

myself that I would rather die than kill on his orders. But what if that was not the choice? What if the choice was – kill, or go back to the Hall of the Whisperers? The mere thought made something inside me curl up and break, like straw in a fire. I was scared. I was so scared that I didn't think I could ever be brave again.

Weak. Sorry. A gutless coward.

Nico wasn't any of those things. I was.

If only I had been able to sleep. But the Whisperers had bored their way into my skull, like maggots in a sheep's brain.

I leaned against the wall next to the window. Outside the wall dropped steeply and dizzyingly down. The moon shone on sharp rocks far below me, and on the black waters of the lake. If someone was to fall . . . there would be silence. No voices. Nothing. But the window was too small, I couldn't squeeze through.

Morning. I stood by the window, watching it dawn, from the first faint rose-gold warning to the full white sunlight of a summer's day. There was such a good smell from outside, of lake winds and warm rock. I had dozed now and then, I supposed, upright, leaning on the wall. But to sleep properly, deeply and without dreams . . . no. It had been beyond me.

Further off, I heard tradesmen reporting at the gates with their goods, and washerwomen teasing each other and giggling over what one's daughter had been doing with the other's son last night. It was so strange to think that all that continued. That the world outside was ordinary and full of everyday living, that there were people out there thinking about what might be for dinner, or what price they might get for two sacks of barley and a cartload of kale. While I was in here, knowing now that I was someone other than I thought I was, and Nico was on the stone floor in the Whisperers' Hall, losing his mind bit by bit, whisper by scornful whisper.

The door opened. In the passage outside stood Master Vardo, accompanied by the same two guards who had dragged me back to the Hall of the Whisperers the last time.

'Come here, my son,' he said.

If I obeyed, would they spare me the Whisperers? Would he give me water again?

'Master,' I said, hoarsely. 'I'm thirsty.'

'Yes,' he said. 'Soon, you will drink. If you are brave and obedient and serve the will of the Prince.'

Brave. I would never be brave again. My heart sank. What did the Prince want me to do?

They led me through the castle and down the long stairs to the dock we had arrived at that first evening. Outside the cavern, sunlight played on the living water, and above our heads, bats hung in clusters from the ceiling, like bunches of dark, furry fruits.

Two more guards came down the steps, holding Nico. His eyes flickered around the cave, from me to the boats by the dock, to Master Vardo, then back to me again. There was an accusation in that look, I thought, and I dropped my glance. Weak. Cowardly. Oh, he didn't need to say it. I knew what he was thinking.

Something stirred inside me, something sickening and nasty. An anger, as slow and cold as a reptile's. Who did he think he was? What gave him the right to look at me like that, so superior and condemning? Just because he had seen me kiss Master Vardo's dragon ring. What was so terrible about that? Under the circumstances, it was the only sensible thing to do. Only fools tortured themselves unnecessarily. Fools like Nico.

Master Vardo put his gloved hand on my arm – the hand wearing the dragon ring.

'Look at me, my son,' he said softly, and I was suddenly reminded of my mother. It shook me, because what could Master Vardo possibly have in common with a Shamer?

More, apparently, than you would think. At any rate, I raised my eyes to meet his, even though I didn't want to.

'What is your deepest desire right now?' he asked.

'Water,' I said without thinking. I was so terribly thirsty. 'And sleep.'

Master Vardo nodded, as if that was the correct answer. I breathed more easily. So far, I had done nothing wrong.

'I can give you both,' he said.

Then he moved over to Nico and put his hand on Nico's arm also.

'Look at me, Nicodemus.'

It took longer, with Nico. But in the end, he too looked up to meet the Master's eyes.

'What is your deepest desire right now?'

Nico stared silently at the Educator for a very long

time. When he finally spoke, there was defiance in his tone.

'Freedom,' he said, glancing at the cave mouth and the blue air outside.

'No,' said Master Vardo. 'Wish for something else.'

Nico just shook his head. Vardo frowned.

'Nicodemus, I'll have you know that the Prince in his mercy has granted me the power to grant a wish of yours. Do you want to mock that mercy with your obstinacy?'

Nico looked gaugingly at Master Vardo.

'Very well, then,' he said. 'Mira's freedom.'

'Mira? Aurelius's daughter?'

'Yes. If the Prince is sincere in his wish to be merciful, then let Mira go home to her parents.'

Master Vardo studied Nico for a very long time. Then he nodded.

'As you wish. It is within my power. If you can earn it. The Prince wishes to test your faith, courage and strength. In the water, a precious treasure lies hidden – a golden cup. He who finds this cup and delivers it into my hands shall be rewarded by the granting of his wish. The one that fails in this task . . . he must return to the Hall of the Whisperers until he has learned to serve better.'

He nodded at the guards, and they let go of us.

'Begin,' ordered the Educator.

Nico was at the edge of the dock in three paces. I was only slightly slower. We both threw ourselves into the water as if we meant to save a drowning man.

The water was cold. It was more than cold. The chill

numbed me instantly, and for a moment I was afraid my heart might stop. But Nico had already begun his dive, and if I didn't find the cup before he did . . . they would drag me back to the Hall of the Whisperers and leave me there, until I lost my mind completely, or found some way of killing myself.

I took a deep breath and dived. The water was glass-clear like ice, and deep. It was a green and white world down here, a mountainscape with rocky spires and deep valleys, dark as night. A little ahead of me, I saw Nico. He was swimming downwards with strong strokes, and tiny bubbles from his hair and clothes rose behind him in a glittering stream, almost like smoke.

I couldn't see the cup anywhere. The blood was singing in my ears, and I was nearly out of air. But Nico still hadn't turned back. If he found the cup before me . . .

I took another few desperate strokes, but my arms barely obeyed me, and there was a burning in my chest as if my lungs were on fire. I couldn't stand it any more. If I stayed down here a second longer, I would drown. I streaked back up to the surface, treading water while I snatched air in huge, sobbing gasps. Then I dived again.

A shadow in the water, a movement . . . Nico streaked past me, on his way up. Had he – no. His hands were empty. He had not found the cup. I swam downwards, further out, towards the opening of the cave. The rocks out there were sharp like fangs and rough to touch. As my hand brushed one of them, the edge rasped away the skin, and a thin thread of redness swirled away from me in the water. Would the Wyrm notice something like that? And did she ever come into the cave? I wished I hadn't thought of that.

There! A golden glint. I scissored my legs and shot downwards, not caring that I got too close to another rocky spire, so that I tore both trousers and skin. Was it – no. Metal, but no cup. A buckle of some kind, from a shoe or a belt. I didn't like to think how it had come to be here, or where its owner was now. In the belly of the Wyrm, it might be.

Air. I had to go back up. But which way was up? Panic writhed inside me. Water, darkness, rock . . . light. That way. Up.

'Hhhhaahhh . . . hhhaaaahhhh . . . hahhhhh . . .' Air whistled in and out of me, and lake water burned in my nose and throat because I had started breathing a second too soon. I coughed and retched and snorted. Damn Prince Arthos and his miserable cup, damn him to the deepest hell. My arms and legs were heavy and stiff, and my chest hurt. But if I didn't find it . . . if I didn't find it . . . I would almost rather be eaten by the Wyrm. Down, down again, closer still to the opening of the cave.

I saw it nearly at once. And saw that Nico had seen it before me. He shot downwards, smooth like a seal. I forced my leaden arms and legs to swim after him, forced them to move faster, faster . . .

Nico curled round a spire, scissored his legs once and seized the golden treasure. He had it. I was too late.

The Hall of the Whisperers. I couldn't stand it. Perhaps, if I simply stayed down here, gave in to the urge to breathe . . . I could drag water into my lungs instead of air, and drown. It wouldn't take very long.

But wait . . . He who finds the cup – *and delivers it into my hands*. That's what he had said. Delivers it into my hands. And Nico hadn't got that far yet.

I caught him just before we reached the surface. He was completely surprised, and I wrested the cup from him before he recovered. Now, I only had to get up on the dock—

Nico flung his arms around my waist and dragged me back down. I swallowed a mouthful of water, coughing and gasping, but I didn't let go of the cup.

'Give it to me,' hissed Nico, gasping just as hard. 'I found it!'

I didn't answer. Instead, I jabbed my elbow into his midriff and tried to wriggle free of his grasp. I couldn't. He was good at this kind of thing, as I had discovered during our water fight back at the Foundation bath house. But this time, we weren't fighting for fun. I clung to that wretched gold cup, and Nico clutched me equally hard and would not let me get on to the dock. Both of us used arms, knees, elbows, whatever came to hand, but neither could get rid of the other. In the end we were so beaten and exhausted that we could do no more than cling to the edge of the dock side by side, like two half-drowned kittens.

'Give it to me,' Nico gasped. 'If I win . . . they'll let Mira go. What did *you* ask for? Water!' He snorted, half in despair, half in scorn. 'Couldn't you have come up with a better wish? Look around you. You're *swimming* in it.'

'It's not that,' I muttered. 'It's the other thing.'

'The Whisperers?' He looked at me. Our faces were no more than a hand's breadth apart. Water was dripping from his dark hair, and his eyes were reddened from tiredness and strain, but he did not let go of my arm. 'Davin . . . Can't you . . . one night. Two, perhaps. Don't you think you could stand that — for Mira's sake?'

I wanted to. I really, really wanted to.

But I was a weak and sorry coward, and a killer to boot. The Hall of the Whisperers — no. I couldn't stand it.

With a last desperate heave, I wrenched myself free, kicked and wriggled, and flopped on to the dock with the cup clutched in one hand. The rough boards rocked and squelched beneath me. I did not have the strength to get up, so I crawled the last few feet on all fours.

'Master,' I said, giving him the cup. 'Here it is.'

His face was completely smooth and expressionless, and I couldn't tell whether he was pleased that I had won. Would he rather that it had been Nico who had brought him the cup?

All he said was:

'Well done, my son. You shall be rewarded.'

The cup glinted faintly in the sunlight from the cavern's mouth. A precious treasure, he had said, but it looked more like brass than gold, now that it wasn't a half-hidden glitter in the murky depths. He held it high, as though toasting somebody. And then he threw it, in a long, lazy arc, back into the waters. There was a small splash, and it was gone.

A hiss escaped me. He had tossed it back in! As if it

didn't matter, as if it was worthless. As if it hadn't cost anything.

'The real value lies not in the reward, but in the test itself,' he said, as if he could hear my thoughts. 'That is your lesson for today.' Then he nodded at the guards. 'Fish out the other one.'

The dock rocked beneath their weight as they moved towards the edge. One of them went down on one knee. And stayed there for some moments.

'Master,' he finally said, in a funny hollow voice. 'He isn't there.'

They took out the boat and searched for more than an hour, until the Wyrm appeared and scared them back into the cavern. They poked and prodded with long stakes in the depths of the cavern pool and dragged hooks through the water, but they found nothing.

'Wyrm ate him,' said one of the unfortunate guards. 'Or he drowned. Can't have made it out of here alive.'

'I see,' said Master Vardo acidly. 'And is that a point of view you would like to report to the Prince?'

The guard flushed and muttered something almost inaudible that ended in a 'No, Master.'

Nevertheless, Master Vardo himself offered more or less the same opinion a little later, in the council chamber.

'I regret deeply, My Lord Prince, but the young Lord Ravens is lost to us, and must be regarded as dead. Whether he drowned or perished in the jaws of the Wyrm makes no practical difference.'

Prince Arthos sat in his high-backed chair, regarding

the Educator with his head slightly tilted to one side. His hard, egg-smooth face did not look inclined to lenience.

'A dead Ravens. A dead Ravens whose unfortunate fate may be laid at my door. Is it the Educator's opinion that I should thank him for this day's work?'

'No, My Lord Prince. The error is mine.' Master Vardo bowed his head.

'Hmm. Yes. I might, of course, have my Master Educator executed to show my public wrath at this misdeed.'

Vardo's face remained smooth. I couldn't tell whether the threat scared him or not.

'My Prince has that right,' he said.

'Indeed, I do. However, I am not convinced that Ravens' followers will grasp the finer points. It will hardly diminish their anger against me or my bastard grandson.'

'Probably not, My Lord Prince.'

'Hmm. We acquired an unexpected pawn, Master Educator. But we played it badly. Go. I have other things to think of.'

'Thank you, My Lord Prince.' Master Vardo bowed. 'Does My Prince wish for the teaching of Davin Tonerre to continue?'

It was as if Prince Arthos saw me for the first time. They had put leg-irons on me again, as if it was somehow my fault that Nico had slipped his tether. A guard stood on either side of me, but they weren't bothering to hold on to me any more. It was as if they knew that I was so broken and harmless now that they hardly needed to guard me. I was still wet and cold all over, and chilled to my soul.

'Is he making any progress?'

'More than young Lord Ravens did. But it may take a few more weeks before we have him fully trained.'

Trained. What did that mean? Was it when there was no longer any trace of the Davin I once thought I was? When I was no longer my mother's son, or Dina's brother, or Nico's friend, but only a tame dog of the Prince's? Or even worse. His executioner.

For one short, wild moment I didn't care about the Whisperers, didn't care about Vardo and his threats. I saw it all clearly. This one moment was all I had. If I wanted to be myself, for however long they let me live, I had to do something here and now.

I spun towards one guard, jerked his sword from its sheath and flung it at the Prince with every last ounce of my strength. It turned in the air like a throwing knife and buried itself in the back of his chair. It stuck there, quivering, for a second, before clattering on to the marble tiles. A single scarlet drop of blood fell from the earlobe of the Prince on to his white lace collar, dyeing the edge of it red.

For a moment, everyone stood frozen. Then the Prince's bodyguard leaped on me, hammering me to the floor. Everything darkened, and I couldn't see any more, but I could still hear. Hear the voice of the Prince.

'I want him whipped,' he said coldly. 'Tomorrow morning, in the main courtyard, so that everyone will see it. And when there is no skin left on his back, he can follow Ravens into the belly of the Wyrm.'

★ ★ ★

They dragged me back to the Gullet, but not this time to Mascha and the old gang. Instead they opened another of the iron gates.

'Hey, Davin,' called Mascha. 'What's goin' on?'

I couldn't talk, but one of the guards answered for me.

'He'll spend the night in the stone coffin. And tomorrow you will see him again, at the whipping post.'

'What did he do?'

This time, Master Vardo answered.

'He attacked and offended the Prince's person. And tomorrow you will see what happens to someone who spills royal blood.'

A murmur spread through the Gullet, and not just from Mascha's gang.

'You mean, he wounded him? Davin, did you stick him?'

'Shut up, dog,' snarled a guard. 'You just mind your own business!'

Another murmur ran round the cellar. And this time, a different sound followed. A firm, rhythmic pounding: *clang, clang, clang*. It was Mascha, hammering at the grille of the gate with his chain.

'Stop that!' roared the guard.

But Mascha didn't stop. And now he wasn't the only one. *Clang, clang, clang*. Scores of prisoners were pounding away, pounding the bars, or the floor, or whatever they could reach that would make a noise. The sound rose and rose, an infernal racket that wouldn't go away no matter how much the guards yelled and threatened.

'Get him out of here,' said the guard captain. 'Or they'll never stop.'

They half dragged, half carried me along a long dark cellar passage. But behind us, the noise kept on, like when people clap and cheer a juggler or a tightrope dancer, and simply won't stop again.

They dropped me into a small cold hole that wasn't even long enough for me to stretch my legs. This, it would seem, was the stone coffin.

Master Vardo stood at the edge of the hole looking down at me. I couldn't see what he was thinking. His black figure was just black, and the pale smooth face was as stony as ever. If I had hit him with the sword, would he even have been able to bleed?

But there was silence in my head now. Blessed silence. The Whisperers were gone. And far away, faint but still audible, I could still hear the prisoners pounding away, strongly and firmly.

'I won,' I told the stone face. 'You lost, and I won.'

He didn't answer. He turned on his heel and left, and the guards dropped the grille on top of the hole and locked me away in the dark.

VI
The Shadow of Death
Dina's story

THIRTY-THREE

Master and Shadow

There was no one on the mountain road except us. No one met us, no one passed us. And all day long, we saw not a single house. Late in the afternoon Sezuan succeeded in catching one of the big red-brown lizards and killed it with a stone.

'Can you *eat* that?' I asked dubiously.

'You can try,' he said, gutting it. 'At least they are not venomous.'

We made a small fire and boiled a little water. We had no real tea any more, but I had picked a little valerian and sweet cicely along the way. There was no real nourishment in it, but it soothed the stomach and made me feel that at least we had *something*. Sezuan wrapped the lizard in some leaves and put it in the embers to cook. I looked unhappily at the small green package as it began to steam and blacken. Was it really something you could eat?

Shadow tossed away his mug so that hot valerian tea spattered across the rocks. 'Taste bad,' he whined.

I eyed him irritably. He sat there scratching at his

chest with one hand, like a dog with fleas. Having hung across the donkey's back for most of the day, he had come to his senses late in the afternoon and had walked on his own for a little while. It had been a relief to be able to tie some of our bundles to the donkey instead of carrying everything ourselves, but I would have been quite happy for Shadow to dream on. The last hour he'd done nothing except whine and complain and get in the way. It was like having a giant three-year-old along. He was worse than Melli had ever been. Ten times worse.

He crabbed his way towards me without getting up. The sour smell of him made my poor stomach turn so that I nearly brought the valerian tea back up.

'Shadow is hungry,' he said, leaning towards me. 'Shadow is really hungry.'

I couldn't stand it. I pushed him away and got up, but he caught at my ankle with one filthy, scaly hand.

'One can eat children,' he said. 'They taste better than lizard!'

'Let go of me!' I kicked my foot to free it, but he was stronger than you would think, considering how gaunt he was.

'Leave her alone,' snapped Sezuan.

Shadow let go of me, but he scowled meanly. 'The Day of Vengeance will come,' he hissed. 'Shadow will be Master, and Master will be Shadow, and on that day, Death will eat his fill of little girls!'

I backed away from him until my back met the donkey's warm flank. My skin crawled all over, as if I had slept some place with lice in the bedding. He didn't mean it, the part about eating children. Did he? No, it was just something he said to scare me. And yet . . . there was something about his eyes, about – about all of him, the bony hands, the scaly skin, the smell . . . if anyone ate human flesh it might be someone like Shadow. Someone who sneaked around in the shadows smelling as if he ate whatever he could get hold of, dead or living, fresh or decayed. A vulture without wings. And Sezuan wanted me to share a camp with this creature?

'This is probably about as done as it will ever be,' said my father, rolling the black leaf bundle out of the embers. He cut it open and split the steaming lizard meat into three portions.

Shadow gulped down his in four quick mouthfuls. I looked more dubiously at my share. The meat was pale, almost like chicken. I put a little in my mouth. There was no particular taste to it, no bitterness or sweetness, just a hint of charred wood. I ate the rest. There wasn't much, and my belly rumbled desultorily – I almost wished we had another lizard.

'Go ahead. Sleep,' said Sezuan. 'You must be tired.'

Tired, yes. To my bones. But . . . did I dare? I glanced at Shadow. Would I be able to sleep at all, with him only a few arm's lengths away?

'Sleep,' said my father again, and I knew this meant that he would watch over me. He would stay awake and make sure Shadow didn't hurt me. I lay down and fell asleep almost before I had pulled up the blanket, despite my unease, and despite a stomach that had been fed nothing except one third of a lizard and a cup of valerian tea.

I was dreaming. I knew it was a dream, because I knew this darkness, this underground chill. The dungeon. But where were the snakes? The last time I had been here, there had been snakes. And where was Davin?

He is not here.

It sounded like a whisper, but no one had spoken. I shivered, both from cold and fear. If Davin wasn't here, where was he? I could see almost nothing. A tiny bit of light filtered down from above, pale and bluish like moonlight. I touched the wall. It was slimy and uneven and damp like the skin of a slug. Where *was* Davin?

I took a tentative step forwards. My heel sank into soft earth. Earth? I had expected stone floors, hard and cold. Where was I? What kind of a place was this? Like a badger's lair, only much bigger.

'Davin?' I called out cautiously, not too loud. No one answered, and the sound of my voice died away at once, with no trace of an echo.

Then my foot sank even deeper into the ground, and I pitched forward into the darkness. The smell of earth and dampness washed over me, the smell of things that were rotting and turning into loam. And my hands touched something that was neither earth nor stone.

Clothes. A body.

'Davin?' I fumbled in the darkness, scraping dirt away with my hands, seizing and lifting . . .

The pale light fell on his face. Dark, damp earth clung to his mouth and nose. His eyes were closed, but not because he was asleep.

He is not here.

No. He wasn't. Not any more. This was no dungeon, and no badger's lair.

This was a tomb.

I was crying. I could feel the hot trace of tears on my cold cheeks. It was a dream. It was only a dream. I knew it, and still I was so terrified and miserable that I couldn't stop crying. It could be true. I had no way of knowing whether Davin was even alive any more. What if he was in some dark place now, dead and half buried? I couldn't bear the thought of it.

'Ssshh.' Something touched me. Touched my cheek. A gentle, tentative finger.

Sezuan. Perhaps he would sing to me again? I wished he would. I would have liked to lie here and listen while my father sang to me and chased away the nightmares.

'Ssshh,' he said, once more.

I opened my eyes. And screamed to the high heavens. Because it wasn't Sezuan. It wasn't my father. It was Shadow who had hushed me, Shadow's scaly finger that had touched my tears.

'Leave her alone!' Sezuan lurched to his feet. His eyes were dark and confused with sleep, but he grabbed Shadow's arm and practically threw him away from me. 'I told you to stay away from her!'

Shadow spat like a cat. 'The girl was crying,' he said. 'Shadow didn't do anything. Shadow was soothing her!'

He looked like a little boy accused of something he didn't do. I felt a pang of compassion. How well I knew it, that helpless anger at being unjustly suspected. Every time people called Mama or me witches, every time they whispered behind our backs and made the witch sign . . . every time something like that happened, I felt exactly like Shadow was feeling now. Or at least I thought so. Who knew exactly what Shadow was feeling?

Sezuan stared at the ground. He was so tired that he was swaying as he stood.

'Forgive me,' he murmured, 'I thought I could stay awake, but . . . I have to sleep, even if only for a little while.' He raised his head and looked at Shadow. 'Come here,' he said.

'Why?' Shadow looked suspicious. 'What does Master want with Shadow?'

Sezuan touched the flute deliberately, with one hand. 'Come here, I said.'

Shadow's eyes were glued to the flute. 'May Shadow have another dream?'

'Come on. Lie down over here.' With a neat twitch, Sezuan sliced off one end of the donkey tether.

'Shadow doesn't want rope. Shadow doesn't want to be tied up!'

'Do as I say,' snapped Sezuan, short-temperedly. 'Or you have had your last dream, I promise.'

Shadow's lip was quivering. His whole body was trembling. 'Master is mean. Master is mean to Shadow!' But he did lie down and suffered Sezuan to tie his hands together and tether him to the same thorny bush that anchored the donkey's line.

I felt as if I ought to defend him. Tell Sezuan that he had only hushed me and touched my cheek. But the mere thought that he *had* touched me . . . if he was left free, he might do it again. While I was sleeping. I bit my lip and said nothing.

Shadow, on the other hand, had a lot to say. Curses and reproachful moans about 'mean Master' came from him in a steady torrent. When he ran out of words, he just whined, a long, drawn-out *aaaaaah* sound, like a worn-out baby or a wounded animal. Sezuan tried to hush him up, but that only made him whine even louder.

'Come on, Dina,' said my father. 'We'll move a little further away. Behind those rocks, I think. Once he can't see us, he'll stop. Sooner or later.'

But he didn't. The wordless whine rose to a keening as soon as we were out of sight. The whole valley could hear him. If there really were robbers somewhere around, they would be in no doubt where to find us.

'If this keeps up, we won't get any sleep,' I said morosely. 'Can't you just . . . give him a dream?'

Sezuan rubbed his forehead with a not particularly clean hand. Filthy, to be exact. Unsavoury. His shirt was blotched and stained with sweat and road dust, and the shadows lay heavily beneath his tired eyes. He didn't look much like the immaculate and self-assured gentleman who had arranged our dinner at The Golden Swan.

'It makes him worse,' he said. 'I think each dream makes him slightly more insane. And it is not easy for me either. It . . . takes effort.'

'Was it Shadow who killed Beastie?'

Sezuan nodded. 'Yes. I . . . please believe me, I never meant to hurt you. I just wanted to . . . see my daughter. Get to know you a little bit. I couldn't know that your mother would . . . that everything would happen the way it did.'

I looked at him, trying to gauge what was going on inside him. I didn't like it that he tried to avoid taking the blame. And particularly not that he almost seemed to blame my mother. The moon was nearly full, and the moonlight made the rocks around us look pale as bones. It glittered in his eyes and caught the silver serpent in his ear. On the other side of the ridge I could hear Shadow moaning about his 'mean Master'.

'So it's not your fault? You've done nothing wrong, it's everyone else's fault. Is that the way of it?'

I knew it was me saying it, but I could barely recognize my own voice. So harsh, so cutting. He jerked as if I had stuck a needle in his flesh.

'I didn't kill your dog! And I . . . I punished him for it.'

'How?'

'I gave him a nightmare instead of a dream. And I told him I never wanted to see him again.' Sezuan looked away. 'But that might not have been wise. After that he . . . after that he couldn't be among people any more. And he still followed me. He was jealous of you, he felt it was you who had driven us apart. That time with the coppertail . . . he nearly killed you, Dina! And when he attacked that little girl . . . it was because of him that the villagers chased you away.'

'All Shadow's fault, then. Not yours? *You have nothing to be ashamed of?*'

I didn't mean to do it. It wasn't something I could control. But suddenly it was there, the Shamer's voice. And Sezuan raised his eyes to mine as if he had to.

'Oh yes,' he murmured. 'I feel ashamed.'

'At what?'

'I did not kill your dog. It was not my hand that dropped the coppertail on you. It was not me. But it is my fault that Shadow is the way he is.'

I caught a glimpse of something he remembered. A small boy unable to sleep. An older boy singing to him.

'He is your brother!'

'Half-brother. My mother's son by another man.'

One hand stole up to touch the serpent earring. I don't think he even noticed it himself.

'My mother bore twelve children,' he said in an odd, flat voice. 'For the sake of the family. Always *for the sake of the family*. To make the gift grow stronger, and our house more powerful.' His lips twitched, but I wasn't sure it was meant to be a smile. 'She was furious when your mother ran off. The whole household trembled for weeks. But even though we searched until we had half killed the horses, we never found Melussina. It was the first time I had ever seen anyone go against my mother's will and get away with it.'

I couldn't help thinking what would have happened if my mother hadn't escaped. How different my life would have been. *The whole household trembled for weeks* . . . No, I had to count myself lucky that I had never had to meet Sezuan's mother. My grandmother. Grandmother. The word sat oddly in my mouth.

'How could she care for so many children?'

'She didn't. Not really. It was only those of us who had the gift that she found interesting. The rest were cared for by servants.'

'That's a strange way to be a mother!'

He shook his head slightly. 'Perhaps it is. But when you are born to the life, you do not wonder at it. Her own mother had done the same thing. For the sake of the family.'

It seemed . . . cold. And I remembered Mama's voice: *Your mother sent you to me the way they send a stud to the mare. Because she thought the offspring might be interesting*.

Cold, yes. And I had been created . . . almost as coldly.

'When I was a boy, I was proud to be one of my mother's *true* children,' said Sezuan in a strangely bitter tone of voice. 'That was what she called us. The ones that did not disappoint her. Sometimes I wonder whether those of us who were raised in the servants' wing were not the lucky ones.'

'Was Shadow one of the true children?'

'Nazim. Nazim was . . . borderline. He went to the servants' wing more than once. But each time he succeeded in doing something that convinced Mother that he was worth bothering about after all. Finally she gave him to me as a sort of . . . test piece. If I could rouse Nazim's gift and make it useful, she would consider me fully trained.'

He looked across his shoulder, in the direction of our old camp. Shadow's keening was still very loud.

'Nazim was twelve. I was twenty-one. We were both much too young.'

I raised my head with a jerk. Was Shadow . . . was Nazim really almost ten years younger than Sezuan? Anyone seeing them today would think it was the other way around. Much of the time, Shadow looked like an old man, even though he talked almost like a child.

'I was strong, and proud of my strength. And Nazim . . . wanted it so badly. He wanted to be one of us, one of the true children. But his gift was weak. No matter how hard he tried, no matter how severely I tasked him, nothing much came of it. And that was when I decided to give him the dream powder.'

Sezuan met my glance. His eyes were like dark caverns.

'I didn't do it for him,' he said hoarsely. 'Or not only for him. It was because I would not suffer defeat. I wanted to pass the test. I wanted to become a master. And . . . I did.' He licked his lips and closed his eyes for a moment. Then he forced himself to open them again. 'I became Master. And Shadow became Shadow. Not all at once. But gradually. Nazim . . . seeped away, day by day, year by year. Until there was only Shadow left. Shadow thinks I have stolen his soul, and that one day he will force me into giving it back. *Master will be Shadow, and Shadow will be Master.* You must have heard him say it.'

I nodded, shivering a little. The Day of Vengeance, he had called it. *And on that day, Death will eat his fill of little girls.*

'In a way he is right,' said Sezuan slowly. 'One may say that I took his soul. But I am afraid that he will never get it back.'

Finally, Shadow fell silent. Perhaps he was asleep. I clutched the blanket tightly around me. The last of the day's heat had left the rocks, and the chill nipped at your ears and nose if you didn't wrap up. I was thirsty, and my throat was dry, but I was too tired and too loath to give up the blanket's warmth to go and find the water skin.

'Sezuan?' I whispered, tentatively. I still couldn't make myself say the word 'father' out loud.

'Mmmh?' His voice was slurred with sleep.

'If we have to bring Shadow along, then . . . we'll never make it into the Sagisburg.'

He sighed. 'No. You may be right.'

'Then . . . what do we do?'

He was quiet for a while.

'Do not worry about it,' he said.

'We have to free Davin and Nico.' I wanted to tell him about my dream, but didn't dare after all. It was almost as if it would become more real if I said it out loud. As if Death would somehow hear me and move closer, if he heard his name spoken. 'You promised!'

'Yes. I promised.' I could hear him stirring – perhaps he had rolled over. 'Go to sleep now.'

'But . . .'

'I shall think of something. Go to sleep.'

It took another six days for us to reach Sagia, the town below the Sagisburg. Every mile was a nightmare. We had very little to eat because we couldn't let Shadow near to other people, and we had very little sleep because we had to tie him up at night, and when we did that, he howled like a dog, like he had done the first night. It is incredible how much you can come to hate someone who keeps you awake night after night. In the end I was wishing desperately that he had never been born. Or at least had been born so far away that I would never have had to feel the grasp of his bony fingers, smell his sour smell, or hear his shrill voice.

Now, here we were, in a small orchard of quince trees just outside town. The quinces were nothing but small, brownish-green knobs, completely inedible. But down there in the town were three inns, we had been told. Oh, to be able to take a room in one of them, to be able to bathe and eat my fill and sleep until I was no longer completely exhausted. Just one night's sleep, I prayed. Just one. Then I might be able to believe again in Sezuan's infallible Blackmaster powers. I might be able to believe once more that he would be able to get into the Sagisburg, free Davin and Nico, and get away with them unseen. We were so close now. If I looked up high enough, I could see the jutting grey ramparts of the Burg. I could see the houses of Sagia, with their sharply pointed slate roofs, stone walls and tarred dark shutters. And the city gates. It would take me less than an hour to walk there. But with Shadow in tow, we wouldn't even make it into town, to say nothing of getting unnoticed through the streets, up the castle road, across the dragon pits we had heard of and through the big black iron gates of the Sagisburg itself.

'You said you would think of something,' I whispered reproachfully. 'What are you going to do? Tie him up? Lock him up in some cave? We have to do *something*.'

'Dina,' he said tonelessly. 'Stop pestering me.'

He didn't look well. Worn out, sick and exhausted. And more than that. His eyes were . . . strangely dead. Maybe I was wrong to pester him, as he called it. But I was tired too. And hungry, and desperate. Davin and

Nico had been prisoners in the Sagisburg for . . . for more days than I could readily count. More than a week. Nearly two. I hated to think what might have happened to them in all that time.

'You made me a promise,' I said. 'We made a deal. If you cheat me now, I'll . . . I don't want to be your daughter!' It hurt unexpectedly to say it. In my own mind, I had begun to think of him as my father.

He was quiet for a terribly long time. I grew scared that he was working up to telling me that it couldn't be done, we would just have to turn back and go home. Perhaps it had never been possible. Perhaps he had made it all up in order to lure me away from Mama? The thought made me cold to the marrow and beyond. But Mama had believed it – hadn't she? She had believed that he could do it. She just hadn't been willing to pay the price.

'Wait for me by the city gates,' he said.

My heart skipped a beat. He *had* thought of something. But why wouldn't he tell me what it was?

'Sezuan . . .'

'Go,' he said. 'It will not take very long.'

He took the flute from his belt, and I nodded to myself. I knew now what he meant to do. He would give Shadow a dream. And when Shadow came to his senses, we would be on the other side of the city walls. Now, if only Shadow didn't manage to sneak in after us. He could be clever when he wanted to. How long could Sezuan make the dream last?

Shadow, who had been trying to eat the inedible quince buds, snapped round as if pulled by an invisible string. It was as if he had some sixth sense that alerted him whenever Sezuan touched the flute.

'A dream,' he whispered. 'Master will give Shadow a dream?'

'Yes,' said Sezuan. 'Dina. Go. Wait for me by the gates.'

I trudged along the road. The dust turned the toes of my shoes pale yellow. On either side of the cart trail the thistles grew higher than my head, and bees were buzzing in the blue and purple flowers.

Behind me, Sezuan had begun to play. I walked on another few paces. Then my feet stopped without any orders from me.

This wasn't like the last time he had given Shadow the dream he so hotly desired. Nor was it like the time he had tried to call him out of hiding. I had never heard Sezuan play like this before.

It was broad day. The sun was shining, veiled only by a thin cover of clouds. And yet I thought of moonlight. Moonlight, and velvet-soft scented summer darkness. A bird hearing those notes would look for its nest. A kitten would seek its mother. *Home*, said the flute. *Shelter. Rest. It is time to sleep now.*

Was it my imagination, or had the day grown darker? A dove in a rowan tree by the road rubbed its beak against its chest and then tucked its head under one wing. The bees had stopped buzzing among the thistle flowers. Even the wind had died down.

Rest now, whispered the notes. *Sleep. You are safe now. Harm cannot reach you here.*

It was beautiful. Incredibly beautiful. Like a sunset. Like icicles just before they melt. But I had begun to shake all over. I was thinking of my dream. Of Davin. *He is not here*. Half buried, his eyes closed . . . and still the flute kept playing:

Rest now, tired eyes.
Heart, be still. Stop beating.

'No!'

I meant to shout it, but no sound came. It was as if the flute had stolen my breath, and with it my voice. I closed my ears with my fingers to try to shut out the sound. I was staggering along on stiff, unwilling legs, not towards the city gates any more, but back to the quince trees. I couldn't hurry, but it didn't matter any more. I knew it was already too late.

The notes died away. All at once, there was wind again, and sunlight, and the sharp smells of dust and thistles and sage. The dove from the rowan tree beat its wings and flew off.

Sezuan was sitting with his back against a quince tree. Shadow's head rested in his lap. But Shadow's body was limp and lifeless, without a heartbeat, without breath. I knew he was dead.

'You killed him,' I said. 'You . . . you *played* him to death.'

At first, Sezuan didn't answer. The flute lay on the ground, and his hands looked empty and powerless without it. He himself looked barely alive.

'I told you to wait by the gates,' he finally said. His voice was no more than a ragged thread, and he made no attempt to deny it or defend himself. Instead he looked at me in wonder. 'Dina? Are you crying? Are you crying because of him?'

'Of course I am!'

'But . . . he did you so much harm.'

I didn't answer. And still, Sezuan kept looking at me as if my crying made no sense to him.

'He would have given us away,' he finally said, as if that were reason enough.

'But you can't just . . . can't just . . .'

But I had practically asked him to. My own share of the blame cut me like glass. I choked back a sob.

Sezuan slowly rose. He came towards me and might have wanted to comfort me, to hold me. But I could only see his hands, his slender, beautiful flute player's hands that had just killed a living human being. I backed away and wouldn't let him touch me.

He halted. He looked at me for a long time, and his gaze hurt.

'I . . . have to hide him,' he said. 'Bury him. Stay here until I come back.'

He bent to pick up Shadow, holding him in his arms like one holds a child. It looked as if the dead body weighed nothing at all.

I still didn't say anything. I was shaking all over like a dog that had just been beaten. I wished I had never set eyes on him. I wished I had never seen either of them, him or Shadow. I wanted to go home. I didn't have a home. I wasn't even sure I had a mother any more, because who would want a child who had him for a father? He had played him to death. He had stolen his breath and stopped his heart and killed him *dead* with his serpent arts. And he didn't understand why I was crying?

365

He stood there with his dead half-brother in his arms, and his face was as closed and strange to me as if I had never seen him before.

'Dina. I mean it. *Stay here.*'

'Yes,' I said. I was afraid to do anything else.

THIRTY-FOUR

A Dead Man

'Are you not going to eat anything?'

Mutely, I shook my head.

'Dina.' He pushed the dish towards me. 'You need it.'

I stared down at the dead chicken lying there with its broiled thighbones jutting into the air. It might have been pecking corn in the yard this very morning, until someone had caught it, chopped off its head and roasted it for supper. There was a sour taste in my mouth, as if I had just thrown up. I couldn't eat a dead chicken right now. I wasn't too sure I would ever be able to eat anything dead again.

'Eat.'

'I'm not hungry.'

He glanced quickly around the inn's aleroom.

'People are looking,' he said.

I didn't care.

'Make them see something else,' I said bitterly. 'You who are so good at lies.'

His hand twitched, but his face was as expressionless as it had been ever since he killed Shadow.

'I am very tired, Dina,' he said tonelessly. 'And so are you. If you do not eat, you will be ill. Can we afford to wait around for a few days while you get well? Think about it.'

I hated him. I hated his hands and his voice and his cold sensible reason that could always line things up in a way that left you no choice. How I hated him. But I ate a little bread.

Getting into Sagia had proved unexpectedly difficult. The guards at the gate wanted to see all sorts of papers that we didn't have. 'Travel documents', they called them. In these parts, apparently one had to have the permission of the Prince in order to go from one town to the next. I would have thought that Sezuan could easily persuade them to see him as a fine gentleman with no need for such trivialities, but he just stood there, looking tired and dirty, as if he were no Blackmaster at all, but just a road-worn common man with a donkey and a scared and silent girl he claimed was his daughter. Finally he had to pay a fine. And we had to sell the donkey to pay for a room at The Black Dragon, the cheapest of Sagia's three inns.

Sezuan ate the rest of the chicken. Six marks it had cost him, and he had had to lay his money on the table before the innkeeper would serve him. And this was the man who was supposed to talk the castle guards into letting Davin and Nico go? A feeling of hopelessness spread through my body.

'I need to sleep,' he said. 'I think you should sleep too. At any rate, you will come upstairs and rest.'

The last bit was an order, that much was clear. I

followed him up the stairs. He was right, people were looking at us. Perhaps they didn't see strangers all that often?

The room could hardly be called a room, we discovered. It was really just a sort of booth closed off with a curtain so faded and worn one could hardly tell it had once been blue. There was a bedstead with a mattress of straw, and two pegs to hang one's clothes on. That was all.

'Get in,' he said. 'You will sleep on the inside.'

Was he afraid I would run off while he slept? Or was he still trying to take care of me? I didn't know. I was so tired I almost didn't care. The mattress had a sour unwashed smell that reminded me of Shadow. But I rolled myself up in my blanket and fell asleep all the same.

I woke later in the afternoon because the bedstead creaked. Sezuan had risen. Had he slept? He looked no less exhausted.

'I am going to look at the castle gates,' he said, when he saw that I was awake. 'I want to know what sort of people they let in and out.'

I didn't say anything.

'Can I leave you, Dina?'

What did he mean? Was he asking me whether I would run away, or whether I was afraid to be left on my own?

'Go ahead,' I said.

But he kept looking at me as if he wasn't sure.

'Go on!' I said.

'Sleep a little more, if you can. I will be back soon.'
And he finally went.

I lay for a while staring at the rough boards of the ceiling. Once they had been whitewashed, I supposed, but now they had an indefinite greyish-yellow colour, with stains where the rain had got in. From the cracks hung strange fronds of cobwebs, dust and other kinds of dirt. There were eleven boards in our bit of ceiling. I counted them. Twice. Then I closed my eyes and tried to sleep again, but even though I was tired, sleep wouldn't come.

I was thirsty. I was also a little hungry. Five mouthfuls of bread were not enough to fill even a belly as shrunken as mine.

I counted the boards of the ceiling once more. Then I sat up and counted the floorboards, those that weren't hidden by the bedstead. That was no great task. There were only four. Then I got up, combed my hair with my fingers and went down into the aleroom.

There weren't that many guests at The Black Dragon that afternoon. A peddler with most of his wares spread out around him was having an early supper, and apart from him there were only two old men playing dice. The innkeeper was hardly rushed off his feet. Nevertheless, he seemed to have a strange difficulty in noticing me.

'Excuse me,' I said. It did no good. Apparently, the dice game took up all his attention.

'Excuse me!'

A little louder this time. Loud enough that he felt he had to look at me.

'Yes?' he said with no hint of friendliness in his manner.

'Could I have a little water? And perhaps some bread?'

'Where is your father?'

'He went out. But he'll be back soon.'

'Right. You'll just have to wait, then, till he gets here.'

For one tiny moment I wished I had Sezuan's ability to twist innkeepers and the like around his little finger. It would have been *so* satisfying to make this mean, unhelpful man bow and scrape. But then I thought of all the rest. The flute. Shadow. Being able to *play* people to death. And then I felt so miserable that I couldn't even be bothered to argue with a stupid innkeeper.

'Just a little water, please?' I asked. I was so terribly thirsty, and this was not exactly one of those nice places that had washstands and water pitchers in the rooms.

'There's a well in the square,' he said, with a jerk of his head towards the open door. 'You can drink from that like the rest of us, can't you?'

There didn't seem to be a lot else I could do. I moved past the old men and their dice game and walked through the door.

The Black Dragon was in a steep and narrow alley, surrounded by unpainted walls and windows with crooked, sun-bleached shutters. Not the best part of town. The alley was cluttered with straw and donkey manure and other kinds of dirt. A little further down I could see the square the innkeeper had been talking about. Steep streets led off in four directions, and in the middle was a single tree – a crooked old rowan tree. I

371

found the well easily enough. Water came splashing through a stone gutter into a trough, and by the trough sat an old woman, knitting. I bent to drink from the water spout.

'Hang on, dear,' said the woman. 'Don't forget the Prince's penny.'

'I'm sorry?' I said.

She peered up at me. 'Oh, you're not from around here,' she said.

I shook my head. 'No. I'm just here with . . . with my father. Passing through.'

'Well, you see, dear, this is the Prince's water. So you have to lay down a copper penny to drink it.'

I had never heard of such a thing before. Not even in Sagisloc where everything was so expensive had they thought of taking money from you before they would let you drink from a town well.

'But . . . it's running all the time,' I said. I couldn't see that it made a difference if I drank a mouthful or two.

'Well, dearie, that's the law,' said the woman, switching needles. 'And how else would a poor well-keeper like myself make a living?'

'But I have no money,' I said.

She looked at me across her knitting. 'Not even a penny?'

'No.'

'Hmm. Go to the lake then, dear. You may drink there for free. But watch out for the Wyrm.'

'The Wyrm?'

'Where are you from, dearie? Everybody knows the Wyrm.'

Not me. But I didn't want to seem too odd, so I just nodded. 'Oh, yes. The Wyrm.' And hurried on before she started asking me awkward questions about who I was, and where I came from. And why we were here.

I could see the waters of the lake glinting at the foot of another steep street. I didn't like to get too far away from The Black Dragon, and Sezuan would probably be angry and perhaps uneasy if he came back and I wasn't there. But I had no money for the well-keeper or the unfriendly innkeeper, and I was so thirsty it was giving me a headache.

I was no more than halfway down the hill when a small bare-bellied boy came sprinting past me, howling his head off.

'Maaamieee!' he cried. 'Maaamie! There's a dead man!'

He never even noticed me, he was so busy crying.

A dead man? I felt a chill in my chest and thought of Sezuan. Or had they found Shadow? I could see a small crowd of people down there on the lake shore, gathered around something. I began to run. When I reached the crowd, I pushed through it, not caring what shoves I gave or took.

'Look,' said someone, awe in his voice. 'The Wyrm had him. But she spat him right out again!'

The dead man lay on the docks, in a pool of lake water. His dark hair was plastered to his forehead and his cheeks, and he was so pale he looked nearly blue, except for the places where he was bleeding from a thousand cuts and scratches.

It wasn't Sezuan, and it wasn't Shadow.

It was Nico.

THIRTY-FIVE

Not One Soul

'Should we get the castle guards?' someone asked.

'What do we want them for?' said someone else. 'Poking their noses into things that don't concern them.'

'But . . . he's dead.'

'So? He won't complain, then, will he? We can always toss him back for the Wyrm to deal with.'

Nico coughed.

It wasn't a very loud or forceful cough, just a small gurgly wet sound, but it made several of the onlookers start back.

'Uuh! He's not quite dead!' said a woman, as if Nico were a mouse her cat had caught.

I touched Nico's hand. It was cold, and I could well understand why people had thought he was dead. He didn't look like a living man. I grasped his shoulder and tried to roll him on to his side. Mama had said that that was what you should do with people who were unconscious. There was another weak gurgle from Nico, and a slightly louder cough.

'Where did he come from?' asked a woman with a large basket full of turnips. 'Haven't seen him before.'

'He's my cousin,' I quickly said. 'He was supposed to meet me here. He . . . he must have fallen into the lake on the way.'

The turnip woman looked at me, suspicion written large on her face.

'They had the boat out this morning,' she said. 'Them from the castle. For over an hour, before the Wyrm chased them back in. What do you suppose they were looking for?'

'I don't know,' I said. 'But it can't have been my cousin, 'cause he's never set foot inside the Sagisburg.'

Come on, I thought. Believe me. And like Mama had taught us when we were ill to imagine that we were well again, I *imagined* that the turnip woman was nodding, she was convinced by my story, and in a moment she would stop taking any interest in us whatsoever . . .

She shook her head as if a fly was bothering her. Then she settled her basket on her arm and turned to leave.

Nico was no longer wearing his grey Foundation shirt, and that probably helped. He did not look like a greyling, or a prisoner for that matter. But one of the men in the crowd, a carpenter to judge from the tools in his belt, had caught sight of something else.

'What's that?' he said, pointing his hammer at some swollen red marks on Nico's ankles. 'Looks like bruises left by leg-irons . . .' He looked straight at me. 'How did your cousin come by those?'

I didn't know what to say. I couldn't think of a single good excuse that would explain away those marks. And I could not even imagine how to get the whole crowd of people gathered there to believe whatever I came up with.

'Maybe we should get the castle guards after all,' said someone.

The sound of the flute came so faintly at first that I think I was the only one to notice. It was another tune I had never heard before, a cheerful little thing that made me think of hot sausages and new bread, of the scent of good cooking and the cool damp feeling of a glass in your hand, a glass filled with something cold and sparkling.

'Right, then, better see what the wife has cooking,' said the carpenter suddenly, apparently forgetting all about the bruising on Nico's ankles.

'Wonder what's on at The Dragon tonight?' muttered someone else and straightened expectantly.

And within moments the small crowd had scattered, and it was just me, Sezuan and Nico on the docks.

Sezuan lowered his flute.

'Strange fish you've caught,' he said.

'It's Nico!'

'Yes,' he said. 'I know. I've . . . seen him with you and your family.'

'But if Nico is here and . . . and nearly drowned . . .' I could hardly make myself say it, 'then where is Davin?'

Sezuan looked down at Nico, who still looked more dead than alive.

'I don't know,' he said. 'But if we can get a bit of life back into the young Ravens, we can always ask him.'

★ ★ ★

Sezuan carried Nico up the steep alley to The Black Dragon. It shortened his breath quite a bit, and the last bit of the way I had to carry Nico's legs. To the mean innkeeper he just said that Nico was his nephew whom he had bumped into in town.

'Had a glass or two too many,' said Sezuan, giving the innkeeper a sort of man–to–man wink. 'You know how it is. I'll lend him my bed and let him sleep it off there.'

And somehow the innkeeper failed to notice that Sezuan's 'nephew' was soaking wet and bleeding all over, and he even refrained from demanding extra payment now that there were three of us using the 'room'.

'Stay with him,' said Sezuan. 'I think it might be a good idea to get some brandy inside him.'

He disappeared down the stairs. I stared helplessly at Nico, trying to remember what Mama had said about nearly drowned people. Something about blowing into their mouths . . . but Nico was breathing on his own, even if he snuffled a bit. Something about keeping them warm, too. The cold water! That would be why he looked so blueish-white. Like the belly of a dead fish.

I started rubbing his hands and wrists to get some life back into them. He was so cold. What was taking Sezuan so long?

'If I raise him,' said Sezuan, returning, 'can you get a little of this down him?'

He gave me a small clay jug. I pulled out the stopper and took a sniff. It smelled powerfully of liquor and juniper berries. Not brandy, that was certain. But whatever it was, I hoped it really was strong enough 'to bring a dead man back to life', as the Highlanders usually put it.

At first it just ran out the corner of Nico's mouth. But at our second attempt he swallowed. And then he began coughing in earnest. Sezuan pounded his back, many times, so hard that it sounded as if he was beating him. But it seemed to be what was needed, because Nico was coughing up water now, water and slimy fluid, and when the coughing finally eased, his breathing was much better.

We took off his wet clothes and tried to get him warm and dry by rubbing him with my blanket, and after a while he started to look less like a dead fish and more like a human being. But he still hadn't opened his eyes.

And the way he looked . . . there was hardly a bit of him that wasn't cut or scratched or bruised. He looked as if something very large had clawed and chewed at him.

'They said the Wyrm had him,' I said to Sezuan. 'What did they mean by that? What is the Wyrm?'

'I told you there were monsters in the lake.'

'You mean . . . the Wyrm . . . ?'

He nodded. 'I have never seen her myself. But plenty of people have. It is why people around here never sail on the lake, or fish in it. Except for the Prince's own boat, which has some way of cheating her. But even they will usually only go out in the evening, when she is most placid.'

'But . . . do you think he . . . they said she had spat him back out!' I looked at Nico's scratched and torn skin. How did lake monsters eat their prey? Did they swallow them whole, or . . . did they chew?

In that moment, Nico's eyes finally flew open. His gaze flickered wildly from side to side, as if he couldn't figure out where he was. Which wasn't so odd if the last thing he remembered was the cold waters of the lake. Or worse – the belly of the Wyrm. I shuddered at the thought.

'Nico,' I said.

He turned his face, and for once he looked into my eyes. And kept looking for a long time.

'Are you alive?' he finally asked.

How that scared me. People didn't say things like that if they were in their right minds, did they? Could the head take damage from too much cold, black lake water?

'Yes,' I whispered. 'And so are you. But you came very close to drowning.' I thought it best not to mention the Wyrm right off.

Then Nico caught sight of Sezuan. It took him only a moment to figure out who he must be, despite the fact that he had never seen him before.

'Blackmaster.'

He made it a curse, an insult. And you could practically see his mind racing, trying to figure out what I was doing here, alone, with Sezuan.

Sezuan didn't say anything. He just inclined his head graciously, as if Nico had just greeted him with perfect courtesy.

'Sezuan promised to help free you and Davin,' I said quickly. It was so confusing. After Shadow's death I had

379

made up my mind to hate Sezuan, and yet here I was, defending him to Nico.

'Where is Davin?' asked Sezuan.

A haunted look passed over Nico's face. 'I don't know where he is now,' he said. 'But I know where he was. And there is no time to lose if we are going to get him out of there . . . safely.' Then his gaze grew so strange and inward-looking that I began to worry once more about head injuries. 'Him,' he said, 'and all the rest of them.'

'What do you mean?' I asked.

'The children. The prisoners. And all the others, all the scared and damaged ones, until there is not one single captive soul left in his whole damn castle.'

It was as if his words hung there in the air, for a horribly long time. It was impossible. He had to know it was impossible. Why then did he say it, in that stubborn I-want-it-to-happen way, when he knew it couldn't be done?

'Nico,' I said, feeling frightened. 'I just came to save my brother. And you.'

'Yes,' he answered. 'And that was bravely done. But, Dina, it isn't enough. It isn't enough at all.'

Sezuan tried to talk some sense into Nico. They fought about it for almost an hour, until Nico's eyes started closing of their own accord, and he could barely speak. And even then he stuck to his impossible decision. I sat listening, feeling more and more miserable. I wanted them to stop fighting. I wanted us to free Davin and go home. That was difficult and dangerous enough, but at least it seemed to me to be just barely within reach of the possible.

I didn't understand what had happened to Nico. He who had not even been able to kill Drakan when he had the chance – how had he come to hate the Educators so much?

'But what is it they *do*?' I asked in the end.

'They destroy people's souls,' he said. 'They destroy the souls of *children*.'

The last was clearly the worst as Nico saw it.

'But . . . how?' Because I simply couldn't understand.

Then he told us about the whipping post. And the key to wisdom. And the Hall of the Whisperers.

'They destroy you from the inside,' he said quietly, 'until there is no will or hope or dream left inside you. Some of the children, and I think even some of the prisoners . . . if you opened the door and said, you're free, you can go now . . . they would still stay where they are. Because they no longer have the simple courage to do anything else. Because they can no longer even *imagine* anything else.'

'But, Nico – how do you expect us to free them, then? If they can't even help themselves. If they just . . . if they just call out for the nearest guard the minute they see us, because they are too scared to do anything else?'

'I don't know,' he said. 'Not yet. But there *has* to be a way. I'll just have to think of something.'

'And how long might it be before the Young Lord has conceived of such a plan?' asked Sezuan in sour tones. 'I merely mention it because even such lodgings as these are not free of charge. Nor are we free from danger. The only reason the castle guards are not already knocking at The Black Dragon's door is because of me and my little *Blackmaster* tricks.' The last words were particularly acidic, because Nico had made no secret of his opinion of Sezuan and his serpent gift.

'Don't call me that,' said Nico.

'What?'

'Young Lord. I am no one's lord, nor do I wish to be.'

'But the title of hero and saviour, now, that would suit His Lordship nicely?'

That did it. They would now begin to fight again, I just knew it. And I couldn't stand listening to another round of it.

'Do we have a little money for bread?' I asked. 'I'll get it.'

Sezuan looked at me, and his expression grew somewhat gentler.

'You must be starving,' he said, fishing a few marks from his purse. 'Here. See what our skinflint landlord will give us for this.'

I trudged downstairs into the aleroom. It was crowded to bursting point, now, and no one paid me any notice. Everyone seemed to be looking at the same man. Something familiar about him, I thought. He appeared to be in the middle of a story.

'Then there was a terrible storm. The wind was howling and roaring and whipping the lake waters into a froth . . .'

I tried to catch the innkeeper's attention, but this was

even more difficult than it had been earlier in the day.
He, too, was completely engrossed by the story the man
was telling.

'Well, it was pitch dark down there in the belly of the
Wyrm, so he lit himself a fire . . .'

The belly of the Wyrm? I stared at the man. But it
wasn't until I noticed his toolbox on the table that I
recognized him. The carpenter. The one who had noted
the bruising around Nico's ankles.

'. . . and coughed and coughed until it coughed him
right back up and on to dry land. A little the worse for
wear, of course, but no more so than he could get
up and walk away. After seven days in the belly of the
beast!'

It was Nico's story he was telling, I suddenly realized.
Or nearly so. With a great deal of exaggeration. Lies,
even. But it made the story all the better, and people
liked a good adventure. They cheered for the carpenter,
and bought him another beer. And even the mean old
innkeeper seemed to be in a better mood and gave me
both bread and cheese and sausage for my three copper
marks.

When I got back, Nico and Sezuan were still in mid-
fight. I interrupted them.

'Nico,' I said. 'Were you in the belly of the Wyrm?
Did it spit you back out?'

'Who told you that?' he said, looking amazed. 'If she
had eaten me, I hardly think I would have been sitting
here, do you?'

'But . . . all those cuts . . . you look as if you've been
bitten. By something very large.'

'They're from the rocks, Dina. They are like fangs, in places.'

An odd disappointment spread through my stomach. I liked fairytales as much as the next person. Particularly those with a happy ending. And if he really had escaped from the belly of the Wyrm, then perhaps he could accomplish other fantastical and impossible things. Like the one he was so determined to do: to get everyone out of the Sagisburg till not one single prisoner, one single child, one single cowed and damaged soul was left.

But it had all been lies and make-belief. The Wyrm had not spat Nico back up. And this adventure did not seem headed for a happy ending.

It was no use.

It was hopeless.

They destroy you from the inside, Nico had said. *Until there is no will or hope or dream left inside you.*

No fairytale.

At that moment, it was as if I heard something inside. A few notes. The beginnings of a melody.

'May I have the flute a moment?' I asked Sezuan.

He broke off in the middle of a pointed remark to Nico and looked at me in surprise. But he didn't ask me any questions, didn't ask why. He just drew the flute from his belt and passed it to me.

I raised the flute and tried to shape the notes I had heard in my head. I pursed my lips and blew steadily but not too hard, the way my father had taught me. The melody began, lightly, like a breath of wind, a whisper . . . and I didn't know how it ended.

I stopped.

Both Nico and Sezuan were staring at me.

'What was that?' asked Nico.

I couldn't quite explain. 'I think . . . I think it is a fairytale. Or a dream.' I passed the flute back to Sezuan. 'You know. You know how to do it.'

'Dina . . .'

'You can do it. You can get them all out. With the right dream.'

For one short moment, Sezuan looked completely frozen. Horrified, I think.

'Dina, it's not . . . how many people are there in that castle? Hundreds. I can't do that!'

'If you did it just a few at a time? Papa, can you? Don't you think you can?'

Something went through him. Through his entire body. Something I had said? He looked at Nico, and then at me.

'Is this what you want, Dina?'

'Yes.'

He shook his head slowly, but not in refusal. It was just a disbelieving headshake, as if he couldn't quite credit what he was about to say.

'Well, then,' he said, with a faint smile. 'We shall have to try, I suppose. Since it is my daughter's wish.'

THIRTY-SIX

The Moonshine Bridge

It was a warm night. The moon was full, and yellow as a buttercup. There was almost no wind, and the air was full of bugs from the lake, and bats hunting them. Every once in a while, one of them would streak by, so close that one could hear the dry rustle of wings without feathers.

It was a good thing we had slept a little earlier in the day, and for a few hours before we left.

'We have to do it in darkness,' my father had said. 'I am going to need all the help I can get.'

Shortly before midnight, we were standing at the edge of the dragon pit, across from the big black gates of the Sagisburg. As it was night, the drawbridge was up, and we couldn't get any closer. There were guards over there, and they were awake. We could see dark forms moving behind the parapets, and in the two embrasures above the gate, torches were burning. It looked uncanny, as if the gates were a black maw and the torches two burning eyes.

Sezuan raised the flute.

He began with the notes I had heard inside. They drifted along on the moonbeams, across the darkened pit at our feet. I thought of spider silk, the first fine thread in a web, a thin and shining silken bridge floating between heaven and earth, then catching hold on the other side.

A bridge. A bridge across the pit, a bridge for angels and spirits, spun from mist and melody, from evening haze and night dew. Oh, to be able to walk such a bridge. To set one's foot on its silver pure moonshine arch, to cross from one world into another, and see what was on the other side. To walk waking into dreamland and look around. There was a yearning to that song, deep as dreams.

The drawbridge was down. The moonshine bridge was real, a solid ramp of timber and iron, strangely commonplace but built to bear the weight of men. And a man was standing on it, a man in armour and helmet, with the Draconis double dragon on his chest. His eyes were full of dreams and moonlight, and he walked as if his feet barely touched the ground.

'That takes care of the bridge,' said my father hoarsely. 'Let us see what we can do, once we get a little closer.'

I was almost afraid to set foot on the drawbridge, as if it might suddenly dissolve back into moonshine and spider silk and melody. It didn't. And our steps sounded quite ordinary against the bridge timbers. But the armoured man stared right through us as we passed him, as if the bridge he was crossing was a different one, in quite another place.

The gate was half open. Nico and I pushed it wide.

And as Sezuan began to play again, softly and dreamily, we entered the dark castle.

The notes drifted across the damp cobbles of the courtyard. Up the jutting ramparts, pale in the moonlight. Through open doors, and closed ones. Through windows. Through gates. They touched sleeping kitchen–maids and stable lads asleep in the hay. They played lazily with dozing guards, and touched the children's cots in the House of Teaching like a half–forgotten caress. Even the prisoners in their damp holes heard them and stirred, so that their chains rattled. Perhaps even Prince Arthos listened. Who knows? But in that old, chilled heart no dreams would have found room to grow.

Sezuan played as the moon rose in the sky and began to set again. He played as the stars grew sharply bright above the mountain, and then began to fade. When the lake breeze crept over the walls just before dawn, the flute was hardly more than a whisper. But still he played on. While the bats returned to their cave, folding their night wings. While the thrush began his morning song. While the sky paled, and the first blush of day touched the edge of the clouds. And only when the sun touched the castle spires themselves did he stop. His lips were so dry they had split and were bleeding down his chin. And as the last note died away, he dropped in a heap in front of the door to the House of Teaching, looking like a man who would never rise again.

'Water, please,' he whispered.

I looked around uneasily. There had to be better places than here, in the first rays of the morning sun, right on the threshold of the Educators' own lair. IN EVERY THING A LESSON, it said, in huge shouting letters right above our heads, and it looked more like a threat than a promise. But when I saw how pale he was, and how his lips were bleeding, all I could think of was to get him the drink he asked for. I ran across the courtyard in front of the House of Teaching and into the next yard, where I remembered seeing a pump.

A man came out of the building behind me, and I jerked in alarm. But he barely looked at me, nodded vaguely and began to walk towards the castle gates. He had no shirt on, and in his hair there were still a few pieces of straw from the bedding.

A second later, a thin boy, his hair cropped close to his skull, came darting along the wall. He looked left and right, then ran across the yard and out of the gate.

A door slammed. Out came a broad, dark-haired woman holding a small girl by the hand. Then a balding man in a butcher's apron. Two guards, without their helmets and armour. Two more short-haired boys from the House of Teaching. A silently weeping man in a black velvet waistcoat. A kitchen-maid with a starched cap and a face that was flushed with excitement.

Every last one of them headed for the gates and the drawbridge. And no one tried to stop them.

'It's working,' I whispered to myself. 'It's *working*!'

And then I ran back to my father, water sloshing in the bucket, splashing my skirt. Four more people passed me before I got there, one of them another guard who had thrown off his armour.

Nico was kneeling on the cobbles, supporting Sezuan in his arms.

'It's working,' I said joyously. 'They are all leaving! And no one is stopping them.'

My father's eyes were closed, and his face was pale as death. Nico had tried to dab the blood away with his sleeve, but it kept seeping from the split lower lip.

'I don't know if he can hear you,' he told me quietly. 'But try and see if he will drink the water.'

All at once, I was cold and scared all over again.

'What's wrong with him?' I asked.

'I don't know,' said Nico. 'Perhaps he is just worn out. Building bridges from moonlight and spinning dreams for hundreds of people . . . I suppose he has a right to be a little tired.'

I cupped a little water in my hand and held it to my father's lips. His eyelids twitched, and he drank the water greedily. Encouraged, I gave him another handful, and another.

Behind us, the great doors of the House of Teaching opened a crack, and five short-haired children, two girls and three boys, slipped through and ran for it, barelegged and in nightshirts.

'We have to move,' Nico said. 'If we could find a place where he can lie down, out of harm's way . . . there is still much to do. Locked doors and shackles don't unlock themselves.'

I knew he was right. And I grew more and more anxious, both that something was really wrong with my father, and that someone would find us, someone who had not taken Sezuan's dreams to heart. Sezuan had warned us that the flute did not affect everyone the same way.

'Can you carry him?' I asked.

'I suppose I can,' said Nico. 'But not too far. Let's try over there.'

He nodded towards a building on the other side of the courtyard, with a white door, two tall windows and a small belfry. I took the bucket, and Nico lifted Sezuan into his arms and carried him the short distance to the white door.

It was a chapel. All of one end was covered in pictures, most of them of Saint Magda, and the floor had tombstones embedded in it, with names and holy words and the double circle of Saint Magda, which always reminded me a bit of my own Shamer's signet. Along three of the walls were galleries where the finer folk could sit, raised above the common herd. But it must have been a fair long while since anybody had sat here. Dust coated the dark benches in a thick layer, and there was a damp and empty smell of cobwebs and cold stone walls.

I brushed the dust off one bench with my sleeve.

'Here,' I told Nico. 'At least he won't have to lie on the floor.'

Nico settled Sezuan on the bench. My father looked so lifeless that it hurt me to look at him.

'I have to go,' said Nico. 'I have to try and find Davin. Stay here, Dina, this is as safe a place as any.'

I nodded. I didn't want to leave my father, and Nico

knew his way around the castle much better than me. It was the only sensible plan. All the same, I had to bite my lip to stop myself from asking him not to leave me.

He slipped through the white door and closed it. I sat by my father's side getting colder and colder. I made him drink a little more, and drank a little water myself. He just kept lying there with his eyes shut, even though he didn't look like someone who was sleeping.

I had no cloth, not even a kerchief, so I dipped a fold of my skirt in the bucket and carefully wiped the blood away from his split lip. Had it stopped bleeding now, or was there still some fresh blood coming? Why wouldn't he open his eyes? It was so odd sitting here watching over him, instead of the other way around. I remembered how he had stroked my hair, once, singing to me to chase the nightmares away.

The flute, I suddenly thought. Where was the flute?

It wasn't in his belt; he must have dropped it when he fell. And we had left it lying there, Nico and I, as if it didn't matter.

I had to get it. If it was still there!

Outside in the courtyard there were people still drifting past, a steady trickle of children, women and men all heading for the gates. I crossed the other way, to the door of the House of Teaching.

It was there. It was still there.

Tenderly I picked it up and blew a few tentative notes, the same ones that had started everything. It sounded all right. Nothing broken, then. Clutching the flute in both hands, I hurried back to the chapel.

My father was still lying on the bench, slackly, his

eyes closed. I touched his hand. His fingertips were bloody, too, I noticed. He had played the skin off them.

Suddenly the white door opened. I ducked automatically, which was as well, because it wasn't Nico standing there, it was a stranger. A stranger in a black cloak, with a close-fitting black hood over his head.

He took only one step inside the chapel.

'Come out,' he said. 'I know you are here, girl. I saw you.'

My heart was pounding. This was an Educator, I realized.

He took another step forward. If he walked much further, he would see us, Sezuan and me both. I cast a wild look at my father's face, but there were still no signs of life, and no signs that he might be about to help me or himself. So I got up, flute in hand, and stepped into the aisle.

'Here I am, Master,' I said. 'What do you want with me?'

He halted.

'A child,' he said softly, as if he couldn't believe his own eyes. 'A mere child.'

Behind him I saw three more robed figures appear, as black-clad as he was. My stomach contracted. What could I do against four Educators of the kind that gave *Nico* nightmares?

'Was it you?' he said. 'Did you do this?'

'Do what?'

He pointed at the flute with one black finger. Even his hands were black, covered by sleek tight-fitting gloves.

'Corrupt the very air with that thing! Fill human minds and souls with sick dreams that it may take *years* to cleanse.'

I was careful not to look at Sezuan. Instead I opened my eyes a little wider and tried to look stupid and childish.

'I was just playing,' I said, trying to sound like Melli. 'Want to hear?' I raised the flute.

'No!'

Catching any expression on his strangely smooth and hard face was difficult. But I was fairly certain that what I heard in his voice was fear.

Was he *afraid* of me?

Without taking his eyes off me he rapped out a string of orders to the other three Educators. 'Lock the door from outside. Hero and Pellio, you keep guard. Aidan, you must go and find the Prince and as many guards as you can scrape together. Tell them to stuff something in their ears: rags, tufts of wool, anything. Hurry! I shall see to it that she does no further damage meanwhile.'

'But Master Vardo—' one of them began.

'Do as I say!'

The other Educator bowed his head and made no further protest. He and the other two withdrew from the chapel. The white door closed, and I heard the rattle of the lock. And then I was alone with Master Vardo.

He took another step forward.

'Give me the flute,' he said, as if he were talking to a dog that had made off with a shoe.

I shook my head. 'If you move any closer,' I said, 'I'll start playing.'

He stopped. I lowered the flute a little. But how long would it be before he tried again? How long would it be before he discovered that it was Sezuan and not me who had played his gates open and set dreams in the minds of all the Prince's men?

THIRTY-SEVEN

The Flute Player's Gift

A sunbeam from the tall windows was creeping slowly across the benches between Master Vardo and me. Dust danced thickly in the light. It made my nose tickle just to look at it. One eye kept watering, and I let go of the flute for a moment to rub it.

'You are tired,' said Master Vardo gently. 'It has been a long night for you. And the flute is heavy. Your arms must be getting tired, too.'

Why did he have to say that? Now it felt as if the flute was made of lead – and my arms as well.

'I have no wish to hurt you,' he said. 'You are just a child. It is not your fault that you have been led astray, but that flute is evil. An evil instrument, my child, that hazes the minds of men and makes them see dangerous visions. Put it down.'

I felt so tired and confused. It was true that the flute made people see things. Things that weren't there, things that didn't exist at all.

'Stop it,' I whispered. 'Please stop talking like that . . .'

'It is not your fault,' he said persuasively. 'You

cannot help it. And you will not be punished, I promise.'

My arms were shaking, as if I had no strength left at all. I rubbed my eye again. If only he would shut up. His words seeped into you, like the time Mama had poured a salve into my ear because I had an earache. Sticky. Stinging. Too warm.

He took a step forward. Then another. I had told him not to do that, but right now I couldn't remember why.

'I only want to help you . . .'

He only wanted to help me. Why had I thought his face looked too smooth, too hard? Now it looked gentle. Like the face of a father who might scold you a bit but would never, ever be really angry with you. Someone who was always constant, always the same. Not like Sezuan who never let you be sure of your ground.

'Give it to me,' he said gently, reaching for the flute. No.

No. It was just the tiniest of voices, inside me, but it was enough to make me take a step backwards. No. This was wrong.

'No,' I said. 'Stay away from me!'

He snatched at the flute with his gloved hands. I jerked away from him, turned and ran, through the aisle, towards the steps leading to the galleries. I flew up the dusty wooden stair, hearing him behind me, on my heels—

He grabbed my ankle. I fell, striking my chin on one of the top steps so that my whole head buzzed with it. I kicked back to free myself, but he had both hands on me now and was dragging me so that I thumped down the stairs, step by step, scraping my elbows and knees. But it wasn't me he wanted, it was the flute. I clutched it close to me and curled my body around it so that he couldn't get at it even though he hurled me against the banister to make me let go.

'Leave her alone.'

Thump. The Educator let go of me all at once, turning around.

Sezuan was standing in the aisle, swaying. A thread of blood was still seeping from his lip.

Master Vardo glanced at me and then turned his full attention to Sezuan.

'I see,' he said. 'So here is the real Blackmaster. No untrained child, of course. True evil. Who is the girl, then? Your apprentice?'

Sezuan shook his head. 'No. Just . . . a servant.'

With a quick movement, Master Vardo grabbed me by the hair and hauled me to my feet.

'No,' he said. 'More than that, I think.'

He held up his free hand close to my face. He was wearing a ring, a heavy silver ring shaped like the two dragon heads of the Draconis family. He made a smooth, quick motion with his thumb, and there was a slight click, like a lock opening. Suddenly something jutted out between the dragon heads, a slim spike or a thick silver needle.

'Do you know what this is, Blackmaster?'

It seemed my father did know, although he didn't answer directly.

'Let go of her,' he whispered. 'If you hurt her . . . If she dies because of you . . .'

'There is no reason why she should die,' said Master Vardo. 'Come closer, Blackmaster.'

Why didn't Sezuan do something? Why didn't he make Master Vardo look at something else? Why didn't he disappear in a haze of dust and morning light? *You see Sezuan only when he wants to be seen.* Why didn't he just vanish? I eyed the needle, less than a hand's breadth from my cheek. It was about an inch long, and sharply pointed, of course. It might leave me with a bad scratch, or even a real cut. Nothing that would kill me. Get on with it, I thought. Do something! But perhaps he needed a bit of help?

Vardo still had hold of my hair, forcing my head backwards. It made my throw clumsy and a little short. But still, the flute sailed through the air, hit a bench and clattered to the floor a few steps in front of Sezuan.

Master Vardo cursed and nearly jabbed the needle into my chin. I could feel the sharp point now, though the skin had not broken.

'Do not touch it,' he told Sezuan. 'Come here. Now!'

Sezuan walked past the flute as if it wasn't even there. A few steps from the Educator, he stopped.

'Now let go of her,' he said.

'Kneel,' said Master Vardo. 'And I'll let her go.'

Sezuan knelt. Master Vardo let go of my hair. And hit Sezuan with the back of his hand across the face, leaving a long, bloody scratch across my father's cheek.

Sezuan made no sound. They were staring at each other so hard that neither of them paid any attention to me. I backed a few steps. Then I crept towards the flute.

Still no one noticed me. Hands shaking, I raised the

flute and blew into it, a shrill and shaky note that sounded like nothing at all.

It was enough.

Master Vardo swung round, holding both hands to his ears. And Sezuan flung himself at the Educator's legs, pitching him forward. They both rolled among the benches, and for a few moments I couldn't see what was going on. Then one bench overturned, and then the next. Sezuan was flat on his back now with Master Vardo on top of him. His hands were clenched around the Educator's wrist – the one with the needle glove. Vardo in turn had his other hand at Sezuan's throat, and it didn't look as if my father was winning.

I could think of only one thing to do.

I raised the flute like a club and hit Vardo as hard as I possibly could.

The Educator collapsed on top of Sezuan, but my father just kept lying there, making no attempt to push him away. Finally I grabbed hold of Vardo's shoulder and tumbled him to one side, so that I could help my father rise.

I couldn't get him to his feet. He ended up sitting with his back against one of the overturned benches.

'Leave me a moment, Dina,' he said, out of breath. 'I just have to . . . rest a little.' He looked at Vardo's prone form. 'What did you do to him?'

'I hit him. With the flute.' It was still dangling from my hand.

'Good.' That was all he said.

I held it out to him. 'It was all I could think of. I hope I didn't break it.'

He shook his head faintly. 'Keep it. It's yours, now.'

'Mine?'

'If you want it?' He looked at me uncertainly.

'I . . . I'm not sure.'

He closed his eyes. 'Take it or leave it,' he said tiredly. 'It's a very nice flute. You don't have to . . . play dreams on it. You can just play music.'

Vardo was stirring. Would I have to hit him again? Or should I tie him up with something? I kicked off one shoe and began rolling down my stocking.

'What are you doing?' asked Sezuan.

'I'm going to tie him up.'

'No!' He spoke very sharply. 'Don't touch him!'

'Why not?'

He didn't answer. With great care he took hold of Vardo's needle hand and pressed it against Vardo's neck, just below the chin. The needle sank in, and a jerk went through the by now only half-unconscious Educator. But it was just a small pin-prick wound, and certainly no more than an inch deep. Nothing like the long bleeding scratch on Sezuan's cheek.

'Why did you do that?' I asked.

'So he won't hurt you. Ever.'

I stared. 'What do you mean?'

At first he didn't answer. It was as if he was growing more and more out of breath, not less.

'Dina,' he said. 'Will you please take the flute? I never really gave you anything else.'

'If . . . if you want me to have it. But what will you do, then?' The flute was so much a part of him, it was hard for me to imagine him without it.

401

He shook his head. 'I don't think I'll need it,' he said. 'Where is Nico? Why doesn't someone come?'

Why was his breathing so bad? And what did he mean, he wouldn't need the flute?

'Papa . . . is something wrong?'

He nodded. 'You mustn't touch that needle, do you hear me, Dina? You had better not touch him at all. Or me. Don't touch me either, not even after . . . not even later.'

Only then did I realize what he meant.

Poison.

The needle had been poisoned.

'Little Dina,' my father murmured, 'who cried for Shadow. Will you cry for me too?'

I was crying already, but I didn't think he could see it.

'Is there . . . anything I can do?'

'Stay with me,' he said. 'For a little while yet. But don't touch me.'

He was quiet for some moments, fighting harder and harder just to breathe.

'Dina . . . if it becomes necessary . . . remember . . . the Wyrm is just a serpent. And in my family . . . we are good at snakes.'

Was he delirious? Why was he talking about snakes now? Did he mean . . .

'Do I have it?' I suddenly said. 'Do I have the serpent gift?'

He opened his eyes and looked at me. For a long time.

'No,' he said.

And then he said no more. Ever again. Because a little while later he died.

I sat on the cold stone floor, with a small space between me and Sezuan and Master Vardo. The sunbeam had crept even further along the aisle and now fell on one of the flat tombstones. 'Edvina Draconis', it said, 'Saint Magda grant her good rest'.

I wasn't even sure I believed in Saint Magda. If I asked Mama, all she said was that that was the kind of thing everybody had to figure out for themselves. But if Saint Magda did exist, I hoped she would grant Sezuan good rest as well. He had been so tired, at the end.

I had stopped crying. You can't cry for ever. But it still felt as if someone had stuck a knife in my belly. It was strange that something could hurt so much without being visible at all.

At some point, I heard shouting and scuffling outside the locked door, but I just closed my eyes. There was nothing I could do. No matter who came through the door in the end, I didn't think I would have the strength to fight them.

There was a splintering of wood, and footsteps behind me. I just waited.

'Dina? Dina – are you all right?'

It was Davin. I turned my head. Davin, Nico and a lot of others, most of them scarred and filthy with wild beards and bits of broken shackles still hanging from their ankles.

'I'm all right,' I said, getting up. 'Can I please go home now?'

★ ★ ★

403

I heard that someone did actually make a fairytale of it later. A fairytale about a flute player who played so beautifully that he melted the stony heart of the Prince, so that all swords were thrown away, and all children became happy and free. It's a very nice fairytale. And I would have liked for things to turn out that way in real life too.

But not all swords were thrown away. And I don't think all the children were happy and free ever after, though some were.

Nico had freed all the prisoners. Some simply walked away; but there were also some who had scores they wanted to settle. When we left the chapel, there was fighting everywhere, between prisoners and castle guards, and between guards wanting to leave and guards wanting to stay. There were even a few fights among the prisoners themselves, I could see. The House of Teaching was burning, and at the threshold, beneath In Every Thing A Lesson, lay a dead Educator. The Palace, too, was on fire, and we later heard that the Prince perished in the flames along with many of his Educators and most loyal guards. Of Dama Lizea we heard nothing definite. Nobody seemed to know whether she had died alongside her father or had escaped somehow.

I don't know what would have happened if the prisoners hadn't helped us – the ones that Davin and Nico had been locked up with. Big bald Mascha had a voice like a roaring bull, and it was he that kept our small group together and blazed a path for us through the ruckus in the courtyard. Nobody wanted to get in

Mascha's way, it appeared. But even he couldn't get us through the press by the drawbridge.

'The boat,' called Nico. 'Let's make for the boat.'

He was carrying a small fair-haired girl who clung to him like some kind of human vine. Mira, that would be, from the house in Silver Street.

Mascha headed for some steps leading down into a cellar. That proved to be only the beginning. The stairs kept going down and down as if they never meant to stop. Finally, though, we reached a cavern, a cavern full of water. And in the water was a boat.

People around here never sail on the lake, Sezuan had said.

'Will it be all right?' I asked Nico. 'I mean . . . the Wyrm?'

'We'll have to take our chances with her,' he said. 'It's less dangerous than trying to get through the gates now. They're half crazy up there, and most of them hardly know their friend from their enemy any more.'

Mascha and five other men took the oars, and the boat shot forward through the black waters, towards the cavern mouth. I ducked involuntarily. Those rock spears looked too much like giant fangs, and it hardly seemed as if there was room enough for us to pass through unharmed.

Naturally, there was. And then we were outside, under a clear blue sky. Above us, on the mountain, we could see the Sagisburg burning. The smoke was the only cloud in the sky.

'What happened?' Davin asked. 'How did they die?'

It took me a moment to realize that he meant Sezuan and Master Vardo.

'They . . . killed each other,' I said hesitantly, because even though it was true, it wasn't really the whole story. 'With poison.'

'How suitable,' muttered my big brother. 'For a Puff-Adder and an Educator.'

I wanted to yell at him or shake him and tell him that it wasn't suitable at all, it was . . . it was terrible. But he looked so pale and battered and exhausted that I didn't even say anything. He wouldn't understand it anyway. Who would be able to understand that there was a dark hole inside me, a horrible *lack* where Sezuan had been? Who would understand that I would miss him, that it felt awful to know that I would never see him again, or even hear his voice. There was so much Davin didn't know. Sezuan was my father, not his. And he had sung to me, and stroked my head, until the nightmares went away. What did Davin know about all that?

The waters of the lake were as blue now as the sky above us. Hardly a breath of wind rippled the surface. If it hadn't been for the column of smoke behind us, and the clenched faces of the rowers, anyone might think we were out for a pleasure cruise. But Mascha, Gerik and the others kept a pace that had their veins bulging, and Mira hid her face against Nico's chest and wouldn't look into the water at all.

'How long will . . . how long do we have to be on our guard?' I asked, deciding at the last moment not to mention the Wyrm by name. Who knew whether she might be down there listening?

'Until we reach shallower waters,' said Mascha. 'Perhaps another hour, if we can keep up this pace.'

No one said anything much. I caught myself staring into the water several times, but all I could see was the sparkle of the sun in the ripply blue of the water.

A heron flew by, on wide grey wings. In front of the keel, where the boat had not yet cleaved the waters, midges and pond skaters danced across the surface.

The boat rose.

At first I thought it was a wave. But there was no wind.

'Hells,' hissed Mascha. 'Not now!'

Then the boat dropped steeply, hammering down so hard that the hull creaked and water cascaded over the gunwale. Mira screamed, clinging to Nico as if she meant to choke him. And in front of us, no more than an oar's length away, the Wyrm rose. And kept on rising. Up. And up. And up.

The Wyrm is just a snake, Sezuan had said.

Perhaps so. In the same way that a dragon is just a lizard.

Sunlight glinted in scales that were almost silver-coloured. Spiky fins fluttered, like tree branches in a storm. Her mouth was . . . I couldn't describe it. Big enough, certainly, to swallow a human being alive. But I didn't think anyone could stay alive inside her, for seven days or seven minutes.

'Do we have anything we can throw?' hissed Davin frantically. 'A lamb or something?'

Of course we didn't have a lamb. Where would we get a lamb?

'Not unless you fancy a swim,' snarled Mascha.

Then no one said anything for a while, because the Wyrm suddenly dropped from sight, leaving only a huge frothy whirl to show where she had been.

Was that it? Was she gone? Maybe she wasn't as dangerous as people said she was.

Then the boat rose again, higher than before. It tilted hazardously to one side, and Mascha roared at all of us to lean the other way. Then we thumped back down with a *whump* that jarred the teeth.

'Leak!' screamed Gerik. 'We've sprung a leak!'

'Then patch it, damn you!' Mascha yelled back at him.

'With what?'

'With a rag, with your shirt, with your arse, what do I care? Just patch it!'

'She's playing with us,' said Nico through clenched teeth. 'She's not even trying to snatch at us, she is just going to smash the boat so that she can pick us off one by one in her own sweet time.'

Mira was weeping. Davin took my hand. His felt warm, but perhaps that was just because mine was so icy cold.

'What about that?' he said, nodding at the flute I had stuck in my belt. 'Can't you throw that overboard? It might fool her for a while.'

I clutched at it and knew at once how loath I'd be to lose it. And then I heard Sezuan's voice in my head once more.

The Wyrm is just a snake.

I let go of Davin's hand. Raised the flute to my lips. And blew.

It was a wild note, like the cry of a seagull when the sky is black with storm clouds. It shrilled across the waters, piercingly loud.

'What are you doing, girl?' yelled Mascha. 'Get that thing away from her, Davin!'

Davin looked stunned for a moment. Then he reached for the flute, but I evaded him. I leaped on to the stern, feet wide apart for balance, and kept playing. Notes full of wind and water, of dark depths and black whirls. Of bird cries and sails, and the whisper of oars through the water.

She came. She rose in front of me and stared at me with her cavernous eyes. Water dripped down her long grey neck, and the scales glistened like mother-of-pearl in the sun.

She stared, and kept on staring. But she didn't attack. And suddenly a sound came from her, a quivering whistle, like the song of the whales off Dunlain.

'Holy Saint Magda,' whispered Mascha. 'She's *singing*!' And then, when he had recovered himself a bit: 'Play on, lass. And the rest of you: row. Row, damn you!'

I played on. The Wyrm sank back into the lake until only her eyes and her nostrils were showing. She didn't whistle again. But she kept following us, until the water became too shallow for her, and she had to turn back. With a last snort of . . . I didn't know – pleasure? curiosity? fellowship? – she dived for the depths, and disappeared.

Davin was staring at me. They were all staring at me. I slowly lowered the flute and sat down again.

'Where did you learn that?' asked my brother. 'Is it him? Did the Puff-Adder teach you how to do that?'

I shook my head mutely. I had no strength left for explanations. I knew now that Sezuan had lied to the very end. His last word to me had been a lie.

I had the serpent gift.

THIRTY-EIGHT

Yew Tree Cottage

We reached Sagisloc shortly before dawn the next morning. We didn't dare approach the harbour, but instead dragged the boat on to the mudflats south of the city.

'What will you do now?' Nico asked Mascha.

'Try and find my family,' answered Mascha and suddenly looked much more uncertain and less bull-like. 'If they still want me.'

He and Gerik ripped out a couple of the bottom planks – not hard after the shakedown the Wyrm had given us – and towed the boat out far enough for it to sink. We didn't know what would happen in Sagis now. At that point, we weren't even sure whether Prince Arthos was alive or dead. At any rate, it didn't seem prudent to arrive in Sagisloc in the Prince's own boat, which we had stolen.

We parted. The prisoners each went their way in the dim dawn, seeking families or friends they still hoped to have, or perhaps just some place where people would let a man chop firewood in exchange for a mug of beer and a meal. Nico, Davin and I headed for the house in Silver Street, to take Mira home.

It was full day before we got there, and I think a lot of curious eyes followed us the last bit of the way. I would have gone to the street door, but Nico and Davin headed instead for the kitchen entrance.

The girl in the kitchen dropped a cup at the sight of us.

'Holy Saint Magda!'

'Good morning, Ines,' said Nico with the peculiar politeness that so rarely left him. 'Are Mesire and Medama in?'

Ines stood there, open-mouthed, and at first seemed to have lost the power of speech entirely.

'Yes,' she finally gasped. 'Wait, I was just about to . . . I was taking up Medama's morning tray, but that probably doesn't matter now. Mira. Holy Saints, you've brought Mira home!'

And then she flew up the stairs, tray-less, and a second later Medama Aurelius came rushing down, barefooted in her morning robe, her hair uncombed. She said nothing at all. She just snatched Mira into her arms and hugged her so hard that Mira finally complained:

'Mama, not so tight . . .'

And then I forgot all about Mira and her mother. Because suddenly my own mother had appeared at the top of the stairs.

I wanted so badly to run to her and bury myself in her embrace. And at the same time I felt like running the other way, out of the house, so that she wouldn't look at me. Wouldn't see me. Wouldn't guess what I now was. I ended up doing neither, but just stood there as if my feet had been nailed to the floorboards.

She knew right away that something was wrong. She looked at me, and then at Davin. And Davin hadn't rushed forwards either, I now noticed.

How I wanted to be like Mira, a child who could cling to her mother and not care about the rest of the world. But I wasn't just my mother's daughter any more. I had become Sezuan's too. My father's child. I stared at the floor and didn't know what to do.

So it was Mama who came to us. And drew us both into an embrace, me and Davin.

'Something's happened,' said Davin in an odd, choked-up voice, and I felt sure he would go on to say *Dina has the serpent gift*. Don't, I thought, do you have to say it right now? But perhaps that wasn't what he meant to say at all, and in any case, Mama stopped him before he could go on.

'That can all wait,' she said quietly. 'For now, just let me be glad that I still have you.'

So it was only later, little by little, that we told her about all the things that had happened, or some of them, at least. Mesire Aurelius came down to the kitchen too, and Melli and Rose, and we sat at the kitchen table while Ines kept putting out food and cold milk and tea and beer for those who wanted it. We didn't see the boy, Markus. I didn't know whether he had gone back to his school or was somewhere in the house, skulking, and I didn't like to ask.

Davin talked most. Nico told parts of the story, too. I didn't say very much. Rose could tell that something

413

was badly wrong, I think, because she took my hand under the table and gave it a little squeeze. I kept my eyes on Mama's face as she listened. When she heard about Sezuan's death, a strange expression crossed her features, and I don't think it was all relief. But when Davin told her about the Wyrm and how I'd played to it . . .

She knew. I could *see* her knowing.

I couldn't stand it. I got up and went outside, into the fine new carriage shed that Davin had built. Perhaps I could stay here, I thought. Perhaps I could help Ines in the kitchen, or something. Would Rose stay too, or would she rather go home with Mama? Perhaps she wouldn't want to be friends with someone who had the serpent gift.

'Dina?'

I turned around. Mama stood in the middle of the yard and looked almost the way she always did, only a little tired and with eyes that were perhaps a little too bright. How could she stand there pretending that nothing had happened, when everything had changed?

'I have it,' I said. 'He said I didn't, but I do.'

'Yes. It looks that way.' And still she looked as if everything was normal.

'You said you wouldn't be able to bear it.'

'Did I? That was a stupid thing to say.'

'You wouldn't be able to bear it if I became like him. That's what you said.'

I was crying now. I could feel the tears on my cheeks. Mama took five quick steps and drew me into a hug.

414

'You aren't like him, Dina,' she said fervently. 'And you won't become like him. You are yourself. And my daughter. Now, come back to the house.'

She took my arm and nearly dragged me back to the kitchen even though I wanted most of all to hide in some hole and never be seen by another human being ever again. She made me sit on the kitchen bench and set a cup of tea in front of me.

'Drink that,' she said.

'Dina is crying,' said Melli and grew teary-eyed herself.

'Yes,' said Mama. 'It has been a rough, bad time. But it's over now.'

We stayed in Silver Street for four days, all six of us. Mesire Aurelius even saw to it that our animals were returned to us, though Belle had to live in the stables for a while with Silky and Falk and Nico's bay mare. Mesire hardly knew how to repay us for bringing Mira back to him. If we meant to travel on, he would buy us a wagon, he said. But we were welcome to stay. For as long as we liked.

When the news of the Prince's death reached Sagisloc, a wave of disorder swept over the tidy, well-kept streets. The city guard didn't know who to take their orders from, and a lot of the greylings simply walked out on the Foundation without being hauled back. You no longer saw little carts drawn by greylings. And many of the good ladies of Sagisloc suddenly found that they had to make their own morning tea.

Ines stayed with Aurelius. But she threw her grey shirt

into the kitchen hearth and burnt it, and began to wear a flame-coloured blouse instead.

Mesire Aurelius fetched Markus home from his Draconis school without debate and spoke hopefully of the future.

'Prince Arthos has no living sons,' he said, 'so it's up to the grandsons now. It's one big tussle, and while they argue, we have a real chance of making genuine changes around here! A better Foundation, and a different kind of school, schools that don't steal away people's children and turn them into alien little creatures!' A fleeting pain touched his face, and there was little doubt that he was thinking of Markus. 'Nico, you could help. You understand about children and learning.'

But Nico shook his head. 'I think it's best that we move on.'

'We could go home, couldn't we?' said Davin. 'To Yew Tree Cottage, I mean. Now that the Puff-Adder is dead.'

'Don't call him that,' said Mama. 'He was Dina's father, after all.'

'Sezuan, then. But we could. Couldn't we?' The longing in Davin's voice was so thick it was almost visible.

'Yes,' said Mama. 'We could go home now.'

By the time we reached Yew Tree Cottage, autumn had already touched the Highlands. There were still warm, sunny days, but the nights were cold. In the orchard behind the house, seven red-gold apples waited for us, looking much too large because the branches that held them were so slender.

Callan was terribly happy to see us. All of us, but Mama most of all, I think. And Master Maunus came running over from Maudi's farm, red-faced with haste and joy, when he realized Nico had returned. Many of the Kensies came by 'just to see how ye're doing' that first week. They had missed their herbwife – and perhaps they were even pleased to have their Shamer back, as well.

A few days after our return, I was on my hands and knees in the vegetable patch, pulling up beets; we had to harvest them before the frost got to them, which would only be a matter of days. Nico and Davin hadn't seen me – and when I heard what they were talking about, I kept my head down and eavesdropped.

'When are you going to start meeting my eyes again?' said Nico.

At first Davin didn't say anything. And when the answer came, it was with such fury and bitterness that the venom of it made me gasp.

'You think I'm a sorry coward. You think I'm weak.'

'No.'

'Don't lie to me. You saw me . . . you saw me crawl to him. You saw me kiss his damn dragon ring. And . . . and I took the cup from you. When you could have saved Mira with it.'

'Davin. I was also with you in the Hall of the Whisperers. I *know* what it was like.'

'You didn't kiss the dragon!'

'No. Nor did I wound the Prince. You did.'

There was silence for a while.

Then Davin said, hesitantly, 'Yes, I did. But . . .'

'You didn't let them win, Davin. Have you considered what that meant? When Sezuan played his dream to the prisoners . . . don't you think that meant something? That they knew that at least one prisoner had not been broken? Mascha said they were pounding at the bars half the night.'

Another silence. I knelt among the vegetables with my dirty fingers and hardly dared breathe. It seemed there was still quite a bit Davin had never told us!

'I sometimes dream about it,' he said suddenly, in a very low voice.

'So do I,' said Nico. 'I hear those damn voices whisper, whisper, whisper. And sometimes when I wake up, I still see blood on my hands. It takes a few moments before it disappears.'

A stone skipped across the yard. I thought Davin must have kicked it.

'I think I understand why you don't like swords,' he said.

Nico snorted with laughter. 'Oh, finally! But . . . actually, I've been thinking. You once asked me to help you train.'

'You said no.'

'Well, I think I've changed my mind. We can train, if you still want to.'

I think he caught Davin completely by surprise. In any case, some moments passed before he answered.

'Thank you. I would like that.'

Well, well, I thought, pulling another beet from the damp earth. It seems Nico and my stubborn brother have become friends now. Who would have thought!

Apart from Mama and me, no one knows about the serpent gift. We never talk about it, and I haven't even told Rose. Papa's flute is in the chest under my bed. I haven't touched it since I played for the Wyrm. I'm afraid to. I don't want to. But I can't throw it away. It is the only thing I have that my father has given me. And once that same flute played a moonshine bridge across the dragon pits and gave prisoners and Teaching House children the courage to dream. And the courage to walk away, and leave the dark castle of the Prince behind.

Afterword

Professor Kimberley Reynolds, University of Newcastle

Every now and then a writer appears who seems to speak to and for a particular moment – in her gripping series of Shamer books, Lene Kaaberbol proves herself to be such a writer. This is first-class storytelling. In these days of political spin, the idea that there could be someone who cuts to the truth and makes it visible to all is deeply attractive; but Kaaberbol's Shamers are more than human lie detectors. A Shamer is a public figure with an inherited power to compel those who meet her eyes not only to confess to wrongdoing, but also to see their actions clearly. To look into a Shamer's eyes is like putting the self under a microscope that filters out and magnifies every petty, mean and vicious action in a person's life. No one enjoys it, but admitting to misdeeds can be a relief, and the certainty it brings to the powers that administer justice is enviable.

Since reading the Shamer books, I have frequently wished a Shamer could be produced to make presidents and prime ministers, dictators and abusive soldiers look to their actions. If we were unable to fool ourselves and others with partial truths, the world would undoubtedly be a fairer and more equable place.

But a Shamer isn't a machine, and as always, power comes at a cost. This series of four books traces the life and trials of Dina Tonerre, who has inherited her mother's ability to shame. Shamers are not popular; few willingly look into their eyes, and even fewer like what they see there. Shamers are social outcasts, and for eleven-year-old Dina, this makes her gift seem like a curse. In the course of the series, however, she learns to understand and value the power she has inherited, and to appreciate the small band of family and friends who support her, including her older brother Davin, who feels responsible for his mother and sisters, and guilty that they have had to deal with enemies while he is left at home.

The Shamer books are fantasies, and they are set in a familiar landscape that contains dragons, swords and castles, and in which the battles between good and evil are not played out on television or computer screens. Although clearly not a realistic reflection of the world we know, like all the best fantasies, the books speak forcefully about this world. Not only is the truth manipulated and corrupted by charismatic leaders, but the distinctions between good and evil are also difficult to distinguish.

By following the events that afflict the Tonerre family, readers are reminded that it *is* important to stand up for what you believe, and that even one person can make a difference in the course of events. The series provides a dose of energy and optimism to counter the apathy-inducing effects of modern life.

The Shamer books also reflect the concerns of modern life in many other ways. Dina's mother is a single parent and a working mother at that. Although she has provided a valuable service to her community for years, when a powerful enemy spreads rumours that she is a witch, the fact that she is a woman with knowledge and power becomes a source of danger to her, as has been true for many women throughout history. In the same way, when Dina's father, who has played no part in raising her (she does not even know who he is) decides he wants what her gift can give him, she is caught between warring parents and forced to make unsatisfactory compromises.

Just as disturbingly and topically, the devastating effects of war and persecution make refugees of the Tonerre family, and they soon find out how difficult it is to maintain life and a sense of identity when you have no home and those in power spread false information and create biased legislation to control or even eradicate you. Perhaps more relevant than all of these issues are the ethical questions the books raise about relationships, power, trust, abuse – and what it means to be a hero. Dina's friend Nico, heir to the throne, has a principled dislike of swords and battles, but he and readers have to decide whether it is sometimes right to fight – and kill – in a good cause.

Though never preaching, the four Shamer books hold up a mirror to us all and ask that we think through the consequences of action and inaction. The books make gripping reads and, when finished, they linger in the mind. This is the stuff of classic fiction.

Another title from Hodder Children's Books

THE SHAMER'S DAUGHTER

Lene Kaaberbol

I couldn't move. I couldn't breathe. I knew now where my mother was. Drakan had her.

And tomorrow he would give her to the dragons.

Who dares look into her eyes? The Shamer is feared and resented for her power to unmask the soul's darkest secrets and crimes. Dina has inherited this gift from her mother, but to her it feels more like a curse.

When her mother disappears, Dina must track down the evil Drakan, and confront the vicious and revolting dragons of Dunark . . .

Shortlisted for the 2002 Marsh Award for Children's Literature in Translation